A STEVE CANNON NOVEL

VEGAS WASH

B. R. LAUE

ISBN: 978-09973419-0-4

Brandy Hill Publishing
P.O. BOX 1202
Morgan Hill, CA 95038

brandyhillpublish@gmail.com

Join the mailing list (no spam) for advance notice of new books in this
series and to periodically receive free Steve Cannon short stories.

Cover by Sandy L. Laue

For Sandy,
my beautiful muse

AUTHOR'S FOREWORD

The Steve Cannon series of novels take place in 1960's Las Vegas, a small city that held 97,591 residents at the end of 1963. The city was comprised of groups of housing tracts, business districts, the Strip and downtown, most separated by large parcels of empty desert. Of all the Strip hotels that existed then, only the Flamingo and the Tropicana remain. Caesars Palace, opened in August 1966, joins them as the last survivors of the 'carpet joints' that epitomized Las Vegas' golden age. Fictional license has been taken in a few cases in respect to the location of various places, their names and in one or two cases their ownership, but in all instances the layout and ambience of the town is accurately depicted as it existed then.

August 16, 1964

The Sahara Hotel glowed pink in the mid-August sun as Steve Cannon drove west up East Sahara Boulevard toward the intersection with Las Vegas Boulevard that was the ending and beginning of the strip. Southward were casinos with hotels and pools, and north was the business district that after a few blocks culminated in Fremont Street, with smaller casinos, fewer pools and more slot machines.

The three-sided, two story black temperature board on top of the Sahara Hotel read 104 degrees. Steve leaned forward in the seat, his damp khaki shirt peeling away from the humid plastic and eased the '63 Jeep Wagoneer away from the light at the intersection and smoothly steered to the far lane and turned right into the small strip mall that housed his destination: Foxy's Deli. He parked four spaces away from the front, just under the smiling fox sign, and waited for a few minutes, lighting up a Pall Mall and puffing slowly. His dark brown eyes occasionally swept the side view mirror whenever a car moved down the row in back of his parking space.

He had just turned forty-three, his black hair showing some slight gray at the temples and his face, though still youthful and tan had several creases and one short scar on his left cheek that sloped toward the strong lower jaw. A three day beard rose from the collar of the wilted shirt that was tucked into a pair of blue jeans. After several minutes with the air conditioning off and the slight breeze blocked by the adjacent cars, the hot interior drove Steve to step out of the Jeep. Dropping his cigarette as he pivoted from the door, he took his time crushing it under his left foot as he scanned the parking lot, looking for anything or anyone out of the ordinary. He moved quickly through the glass front door of the deli, and bypassing his usual seat, he took one farther down the wall in a small alcove outside the men's room where he could see anyone that came in through the front door, but was out of sight of anyone passing by the big glass windows or coming through a side entrance from the small casino next door.

There had been three phone calls in the last two weeks. The voice was deep and gruff and the threats were starker with each call, though the transgressions that motivated the caller went unspecified. Though there was a likely and not small pool of possible enemies, accumulated over fifteen years in a town full of wise guys and petty criminals, Steve's intuition honed over those same fifteen years told him that this was something different. If there was trouble from familiar quarters, he would have heard about it from the numerous contacts his usual occupation as a private detective required, and no one offered anything, not even the two or three people he occasionally took into his confidence and who could be counted upon to readily contact him with any serious information. As he mulled over the possibilities, his reverie was broken by the sight of a waiter, weaving through the empty tables towards him. The waiter bent down slightly towards Steve when he reached the table, and waited for Steve to complete his scan of the windows and the four other patrons present before addressing him.

"Bernie said to tell him when you came in." His voice was low and his head was turned carefully away from the closest customer two tables away.

"Is that OK by you?" Steve nodded, and before he could speak, his attention was drawn toward two men spilling into the deli from the casino, each holding onto the same small wad of bills as if it were a wishbone, one pulling the other towards a table in the deli, the other attempting to turn his smaller friend back towards the door they had just entered. Just as the first man had almost reached the table he had selected as their destination, his dance partner pulled the bills away with one quick jerk, and throwing a laugh over his shoulder made three rapid steps back through the door into the brightly lit casino. Watching him disappear, the smaller man shrugged his shoulders, slumped into the red upholstered chair and slid a plastic menu off the table into his lap.

In the time it took to observe this interlude, a medium height, stocky figure moved behind Steve's chair and rested a dish water reddened hand on his shoulder. The hand belonged to Bernie Gold and though connected to large shoulders that bulged a wet, spotted cotton shirt, a large smile beamed from the round face as the pale blue eyes fastened their gaze on Steve. Steve began to stand from his chair but the shorter man laughed and pushed him back down, slapping the glass of beer he had been holding in his other hand down onto the table. Steve relaxed, and glad to see his old friend, did as he was bid. He slid his hand up the big shoulder and squeezed it warmly. Bernie sat down across from Steve and shoved a place setting to the side.

"Steve my boy, how are you? I haven't seen you for a week, and I have been needing to talk with ya. Christ, you look like hell," he added.

Steve raised the cold glass of beer and emptied most of it in one go, the bottom half of his friends' face disappearing over the rim as he tipped it farther back. Bernie was from Chicago, a Jewish immigrant that had arrived in 1940 sans parents or any family, the only scion of a jewelry making family in Cologne and the only member to survive the Hitler years that had devoured Europe.

"Been out in the desert for a few days," Steve offered as he finished the beer with the second gulp.

Bernie signaled the waiter for a refill with a quick gesture of his left hand and with two fingers of the other hand fished a small piece of paper from the one dry pocket on his shirt.

"Here, this is for you. Geez, I don't know how you can run around out there especially this time of year, but here it is: Tam Polhaus from downtown said you might be able to help on a case he has, couldn't get you on the phone, so he called me." Bernie's words came out in a long staccato string as he pushed the newly arrived beer towards Cannon. Steve spread the wrinkled paper flat and read it over his glass as he took another long draught on the new beer.

Audrey Sizemore, Desert Inn Hotel room 335

"So what is the story, Bernie, I haven't heard from Tam for months, not since the jewel caper downtown?" Cannon again surveyed the room and the glass windows that now captured the low slant of the afternoon sun.

"This woman came in two weeks ago, hasn't heard from her brother in a month. They are from Detroit, or St. Louis or somewhere, anyhow, Tam must have felt bad about it, I don't know, but he thinks this may be more your type of operation, plus she apparently has money, so…"

Bernie was interrupted by the loud ding, ding, ding, of a slot machine bell in full payout mode just inside the door of the casino. Almost as suddenly as the noise began, the small man who had been eating quietly, bolted from the table back into the casino and a few seconds later loud arguing could be heard coming through the open door. The waiter who had brought Cannon his beer looked at Bernie who made a slight movement of his head in the direction of the casino door. The waiter moved in a casual but quick motion out of the restaurant and into the casino. Bernie turned back to Steve and pointed to the piece of paper still lying in front of the now empty beer glass.

"What you gonna do about that? Hey, how about a sandwich?" Bernie leaned back in his chair tilted his head up and caught the attention of a tall slender man behind the counter.

"Walter, a pastrami on rye with kraut over here." He motioned to Steve's side of the table. Steve Cannon waited until Bernie had pivoted back in his chair and was again facing him.

"I guess I will give it a try. If it is a bona fide deal, then I won't have to throw blackjack for Nick Montero down at the Golden Nugget for a while." Steve laughed.

"When I couldn't reach you, I thought that was where you were, but Nick says nope, hasn't seen you in three weeks. Said security there was getting lax and they had some bad types that needed to be discouraged from playing…"

His words trailed off as he spied the waiter returning from the casino. Bernie motioned him over to the table and made a small inclination of his head towards Steve, indicating that it was OK to talk in front of the private detective. The waiter approached the table from Bernie's side, picked up the empty beer glass, held it up and peered at it as if he saw some dirt on the rim. He wiped it carefully with a hand towel he carried on his shoulder. At the same time he spoke to Bernie in a low voice.

"Machine 23 sevened out for 5 bigs, two guys arguing over splitting the pot, Joe took them back into the office to sort it, should be no big deal."

Bernie nodded and as the waiter left the table, flashed a smile and a conspiratorial wink at Steve. Steve smiled back and let out a long low whistle silently to himself. He was impressed and a little surprised at being party to the quick conversation that in six seconds confirmed for him a long standing rumor that Bernie Gold was indeed the man behind the small strip mall casino. He looked across at his friend who was now knoshing on the large dill pickle from the sandwich plate that Walter had just handed to him, and he was in the act of passing on to Steve. A few minutes later he picked at his sandwich and mulled over the new information as Bernie was relaying some instructions to another waiter behind the counter.

Bernie had always been somewhat of an enigma. He was not "juiced" per se. Which is not to say he didn't have clout, he had something perhaps better than that: respect. He had made his living as a young man in a tough part of Chicago and undoubtedly knew some formidable people early in their careers, some he still knew and consorted with even today. But he had never been 'connected and protected', he had always been his own man. But he was vulnerable, especially if the rumor that he was the de facto owner of the casino became common knowledge. Kennedy had been killed nine months before, but the effect of his administration was still being felt in Las Vegas. The Feds push against the crime organizations had lost some steam but the gaming commission saw the future and would love to tack an unprotected scalp like Bernie's to the wall. But Bernie had other friends, in some ways even more powerful than the gaming commission and the crime syndicates put together. For years Bernie had run high stakes poker games for many of the more famous entertainers in town. Steve had been invited many times over the years as the main players always liked to mix with some of the locals and have someone else from whom to take money. They also used the games as an initiation of sorts for other entertainers new to town. They had once taken fifty grand from a young singer who had a hit TV show, and there had been some short nastiness back and forth, that eventually involved the assistant DA, but Bernie had reportedly smoothed things over and continued to enjoy the patronage of most of the big names that played the casinos. For his part, Steve could take or leave most of the celebrities he had met. Sooner or later they pulled rank on you and he had seen enough of that in the war.

Bernie left the table to take care of more business and Steve finished his sandwich. As his six foot two inch frame stood up from the table, he waited until Bernie's back was turned, then slipped a five dollar bill from his pocket and hid it under the plate. He waved to his friend, now standing behind the counter and talking on the phone as he crossed the restaurant to the front door and out onto the hot cement sidewalk. Just as he reached his car he heard Bernie call to him from the front of the deli.

"Hey, Steve, I almost forgot, I heard Angelo Sorelli is back in town. Nick told me to tell ya, he's living in Francisco Park."

"Old or new?" Steve stood in the shadow of the open driver's side door, his brow furrowed at the mention of the name.

"Old, a few blocks from Gorman High School." Bernie disappeared back into the coolness of the deli, his right arm waving a farewell as the glass door swung shut.

Steve Cannon drove back up East Sahara Boulevard, turned left onto Nellis Boulevard, and two miles later pulled off Ringe Lane onto a semicircular gravel driveway that swung back onto the street fifty yards ahead. Halfway there it passed a low slung, dark brown one story house built on an old stone foundation, a newly added garage, painted lighter beige was attached to the near side. From the back of the house there was nothing but desert all the way to the Nellis Air Force Base and Sunrise Mountain, the top third of the peak golden in the setting sun.

Steve noticed several sets of tire tracks in the gravel along the inside of the curved driveway, far outside of the line that he consistently took when leaving. Most of the time it was lost drivers turning around, but today it seemed there were more than usual. Steve left the Jeep in front of the house making sure it obscured the view of the front door from the road and unlocked two large padlocks on the beige garage. With both arms he shoved the heavy door back to the end of the metal track.

The late sun glinted from the bright bumpers and the chrome blower which rose from the middle of the '61 Corvette. The white coving swept back along the sides of the bright red car and the sweet, dark smell of motor oil enveloped him as he stood in the entrance of the garage. He reached under a wooden workbench along the wall and pulled out a pair of keys that hung from a small hidden hook. He swept a leg over the low driver's door and settled into the warm black leather seats. Steve jostled the large shifter knob to make sure it was in neutral and turned the key. As the engine rumbled alive, he placed his hands over his ears and pressed down on the gas pedal. Even through his hands he could hear the sound of the big V8 lashing back from the brick walls. He let the car idle for a few minutes then shut it down, replacing the keys and closing and locking the garage door. He walked to the front of the house and unlocked the thick oak door.

Inside the house the air was only slightly cooler. Steve dropped his olive green duffel bag on the wooden floor, and carefully locked and bolted the front door behind him. He was in a small foyer that opened directly onto a rectangular living room with a fireplace in the middle of the opposite wall made of the same stone as the foundation. To his left was the door to a narrow room he used as an office, beyond, a short hallway to the kitchen, and behind the kitchen was the bedroom. He moved to his right and flipped a switch just outside the office door. A low swishing sound came from a vent in the ceiling of the living room as the swamp cooler began to blow moist air through the room.

Steve continued on to the kitchen, retrieved a Coors beer from the refrigerator and returned to the office. After turning on a stereo receiver in the corner of the darkened room and dropping the needle of the turntable on a record that was covered with a light layer of dust, he flopped onto a small brown corduroy couch that faced the only window at the far end of the room. The blue lights of the Marantz amplifier glowed and the sweet smooth vocals of Ella Fitzgerald rose from the speakers in the far corners of the room.

Three hours later the ringing of the black phone on the narrow table along the near wall brought him out of a deep sleep. Rolling into a sitting position on the couch he stared at the instrument, a yellow light blinking on and off with each ring. It stopped after seven rings. Steve stretched his left arm out and rubbed his knee that was throbbing when he awoke. Before he finished, the phone began ringing again. He hobbled quickly over to the table and before the third ring he pressed the large black receiver to his right ear.

"Steve, is that you?" In the blackness, the low female voice seemed to float in through the door from the next room.

"Yeah, Remy, It's me alright." He could hear his breath rasping back at him through the mouthpiece.

"It's good to hear your voice, Steve, I miss talking to you and I miss…" He interrupted her.

"I know Gem… I know…., it's the same for me." He wrapped the long phone cord around his arm and sat back down onto the couch. "I was hoping you would call tonight." He looked at his watch. It had been six when he had arrived home, it seemed like ten minutes ago.

"I saw Bernie at the party they had for the opening of Danny Kaye at the hotel and I wanted so badly to ask him if he had seen you." She stopped and waited for his response. She could hear him breathing softly and sensed a weariness she had not seen or heard before.

"Good thing you didn't, I don't think your husband would have appreciated that very much, and besides, you would have given ol' Bernie G. a heart attack." They laughed softly together and she waited for his to stop before she went on.

"Nash wasn't there, he was in L.A. again, he made me stand in for him….thank god Bernie and some of his pals were there." She paused. "You could have been there too, Steve." Her voice was unsure and she added a small laugh that came a split second too late.

Her image suddenly welled up in front of him, as he had last seen her, and though the room was still warm he shivered. He pressed his thumb and forefinger to the bridge of his nose and quickly rubbed his eyes.

"That isn't for us, Gem." He said quietly. He hesitated then continued.

"I wish it were different, but it isn't, and I don't like living with it, but I have to."

"I have to live with it too, Steve."

For several seconds neither spoke. Remy broke the stalemate.

"Nash is back in L.A. for the next three days. Can I see you?"

"Sure, Gem, sure……. We can work it out"

A few minutes later, he sat alone in the room. A car's headlight flashed in the mirror that he had leaned against the wall at just the right angle to catch any lights that made the jog off of Ringe Lane but not those that continued on. Steve heard the engine gun as the driver realized his mistake, backed up and left in the opposite direction. He looked back down at the phone. He pressed the receiver to his cheek and dialed the number of the Desert Inn Hotel.

August 17

AUDREY SIZEMORE SAT alone at a table for four in the bustling coffee shop of the Desert Inn Hotel. Her pale gray eyes set in the fine features of her face watched as a group of dealers exited noisily from the front of the shop heading for their morning shifts. They passed in front of Steve Cannon as he observed the woman through the glass wall that separated the restaurant from the main lobby of the hotel. He had reached his vantage point after parking his car just inside the large wooden arch that guarded the entrance to the resort. He walked under the marquee that proclaimed Jimmy Durante as the headliner along with Phil Harris and the stage revue, 'Hello America!' underneath in smaller letters. He entered the revolving glass doors and stepped onto the marble floor of the main lobby. From there he passed by the front desk and took a right turn down a short wide hallway to the coffee shop. Steve waited until a waiter had delivered a pot of coffee and two cups to the table and removed the two extra settings before he entered the room, nodding to the manager on his way past the hostess station. He stood silent for a few seconds in front of the table until he was acknowledged by a small tight smile and a motion to sit directly across from her. She took a few moments shifting the coffee cup and saucer from her side to a spot in front of the chair that Steve Cannon had turned sideways and slid into, crossing his legs and staring silently at the dark haired woman.

"You are Mr. Cannon, I presume?" She spoke with a low even voice her eyes fastened on his.

Steve returned the gaze. "Yes, that's me," he said just as evenly.

"Are you related to..?"

"No." Steve cut her off sharply before she had finished.

"Sorry. It's just that I get tired of that question." He purposely removed the look of irritation from his face, a move he had used many times in similar situations. The Cannon clan was very large and well known in the region and the family counted the senior senator from Nevada as a member. Steve's family was not related.

"I'm sorry... I didn't mean...."

"It's all right, let's skip it." Steve broke her gaze and turning slightly in his seat surveyed the half of the room he had been unable to see from his vantage point on the other side of the glass wall. She waited until he had squared himself back in his seat and was again looking at her.

"How did you know I was the one you were meeting?" Her eyebrows arched as she carefully placed her cup back onto the saucer.

"I didn't. I just picked out the only person that was obviously not a local, but not your typical tourist either. I figured that had to be you."

"I see, part of your job as a private detective." Her manner had softened somewhat and as she spoke she lifted the pot and poured Steve a cup of coffee than refilled her own cup.

"Mr. Polhaus has great confidence in your abilities and I need your help." Her voice cracked and trailed off, she dropped her hands in her lap and her eyes drifted down.

"I doubt that Detective Polhaus has any real idea of my abilities one way or another, but what is it, Miss Sizemore; exactly, that you and Tam think I can help you with? I thought I heard mention of a brother,… your brother." He took a long slow sip of the coffee and waited for her to regain her composure.

She looked up from her coffee cup, her eyes glistening and for a few seconds, she studied the tan, sturdy face before her. When she spoke, her voice was heavier and even more deliberate.

"My brother has disappeared, and I am afraid that something is terribly wrong. I need you to find him for me. I can't go back to my parents without knowing where he is and that he is OK."

"What makes you think he is missing?" Steve took a small notebook from his right coat pocket laid it on the table next to the coffee cup and retrieved a pen from the breast pocket of his shirt.

"Do you mind if I take notes?" He waved his hand towards the notebook.

"No, not at all, I need to tell you everything I know. I don't quite know how to go about this."

Steve took a deep breath, opened the notebook on his knee, and looked up at her for a few seconds, then scribbled a few lines on the top of the first page before answering.

"Let's start by me asking the questions one by one. If you think of anything you may have left out of one of your answers, stop me and we'll go back over it. Agreed?" He looked at her as she brought her cup slowly to her mouth.

"Yes, Mr. Cannon, ask me anything you like."

When Steve arrived back at his car, he pulled the notebook from his pocket and quickly flipped through the pages. He carefully slipped a photograph between the last two pages of the book and leaned across the front seat and opening the glove compartment lid, placed it under several maps. He lit a cigarette and waited for ten minutes. When he was sure that Audrey Sizemore had enough time to leave the coffee shop, and had not come out of the front door of the resort he locked the car and strolled back towards the entrance.

On the way in he had seen a familiar face at the small taxi stand that stood a ways off from the main entrance. He walked under the portico between the cobbled pillars until he was just opposite the line of yellow taxis waiting for fares. A large black man was ushering a couple into the back of a cab while at the same time signaling for the next cab in line to move forward. He indicated to the new cabbie a group of three men who had just come through the spinning door and were now standing on the curb blinking in the bright morning sun. He flashed a smile at them, pointing them towards their taxi, carefully folded the woman's long scarf in before the door swung shut and with a small quick pivot grabbed the door of the cab just as the three men stepped off the curb. When the cab had sped off, Steve stepped out from the pillar he had been leaning on.

"Well if it isn't the big gun, Mr. Cannon!" The large man laughed, his mouth open, as he shook his forefinger in Steve's direction. Steve crossed over between two waiting taxis and reached for the man's outstretched hand.

"Shelly, baby, how are you doing?" Steve called out as he arrived, matching the vocal intensity of the younger man.

"Not bad... not bad." Shelly took two steps back opening his arms and indicating the immediate area with a large smile. Steve laughed at the gesture.

"Yes, my man, you have definitely got it made now. No more parking pick-up trucks down at the Nugget for you."

"You got that." Shelly laughed.

After catching up with the doorman for a few minutes, Steve waited as Shelly returned from depositing another group of late night revelers into their cab, no doubt heading back downtown to sleep it off where the room rates were lower.

"Shelly, do me a favor if you can," Steve began. "Actually two favors. Do you know anyone inside that can give me some info on a guest that stayed here last month without asking too many questions?"

"A big whale or small fish?" The larger man cocked his head and pulled at the brim of his red cap to block out the sun as he looked at Steve.

"Don't know, but probably no juice. The guy's name is Ralph Sizemore and whoever he is, he probably looked like a typical visitor to the boosters."

"Boosters? Are you from the Chamber of Commerce, or what? Yeah, man, I think I can help." He started walking backwards towards the bellman's booth, spun around and picked up a phone that rested on top of the green podium.

Shelly returned a minute or two later. "Go on up to the offices on the second floor. See a Mr. John Bonine, he might talk to you."

"Thanks, Shel, are you going to be here awhile?"

"Til noon, my man, til noon." The last words trailed off as he started walking towards another 'visitor' who was busy trying to create a parking space between two yellow cabs.

John Bonine turned and thumbed through a large file cabinet behind his desk. Steve leaned on the edge of the open doorway. The walls were all glass from halfway up and from where he stood he could see a half dozen people moving about the offices and he felt very conspicuous.

"He should be in this file," the reservation manager said half to himself.

"Why that file?" Steve moved farther into the room and took one step to the right where he could see part way over the man's shoulder. Bonine turned back from the cabinet and looked at Steve. "Because he was asked to leave." As he spoke he turned around and continued his search.

"Why?" Steve asked flatly. "And why would you remember that?"

Again the man turned from the cabinet, but this time he clutched a thin piece of onionskin paper in his left hand. Steve could see that half the page had single spaced typing on it. Bonine sat down in his chair and read the two paragraphs to himself, as he answered in a matter-of-fact tone.

"Because I was the one who told him to leave." He finished reading and looked up at Steve. Something in his manner gave Steve the impression that the interview was in danger of coming to a close.

"Some sort of ruckus?" Steve was hoping he could rekindle the man's interest and keep him from wondering why he was giving out this kind of information on a former guest. Steve decided he needed another distraction. Before Bonine could answer, he quickly continued on. "Well, you know, in any case, he's probably some other hotel's problem now... It's just that...." Steve took a conspicuous breath and waited.

"It's just what?" Bonine took the bait and clearly showed some interest again.

"Well it's just that he's come up missing... and the police...well they..." Steve looked down at the floor. Bonine cut him off.

"He looked just fine when he left here." His voice was elevating defensively as he half stood and placed the piece of paper on the front edge of the desk. Steve took one step forward and quickly interjected. "What date was that?" He scooped up the paper and answered himself. "July 17th, it says here, is that how you remember it?"

"Yes, it had to be right around then." Bonine put his hands in his pockets and waited while Steve quickly read the rest.

Steve looked up, his brow furrowed. His eyes bore straight into the other man's.

"He was comped into the Sky Room Suite?" Steve's husky tone betrayed his surprise. The Sky Room Suite was the hotel's best and anyone staying there for free was someone who lost big at the tables or was important enough to warrant the favor.

Bonine sat back down in his chair and began to rearrange a stack of papers from his 'in' box, looking at each in turn. He looked back up at Steve who had both hands flat on the desk and whose face was now only two feet from the uncomfortable man.

Bonine spoke quickly. "Orders from the casino manager, no play no stay, you know how it works." He tried to inject some confidence into his voice.

Steve stood up and straightened to his full six foot two. He did not break his gaze as he spoke. "Who requested the comp?" he asked, most of the stress falling on the first word.

Bonine slid his chair back until it touched the still open cabinet behind him. He folded his arms and looked up at Steve who now loomed only a little less menacingly from his place squarely in front of the desk.

"I wouldn't give out that kind of information even if I had it….. which I don't", he added a half second later. Steve gazed down at the man for a full five seconds.

"Do you know Detective Tam Polhaus?" The words were relayed in a normal voice, but the hard gaze behind them held Bonine's attention. Before Bonine could answer, Cannon continued.

"Because I am going to have to tell him about this, and when I do, it will be him doing the asking. So if I were you Mr. Bonine, I would get permission to release the name to me before that happens." He gazed at the seated man for a few more seconds.

"I will call you tomorrow and I think it would be wise to have the right answer."

Steve dropped the paper onto the stack that Bonine had been neatly arranging and stepped back into the corridor.

On his way back to see Shelly, he retrieved his notebook from his car.

"Yeah, man, I remember him." Shelly held the black and white photo at arm's length before handing it back to Cannon.

"As will most of my boys, if you were to ask 'em. Terrible tipper." He handed the photo back to Steve.

"What else do you remember Shelly? Did he ever go out?" Steve slipped the picture back into the notebook and carefully dropped it into the inner pocket of his sport coat.

"Only once when I was here." Shelly motioned to one of the car runners to take a ticket from an older woman who had just exited the front door.

"Yeah, he left late one night about a week before he checked out with two men." Shelly added as if Steve's question had triggered a memory.

"Recognize them?" Steve asked hopefully.

"Nope, but they looked like outta town wise guys to me." Shelly turned to face Steve directly and dipped his chin knowingly.

"Out of town wise guys..... in this hotel?" For the second time that morning, Steve was surprised.

"Yep, sure looked like it. Talked like it too."

"Friendly with Sizemore?"

"More like business, everyone clammed when I came up."

"Where did they tell the cabbie to take them?"

"I don't remember, but it wasn't another hotel, I know that."

Steve turned and looked at the strip where the morning traffic was thickening. He stretched and rubbed the back of his neck before turning back to Shelly.

"Shel, were you on duty when he left for good?"

"Yep, Steve, right here, morning just like this one."

"Do you remember where the cab took him?" Steve figured this might be a long shot, but if anyone could know, Shelly would.

"Wasn't any cab." Shelly said quietly. "He walked out of here."

"He walked off on the Strip?" For the third time Steve was incredulous.

Shelly nodded, in full agreement with the other man's surprise.

"Last time I saw him, he was toting a brown leather suitcase towards the bushes over there." Shelly turned and pointed to the extreme north end of the property where a long line of dark green oleanders met the strip and hid a parking lot alongside the hotel that mostly served the golf course.

Steve bid goodbye to Shelly and walked around the end of the shrubbery and gazed into the parking lot. He turned and looked up the strip towards the Thunderbird Hotel. Then he turned and looked south. In almost a half mile of concrete sidewalk, there was not one pedestrian to be seen. He waved again to Shelly and returned to his car.

*

TAM POLHAUS WAS not in a good mood. Under most circumstances he was not too pleased to see Steve Cannon, but today his demeanor gave no doubt he thought his time was being wasted. Steve was tempted to remind him of the one or two times when Tam had been glad, even grateful to see the private eye. But today he thought better of it.

"I sent the Sizemore woman to you because I couldn't help her anymore, so why are we having this conversation?" The detective's face was reddening as he continued. "You found plenty of skips before, so why is this one breaking your pick?"

Steve sat back in the green vinyl of the steel chair and carefully put his right foot up on the corner of the desk and folded the left foot over it. He retrieved his cigarettes from his shirt pocket, selected one, helped himself to the gray metal lighter that was sitting on a green blotter and slowly lit the Pall Mall. As the smoke from his first exhalation cleared, he stared at the detective in front of him.

"Just want to compare notes, that's all." Steve tried to make his voice sound friendly.

With his left hand he removed a small bit of tobacco from the tip of his tongue and deposited it into the half full glass ashtray that

Tam had pushed to his side of the desk when it was clear to the cop that Steve was not leaving soon.

"So compare." Tam leaned forward on his elbows and glared at the private eye.

Steve ignored the glare and looking up at the stained ceiling tiles, took a long drag on the cigarette, releasing most of the gray smoke back across the desk before he spoke.

"I guess I better cut to the chase, Tam. Wouldn't want to waste the time of one of Las Vegas's finest." He reached out, tapped some ash into the tray and met the glare with a harder one of his own. Tam opened both of his hands, sighed and sat back in his chair.

"Don't you find it curious," Steve began, "that Ralph Sizemore would spend two weeks comped into the Sky Room suite of the D. I. and then be asked to leave for not playing?" He stopped and waited for a reply.

The detective crossed his arms and continuing to glare, looked across at Steve.

"So? Who cares what they do with their big shot rooms? She said he was there, called her or her folks every other day and then when she didn't hear from him for two weeks she came out here looking for him." He shrugged and then continued.

"What's to figure on anyway? You know as well as I do how this usually goes. It's a dame, it's the booze, it's the horses, it's the wheel, or the slots, pick one. They eventually go back home, or they keep on going and never come back. What do we care? Take her money, trace the skip, but try and leave me out of it." Tam tossed a pencil on the desk and sighed. Steve chuckled.

"Well that was quite a little speech, Tam, especially coming from you, a man famous for few words. But here is something that may not be in your report: Shelly Cointreu saw Ralph Sizemore come out of the D.I. with two out of town tough guys and leave in a cab."

Steve removed his shoes from the metal desk and sitting forward in his chair, stubbed out his cigarette for emphasis and waited for a reaction.

"I don't suppose these goombas have names?" Tam said casually, but he wasn't glaring at Steve now and his tone had softened. Steve sneered.

"No, Tam, those types aren't in the habit of introducing themselves to doormen, but you're missing the point aren't you? Why were they coming out of the D.I. unescorted? If they were in town uninvited that would be the last place they would show their faces. And if they were invited, why wasn't some of the D.I. talent with them? And why comp a guy you know isn't a whale, only to kick him out two weeks later? No real gambler can resist the tables. He was no gambler and whoever comped him into that suite, knew it."

Tam snorted, and pointed a forefinger at Steve.

"I'll tell you why. All this is what Shelly says he saw. He should have stayed in New Orleans. He has haunts on the brain. And if these guys were there, what's the big deal? They are all thick as thieves. This nonsense about turf and who has to ask permission to be in town and who can't..... ah...." He waved a dismissive hand towards Steve. Steve laughed.

"Twenty says you follow up by the end of the week, and Shelly will tell me if you do. I think he could give you a pretty accurate description of the two mugs. You know how this town works and why it works the way it does, same as I do." Steve sneered again, and extended his hand to shake on the bet. Tam ignored the gesture.

"Look, Cannon, I got too much to do as it is. The Beatles are hitting town this week and everyone is on short rations, and the same night, Sinatra opens at the Sands again. So I got no time for anything Shelly saw." The detective stood up and pointed to the door.

"Gee, I bet Frank hates that." Steve laughed, slid his chair back, stood up and headed for the door. He stopped halfway, turned around and faced the detective who was coming around the side of the desk. Polhaus stopped short and grimaced slightly when he saw the private eye still inside his office.

"Hey Tam, I almost forgot. What do you know about Angelo Sorelli being back in town?"

Steve deliberately kept his voice as light as he could. Tam's head gave a slight jerk backwards and a perplexed look replaced the irritated one he had worn just two seconds before.

"What? Who told you that?" The detective was now clearly more interested than at any point in the conversation.

"I just heard, it that's all and figured if anybody would know if it was true, you would."

Steve shrugged his shoulders and turned again to leave. The detective reached out and tugging on his sleeve, stopped him. He had an earnestness about him that had not been present before.

"I haven't heard that. Are you sure that's what you heard?" Steve noted the lack of sarcasm that had met his description of the men Shelly had seen.

"Yep, living as big as you please in some house in old Francisco Park". Steve leaned against the door frame enjoying the new found curiosity of the detective. Tam blinked several times.

"But he was excluded six years ago. I didn't think he would show his face here again, not after the showgirl thing." Tam turned and stared at the wall for a second and turned back towards Steve.

Steve crossed his arms and shrugged. "Well, everyone on the commission that excluded him is gone, and he wasn't sponsored then, so it's nobody's tuchis in a sling if he shows back up as far as I can see."

Tam was now deep in thought as if he was the only one in the room. Steve chuckled and slid off the door frame and started out the door. He paused just before he stepped into the hallway.

"Well Tam, you think about it while you're ducking jelly beans at the concert." Tam did not reply.

Steve left the detective deep in thought and walked down a long corridor and back out into the searing midday heat. As he navigated the large Jeep back onto Fremont St., he thought about the last part of the conversation he had just ended. Tam's face had paled at the mention of Angelo Sorelli. The usual pink complexion of the German-Irishman had gone at least one shade whiter. Tam had made the collar on Sorelli and testified to what he had found in the apartment after the arrest. Pretty routine. For his part, Steve had testified to his findings on behalf of the showgirl and her boyfriend, but that had been pretty routine as well, mostly dates, times and so forth. Maybe Nick knew more.

The parking lot behind the Golden Nugget casino was three quarters full when Steve swung into a space that was reserved for employees. He walked quickly up three concrete steps and entered a long red-carpeted hallway through the glass door. The wave of air-conditioning hit before he had closed the door behind him. He shivered for a few seconds until his body adjusted to the frigid air. He pushed open another door halfway down the hall and spoke to a middle-aged woman sitting at a desk.

"Hi, Martha, is Nick around?" She looked up from her paperwork and smiled.

"Hi, Steve, how you been? We haven't seen you around here for a while. Nick is down on the floor. When you see him, remind him he needs to be back up here by two, will ya?"

"Sure, I'll tell him." Steve nodded, and letting the door swing shut continued down to the end of the hallway, descended two sets of wide carpeted steps, his hand brushing along the brass railing in the middle of the staircase and entered the main floor of the casino. He weaved through the parallel banks of slot machines, the constant coin rattle and bells making him acutely aware of how silent his three days in the desert had been. He strode along beside the blackjack tables catching the eye of the pit boss stationed in the middle who acknowledged him with a quick upward nod of his head. Over the din Steve mouthed the word 'Nick' and the pit boss pointed in the direction of the cashier cage. Steve waved and continued on toward the back of the casino.

Nick Montero was a Basque from the northern part of the state. He had begun working in the business while still a teenager and in the subsequent forty years had seen downtown grow from mud choked streets lined with thin timbered joints to the big flashy casinos that now stretched down both sides of Fremont street all the way to the Boulder highway. He was standing inside the door of the cage talking on the house phone when he spied Steve just behind a line of gamblers buying chips through the cage window. Without stopping his conversation, he waved Steve inside and after Steve squeezed by him into the small room, closed and locked the door with a string of keys he held in his free hand. He pointed to a chair in the corner next to a small door that led to the counting room.

While he waited, Steve watched the steady line of patrons transacting business with the two cashiers through the small cage windows. He kept track of those who were cashing in and those who pushed their wad of bills across the black line and received a stack of chips in return. Only one in twenty traded their chips for cash. Steve knew all too well how hard it was to leave the table with chips.

Nick hung up the phone and with his hand still resting on the receiver, looked pensively at Steve.

"Let's go somewhere where we can talk." He swung the set of keys up in front of him, selected one, and inserted it into the large double lock on the door and then held it open for Steve. Steve smiled and walked through the door, turned and waited for Nick to lock it again from the outside. Nick indicated with a slight movement of his head that Steve should follow him. Nick led the way past the cage and off the casino floor and down another short narrow corridor. Steve guessed they were going to the 'conference' room, the one in which they held the cheats and other malcontents until the cops came or security threw them out. Nick threw one leg up on the large table in the middle of the room and motioned Steve to one of the two chairs opposite him. Steve settled himself in the chair and studied the Basque's face.

"Cheer up Nick, business can't be all that bad," he joked, hoping that might lighten the mood.

"We got other things to talk about, Steve, but now that you brought it up, we have been getting hit pretty hard by at least one, maybe two crews. Sometimes card counters, sometimes riot boys, but never two nights in a row. I think they hit the Mint when they aren't here, and I have heard rumors they hit the Stardust and the Sands on the strip." Steve was not smiling now.

"Nick, let me know what nights you need me, I am always glad to help."

"Yeah, I know. But you might have to deal 21 for a few nights. You up to it?"

"I can be," Steve replied. "Just tell me when."

"OK, I will keep you posted, but let me ask you something." Nick shifted from the table and pulled out one of the chairs opposite Steve and once seated, scooted in close. Nick's rugged face held a concerned look.

"How much history you got with Angelo Sorelli?"

Steve rocked back slightly in his chair. He had expected to bring up the subject of Angelo.

"Not too much," he replied, looking for clues in the other man's face.

"Same as any of us," he continued when Nick's silence indicated he wanted more. "I knew him slightly back in '55 when he started coming here after the pro wrestling thing petered out. When he began body guarding for the Hollywood types I would run into him once in a while, and there were one or two times he figured in something I was looking into, but the only time I was on the other side of him was the showgirl thing, and they certainly didn't need me to send him up for that one. He cooked that goose himself."

Nick nodded, looked at his hands for a few seconds and then leaned in closer to Steve.

"Let me tell you what I heard." Nick's voice took on a slight tone of conspiracy. "You know Tammy Grimes, cocktails on the swing shift?" Steve nodded his head.

"Well, Sorelli is in here three or four nights in a row last week, takes a shine to Tammy and hangs around and takes her out for drinks after shift and shoots off his mouth a little too much. Says he has been called in to take care of some situations and that in the process some people who play it a little fast and wise are going to get payback. Mentions you, Tam Polhaus and Mike.. Mike.. that guy who used to run the floor at the Castaways, what's his name...?" Nick looked up at the ceiling and snapped his fingers a couple of times trying to recall the name.

"Hunter", Steve offered.

"Yeah, yeah, him." Nick pointed a finger at Steve.

"So, Tammy gets a little scared, comes to me." Nick threw up his right hand over his shoulder with the thumb extended. "He is on the excluded list so that was an easy call, Stan and Jay threw him out, 'cept he comes back the very next night and starts in at craps as big as you please. I pull him in here and talk to him myself. He's acting like he don't care and saying I can't touch him 'cause he is working for the right people now, and so on and so on. So I pick up the phone in here, called one of the Mormon boys over at the commission, and two sheriff deputies haul him outta here twenty minutes later."

Nick sat back in his chair, opened both of his hands and shrugged. "So there you have it, Steve, with the exception of the small fact that he didn't even spend the night in custody and by all accounts is still out there walking around. Moe over at Binions saw him in there two nights ago." Steve remained impassive in his chair.

"Well, Nick, I wouldn't worry about it, Angelo was always a big man in his own mind and was always shooting off his mouth." Steve was hoping the normal tone of his voice was also apparent in his face. Nick furrowed his brow and squinted slightly at Steve.

"Maybe, maybe not." Nick held up his hand and continued. "But why come back here after six years? And why didn't the commission have him escorted to the border?" Nick's eyebrows arched as he let out a deep breath.

"I tell you what, Nick, I will watch myself and mention our little chat to Tam. Doesn't pay to get too crazy about this stuff. By the way, Nick, Martha said to tell you to make sure you are back upstairs by two." Steve moved his chair back to leave. Nick reached out and clasped Steve's left wrist and gently stopped him from rising.

"Have it your way, Steve, but I thought you ought to know." His voice was lower and softer now.

"I appreciate it more than you know Nick, and I will be careful." Steve began to rise again but the older man still held him by the wrist. The voice was still low and soft.

"Steve, you gotta do something about Skipper. Stan had to throw him outta here two times this month and one of the bartenders saw him yesterday laying down drunk in front of the Sal Segev club, and the cops were having to scrape him up off the sidewalk." Nick released his grip but still held a steady gaze on Steve.

Steve slumped back down into the chair as Nick rose, straightened his jacket and put his hands in his pants pocket and looked back down at Steve.

"Yeah, I know, things have been getting worse for him. He seemed like he was making a comeback a few years ago, but not anymore." Steve's voice trailed off. He looked down at his hands folded in his lap and let out a long breath. He took out a half pack of cigarettes, tapped one from the cellophane, pulled a battered zippo from his back pocket and lit the smoke.

"See ya kid," Nick said as he squeezed Steve's shoulder and closed the door behind him.

"Yeah, see ya, Nick," Steve said quietly a few seconds later to the empty room.

After several minutes he crushed out the butt in a tray at the far end of the table and walked back down the long corridor to the parking lot. He stopped just inside the door and picked up the house phone.

"Outside line please," he requested when the operator came on the line.

A few minutes later, Bernie's voice came through the receiver.

"Bernie, can you do me a favor? Can you get me two,..no, make it three tickets to the Beatles concert this week?" He waited as Bernie said something to someone who had come up to him.

"Sure thing, Steve, I'll call Stan Irwin, since this whole Beatles deal was his idea. I can pretty much guarantee I can get them for you, he owes me, though everybody and their brother thinks their kid should go. Gotta hand it to Stan, flies them guys in for only two shows. Two shows? In Las Vegas?" Bernie laughed. "Check with me later tomorrow, I will have them here for you. Gotta go."

Steve drove out of the parking lot and turned left when he reached Fremont Street. Just past the Showboat Hotel he turned right onto Boulder Highway and settled back, his right arm draped along the top of the bench seat.

*

STEVE CANNON STOPPED his car in front of the large stucco edifice, the yellow stone bright in the afternoon sun. Several teenagers were still straggling out from the three sets of double doors that sat atop the long concrete steps. As a group of four swung open the middle doors, Steve caught a glimpse of the silver trophy case that ran along the entire length of the inside wall. The championship game footballs would still be in there. The large gold trophies would be beside them and up on the third shelf would be the faded black and white picture. In the back row was a six foot but skinnier Steve Cannon, his mouth and jaw set in a grim try at a game face, beside him a slightly smaller boy grinning up at him and not looking at the camera.

Steve pulled away from the school, and circled the city park a few blocks away. The sign at the entrance proclaimed Boulder City as the gateway to the Hoover Dam. Five blocks away from the park, Steve turned into a two track dirt driveway with a strip of grass running down the center. He shut off the engine and sat for a few minutes as the big motor cooled and ticked.

He looked up when he heard the screen door of the house close with a bang. A slim, brown haired woman descended the three wooden steps and stopped. With her left hand on her hip, she looked at the car, her face impassive and watched as the occupant closed the driver's door behind him and came towards her. When Steve got close enough to see her face he stopped.

"Hello, Val," he said as he raised his left hand in a small half wave and waited.

"Hello, yourself." The woman answered, but didn't shift her position or change her expression. Her voice was husky and constricted.

"If this is a bad time, I understand, I just wanted to see how you and the girls were getting along." He deliberately relaxed his body and smiled.

"They're not here. I sent them on an errand after their piano lesson."

"I don't mind waiting."

"Well maybe I do, Steve." The woman's voice was tighter and she crossed her arms as she spoke. "Why didn't you show up for Horace's birthday? You could have called at least."

"I was busy and out of town around then, sorry, I will make it up to him." He took a step backwards, but still kept the smile. The woman sighed, dropped her arms, turned and started towards the steps.

"I doubt if he cares much one way or the other, but the girls were sorely disappointed, that's all." She stopped at the steps, turned and looked at Steve still standing six feet from the car.

"But if you want to come in and wait, they shouldn't be too long." She grasped the handle of the screen door and entered the small wooden porch attached to the front of the house. Steve followed her in and waited just inside the front door while she took a basket of clothes from a small divan and placed it on the floor next to an ironing board that stood in front of the picture window.

Steve sat down on the end closest to the window. He watched as she selected a shirt from the basket, sprinkled a few drops of water over the collar, and after testing the iron, began to slowly press the light blue fabric.

"How's the job, Val, still working swing at the plant?" The iron hissed and released a cloud of steam as Val quickly set it upright and turned to her brother.

"Why do you have such a hard time being part of this family?" Val caught a quick sob and pressed the knuckles of her right hand against her lips. She turned back to the board and grabbing the iron began to forcefully press the steaming collar.

Steve rose slowly from his seat and took the iron gently from his sister's hand. His left hand turned her by her shoulder. He caressed her neck and pulled her towards him until her face was against his upper chest. She let her arms go limp at her sides and sobbed into the soft fabric.

"I am sorry, Val." He held her for a few moments and released her as they heard excited squeals and the banging of the screen door.

"Uncle Steve, Uncle Steve!!!" The two young girls rushed across the front room, both wrapping their arms tightly around Steve's legs as he bent down to pick them up. With his right arm he swung the smaller child over his left shoulder, and turning, he collapsed onto the divan, the older girl still clutching his right leg. He lowered his youngest niece and as he did so she placed her hands on the floor and did a small hand stand to an upright position and then scrambled back into his lap. The older one climbed up beside him and snuggled in under his right arm.

"Uncle Steve, where have you been?" Betsy, the younger girl asked as she looked up at his face from her seat on his legs.

"We miss you," Susan chimed in from under his arm.

"I missed you two even more." Steve gave Susan a hug and patty-caked both of the out stretched palms of the younger girl.

"Mom, can he stay for dinner? Please?" Susan implored.

Val watched from behind the ironing board, her arms crossed. "I am sure he has things he has to do, honey." She looked at Steve, at the same time arching her brows.

"Your mom is right, I have to get back to town, but I wanted to come out to see you how you are doing and see if you have been behaving your parents." Steve looked from one to the other and then back again. Both girls gravely nodded their heads. "Well in that case, I think you should be rewarded, but only if it is OK by your mom." He looked up quizzically at his sister who shook her head slowly back and forth.

"How would you like it if your mom took both of you to the Beatles concert this week?" As he spoke he hoisted Betsy up in the air. She began to wriggle furiously and squealed when she heard the word, 'Beatles.' Both girls jumped off the divan and running to their mother began to implore her to assent to the request. Val ignored the pleas, hugged both girls to her waist and frowned at her brother.

"When did you come up with that idea?" She asked. "And how were you able to get.....never mind, I am sure I don't want to know." She stopped for a second, shushed the clamoring children and spoke evenly to Steve.

"That is in the middle of the afternoon on a weekday. How did you think I was going to swing that with work?" She waited.

"Well Val, I figured you could call in sick for that one day." Steve paused and Val interjected.

"Steve, I used my sick leave when Horace hurt his back in May and I had to take care of him and the girls right before school got out for the summer." She removed both girl's hands from her waist and directed them to sit on the divan next to their uncle. When they were seated, she looked at Steve with a bemused expression.

"I guess if they are going to go, their uncle is going to have to take them."

Steve's half-hearted try at a protest was drowned out by squealing as the girls raced from the living room and returned a few seconds later, their hands filled with teen magazines. They flopped down on the rug in front of Steve and began to flip through the pages, laughing with each other and ignoring the adults. Val looked at her brother who had slumped back in his seat surveying the scene.

"Well it was your idea," she said as she put her hands into the shallow front pockets of her skirt. "If you would rather not take them, I think you better tell them now." For the first time in a half an hour, Val smiled. She turned and walked toward the small kitchen. "You are welcome to stay, I have plenty."

Steve drove down the highway as it sloped gently away from Boulder City. Though sunlight still tinged the top edge of the Spring Mountains in the west, lights were already visible the entire length of the valley and two or three of the larger neon hotel signs could be seen in the twilight. He pulled off the highway and by the time the tires of his car crunched onto the gravel drive it was nearly dark.

Seated in his office, Steve pulled out his notebook, removed the picture and began to read the notes he had taken when he had questioned Audrey Sizemore. He pulled a large calendar out from one of the desk doors and began to fill in some of the empty squares with dates and times. He included the date he had been given by Bonine for Ralph's departure from the hotel. When he had finished, he retrieved a magnifying glass from a cup on the desk top and lifted the lamp closer to the middle of the desk.

The picture was of a man from the chest up that filled most of the frame. He looked to be about 35 and was slightly smiling, and though it was in black and white, it was obvious his hair was light brown. Behind the man several doors of a one story apartment building could be seen. Most of the apartments of recent vintage in the city were two or three story.

Steve moved the glass to the far left bottom corner of the picture. There was some sort of fence, though it was a high chain link one, not the short variety that you would expect to find for safety around the swimming pools. Steve moved the picture closer to the glass.

Just inside the frame of the photo was the corner of a thin white line. A tennis court. There was only one property in Las Vegas that could be the background for the photo. The Bali Hai apartments. Steve put down the glass and continued to look at the picture. He smiled. The Bali Hai apartments were on Desert Inn road as it narrowed alongside the Desert Inn golf course, three hundred yards from the strip and the entrance to the hotel.

*

STEVE TURNED OFF Paradise road onto Desert Inn. It was nearly ten o'clock. He drove slowly down the street until he was opposite the Bali Hai. There were a few lights still on in the small parking lot that was right off the road. The U-shaped building sat farther back from the street and there was a small sign near the sidewalk entrance. 'Weekly Rates Available'. There were a few rooms with lights in the window, but no one was about. Steve pulled partway into the parking lot, turned full circle and headed back towards Paradise road. He drove four blocks down Paradise and turned right onto Twain. Five blocks later, he turned the Jeep right again, this time onto a narrow asphalt strip that ran the length of the first hole of the Desert Inn golf course and terminated at a chain link fence that encompassed the course maintenance shacks. He parked the car just off the road in a strip of desert that lay behind the hotel. He switched off the lights and waited.

When he was satisfied that no one was around, he locked the car, quickly crossed the road and opened a small gate in the chain link fence that allowed golfers to retrieve errant balls that ended up in the desert. He was just inside the circle of light from the yard, so he moved swiftly into the darkness and across the damp fairway until he reached a cart path eighty yards ahead. He slowed his pace on the path as there was no ambient light beneath the trees and the roots had pushed up the asphalt into irregular bumps. He continued for two hundred yards until he reached the second hole of the course. Across the wet grass several large houses lined the fairway, and just beyond them stood an eight foot high stucco wall.

At the house directly across from him a pool party was in progress, the sound of laughter and the tinkling of glasses came clearly to him in the warm summer night. He moved across the fairway towards the house just to the right of the party goers. When he reached the low wall that separated the property from the golf course he hesitated.

Just beyond the wall was a shallow slope covered with decorative rock and several small palm trees. A large kidney shaped pool threw bright turquoise light against the dark house. Steve slipped quietly over the wall, kept to the shadows at the far end of the pool and approached the back of the house. The light from the pool illuminated the sliding glass door in full view of several of the nearby guests. Steve waited until several peals of laughter erupted, then quickly slid the door open, stepped inside and drew it noiselessly closed behind him. The darkness of the interior and the icy cold of the air conditioning enveloped him at the same time. He shivered and at the same moment that his body grew accustomed to the chill, he felt a slight movement beside him. He turned to his right as Remy slipped her arm around his waist. He reached out and touched her bare shoulder and then the soft silk of her long chemise. She moved forward and pressed her body firmly to Steve's. He stroked her long dark blond hair and leaned down to her, searching for her lips. Together they gently fell back against the glass of the door Steve had just entered.

Later, Remy lay with her head in the crook of Steve's arm as they watched the waves of light from the pool play across the ceiling of the large bedroom. The revelers next door had called it a night and there was no sound except for their own breathing. Steve slid from under the single sheet and buried his toes in the plush carpet. He reached for the pack of cigarettes in the pocket of his shirt that still lay on the floor. In the glow of the lighter he held to his mouth, he saw the long willowy body and the full expectant lips. He could not see the dark eyes, but he felt them and knew the provocative look they probably held. He carefully lifted the sheet and rejoined her in bed.

"Do you remember when we first met?" He offered the cigarette as he spoke with the hand that was not cradling her head. She took it from him, inhaled shallowly and then handed it back.

"Yes, it was in the showroom of the Dunes. It was early in the morning, the room was empty, we were rehearsing a number. We had just opened Casino de Paris two months before and it was being expanded. It had just rained and you were wearing a trench coat."

"You were wearing a long green flowing gown over your costume. You smiled at me as you came down from the stage, though it was not really a day for smiling." He stopped when he saw her expression change.

"Cheryl was a friend of mine and a sweet girl. I was the one who persuaded her to leave France and come here to dance. I felt I was in some way responsible for what happened." She reached for the cigarette, took a longer drag and looked away as she handed it back to him. Steve took a deep breath.

"One question I didn't ask you then, because it didn't seem important at the time, but it has been bothering me lately. How did Angelo and Cheryl meet?"

Remy sat up and turned her face toward him and away from the light.

"Why do you ask that?" She pulled her knees to her chin and wrapped the sheet tightly around her body. "I don't like talking about him, Steve, why is this important now?"

"Angelo Sorelli is back in town, that's why." He leaned over to the nightstand and stubbed the cigarette out in a glass ashtray. He could feel her eyes on his back. When he turned back, she held his gaze for a second and then looked away.

"Angelo knew my husband." She said quietly. "He met him at one of those Hollywood parties he was always going to." She leaned forward and pushed a strand of hair behind her ear.

"But why was Angelo hanging around the Dunes?" His voice was insistent.

"I don't know, Steve, why does anybody do anything?" Her voice became slightly elevated and she pulled the sheet even tighter to her body. "You ask questions as if there is always a reason for everything that happens. A reason that is right there and obvious to everyone, except it never is, but you're the only one that doesn't see that." She quickly put her hand up to her chin and turned her face away from his. A few seconds later she turned back to him.

"I'm sorry, Steve, I can't talk about it. He beat her within an inch of her life. She was a beautiful young woman and a talented dancer, and now she lives with her parents and can barely walk." She leaned forward and began to cry. Steve lifted her gently and rolled her against his chest. He wrapped both of his arms around her body and held her tightly. After a few minutes she drifted off to sleep. Two hours later, he slipped from the house and retracing his steps he made his way back to his car.

August 18

THE OFFICE DOOR creaked as Steve swung it open and stepped inside. Though it was barely ten o'clock, the temperature was nearly ninety and there was more than a touch of humidity. The air inside the office was only a little cooler. Four feet away from a tall counter, a balding, pudgy man in his forties was sitting at a desk looking over his glasses, methodically pressing the keys of an adding machine. While he waited for him to finish, Steve looked through a stack of postcards on the counter. Each was a full color shot of the Bali Hai motel apartments from different perspectives. Steve looked down at the dirty linoleum tiles and then back at the cards covered with palm trees and blue skies.

"Can I help you?" The man had stood and moved to the counter opposite Steve.

Steve dropped the postcards back onto the counter, retrieved a brown wallet from his back pocket, pulled out a small white card and slid it across to the other side. The man, who had been smiling, frowned as he looked at the card.

"I don't talk to cops." He pushed the card back across the counter to Steve.

"I am not a cop. I am a private detective." Steve ignored the card, but leaned forward until his face was less than a foot away from the other man's face.

"I need some information on a man who may be a guest of yours."

When the clerk didn't say anything more, Steve reached into his coat pocket, pulled out the photograph of Ralph Sizemore and held it under the man's nose.

"This is the guy I am looking for. Ralph Sizemore, now what about it?" Steve demanded.

The clerk took two steps back towards his desk and when he was out of Steve's reach, folded his arms and nodded towards the picture Steve still held out at arm's length.

"Yeah, he stayed here, but he is gone now and that's all I know except he owes me eighty-four bucks." The man reached over his desk and selecting a small piece of paper from the stack in front of the adding machine, waved it in Steve's direction.

"'Cept that's not his name. His name is Beech, Wallace Beech, or at least that was the name he gave me. Haven't seen him for two weeks." The clerk moved around his desk and sitting down again, prepared to resume his work.

"When did he check in, how long did he stay, and what possessions did he leave behind?"

Steve's voice held the same demanding tone as before but this time he punctuated it by moving into the small opening that allowed access behind the counter. His six foot-two frame blocked out most of the sunlight that came through the glass door. The clerk stopped pressing his keys.

"Look, I don't want any trouble." He sat back in his chair, raised his arms and turned his palms outward. Steve leaned casually against the edge of the counter.

"No trouble, no trouble at all, pal." He smiled and pulled out his pack of cigarettes, offering one to the seated clerk with the same motion. When the clerk demurred, Steve tapped a cigarette softly on the counter and looked out the dirty window at the tennis court.

"How would you like to get your eighty-four bucks back?" He turned back to the clerk but this time without the smile.

"Sure, you bet I would. Are you going to take care of it?" The clerk picked up a lighter from the desk and held it up to Steve. Steve shook his head and placed the Pall Mall back into his pocket.

"No, that won't be me, pal, but I do know where his sister and your money is." Steve smiled again and waited.

"What do you want to know?"

"I want the date he got here, what he did, who he talked to, and I want to see what he left behind." Steve moved out from the opening and gestured towards the door.

The clerk opened a drawer in the desk, pulled out a ring of keys and shuffled past Steve and pushed through the glass door. As he led Steve towards a small hallway and a brown door with no room number on it, he spoke back over his shoulder.

"He checked in on the 17th of July, last time I saw him was on the 4th of August when I stopped by his room to ask for the rent. He only went out at night as far as I know, didn't socialize with anyone, though he must have gone to the Orange Julius up on the strip, judging by the trash he left in his room. Here we are."

The clerk stopped before the door and pushed a small brass key into a padlock that hung from the door at shoulder height. He swung open the door, stepped inside and pulled the small chain beneath a single light bulb that was suspended from the ceiling. Steve stepped just inside the doorway and watched as the man sorted through several suitcases and duffel bags piled on a low table. He selected a medium sized brown leather case and clearing a space, spread it open. Steve stepped forward but the clerk turned from the table and blocked his way.

"Are you sure I am going to get my 84 bucks? It's just that the last guy said he was going to pay, but he never showed back up here." The clerk bit his lower lip and rested his hand on the edge of the suitcase.

"What last guy?" Steve stepped forward, removed the man's hand from the suitcase and at the same time rotated his hips against the man's side moving him away from the case. Steve now stood in front of the case and was staring intently down at the clerk.

"What guy?" He asked again. The clerk blanched and stepped away from the table.

"A guy. Ten days ago. Big ugly guy with a deep voice. Said he was a friend of Beech's and that Beech had something of his...so... I."

"You let him go through the suitcase?" Steve hissed.

"He said he would pay me." The clerk replied weakly.

"Great." Steve looked disgustedly down at the case.

"Did he find anything?" Steve picked up a wrinkled shirt and a brown wingtip shoe. He held them up as he waited for the man to reply.

"I don't know. He didn't seem real happy with anything in there, like what he was looking for wasn't there." The man inched toward the door in an attempt to again get out of Steve's reach. Steve put the clothing back in the suitcase and closed the latch.

"Come on, we're going back to the office." He used the suitcase to push the clerk through the door and out into the hot concrete hallway. When they were back in the office, Steve motioned for the man to sit down in the desk chair. He reached down and pulled the phone over to the counter and then turned back so he could see the clerk. He dialed the phone and a few seconds later the connection was made.

"Miss Sizemore?" Steve put his hand over the receiver and motioned for the clerk to hand him some paper and a pen.

"Cannon here, I need to talk with you." He waited while she replied.

"No, the golf lesson can wait. I found out where your brother went after he left the D.I. and I have some things here that might belong to him."

"Yes, I need to come over now." He emphasized the last word. "But there is one thing. Your brother left owing money. I will take it out of the money you gave me the other day and you can reimburse me when I see you." As he spoke, he cradled the phone with his shoulder next to his chin and wrote down the amount on the piece of paper under the words: 'Received by' followed by a short line.

"Yes, ten minutes, and don't go anywhere until I get there." He hung up the phone and looked down at the clerk. Steve opened his wallet and extracted six twenty dollar bills, spread them out evenly and held them up for the clerk to see. He handed him the piece of paper and the pen.

"Sign your name and write: 'Paid in Full' underneath." He watched while the man quickly did as he was told and handed the paper back to Steve. When he had safely placed the paper in his sport coat pocket, he leaned back on the counter and once again held the wad of bills up in front of the clerk.

"Now, you're going to tell me everything you remember about the big ugly guy."

The entrance to the Desert Rose suite at the D.I. was at the end of a long corridor accessed by a private elevator. Steve had waited for several minutes until the floor manager arrived and after securing permission from the suite's occupant, had escorted Steve personally to the door. The manager pressed a hidden button in the door frame and the glossy wooden door slid open to the right. He waited until Steve had stepped into a marbled foyer before closing the door behind him using the same button.

Steve stood three steps above a sunken living room that ended in a glass wall that ran the entire length of the suite. Even from where he stood the whole eastern side of the valley was spread before him, punctuated by the space-needle inspired Landmark Hotel, which was only partially built and seemed to loom just outside the window. Beyond the Landmark, the Convention Center dominated a large parking lot with its' spaceship like presence, and lying just east of that was the pink stucco façade of the horse track: Las Vegas Downs.

Steve turned as he heard the sound of ice in a glass and watched as Audrey Sizemore glided into the room. She wore a pink Izod golf shirt over a pair of black pedal-pushers, her dark brown hair was pulled back into a pony-tail and she was barefoot. She stopped halfway into the room at a mirrored bar, selected a decanter filled with a clear liquid from the array and poured herself another drink. She retrieved a second glass from under the bar, filled it with ice from a crystal bucket and held it up in Steve's direction. When Steve shook his head, she placed it back on the bar and crossed the room and sat down on a low couch that was against the long window. Steve descended three steps, crossed in front of her into the room and sat down in a chair opposite the woman. Audrey Sizemore took a small sip from her glass and pointed to the floor by Steve's feet.

"Well, where are they?" She rubbed the glass against her cheek, her eyes narrowed as she spoke.

"Where is what, Miss Sizemore?" Steve leaned back in his chair and crossed his legs.

"You said on the phone, that you had my brother's things. I

would like them now." She pointed the glass at Steve as she finished the sentence.

"I said I had some things that might belong to your brother. I can't be sure until I have had some time to examine them, and then I will decide what happens to them." He stared at her coldly and held her gaze until she looked away.

"Before I forget, you owe me eighty-four dollars." He reached in his coat pocket and after pulling out the small sheet of paper, laid it on the round table by his chair. Audrey Sizemore didn't glance at the paper but took another sip from her glass and looked back at Steve.

"So, you haven't found my brother, is that what you are trying to tell me, Mr. Cannon?"

"I'm not trying to tell you anything, Miss Sizemore. If I had found your brother or knew where he was, you would be the first to know." Steve stood up from the chair and walked to the window.

"The truth of the matter is this, Miss Sizemore: Your brother has gone missing and there is at least one very bad character also looking for him. So I think our time together is best spent going over some of your answers to my questions. And this time let's see if you can do a bit better."

Steve turned from the window, walked to the bar, and selected a decanter that looked like it might contain scotch. He poured himself two fingers of the brown liquid into the glass she had left and then sat back down in the chair. He took a small sip and leveled his gaze at Audrey.

"I don't have to sit here and be spoken to in this manner." She leaned towards Steve, her small chin jutting forward. "I can have you thrown out of here." She placed her glass on the table in front of the couch. "I will pay you the agreed upon amount and then we part company right now." She stood and crossed the room to where her purse sat on a narrow table below a beveled mirror. Steve stood and again walked to the window. He could see the traffic moving slowly on Paradise road, the heat waves shimmering just above the asphalt. He turned and watched while Audrey pulled her check book from her purse, holding it with one hand while she searched the interior pockets for a pen.

"If you are going to write a check, you better make it for double." He took another sip of whiskey and smiled into the glass as she stopped her fumbling and looked at him in surprise.

"You don't seem to fully appreciate your situation, Miss Sizemore, so let me spell it out for you." He motioned with the glass for her to take a seat in the chair he had just vacated. Audrey slowly walked over and sat in the chair, letting her purse slip to the carpet. Steve continued.

"Here is how I see things, Miss Sizemore: Your brother did not come here as a sightseer or gambler, but for some other purpose. What that was or is, I don't know, but this I do know: He is in some kind of trouble or shortly will be, and if the people he has been seen associating with don't find him, they most certainly will find you." He paused to let the message sink in. Audrey's face had gone blank, but her hands were twisting the leather straps of her purse.

"So this is how it is, Miss Sizemore: I am your only hope to keep bad things from happening. I hope it is not too late for your brother, but you and I sitting here chatting proves it might not be too late for you. The choice is yours." Audrey pulled the bag back up onto her lap.

"I will give you what you want," she said quietly.

"The money is not as important as information, so suppose you tell me why your brother was here in the first place. The first time I asked, you said you had no idea. Now is the time for a better answer." He walked over and stood two steps away from her chair. She looked down at the strap in her hands. She could see his brown shoes motionless in front of her.

"He came out here to invest in a land deal." She looked up at Steve, her eyes were wide open.

"What kind of land deal and with whom?"

"I don't know, but when he told me about it, two days before he left, he was very excited. He said that his timing was perfect and that his money was going to save the deal and in return he was going to own half the project."

"So you have no idea who any of the players here are?" He stepped back and leaned against the couch.

"No, I don't. The only other thing I should tell you is that I am here partly out of concern for my brother, but also because of my family interest. He took a large sum of money out of the trust we control for the benefit of my parents. They don't know yet. I came here to try to get it back."

"How much money, Miss Sizemore?" His voice was calm, but he kept his eyes locked on hers.

"$500,000, Mr. Cannon." She rose and went to pour herself another drink.

"In cash?" Steve downed the last of his drink and joined her at the mirrored bar.

"Yes. The bank confirmed the withdrawal the day I flew here." She filled his glass from the same decanter he had selected earlier.

"Well, Miss Sizemore, I don't have many answers in this deal, but I can tell you that the cash is nowhere in his belongings, if it ever was." He took the glass from her hand and returned to the couch, sitting back against two gold silk pillows. He looked at her back as she poured more of the clear liquid.

"Have you ever heard the name 'Wallace Beech'?" Steve said the name slowly and watched for a reaction.

"No, should that mean something to me?" She looked down at the drink in her hand and swirled the ice around in the glass.

"Don't know, it was just the name your brother used when he checked into the motel down the road. I thought that you might know why he would do that." Audrey remained at the bar. She took a large drink from her refilled glass before she answered.

"I have no idea why he would do such a thing. But if as you say he was mixed up with bad people, he might be afraid." She turned and looked at Steve. He lowered his eyelids and waited before he spoke again.

"Yes, he might be afraid, Miss Sizemore, or there might be other reasons." He looked up and held his gaze on her.

"If he indeed used another name, Mr. Cannon, I don't know why and I have never heard of Wallace Beech."

"Well for now, Miss Sizemore, it matters less what he is calling himself. He is missing in a town where that sort of thing happens frequently." Steve dropped his gaze, and deposited his drink on the table.

"What should I do now, Mr. Cannon?" She watched him settle back into the pillows.

"Well, this hotel is either the safest place in town for you or the most dangerous. I don't know which. But either way, a change couldn't hurt. Where is your phone?" She indicated a small room off the foyer where a white phone sat on a marble table. Steve walked across the foyer into the room and picked up the receiver. After several minutes he returned and sat back down on the couch. He pulled out his notebook and ripped out the last page. He wrote for a few minutes and then placed the page on the table in front of him.

"Give this to the cab driver. Pack up and leave this afternoon. Don't tell anyone where you are going. The cab will take you to a townhouse development farther out in the valley. A friend of mine has a penthouse there and the complex is gated. There are people there who are expecting you and can bring you anything you want. Do not leave the penthouse until you hear from me. Do you understand?" She nodded.

"What are you going to do, Mr. Cannon?" She still stood at the small bar holding on to her glass.

"I am going to try to re-involve the police in looking for your brother, and while I am doing that, I will ask around and try to get a line on the deal that you say your brother was here for."

"I will write you a check, Mr. Cannon." She walked to the chair and picked up the checkbook from the small table.

"Skip it." He looked across at Audrey.

"I am going to do the same as I would have anyway, money or no money. My neck is on the line here just like yours." He put his notebook back into the inside pocket of his sport coat, and gazed at her with a blank expression for several long seconds.

"Remember, don't go anywhere or talk to anyone until you hear from me. My number is on the back of the paper. Best time is after ten at night, or early in the morning." She followed him to the door at the end of the foyer and pressed the button. He walked back down the long corridor and descended in the elevator alone. When he reached the lobby he stopped at a small cubicle and picked up one of the white courtesy telephones. A few seconds later John Bonine picked up the phone in his office.

"Well, Mr. Bonine, I hope you have something for me." Steve waited for a response from the other side of the line.

"I do." He replied in a quiet voice.

"Who is it? I'm not going to stand down here in the lobby and guess."

"You're here?" The voice became panicky and not so quiet.

"Yeah, I'm here. I thought we could do this easy. You know, no big fuss. Right?"

"The name you want is 'Nash Brannock'." Bonine answered quickly and his voice had gone quiet again.

"Are you sure?" Cannon looked up and down the two hallways that intersected the part of the lobby where he was standing. Seeing no one suspicious he turned his attention back to the phone.

"Yes, I am sure. Just don't mention to anyone that I was the one who told you."

"Wait. Are you trying to tell me that you didn't get permission to tell me the name?"

'No, I got permission." The voice was even quieter now.

"Then, I don't see your problem, Mr. Bonine."

"I just don't want to be involved anymore. They told me to give you the name and I did."

The phone clicked twice in Cannon's ear. Cannon picked up the phone, got the operator again, thought better of it and hung up the phone. Two blocks from the Desert Inn he pulled into the parking lot of a coffee shop and parked by the phone booth fifty yards from the entrance.

"Hello, Tam?" He spoke quickly into the receiver when the detective answered his phone.

"Let me buy you dinner tonight. There are some things you need to hear."

"What time?" The cop seemed distracted.

"9:00 at El Cholos."

"Fine. See you then."

The phone clicked again and Steve walked back to his car. As he swung open the front door he noticed a new dark blue Ford sedan pull slowly into the parking lot. Two men were in the front seat. When the passenger saw Steve, he turned his head and said something to the driver. A few seconds later they pulled up to the curb opposite the front door of the café but didn't cut the engine. Steve backed his car slowly out of the parking space until he was directly behind the Galaxie. He stared through the rear window of the car as the two men looked straight ahead and remained motionless. He committed the plate number to memory and after a few seconds he put the transmission into drive and slowly pulled back onto the Strip. When he had gone a block, he abruptly turned left across two lanes and made a U-turn in front of the Riviera Hotel. A few seconds later he passed in front of the entrance to the coffee shop. The blue sedan was just leaving and heading in the opposite direction. Steve smiled and when the traffic in front of him cleared, he made another U-turn and within three blocks was behind the blue Ford as it approached the intersection with East Sahara Avenue. The sedan drifted into the far right lane and then turned abruptly into the parking lot beside the Sahara Hotel. Steve watched as it sped to the back of the lot heading towards Paradise Road. Steve slowed down and drove through the intersection and continued north on Las Vegas Boulevard.

Two blocks below Fremont Street, Steve parked the car, put a dime in a nearby parking meter and walked half a block towards Fremont before reversing course. After passing his car, he walked for another two blocks before he stopped in front of a rundown one story motel. Most of the windows facing the street were covered with aluminum foil. Garbage and old keno tickets littered the small brown patch of dirt outside the gray cinderblock office. Steve walked down the cracked sidewalk under a canopy of green corrugated plastic sheets and stopped in front of a door. The number 9 hung upside down on the peeling black paint. He stepped forward and put his ear carefully to the door. When he heard no sounds from inside, he rapped several times with the back of his knuckles. After a few more seconds he knocked harder, then stepped back into the sun and looked up and down the deserted corridor.

"Can I help you?" The voice came from behind him.

Steve turned and watched as a thin middle-aged man approached across the dusty asphalt from the far side of the motel.

"Oh, it's you." The man slowed his stride and smiled. Steve stepped back into the shade and waited for the man to join him.

"You seen him in a while?" Steve rubbed his jaw and indicated the door behind him, when the man had reached the narrow sidewalk.

"Nope, not since late Sunday night when the cops brought him home. Had to wake me up to open his room." The man kicked half-heartedly at a small weed that was sprouting from a crack in the sidewalk.

"You got the key on you?" Steve asked.

"Well now that's a problem... because I can't..." Steve cut him off.

"You got the key or not?" He sighed and looked at the man.

The man looked up at Steve and smiled.

"Sure, I'll get it. After all, you're paying the freight." He chuckled and trying to stay out of the sun, squeezed past Steve and disappeared into the office three doors away. When he returned, he held out the silver key to Steve, but pulled it back slightly as Steve stepped forward to reach for it.

"Oh, I almost forgot, the rent's gone up, starting the first of this month." The man grinned sheepishly and held the key out to Steve. Steve took the key and looked at the man for a few seconds.

"I'll stop by the office before I leave," Steve said flatly and continued looking at the man. After a pause the man straightened up quickly and started to back away.

"Oh sure…sure thing, you go right ahead, I will be in there if you need me." He pointed to the office over his shoulder as he continued to walk backwards away from Steve. When he had retreated through the door and closed it, Steve turned the key in the lock.

A rush of hot stale air pushed past the door as Steve opened it. Coming in from the bright sun, the room was pitch black. Steve stood in the doorway and waited for his eyes to adjust. Across the brown linoleum, a bed was shoved into a corner. Next to the bed was a red leather chair, the only other piece of furniture in the room. When he could see clearly, Steve walked over to the bed and looked down at Skipper who lay sideways, one foot on the floor and one arm flung over his face. He walked around the bed and into the small bathroom just beyond. There were several empty pint whiskey bottles in the white porcelain sink and several more behind a shower curtain in the bathtub. He filled one of the bottles with water from the faucet and returned to the main room. He gently removed the arm from Skippers face and slowly poured the water onto his head.

Skipper groaned slightly and rolled off his back onto his side. Steve walked over to the chair and after removing a newspaper and placing it on the floor, sat down. Several minutes later, Skipper blinked his eyes a few times and looked across the bed at his visitor.

"Stevie." He spoke weakly, but his face held a small smile.

"You know, I was going to take a cab out to see ya, but…" He groaned as he tried to lift his head from the bed, laid back down and sighed deeply.

"Don't get up, Skipper, just lie back and take it easy." Steve rose halfway from his chair in case his advice went unheeded.

"Yeah, OK, Stevie, I'll just…." His words trailed off as he drifted back to sleep. Steve waited for the five minutes it took his friend to come around again. Skipper looked over at Steve, his eyes a little wider than they had been earlier.

"I needed to tell you, that I saw Johnny Spivey the other night coming out of the Pioneer Club. He looked swell, Stevie, says he has two kids, one in college already." Skipper carefully bent his elbow and slowly propped his head up. He looked across at Steve and smiled.

"What do you say to that? Huh?" Skipper laughed softly to himself. "Say, you got any smokes?" He looked expectedly at his friend across the room.

"Sure, Skipper, here you go." Steve pulled a pack from his shirt pocket and put them into the outstretched hand along with his lighter. Skipper's hand trembled as the lighter tumbled onto the bed. Steve picked it up, pulled one of the cigarettes from the pack, lit it himself and handed it to Skipper. As Skipper took in the first deep drag, Steve picked up an empty food carton from the floor by the bed and placed it near Skippers hand. When he had settled back into the chair, Skipper looked up at Steve.

"I need a drink bad, Stevie." He closed his eyes and pressed the side of his temple with his free hand.

"When was the last time you had one?" Steve said gently. Skipper opened his eyes.

"This morning, I think." He dropped the cigarette into the food carton and closed his eyes again.

"And when was the last time you went to meeting?"

"I don't know. Bill was supposed to come and take me, but I haven't seen him." Skipper opened his eyes and picked the cigarette up again and took a short puff.

"Bill called me two weeks ago, and said you are never here when he comes around." Steve spoke quietly and watched as his friends eyes shifted away.

"Ah... he knows where to find me. Just doesn't want to go into those joints. I understand." Skipper sighed and stared at a gap in the curtain which let a small shaft of light into the room.

"You know, I asked Johnny why we were the lucky ones that got off that island alive...you know.. how you and I talk about who did and who didn't sometimes...." His voice trailed off for a few seconds.

"Didn't want to talk about it... told me to forget it." Skipper looked down at the cigarette that had burned close to his fingers.

"How can he say that, Stevie, he was there...we were all there." The shaft of light had moved down and it now fell across Skipper's face illuminating three days growth of beard.

Steve stood up, crossed the room, pulled the cigarette butt from Skippers hand and stubbed it out in the carton. He looked down at his boyhood friend. Skipper looked up at Steve, tears were streaming from the dark brown eyes.

"It was bad, Stevie,...it was real bad." Skipper's chest came off the bed as sobs convulsed his body. Steve knelt on the bed and wrapped his arms around Skipper's shoulders. Skipper buried his face in the back of Steve's hand. Steve could hear the muffled sobs.

"I know, Skip, I know..." Steve held on tightly until the sobbing slowed. He waited until Skipper grew quiet, and then pulled a thin blanket over his shoulders. He bent over from his position at the end of the bed and spoke softly.

"Skipper, I am going to call Bill. Today is Tuesday. He will take you to meeting." He smoothed the hair on the side of Skippers head and waited for the small nod. A few minutes later in the motel office, Steve dialed Bill's number. Bill's voice was quiet when he realized who was calling and why.

"I have tried everything, Mr. Cannon. I don't see what else I can do unless Mr. John himself makes the commitment." He paused and waited for Steve's reply.

"If you don't take him tonight, I will." Steve put a strong emphasis on the word, 'will'. After another pause, Bill reluctantly agreed.

"If he is not there at six, I will leave without him." Bill emphasized the same word.

"I will stay with him until you come." Steve hung up the receiver. He turned around just as the motel manager spun quickly in his chair and pretended to look for something in a large stack of papers. Steve's eyes narrowed as he spoke.

"So what's the rent now?" He didn't intend his tone to be as gruff as it sounded.

"Well," the man replied as he held out a folded piece of paper to Steve. "As you can see, it has gone up to fifty-five dollars a month." Steve glanced at the paper without taking it and looked back down at the man.

"And five dollars for laundry." The man added, tapping the paper. Steve opened his wallet and counted out ten twenty dollar bills. He looked again at the man and pulled out another. He placed them on the desk in front of him.

"There's three months, plus more in case your beauty sleep gets interrupted again."

Steve's lips twisted into a slight sneer. The man quickly scooped up the bills and didn't look at Steve.

"I will need a receipt for that." Steve tapped a blue receipt book near the man's elbow. While the receipt was being written, Steve stepped outside and lit a cigarette. He looked at his watch. It was 3:35.

When Steve went back into the room, Skipper was fast asleep.

Steve slumped into the chair and listened to his friend's shallow breathing. Skipper was right, they had all been there. All thirteen had joined the special outfit together and all but one had made it to that stinking island jungle in the Pacific. Only six left it, and he sometimes wondered if Skipper was right when he had once told Steve they had all died on that island, and they were just six guys that possessed that knowledge a little longer than the others.

While he waited, Steve flipped back through his notes, adding the new pieces of information he had learned today. Audrey Sizemore had lied. Did she do it to protect her brother? And if so, was she telling the truth now? And why had she not seemed too surprised when Steve mentioned that there were bad characters involved and that his own neck was on the line? Why had Angelo Sorelli not paid her a visit? If he was looking for her brother, Audrey Sizemore ensconced in the third best suite at the D.I. was too conspicuous to be missed. She was also supposedly from the east, so how would she know about the Cannon family? And lastly: Nash Brannock. Steve suddenly thought of Remy, sitting alone most nights in that large empty house. What was his connection to Sizemore? What would compel Nash to comp Sizemore at the D.I.? And why not at the Dunes, his own turf? Steve slid down farther into the chair and closed his eyes.

Two hours later, Steve helped Skipper into a cab. Skipper's face was ashen as he sat in the back seat beside Bill. Though it was still 95 degrees out, Skipper had a long brown coat on with the collar button closed. Steve handed the cab driver some money, patted Skipper on the shoulder and watched as the cab pulled away from the curb and disappeared around the corner.

Steve walked to his car, pulled a parking ticket from under his windshield wiper and crammed it into his coat pocket. He drove for three blocks and turned into a Terrible Herbst gas station when he saw the sign that advertised regular for 17 cents. Even though Steve was too preoccupied with the gas pump to see the blue Ford pull up behind him, he saw the face of Angelo Sorelli reflected in his side mirror before he heard the distinctive gruff voice.

"Well, look who we have here boys," Angelo rasped as he turned partway back towards the car indicating Steve at the same time with his left hand. The man who had been sitting in the front passenger seat was standing by his door, surveying the immediate area of the gas station. Steve had never seen him before and even though the driver was partially obscured by sun glare off the windshield, Steve was pretty sure he had never seen him before either.

Steve's shoulder muscles tightened and his grip whitened on the pump handle. Angelo turned back to Steve. He was wearing a dark blue sharkskin suit which had a sheen of green iridescence. His pink shirt was open at the collar and barely contained the thick fleshy neck. His eyes were widely spaced above the puffy oft-broken nose, and long sideburns crept two inches past his ear and were dyed jet black as was the rest of his hair. His lower lip fell away slightly from the upper one resulting in a permanent sneer. He was at least two inches taller than Steve.

"I told the boys here that all we had to do was cruise by the rummy's dive once in a while, and bingo! I was right." He shot both hands forward in the manner of a gunslinger and laughed. He opened both of his hands out in front of his chest and smiled.

"What do you want Angelo?" Steve's voice was a low growl. He fastened his eyes on the gangsters' and slowly pulled the pump from the gas tank. Angelo stopped laughing when he saw the nozzle pointed at him from two feet away. His dark eyes narrowed as he straightened his suitcoat.

"Just this." He hissed, and pointed at Steve. "You better get out of this town while you can still walk. You have stepped out of bounds, buddy boy, and there ain't nobody gonna save ya. Not that schmuck Bernie or Tam O'Shanter, your cop buddy, nobody." Steve laughed.

"Well, Sorelli, at least you are threatening men these days. Did you run out of showgirls to beat up?" Steve punctuated the last word with a quick forward movement of the gas nozzle. Angelo involuntarily backed up a step as Steve smiled. Angelo turned slightly, straightened his coat again, and pointed at Steve.

"Make it soon, dead man." Angelo turned and walked to the back of the car and got in behind the driver. As soon as the other man closed the front passenger door, the blue sedan backed quickly out of the gas station and raced off toward Fremont Street.

Foxy's was almost deserted as Steve pushed open the heavy glass door. He had called Bernie from the gas station and Steve now waited in front of a double wooden door in back of the lunch counter while the waiter fumbled with the keys. Before the waiter could open the lock, Bernie opened the door from the other side. He was wearing a smile and a dark green Hawaiian shirt. Steve followed him into the private casino where two or three nights a month, depending upon who was in town, legendary poker and craps sessions would take place. It had been at least six months since Steve had been in the spacious backroom. He preferred to play his poker with strangers downtown or with a close group of friends. He had little patience for the clannish and rude behavior of several of the entertainers that frequented the games. Bernie led him to a card table covered in green felt and surrounded by four leather chairs. Nearby was a small refrigerator filled with beer and on the far wall was an eight foot long bar. Bernie stood by the chair nearest the refrigerator and Steve sat in the chair across from him.

"Well you are certainly in it now my friend." Bernie spoke into the refrigerator as he extracted two cold bottles of beer. He opened them quickly with an opener built into the side of the appliance, and put them on the table in front of Steve. Condensation ran from the bottles and made dark rings in the felt. Steve picked up the one nearest him and took a big swig. Bernie sat down and grinned across the table.

"Was he as ugly as you remember?" Steve and Bernie both laughed heartily, the beer threatening to come out of Steve's nose and he had to concentrate to keep it in. When he recovered, he pointed his beer bottle at Bernie.

"Yeah, except, he is dyeing his hair." They both laughed again. They clinked bottles and took long slow drinks of the beer.

"Why do you think he is having such a conniption fit about you?" Bernie waved his bottle in Steve's direction. "He is being pretty brazen for an ex-felon in a town that don't like his kind of trouble." Bernie's brow furrowed as he waited for an answer. Steve paused and thought for a moment his beer bottle poised in mid-air.

"Unlikely to be the Sizemore deal. I just found out about his connection to that today," Steve mused. He looked across at his friend.

"How is our guest doing? And by that I mean what is she doing? Has she made any contact with anyone?"

"No, I got Rocco from Morocco out there keeping things running smooth. The place was due to be rented this weekend, but we took care of that and got the guy and his wife a house on the Stardust golf course for the same price, so he will be happy. I talked with Roc an hour ago and she hasn't made any calls or received any. He will let me know if that changes."

"Thanks Bernie, I owe you a big one." He reached across and clinked the smaller man's beer bottle. Bernie smiled.

"You know I always try to support our veterans." They both chuckled. Steve took the last swig of his beer and placed the empty bottle on the table.

"Bernie, tell me about that land deal you were talking about six weeks ago. The one you thought had to be shady. Who was it suggested that you look into it?" Steve spoke to Bernie's backside as the deli owner was pulling two more beers out of the fridge. Bernie straightened, looked at Steve and then at the wall and thought for a minute.

"It was Nash, pretty sure. At his pool party, which you missed by the way, it was one of his best." Bernie stopped and pointed a finger at Steve with the hand holding a beer bottle. "But no, before that it was Mike Hunter who first came in here talking it up. I wasn't too interested, but it turns out that Nash's whole party was people who had invested or ones that Nash was trying to get to buy in." Bernie handed the bottle to Steve and sat down. Steve waited until Bernie had taken a sip of his beer.

"Who was there that you remember?" Steve put the bottle to his lips, thought better of it and placed it inside the dark ring the first bottle had made.

"It was a mixture, but most everybody I was introduced to was from LA or Hollywood. Not any big names you would know; mostly producers, and executives from the studios. Not really my kind of crowd. Does this figure into something for you?"

"Maybe. Miss Sizemore came across with another story today about her brother taking family money that didn't belong to him to invest in a land deal out here. Thought there might be a connection." Steve looked at Bernie and shrugged.

"So why were you so uninterested? You own more real estate around here than anybody I know."

"Are you kidding? They had options on four big tracks right in the middle of the wash. You know where Vegas Valley road peters out into the desert?" Steve nodded. "Well right there." Bernie moved his fingertip along the green felt and stabbed it at the imaginary point on the table.

"Would take an act of congress and maybe the whole Army Corp of Engineers to fix that floodplain. Might only flood once every twenty years, but it will take everything with it when it does."

"Did you share your opinion with Nash?" There was more than a hint of concern in his voice.

"Naw. No point. I don't think Nash cared if I threw in one way or the other. There were just a few of us included for local color. He was schmoozing the LA people all night, you know, being the big wheel. They were lapping it up."

'Was....?" Steve stopped himself, reached for the beer and took a quick sip. Bernie looked at him quizzically.

"Was... What? Bernie held his hands out, one holding the beer.

"Nothing, Bernie, I just have a lot on my mind."

"I gotta go. Meeting Tam at El Cholos. Wanna come?" He smiled warmly at his old friend.

"What? And watch you two eat Mex food? Nah, no way, but be my guest." Bernie laughed and removed the bottles from the table. He reached into his pocket with his free hand and tossed a small envelope to Steve. Steve opened the packet partway and saw the three light blue tickets. Steve smiled at Bernie.

"Damn, Bernie. Seems I owe you again." He held up the envelope.

"Ah nothing to it." Bernie waved his hand dismissively. "Stan owes me a gazillion favors and this is one of the few times I could collect for real. He usually only wants to take me out to Winterwood, that crappy golf course he likes to play."

"What? You're always telling me how well you score there." Steve laughed.

"I do, I do, but the smell, when the wind blows and it always blows." Bernie made a face.

"Right by the sewage plant, ugh."

As they talked, they walked to the front door of the deli and shook hands as they usually did when parting. Bernie walked through the open door into the casino which was filling up with the local after work crowd. Steve looked at his watch. 8:40. Just enough time to get downtown to El Cholos. Before he drove off, he sat for a few minutes and smoked a cigarette. He was one of the few people that knew Bernie didn't like smoking. Bernie didn't make a big deal to anyone about it and certainly never made anyone feel uncomfortable. Steve made a point to never smoke around his friend and he always had the idea that Bernie appreciated it.

*

EL CHOLOS SAT on a side street just off of Main, five blocks below Fremont Street. It was a medium sized restaurant run by the extended Dominguez family. Steve would stop by occasionally around eleven and join the family for a meal just after closing. On this Tuesday night it was only a quarter full.

When he entered through the glass door from the street, he saw Tam sitting at one of the small tables with a beer watching a nearby family celebrating one of the kid's birthdays. The owner's son immediately came up to him and greeted him warmly. He asked the young man if they could use one of the quieter tables in the back. He led him to the table where the detective was sitting. Tam looked up at the two men.

"You're late Cannon." He growled. Steve looked at his watch. It was two minutes past nine.

"Gee, Tam. Let's not let that spoil our evening." He picked up the detective's beer from the table. "Come on. We're going back here where it's quieter." Steve walked down two short steps without waiting for Tam. He selected a table that couldn't be seen from the door and sat down with his back to the wall. Tam plopped down across from him in the only other chair. He reached across and took his beer from Steve's hand. When the waiter brought a beer for Steve, he handed the menus back to the man and told him that they would have the usual.

"What is it I am going to be eating or is it too impolite to ask?" The detective asked when the waiter had gone. He had a sour look on his face.

"Tamales and chile rellenos." Steve replied as he took a sip of beer and looked directly at Tam until he had his attention.

"What?" The detective was still irritated. Steve decided to go with no preliminaries.

"I ran into Angelo Sorelli today." He held the beer bottle up in front of his face and began to examine the label.

"What? Where?" Tam reached out and took the bottle from Steve's hand and put it out of reach on the far side of the table.

"At the Terrible Herbst downtown." Steve picked up the rest of the detective's beer and emptied it in one gulp. He held up the bottle and caught the attention of the waiter.

"Here is the plate number on the car they were driving." He pulled out a pen, printed the tag number in block letters on the edge of the paper place mat, tore off the corner and pushed it across to the detective's side of the table.

"Who is they?" Tam picked up the scrap of paper and squinted at it as he held it next to the hurricane glass holding a candle on the edge of the table.

"Two guys that followed me out of the D.I. this morning. I didn't recognize either of them. I'm guessing there is a good chance they are the same guys that Shelly saw with Sizemore. Which means they have Sizemore or..." The two detectives exchanged a quick glance across the table.

"What did Angelo have to say?" Tam folded the corner of the placemat and put it in his breast pocket.

"Well, among other things, he said I was a dead man if I didn't leave town and that you and Bernie would be unable to save me, try as you might." Steve snickered and brought the beer bottle up to his lips, then paused.

"Oh and he referred to you as Tam O'Shanter." Steve then took the sip.

The detective scoffed.

"Yeah, he always call..." He stopped himself. He quickly looked up at Steve. A look of dismay crossed his face when he saw that Steve was gazing back at him intently. For several seconds neither man said anything. Finally, Tam sighed, and rubbed his face with both hands.

"Well I guess you deserve to hear the sad story if anybody does." Tam leaned back in his chair and took a deep breath. "OK, here it is. Short and sweet."

"My father was a cop in San Francisco in the 30's and 40's. He worked robbery for a while, but mostly vice. He was involved in some high profile cases at one time. Angelo and I went to the same catholic high school. His uncles were number runners and middlemen for one of the major drug dealers on the wharf. My father busted them for numbers and the dealer was coincidently arrested the next day by the drug squad. Some people assumed that the uncles had ratted out the dealer. Others said my father orchestrated the arrests to make it look like that. One of the uncles was murdered in jail. The other got out but disappeared two days later and was never heard from again. Guess which version the rest of the Sorelli clan went with?" Tam stopped just as the waiter arrived with two large platters of food and another beer. Steve gave out a low whistle and looked down at his plate.

Steve picked up a fork and looked across at Tam. The older man was clearly waiting for a reaction. Steve loaded the fork with a piece of tamale and looked back up at Tam.

"Well that accounts for you and he was pretty direct with me about his beef, and I figured out why Mike Hunter from something Bernie said today, so I guess we just need to figure out how he is going to make his play." He put the forkful of food into his mouth and smiled across the table. Tam looked at him with a bemused expression.

"So that's it then, no questions?" He watched as Steve ate another forkful. Steve looked up and shrugged.

"Stuff happens in high school."

The two men finished their meals in silence. Afterwards, Tam ordered coffee for both of them, and they watched the family gather as the last of the other customers paid their bills and left.

"So, you are pretty sure it was Sorelli that paid a visit to the Bali Hai looking for Sizemore?" Tam put his cup down and paged through a tattered notebook he had pulled from his suit pocket.

"The clerk described him down to the same suit and shirt that he was wearing today. Though if Angelo were sitting right here, I don't think he would know who we were talking about." Steve watched as the detective looked up quizzically from his notebook. Tam snorted.

"He's not too bright, but he ain't that stupid." Steve shrugged.

"I think he knows him as Wallace Beech. I get the feeling that whatever game is going on here, Angelo is somewhat of a latecomer to the party." Of the three names he told Nick's cocktail waitress, he didn't mention either Beech or Sizemore. He did mention Mike Hunter." He looked down at his half full coffee cup and then back across the table at Tam.

"I think you and I are freebies." Steve watched as Tam sighed deeply and tossed his notebook on the table in front of him.

"Freebies? As in: I'm going up for one murder, might as well make it three?" Tam rolled his eyes and scoffed. Steve smiled across the table.

"Yeah, something like that. But let me ask you something. If you were connected to one of the organizations but more one of the clean guys out front for the benefit of the commission and you needed to bring someone in to do some nasty work, who better than someone like Angelo? Very few people here remember him. If he gets his schvanz caught in a ringer, no one is responsible for him, and the fact he has it out for you and me is a good cover for whoever is paying him and muddies up the waters if he gets caught." Steve sat back and took another sip of his coffee. Tam shook his head.

"I knew we weren't going to get through this night without more of your 'Greenfelt Jungle' conspiracy crap. Where do you come up with this stuff? This ain't the old Costra Nostra. These guys are like corporations only smarter. If you want the truth, here it is: These guys work for the state and the state gaming commission. The price is the skim. Simple as that. Why don't we have a 'prostitutes walking around on the streets' problem? Why does every drug dealer above dime bag stuff leave town without us cops doing anything? I'll tell you why. Because all that crap is messy and bad for business. And your Angelo as some sort of Frankenstein they have unleashed is a fantasy. He is just a common criminal that got wind of something he can exploit and he's out to settle old scores while he is here. And like most of these goombas he hasn't got any smarter as the years have gone by and we are going to catch him." Tam let his cup clatter onto the saucer for emphasis. Steve held up his hands in mock admiration.

"Did you stay up last night writing that one Tam?" He laughed, but then grew more serious.

"You are right about one thing, though, Tam. Someone like Angelo running around is not good for business or anybody. Sooner or later he is going to come to the attention of the wrong people. Did you come up with any more information on him?"

Tam scowled and pulled a pair of reading glasses from his shirt pocket, picked up the notebook and skimmed through several pages before he stopped.

"We found where he was supposedly living in Francisco Park, but he vacated the premises ten days ago. We contacted the owner but he didn't know anything, he used an agency to rent it out, some property outfit called....." Tam turned the book upside down and squinted at the scribbled writing on the back of one of the pages.

"Blue Diamond Realty." He looked over his glasses at Steve.

"No other trace of him. If you hadn't seen him yourself, I would have said the whole thing was hogwash. It's getting late, I gotta go." Tam took off his glasses and pushed them and the notebook down into the inner pocket of his sport coat, and stood to leave. Steve stood up with him, reached into his coat pocket and handed Tam a small yellow piece of paper.

"What's this?" Tam held it as far away as he could in a vain attempt to read the small print.

"It's a parking ticket, Tam, I thought maybe you could help me out." He grinned widely at the detective.

'What the...!!" Tam threw the paper onto the table and marched up the two steps and passing the owner's family enjoying their meal, slammed the door as he left the restaurant.

It took an extra fifteen minutes for Steve to arrive home. Though he traveled his usual route, he made several U turns and double backs whenever a car followed his for more than a couple of blocks. There was no further sign of the blue sedan. He parked the car at an angle to the door so any onlookers would be unable to see what was being unloaded and taken into the house. He pulled the brown suitcase out of the back cargo space of the Jeep. He quickly placed it inside the front door, returned to the car and locked it. Once inside, he set up a card table in the office and began to take items out of the case one by one. When he had finished, he had three pairs of pants, six pair of jockey shorts, seven shirts, two sport coats, one suit coat that matched one of the pair of pants, two pair of shoes, several pairs of socks, two undershirts and a dop kit. He opened the shaving kit. Underneath a shaver and a bottle of hair tonic there was a piece of paper in a small plastic bag. Steve unfolded it carefully under the desk lamp. It was a return airline ticket to Phoenix, Arizona. The return date was blank. He set aside the case and began a thorough search of the clothing. A few minutes later all he had found was a $10 Desert Inn casino chip, until he felt a lump in the inside pocket of one of the coats. He pulled it out and held it up to the light. It was a man's kerchief that had been wadded up and stuffed down into the pocket. It looked like it had been there for some time and maybe had even gone through a dry cleaning process. When he spread it out on the table he smiled. In one of the corners were the initials WB in maroon stitch. He opened the drawer of the desk, pulled out a large manila envelope and put the now carefully folded cloth inside along with the airline ticket and bent the metal flaps closed.

He turned his attention to the suitcase. He felt around all four sides and the corners of both the top and the bottom. Only when he set it down on the table did he notice that the silk cloth lining seemed to be pulled tighter on the bottom of the case than the top. He felt both areas. There was definitely something under the lining on the bottom that was not on the top. He rummaged through the bottom drawer of the desk until he found a small silver X-Acto knife. He removed the protective plastic tip and carefully sliced the lining along one side of the case. He was just able to slide his hand under the lining and touch the edge of something. He returned to the desk and pulled out a pair of white cotton gloves. He also carried a pair of long tweezers back over to the case. With the tweezers inserted under the lining, he was able to pull a thin plastic sleeve away from where it had become stuck to the back of the case. Steve carried the sleeve over to the desk and sat down. Inside the sleeve were six pieces of paper. The one on the top and the bottom were blanks designed to protect the inner sheets from transferring to the plastic sleeve. Steve spread the four sheets out on the top of the desk. The first sheet was a mimeographed copy of a land contract that stipulated the terms of the option agreement on several parcels of land. The second was also mimeographed and two thirds of the page was taken up by a map that had a dotted line indicating the four tracts of land. The top third contained handwritten notes that the mimeo machine had rendered indecipherable. The remaining pages were two pages of the same document and were originals, not copies. Steve read both of the pages twice. He went into the living room and retrieved his notebook from the pocket of his jacket that had been lying on the back of a chair. When he sat back down, he copied several lines from the document under the heading: 'Certification of Land Use Feasibility'. He noted that the document had been signed in ink by Herbert Slater, County Board of Commissioners.

Steve replaced the sheets as he had found them in the plastic sleeve and took them into the closet of the bedroom. He opened a small safe that was wedged between a dresser cabinet and the wall. He put both the plastic sleeve and the envelope containing the kerchief inside and closed the door and spun the black numbered dial.

August 19

STEVE AWOKE WITH a start and sat straight up in bed as the image of the dark green jungle faded on the sun lit bedroom wall. He was bathed in sweat and his pulse was racing. He lay back down on the pillow and forced himself to breathe slowly and deeply. After several minutes his breathing returned to normal, he left the bed and walked slowly down the hall to the bathroom and the shower.

Fifteen minutes later and fully dressed he walked through the kitchen on his way to the office. As he passed in front of the window that was over the sink, his eye caught something shiny in his peripheral vision. It was something that shouldn't be there. He stopped cold, crouched, and duck-walked over to the wall and slid slowly up beside the window and peered through a thin space between the edge of the window and the white lace curtain.

Directly in front of the house was a bright red '63 Cadillac convertible, the white top up and the massive chrome grill gleaming in the sun. It was the grill that had caught Steve's attention as he had walked through the kitchen. In spite of the adrenaline that was still surging through his body, a small smile played on Steve's lips.

In this town there were certain people that were rarely mentioned by name. At least not by anybody that knew how the power structure of the valley was set up, and who also wanted to keep their place in that structure. It was also a sign of respect to the supposed anonymity of the personage. There was one man in particular who fit this category to a T. He ran the Desert Inn Hotel and Casino and the only man in Las Vegas who could bandy his name about freely was standing in Steve's front yard smoking a cigarette.

Steve crossed the room, picked up his sport coat from the back of a kitchen chair, walked into the foyer and opened the front door.

Tommy Carmino turned around when he heard the door close. His face wore a bemused expression as he watched the private detective walk around the front of the car, lean back on the hood and light up a cigarette. He snorted.

"Cannon, I'm surprised you're up this early, I always took you for a night owl." Tommy dropped his cigarette in the gravel and after crushing it underfoot, retrieved a maroon silk kerchief from the breast pocket of his dark gray suit and swept the dust off the shiny black shoe leather. He turned and looked around.

"People are always telling me what a dump you live in, but I see the point, it's wide open out here. Quiet." He put his hands under his suitcoat and into his pants pockets. His posture was casual but extremely self-confident. Steve was reminded of a General Motors executive he had once met, the head of one of the divisions. He had carried himself in exactly the same way, supremely confident that his world was just as he liked it, and even more confident that it was going to stay that way. Tommy was as impeccably dressed this morning as always, a white crisp shirt collar hugging the strong neck. His tanned open face and light sandy brown hair would have pegged him as a surfer if he hadn't just turned 40.

He smiled widely at Steve. "How's things Slick?" He bounced a little on his toes.

"Well, Tommy, I can't complain. But having such a luminary as yourself visit me,…I don't know…" Steve gestured towards Tommy with an open palm. "Makes me wonder which way my luck is turning." He exhaled and looked down at the cigarette in his hand.

"You worry too much Cannon. You have to trust your training just like they taught you in the Corps. If I had ill intent, would I be standing here by myself?" He laughed, held up his hands and took two steps nearer to Steve. Steve's gaze was steady as he watched the man come closer.

"As it happens, Cannon, I come bearing gifts. 1,500 of them to be exact." Tommy reached into his left breast pocket and brought out a fat envelope and held it up briefly before tucking it back into the suit. Steve chuckled and flicked the cigarette butt out into the gravel behind the gangster.

"I am sure there are more strings attached to that envelope than to a kid's kite, but I'll humor you." He smiled just as widely back at Tommy. Tommy turned and looked at the long line of purple mountains that stretched across the horizon beyond Steve's house. He turned back to Steve.

"Well here it is, Slick. You need to do a little job. No big deal, won't take much of your time, in fact, by my calculations you will end up making a couple hundred an hour."

"And whose diapers need to be changed for that kind of dough?" Steve ran his fingers along the hood seam of the caddy and squinted down the side, looking to see if any of the panels were out of alignment. Tommy ignored the wisecrack.

"There is a car waiting at McCarren Field. Needs to be in LA by tomorrow night, latest." Tommy took a silver key from his pocket and held it up in front of Steve. When Steve didn't take it, Tommy shrugged, walked over to Steve and the car and placed it on the edge of the hood. He took two steps back.

"Like I said, leave here now, be back by tonight." Tommy's voice was quiet and he waited for Steve's answer.

"Too busy right now, Tommy, maybe should have caught me earlier in the week." Steve's voice was even but not quite as quiet as Tommy's had been.

The color in Tommy's face got a little redder under the tan, but he again put his hands in his pockets, took a deep breath and with a smile repeated the little bouncing on his toes. When he spoke his voice was lower and harder.

"I don't think so, Cannon. You ask for information. You were given information. Some people aren't real sure why you wanted it, but there it is. Personally speaking, I wonder why you just didn't come directly to me if you wanted to know something, but hey, I'm not one to grind on things like that. But the opportunity I'm offering you, I think is what they call a quid pro quo." Steve looked at Tommy without changing expression. Tommy snorted.

"I think you are going to do this Cannon, because we are both good little boys who do what we are told, and that is why we get to play together in this sandbox. I have been given a task and I am giving it to you. I think they call it delegation." Tommy was still smiling, but not nearly as big as before.

'Or maybe you are just twisting my tail a little bit here, huh?" Tommy's smile was brighter now, and his eyes were not set as hard. Steve laughed and crossed his arms and leaned farther back onto the hood of the caddy.

"Yeah, Tommy, just a little. Give me the envelope." Steve held out his hand as Tommy slipped the packet from his pocket and slapped it into the outstretched palm. Steve put the envelope in his back pocket and picked up the key and held it up with a questioning expression on his face.

"Row 53, space 11. Black '63 Chevy Impala. That key only opens the doors and the ignition. No trunk key. The spare and the jack are in the back seat. Don't get stopped." Tommy smiled and hitched up his pants and straightened his burgundy tie.

"Where am I leaving it?" Steve put the key in his front pocket.

"Santa Monica. The address is in the envelope. Also the name and number of the guy it is registered to, in case somebody else needs to verify that. After you park the car, call the number and tell them the car is there." Tommy seemed in no hurry to leave.

"What's in the trunk, Tommy? Want a beer?" Steve motioned over his shoulder towards the Jeep and the front door.

"Naw, too early. Nothing, I know of. I wouldn't worry about it if I was you. What I would worry about, though, is what Angelo Sorelli is up to." Tommy's eyes narrowed and he pursed his lips and looked directly at Steve.

"I would think that you know exactly what he is up to." Steve leaned forward at the waist and spit into the gravel at his feet.

"Not in this case, Cannon. We don't have responsibility for him. He hasn't crossed any lines I know of, and it's still a free country last I heard. But I do hear things. A lot of things." Tommy lowered his jaw and when his eyes met Steve's, he nodded his head slightly.

"Don't think anything about it Tommy, I can handle Angelo Sorelli." He stepped away from the car as Tommy moved forward and swung open the big door of the Caddy and paused with one leg inside the car. When he looked up, there was no trace of a smile on his face.

"I don't have to think about nothing, Cannon. I'm not the one sleeping with the wrong woman." Tommy sat down in the white leather seat and closed the door. He started the car and circled around stopping next to Steve. The glass of the automatic window fell silently into the door. Steve could feel the rush of air conditioning from four feet away. Tommy looked blankly up at Steve for a few seconds.

"LA by tomorrow night." He swung the Caddy off the gravel and onto the road.

Steve watched the big car wallow down the narrow street taking up both lanes until it disappeared over a small rise. He walked back into the house, pulled a black leather valise from the bedroom closet laid it open on the bed and then picked up the phone that sat on a small table by the headboard.

"Tam? Cannon here. See what you can find on Wallace Beech. I would try the Phoenix area first. Yeah, I'm out of town until tomorrow. I will call you from the airport when I get back."

Steve held down the receiver buttons and then slowly dialed the next number. He was relieved when Remy answered after three rings.

"Hi Gem, how are you doing?" His voice was a little stilted.

"Steve?" Remy replied.

"I'm surprised. I mean…. I just never expected you to call…" She trailed off and Steve forced his voice to sound more normal.

"Remy, listen. I know this is short notice and I have no right… but I'm taking a quick car trip to LA and I want you to go with me." He waited and listened to a low buzz on the line.

"Right now, Steve?"

"Yes, this morning. But I guess I have no right to ask…." Remy cut him off.

"How soon do I have to be ready?"

"Meet me at the Bonanza Airline counter at McCarren Field in an hour. We'll be staying at a hotel in Santa Monica and flying back tomorrow morning. If you change your mind, I'll understand."

"I'll be there, Steve." Remy hung up the phone.

Steve went to the closet and put his hand on two shirts then paused. He crossed back to the bed and picked up the phone again. He dialed the number Bernie had given him the day before.

"Hello, Miss Sizemore? Cannon here. I examined the contents of your brother's suitcase and I came across some evidence that suggests he may have been involved in the sort of land scheme you mentioned." His voice was business-like and detached. He listened as she asked several questions in a rapid fire fashion.

"No, I don't know the names of any of the principals, at least not yet. No, there is no sign of the money or your brother for that matter. I am taking a quick trip to LA. When I come back tomorrow I may have more answers. I don't know how long you may have to lay low, but I believe you are in danger and the less you move about the better." Steve concluded the conversation quickly and returned to his packing. Before he closed the door behind him, he made one more quick call and then called Bernie.

Forty-five minutes later he pulled into McCarren airport and found a parking spot six spaces away from the Chevrolet. He locked the car, walked over to the black Impala and twisted the key in the door lock. The car had been freshly washed and looked brand new. Someone had thought to put a white towel over the steering wheel and left the windows part way down. Steve opened his valise and took out a large towel and spread it over the spare tire in the backseat and placed the black case on top. Twenty minutes later he locked the car and walked the hundred yards into the terminal.

He was only five steps inside the door when he spotted Remy

twenty yards away standing in front of the counter looking through the green tinted windows into the parking lot. She was wearing a red polka-dot dress belted at the waist that ended just above her knee. She had a large brim white floppy hat on her head and the white frames of her sunglasses matched the color of her opened toe sandals. She was carrying a large rattan purse and a soft beige leather overnight bag sat at her feet. She turned in his direction, smiled warmly and waved slightly with the arm that held her handbag. For a brief moment, Steve felt a little lightheaded and he found himself smiling almost in spite of himself. He crossed the small interval between them and then stopped. They had moved towards each other as if to embrace, but caught themselves and stopped self-consciously when they realized they were in public. Remy laughed nervously and held out her hand to as if to shake. There was a small crowd of people next to them waiting to transact business at the counter.

"How are you Mrs. Brannock?" Steve clasped her outstretched hand and turning it slightly placed his other hand on top of hers. He caught a faint scent of her perfume.

"I'm fine, Mr. Cannon how are you?" There was more than a hint of her French accent, and her voice was just loud enough for anyone that was listening. Steve released her hand, bent down and picked up her bag.

"Right this way." He pointed with the bag toward the door he had just entered. They walked side by side out into the sunshine. When they got to the curb, Steve gently grasped her elbow and together they crossed the street into the parking lot. When they reached the car, Steve quickly deposited Remy's leather bag on the towel next to his and closed the door. He walked to the front passenger door and opened it for her. She slid onto the black leather bench seat and placed her purse next to her. When Steve had settled in behind the wheel, Remy placed her hand on the back of his neck and pulled him towards her. They kissed passionately for several minutes. Remy nestled under Steve's right arm as he swung the steering wheel around with one hand and guided the car out of the parking lot and onto Paradise Road. The car turned left on Tropicana and made another left hand turn onto Las Vegas Boulevard. Two blocks later they passed the Hacienda Hotel, the last resort on the strip.

"I was surprised to get your call, Steve." Remy looked up at him and he felt her eyes on him and he looked away from the road and down at the smooth skin of her cheeks and her pale pink lips.

"I thought it might be good for us to get away together, we haven't ever been out in public or really been with each other like normal couples." He nuzzled the top of her head with his chin.

"But you're working on a case, right, at the same time?"

"More like doing a favor for a friend." Steve removed his arm from around Remy and changed lanes to get around a slow moving truck. Remy curled her legs beneath her on the seat and laughed quietly.

"Does the favor have anything to do with the spare tire being on the back seat along with our luggage instead of in the trunk?" She looked out her window and watched as a billboard for the Sands Hotel swept by. She turned back to Steve with a smile in the corners of her mouth.

"I don't know anything about that, Gem, just getting this car to LA, that's all." He looked over at her and smiled. Remy smiled back and they were quiet for the next several miles. Up ahead, the desert was obscured by a brown fog. A sandstorm was bearing down upon them. Steve broke the silence.

"What is the name of that realty company that Nash's sister owns?" He kept his eyes on the road.

"Blue Diamond Realty. Why do you want to know that?"

"I just heard the name mentioned last night and I was curious." He turned his head and watched her as she gazed out her window at the yellow desert.

"I have never known you to be curious about just nothing, Steve. It must have something to do with a case you are working on or you wouldn't ask." Her voice was quiet but she turned her face towards Steve and took off her sunglasses.

Steve returned her gaze and placed his hand on her knee. Her skin felt cool underneath the thin cloth of the dress.

"Gem, listen to me, I need to ask you something important." He waited until she nodded.

"If anything were ever to go wrong, do you have someplace you can go to where you will be safe?" He reached up and held her chin, gently turning her face so that she was facing him directly. Her eyes widened and she nodded slightly.

"Steve, you are scaring me. What do you mean?" She grasped his hand and held it tightly to her chest.

"Nash is connected to Angelo Sorelli being back in town. Sorelli has threatened me on the phone and yesterday in person. I think Nash is involved in a fraudulent land scheme and I think he knows about us." As he finished he squeezed her hand. Remy looked down at their hands and shook her head slowly. She looked up at Steve.

"How could he know?"

Steve relayed the last part of his conversation with Tommy Carmino. After that they were both silent for a few minutes. Remy put her sunglasses back in front of her moist eyes. Her voice was quiet and without accent.

"I have my sister in Hollywood. I can always go to her." She stared straight ahead, reached over and felt for Steve's hand. When she found it, she looked up at him, her lower lip trembled very slightly.

"Let's stay in LA together, Steve. Why do we have to go back?" She searched his face with her eyes wide. Steve shook his head slowly.

"Because of who we are, Gem, and the choices we've already made." He looked over at her and pulled her closer with his free arm. "It won't work for us if we start our life together this way. We may not have much of a chance at making each other happy, but if we do, it will only come if we see the things that have been started through to the end."

Nothing more was said for several minutes as large billowing clouds of dust enveloped the car wrapping everything in a yellow-brown curtain. Steve slowed his speed and concentrated on keeping the heavy car between the white lines. Ten minutes later when the air was again clear, Steve looked down at Remy.

"So tell me anything you can about Nash and the land deal." She pulled away and turned her body toward the door and looked out at the horizon.

"I don't know anything, because I am never told anything." Her voice was flat and quiet. "The only thing I know about Nash's business activities is what I pick up from pieces of conversations and put together myself or what other people tell me from time to time." She sighed.

"But I see the people who come around and the ones who answer to him. I am not blind."

"Were you at that pool party several weeks ago that Bernie told me about, with all the Hollywood people?" Remy let out a short sardonic laugh.

"That would describe most every social occasion we put on. Why do you think he spends so much time in Hollywood? He thinks these people are special because they are in the movie business. They think he is a gentleman gangster, kind of a safe guy they can hang out with and tell all their friends about at their Bel Air parties."

"So you never heard any talk about the land deal?" He slowed down as the car undulated in a series of small hills just outside the small town of Baker. She looked over at him. He could not see her eyes behind the sunglasses.

"Yes I know a little about the land deal, Steve. But if I tell you it will only get you in deeper to whatever you are doing, and I don't want that. I don't want that for you and I don't want that for us.

Can't you just forget about all this and leave it alone?" Her voice had a soft pleading tone. He was quiet for a few seconds.

"No, Gem I couldn't even if I wanted to. The minute Angelo showed up in town all those choices were gone. I'm sorry."

Steve pulled the car into a gas station just off the highway. As the gas flowed into the tank, Steve watched the cars and trucks that passed on the highway, paying special attention to those that pulled into the station or the restaurant that sat fifty yards away. After paying the attendant for the gas, Steve drove the Chevrolet over to the side of the restaurant and parked in the shade. They left the car and walked into the rambling building. Neither said much as they ate their burgers and fries.

Twenty minutes later they were back on the road. The desert landscape was bathed in a gray light as smog from the LA basin crept through the canyons and obscured the blue mountains on either side. The highway straightened out and the traffic began to thicken.

"Nash has $800,000 in cash in a safe in the garage." Remy was looking through the windshield at an approaching thunder storm. Her voice was low but not soft. Steve watched the road and did not look at her. He waited and did not say anything.

"He has another $450,000 in an account he opened two weeks ago at Valley Bank on Tropicana." Large raindrops splattered onto the thick layer of dust on the hood and windshield. Steve turned on the wipers, the first few swipes were muddy smears until the rain came down harder and ran down the sides of the windshield in clear rivulets.

"The name on the account is 'Vegas Wash Land Development, Co.' He was just an investor six weeks ago. Now he is running the whole operation and taking money from all his contacts in LA." She looked across at Steve. The pale blue light from the rain made his face look older. "That's all I know. He has never mentioned Angelo." Steve waited for a few seconds.

"There is a man missing, Gem. He came to town the day before the fourth of July, and hasn't been seen since the 4th of August. In his possessions I found papers connecting him with the land project in the Vegas Wash area." He spoke quietly and kept his affect as flat as he could muster. Remy looked out the window where sun rays were streaking through the thinning rain clouds.

"I know my husband, Steve. He is not a killer."

The highway turned from two lanes to four and the black slickness was the only sign that there had been any rain. The wind had pushed the smog away from the valley floor and the air sparkled as the desert gave way to the foothills just east of LA. Steve stopped one more time for gas in western San Fernando Valley and an hour later parked the car on Ocean Boulevard in front of a beach cottage. He pulled their bags from the backseat and placed them on the curb. He also took a small black towel from the floorboard behind the driver's seat. He locked the car, placed the car key inside the towel and rolled it tightly. He knelt behind the car and gently pushed the towel into the tailpipe far enough so that it could not be seen by passerby. They then walked a half block down to the corner and stepped through the doors of an oyster bar. Remy sat on the small veranda and drank an iced tea while Steve used the owners phone to call for a taxi cab. He also called the number on the paper that Tommy Carmino had given him. Business done, he settled into a seat beside Remy and waited for the cab. She looked at him as he tried to see her eyes behind the dark lenses of her sunglasses.

"How far are you going to take this, Steve?" She reached out and took his hand and rested both on the small ice cream table between them.

"All the way to the point where I know what happened to Sizemore and I get Angelo Sorelli off my back." He reached over and took the sunglasses from her face and pushed a stray strand of hair from her eyes. "I don't have any special interest in the land deal, though the district attorney might if he was asked."

"Are you going to ask him?"

"No, but Tam Polhaus might. I have an obligation to share

whatever information I uncover that pertains to the case. Just as he keeps me informed." He searched her face but saw only an empty sad expression.

"Nash has been good to me." She was looking at the ocean a hundred yards away. "He isn't the best husband in the world, not by a long shot, but he has tried to make me happy in his own way." Steve also turned his gaze to the blue water and the green curling waves and said nothing. Remy took a deep breath and looked at Steve. He turned and met her gaze.

"I knew what I was getting into when I agreed to marry him. I know the world he is a part of and I convinced myself that he could keep it separate from us. But it doesn't work. Over the years it has become more of who he is and what he wants. Nothing I did could change any of that." She again looked back out across the small patio to the ocean.

"We all make bad choices, Gem. You, me, Nash, all of us. That's kind of a given in this life as far as I can see. But that doesn't mean that we still can't love each other the best we can. Nobody gets what they want, there is always a shortfall no matter how you slice it. You just have to be ready to do the best you can as you take the next step." He took a sip of his ice tea as a yellow cab pulled up to the curb. Remy gathered her purse and stood up from the table. She looked down at him.

"Even if all the steps you see in front of you lead to pain?" She put her sunglasses on and stepped from the patio onto the sidewalk. Steve followed her and opened the passenger door of the cab and helped her in. He threw both bags onto the front seat and joined her in the backseat. The cab pulled away from the curb and passed the beach cottage. The black Chevrolet was already gone.

A few minutes later the cab pulled into the wide sweeping driveway of the Palihouse Hotel. Steve paid the cabbie while a red-capped doorman placed their bags on a brass trolley.

Remy looked up at the three story structure. "How did you

know about this place, Steve? He put his arm under hers as they walked into the airy lobby.

"I didn't, but Bernie did. He made all the arrangements. Remind me to thank him." Though Steve had requested modest accommodations, Bernie had thought otherwise and they were escorted up the elevator to the third floor and the largest suite in the hotel. The wide spacious deck seemed to float on the ocean, and the long white curtains in the open glass doors swayed in the salty breeze. Their bags were followed closely by the manager of the hotel. He welcomed them warmly and inquired what time they would like dinner and where on the deck would they like their table to be placed. As he left, a waiter arrived with a bottle of Dom Perignon in a bucket of ice. Steve moved the bottle and two glasses to a small table at the edge of the deck. He opened the bottle, poured the two glasses half full and handed one to Remy. For a brief second their gaze fastened on one another. Steve tipped his glass forward and gently tapped it against hers.

"Here's to you Gem, and to our future." Remy turned her face toward the ocean but left the champagne untouched. The breeze caught her hair and swirled it around lips set tight below her high cheekbones.

August 20

STEVE MOVED HIS valise along the floor with his foot as the line to board the flight to Las Vegas wound toward the gate. Through the big silver windows he could see the gray morning as the mist of drizzle and fog obscured the planes as they climbed into the gun metal clouds. He looked down at his watch. 7:41. He had put Remy in a cab an hour ago and watched as it moved down the short street, turned, and left only the morning fog swirling above the ocean. He felt alone and far from home. The thin jacket he had brought was no match for the chilly LA morning, and the Bloody Mary he had chosen for breakfast in the airport bar had only sharpened his sense of loss.

He entered the long tube of blue seats and found his in the rear of the half empty plane. He put the valise onto the seat next to him instead of placing it in the overhead bin. He settled back and watched as his fellow passengers busied themselves with their bags and other belongings. Though it was only eight in the morning, Steve could feel the small current of excitement that most of the travelers betrayed by their quick movements and elevated voices. He could also pick out the inveterate gamblers. Those people for whom the flight was just a high altitude precursor to their drug of choice and whose daily lives were mere holding patterns for their next moments at the tables. It was likely some of them would never return, instead living in small, under furnished apartments and working as dealers and cocktail waitresses to be near that which they held dear and that which they would always serve. Since the twenties it had always been that way, and once exposed to the games few were immune, though like Steve Cannon himself, most went through an infatuation period and rarely if ever gambled the casino games after that. Was Beech just a unlucky gambler, or something else entirely? Steve reclined his seat and pondered this and other things as visions and thoughts of Remy mixed with the shuddering throb of the engines and the small talk of the few people around him.

The sudden heat could be felt by Steve even in the back of the airplane as soon as the doors were opened. He waited patiently for his turn to descend the metal staircase and cross the short length of tarmac into the green windowed coolness of the main terminal. He headed for a bank of pay phones that were off the main hallway and offered some privacy. He dialed Tam's number and waited for the detective to come on the line.

"Hello, Tam?" The connection was bad and it was several

seconds before either party could hear the other and begin the conversation. Tam went first.

"The first thing I need to tell you is that we found the car with the plate number you gave us. It was abandoned in the parking lot of that big shopping center on East Charleston. It was stolen out of Reno five days ago, the print guys worked on it, I'm not hopeful, but at least next time you see them they will be driving something else." Steve snorted at the small joke and waited for more.

"The name Wallace Beech came up bingo. He is a major con man and swindler that has done time twice for fraud. Last known address was Tucson. He is still on parole and can be picked up anytime we see him. That's all I got so far, what spice if any, do you have to add to this stew?"

Steve quickly thought back over the last twenty-four hours and took a deep breath.

"I have found documents that show that Sizemore or Beech or whatever he is calling himself now is up to his old tricks and is running a land scheme involving land in the Vegas Wash area. Blue Diamond Realty is run by Nash Brannock's sister, Denise. Nash himself has nearly 1.3 million in cash and an account at Valley Bank under the title of the land deal. He has taken over the deal and is peddling it to all his new friends in Hollywood. I think this is the stew, not the spices." He grinned slightly into the phone.

"You found all this out in LA?" The detective's voice was incredulous.

"Some there, some on the way and some before I left." He pivoted and looked up and down both concourses as the detective pondered the last statement. "I wonder if you can check and see if Wallace Beech has or had a wife?" Steve waited as he could hear the detective rustling some paper.

"Yeah, I will check. It isn't anywhere here on his probation report. I will get back to you on that. Are you liking Audrey Sizemore on this deal?"

"Fine, I would appreciate that. I am going to drop off Beech's suitcase later so your fingerprint guy can make it official. As far as Miss Sizemore is concerned, she and I need another powwow."

"Good, see you then."

Steve hung up the phone and waited until a large crowd of passengers passed his location then fell in with them, veering off as they headed for the luggage area. He walked behind the big windows that looked out on the street, then quickly double backed and pushed through the glass door. When he reached the Jeep, he opened all the doors and let the hot air dissipate. He then sat for a few minutes and let the air conditioning run before backing out and driving slowly down the rows, making three right turns before heading for the exit.

It was after ten o'clock when he pulled in front of Foxy's and shut off the engine. The last of the morning breakfast crowd was scattered throughout the restaurant when Cannon opened the door. He walked to the counter and waited until he caught the attention of one of the two men working there.

"Is Bernie in?" His voice was weary and flat.

"Yeah. He is in the back. Want me to call him?" The waiter motioned toward the door to the private gaming room.

"No, I'll do it myself." Steve walked around the counter and knocked softly on the door.

The door cracked a few inches and Bernie smiled when he saw who it was. He opened the door all the way inwards and stood aside as Steve walked through.

"How about some breakfast, my friend?" Bernie stood at the door and waited for an answer.

"Sure, Bernie, that might hit the spot." He sat down wearily at one of the tables and pulled out a pack of cigarettes, thought better of it and put them back. Bernie said something to one of the men and closed the door.

"I got coffee right here, just made it." He walked over to the long bar, reached over and pulled out a silver pot and placed it on a coaster near the end of the bar. He reached again and held up two white coffee cups, hooking them both onto one hand and picked up two saucers that were sitting on a rolling table at the foot of the bar. He deposited all of them on the green felt of the table, returned with the coffee and poured the steaming black liquid into both of the cups. He held up his cup, waited for Steve to raise his, clinked the two together and took a long sip.

"I hope I'm not interrupting anything, Bernie, I can come back later."

"No, man, not by any means, I was just going over paperwork which never ends and I need the break. How was the ocean?" He smiled at Steve and took another sip.

"Not as great as the room you ordered up. You really didn't have to do that, but thank you very much, it was grand." He smiled, reached over with his cup and touched the one in Bernie's hand.

"Well I thought you might think it funny having all that to yourself. But I know the owner pretty well and I liked it when I stayed there, so I'm glad you enjoyed it." Bernie's smile faded as he saw something in Steve's face. Before he could ask, Steve forced a smile of his own and chuckled.

"I wasn't alone, Bernie." He quit smiling and buried his nose into his coffee cup.

"No kidding? Well good for you, kid." Bernie reached to slap Steve's left shoulder. Something he saw in Steve's expression made him draw his hand back slowly.

"What?" Bernie's voice held a small note of concern. Steve sighed and looked down at his coffee cup.

"I was there with Remy Brannock". The words were flat and spaced out. He looked back up at his friend's uncomprehending face.

"You were there with Remy Brannock." Bernie's eyes were wide and he spoke slowly and quietly and spaced the words out exactly as Steve had done as if he was trying to make the syllables fall into some kind of sense. When he spoke again, it was with full comprehension of what he had just been told.

"My god, Steve….Nash is…" Steve cut him off.

"I know, Bernie, but that's not the point. I needed to tell you that as background because there are other things I need to tell you and I need your help." Just then the door opened and one of the waiters came through the door backwards with two large platters and two smaller plates balanced on his arms. The smaller plates each held several pieces of toast, the larger ones, eggs and one held several strips of bacon. He placed all the dishes on the table, retrieved two sets of silverware wrapped in cloth napkins from his apron and placed one beside each large platter. He stood back from the table. "Anything else, Boss?" Bernie was peering intently at Steve as he slowly waved his hand absent mindedly toward the waiter.

"No,…No.. Walter, that will be fine…Thanks." When the door closed behind Walter, Bernie leaned forward and looked up into Steve's eyes.

"Look, I don't know what this is all about or what you have gotten yourself into, my friend, but I will do whatever it takes to get you out of it. I mean that." Bernie held Steve's gaze for a few seconds longer, then picked up a knife and fork and pierced one of the over easy eggs on his plate. Steve did likewise and slowly chewed a piece of crispy bacon. After he swallowed, he looked over at Bernie.

"I know I can count on you Bernie, I always have. Hopefully, I can get Remy out of this with as little fanfare as possible. The problem is that it is not a secret anymore as I was informed by no less than Tommy Carmino himself yesterday." Bernie shook his head.

"Not good. That means everyone across the street at the Dunes knows, all the wise guys and Nash's employers, all the wrong people for something like that." He shook his head again and pushed the half-eaten platter a few inches across the table and picked up his coffee cup. He watched as Steve finished off the three eggs and sat back in his chair.

"How long, Steve?" The voice was kindly but concerned. Steve picked up his cup and answered before he took a sip.

"Year, maybe fourteen months." Bernie whistled softly, then smiled.

"Gotta hand it to you kid, you can pick 'em." The smile turned into a laugh. Bernie got up and walked to the far side of the room. He returned holding an 8x10 black and white picture in a silver frame. He handed it to Steve and then sat down again. Steve pushed his plate away and looked at the picture. It was a glamour shot of the showgirl, Line Renaud in full costume for the Casino de Paris revue at the Dunes. She had been one of the first of the French beauties to grace the Las Vegas stages. In the corner there was a loving inscription to Bernie.

"I remember when Remy DeMarche came to town, she made Line Renaud look second rate and that is damn hard to do." Bernie shook his head again and chuckled. His face grew quiet and he looked back at Steve.

"You are a lucky man, Steve, Remy is a beautiful person."

"Was a lucky man, Bernie. Was. She walked out on me this morning. I don't think she is coming back to Las Vegas." His voice was quiet as well. "But I need you to see if you can find out where her sister lives in Hollywood. Not for me, I just want you to find her, contact her once in a while and make sure she is all right. I know you two are good friends and I think she will need one soon." He watched as his friend nodded.

"Sure, sure Steve, I will do that. She is almost like a daughter to me. I met the sister once, I don't think I will have any trouble finding her."

"Thanks, Bernie." Steve reached out and squeezed Bernie's forearm. The phone on the bar near the wall buzzed and one of the lights below the dial began to blink. Walter opened the door at the same time and waited until his boss looked in his direction.

"Boss, Rocco's on the phone." He indicated the bar with a nod of his head and then disappeared closing the door behind him. Bernie went over to the phone, talked quietly for several seconds, looked at his watch and then returned to the table.

"The Sizemore dame is gone. She sent Rocco out to get something, when he returned a half hour later, she was gone. Ronnie was there cleaning the pool, but he didn't see anything, but he wouldn't have had a view of the parking lot the whole time. Sorry, Rocco is not usually that careless." Bernie shook his head.

"Don't sweat it Bernie, I had a small hunch she might skate. Thank you for doing me that favor, at least I was able to see what her play was going to be." Steve leaned forward and in a low voice quickly brought his friend up to speed on everything he knew about the case he was working on. When he was done, Bernie went to the bar and returned with the pot and emptied half of what was left into each of their cups. He took a sip of his and sat back in the chair. He was frowning.

"I don't get it, Steve. Why would Nash get involved in a crooked land scheme? His job is to meet and greet, pretend to be a squeaky clean owner and keep the commission happy. For that he gets the big coin and a lot of 'atta boys'. Why go off the reservation like this? His employers aren't exactly the kind of guys who give you a letter of recommendation for your next job and a nice going away party when you screw up." Bernie threw his hands up in the air and shrugged. Steve looked down at his cup.

"I don't know either, Bernie, but Remy said something that made me think that all his paling around with the Hollywood biggies made him think that this scheme might get him into their league. At this point, I am less concerned about his motivation or motivations, as I am about how Sorelli plans on convincing me to leave town."

"Well if what you tell me is the way it is, I see at least two reasons he has for leaning on you. What are you going to do now?" Bernie got up from the table and stacked the breakfast dishes on the bar.

"Tam is interested again and I am pretty sure that Audrey Sizemore is somehow connected to Beech in a way she has not revealed and if we can find her, we will definitely know which way this wind has been blowing." He looked at his watch.

"Hey, Bernie, I better go. I have to drop by my place, pick up Beech's suitcase and drop it off downtown. Then I got a concert to catch." He grinned over his coffee cup at his friend as Bernie turned around with his mouth open.

"You what? You're going to that madhouse Beatles concert? Since when?" Bernie started chortling. "Man, you are a nut case. All them screaming girls? Oh man, oh man." Bernie held the back of the chair, bent over and continued to laugh. He picked the coffee cups off the table and was still laughing when he turned and placed them on the bar. Steve stood up and swung his jacket over his shoulder.

"I got two little girls I can't disappoint. I'll bring them in soon and they can thank you in person for the tickets." Steve slapped Bernie on the shoulder and turned to leave. He stopped halfway and waited until Bernie turned around and he was able to look his friend in the eyes.

"Thanks for breakfast, Bernie. Thanks for everything." Bernie waved his hand as if to shoo him off and was laughing again when Steve closed the door.

*

TAM WAS NOT in when Steve brought the case and most of the contents to the station. He left it on Tam's desk with a note. He also left a set of his finger prints to help the detective eliminate at least one of the half dozen sets of prints that were likely all over the brown leather. He looked at his watch and figured he had an hour to spare before he had to pick up the girls for the three o'clock concert. All three radio stations that Steve could get on the Jeep's small radio were filled with non-stop updates on the doings of the fab four and their one day visit to Las Vegas. He drove three blocks and parked in a small lot next to the city offices. He studied the black board on the wall just inside the door and then took the cool marble stairs to the second floor. From a row of several stipple glassed doors he picked one and walked in.

He found himself in a deserted outer office, a large ceiling fan circulated slowly, moving a musty smell through the air. The sound of the door latch closing behind him brought activity from the adjoining room and a young man with a thin black tie and shirt-sleeves soon entered through the archway and stopped. He was holding a sheaf of papers in his hands and he had a small yellow pencil behind his ear. He stared blankly at the private eye. Steve waited for a few seconds and when it was obvious the young man was not going to say something, he grinned slightly.

"Hi, how are you? I was wondering if someone here could give me some information?" He widened the grin into a smile. The man put the papers down on the desk and looked up at Steve.

"What kind of information? These are the chambers of the county commissioners. Are you sure you are in the right place, Mr...?" Steve held out his hand across the desk and waited until the young man reluctantly grasped it.

"Cannon, Steve Cannon." He continued to hold the man's hand, pumping it slightly. The man's bored expression changed to one of concern.

"Cannon?... Are you related to the Cannons?" He placed heavy emphasis on the 'the'.

"No, I wouldn't say that I was. But if I was, would I get bet-ter information?" Steve's voice had an edge, his smile was gone and he increased the pressure on the man's hand. The young man extri-cated himself from Steve's grip by backing up and sitting down in the chair behind the desk.

"No, why would you ask that? If I can be of help, I will, oth-erwise I will direct you to the right place. So why don't you tell me what kind of information you are looking for?" The bored expres-sion had returned but the voice held a more conciliatory tone than before.

"Fair enough." Steve pulled up one of two chairs from against the wall by the door and sat down. He looked across at the pale young man who was waiting impatiently.

"Well here is my situation. My brother and I are looking to buy a tract of land and build a small group of houses and maybe a strip mall. We have several parcels in mind and I thought we had better get acquainted with the process the city and the county will require before we go in any deeper. So, I have been delegated to do just that." He smiled across the desk and sat farther back in his chair. The young man sighed and looked at the clock, leaned forward and began to speak rapidly.

"Well, all I can do today, is give you a rough outline of the process and a forms packet. You would have to fill those out with help from the seller and file them with the clerk downstairs. They will contact you and inform you if there is a need to put your item on the monthly meeting agenda for discussion." The young man had reached into his desk as he spoke and now handed Steve fifty pages of paper held together with two long metal fasteners. Steve took the papers from the outstretched hand and flipped through them quickly.

"I see. Thanks for the information, I just have another quick question if you don't mind." He rolled up the packet and tapped his knee softly several times and looked at the young man waiting for an answer. When the bored expression across the desk did not change, Steve continued.

"Does Herb Slater have a financial interest in any deals that involve land in the Vegas Wash area?" The low hum of the fan and the tapping of the packet on Steve's leg were the only sounds for several seconds. The young man's face reddened and he sat more upright in his chair.

"What….what…would you ask… where did you come up with that?" The man's face showed intense irritation at his stuttering reply and tried to reassert himself. "Now look here…" He stopped in mid-sentence as Steve stood up and leaned across the desk and tapped him gently on the nose with the rolled up packet.

"No, sonny boy. You look here. Herb Slater's name is on a piece of paper I have certifying that the Vegas Wash area is suitable for a housing development. I want to know how he explains that. His family has been here as long as the Cannons and anyone in town more than a year knows what happens to that area when it rains. Here is my card if Mr. Slater wants more details." He took the pencil from behind the man's ear and wrote 'Vegas Wash' on the back of the card and stuffed it into the clerk's shirt pocket. His face twisted into a sneer and he leaned closer to the now red face in front of him.

"Slater's running for mayor. Maybe he would rather I take my questions over to Hank Greenspun at the Sun." He threw the curled packet of papers on the desk, opened the door and closed it softly behind him. He chuckled a little to himself as he walked down the hall toward the stairway.

Even though it was two o'clock in the afternoon, the convention center was lit up, the bottom half of the saucer shaped building glowing green in the 97 degree sunshine. The girls had been waiting impatiently on their front lawn when he had driven up and their level of excitement had only increased on the ride into town from Boulder City. He had spoken briefly with his sister and promised to deposit the girls back home after the concert which he estimated to be around eight or nine o'clock. He also asked permission to take them out for dinner as they would be arriving home too late and would miss their regular mealtime.

The line for ticket holders was wrapped around the main building as well as the flat roofed exhibition hall that was connected by a large breezeway. Though the main floor normally held a little over seven thousand people, Stan Irwin had reconfigured the seating pattern and it now held nearly eight thousand five hundred for each of the two shows. As Steve stood in line, he estimated that nearly twice that number had shown up and were arranged in large screaming groups at the curbs and spilling into the parking lot. At regular intervals the screaming would reach a crescendo, die down only to rise again and last for even longer. The line was moving slowly and after a half an hour, Steve and his two nieces moved inside the main lobby of the venue. The orderly line that had waited outside turned into a milling mass once they had gained admittance behind the bank of glass doors. Steve noticed the same wide-eyed look on most of the adults that were accompanying underage kids. Though for the moment there was less screaming than there had been outside, it now echoed off the ceilings and the concrete floors and transformed into one long howl. Luckily there were large numbers of ushers that scurried around examining the light blue tickets that were thrust towards them and directing the holders through the various doors to the general area of their seats. Steve was glad that the seats they were shown to were in the twentieth row as the first four rows were filled with swarms of teenage girls hopping up and down and shrieking at each other, confounding the efforts of the ushers to seat the patrons who held tickets for those rows. He held the hands of both girls tightly. They had both been rather quiet since they arrived and even they were impressed by the volume of noise that bounced off the walls and the rafters making normal conversation impossible. Stan Irwin, in an unnecessary attempt to build up excitement, had booked no fewer than six acts that preceded the actual appearance of the Beatles. Each act was met with more impatient derision than the act preceding it until the penultimate performer, Jackie DeShannon, was nearly booed from the stage. From where Steve and the girls sat, nothing could be heard for the screaming and precious little could be seen as virtually no one sat in their seats. Steve resorted to lifting each girl in turn above his head for a few moments so they could at least get a glimpse of something other than the back of the seats. By the time the Beatles themselves took the stage it was nearly five thirty and they had been preceded by a doubling of the police directly in front of the stage. What had been merely chaos for the last two and a half hours now turned into pandemonium. Whole sections of young girls left their seats and rushed towards the stage tripping over those that had gotten there ahead of them as well as the cops who were constantly coming up the aisles carrying out those who had actually tried to get on the small stage. The sound system was under powered and few other than those directly in front of the stage heard more than a note or two above the din. Steve held Betsy against his waist at several points and protected her ears with his hands.

The actual concert lasted little more than a half hour and then it was over. But it was not until Steve bundled both girls into the back seat and strapped them in with the seatbelts did they get some relief from the noise. It took Steve longer to negotiate the long tangled lines of traffic out of the parking lot onto Paradise road then the Beatles had been on stage. His task was made harder by the throngs of cars attempting to get in for the nine o'clock show. It was nearly seven thirty when he was able to turn left onto East Sahara and make his way to the small strip mall that held Foxy's Deli. For the second time in a day he stood in front of the glass doors, then opened them to the comfortable dining room and held it as the girls walked in. They were still excited from the concert and were chattering excitedly as they tried to decide where they wanted to sit.

Bernie came in from the casino and seeing the two little girls, came up from behind and scooped both of them up into his arms. They both laughed and threw their arms around his neck as he carried them over to the large round table set for eight in the middle of the dining room. Bernie sat the girls on either side of him and motioned one of the waiters over and ordered them each a Shirley Temple. Steve asked for an ice tea when the waiter handed him a menu. He watched as Bernie went over the menu with the girls, offering to make something for them if they didn't see it on the menu. As the girls read the menu to each other out loud, Bernie looked over at Steve six feet away at the other side of the big table.

"Well how was that?" Bernie was grinning widely.

"Loud." Steve laughed and tossed his menu into the middle of the table. "But the seats were fantastic, I can't thank you enough." Bernie looked at both girls, still engrossed in their reading.

"It was my pleasure, especially to see these two so happy." Steve called each girls name to get their attention. When they were both looking at him, Steve smiled and pointed at Bernie.

"Don't we have something we want to say to Mr. Gold here?" His eyebrows arched. "Hmmm?" Betsy laughed and hid her face behind her menu.

"Mr. Gold." She laughed again. "His name is Bernie". Both girls again hugged Bernie's neck and said "Thank you" in unison with their high pitched voices. Bernie laughed and hugged them back. "Why didn't you come with us, Bernie?" Susan asked as Betsy chimed in. "Yeah, why not?" Bernie laughed again. "It is bad enough your uncle had to lose his hearing, I'm way too old for that stuff. Besides, someone has to stay behind and make the sandwiches." The three of them laughed as Steve smiled at the odd little grouping. The girls decided that they both wanted hamburgers, not a particular specialty of the restaurant, but Bernie went back into the kitchen to make sure they were up to snuff. Betsy had requested a burger like the ones they make at McDonalds and Bernie had taken it as a personal culinary challenge. While they waited, Steve and his nieces shared their impressions of the concert. Both girls were disappointed that they had been unable to hear the music and weren't even sure what songs had actually been played. Susan thought the concert was way too short and that the Beatles had appeared as if they were in a hurry to get off the stage. In the end, they were both happy that they had gone and they both agreed it was far more fun with their uncle than it would have been with their mother.

Bernie and a waiter returned with three burgers and a roast beef sandwich for himself. The burgers were at least six inches high with not two but three layers of meat and separated by carefully sliced buns all seated on a mound of golden fries. The girl's eyes were wide as the waiter set the food down in front of them. The girls ate their burgers and chatted with Bernie while Steve leisurely picked at his meal enjoying being able to relax with most of the people he considered family. Bernie left the table after a half an hour and Steve encouraged the girls to finish their meals and get ready to go. Before they could make much progress, Bernie returned with two large glasses filled with ice cream and strawberries with a mound of whipped cream on top. He placed one in front of each girl and handed them both long handled spoons. Steve shook his head. "Val is going to kill me Bernie, if they eat all that." Bernie laughed and smiled down at the girls as they dug into the sundaes.

"Well, you don't bring them in often enough for me to spoil them, so I gotta do it all at once." He quickly scooped up a napkin and wiped a small spot of whipped cream from Betsy's chin. The restaurant was now almost full with concert goers, so Bernie said his goodbyes and disappeared with Walter into the kitchen. Steve got the girls organized and steered them through the maze of tables and out the door onto the sidewalk. The lights had begun to come on up and down the strip and a full moon was rising in the dark part of the desert sky. The girls clamored into the back seat of the car and Steve settled in and turned on the radio. One of the three stations was playing Beatle music and Steve turned it up so the girls could hear in the back. They were singing along to 'If I Fell' as he drove east on Sahara toward the Boulder Highway.

Steve had driven two miles from the turn-off onto the highway when he saw a pair of headlights in his rearview mirror come up rapidly from behind, close to within three feet of the bumper and then veer into the lane next to the Jeep. Steve immediately swiveled in his seat and grabbed Susan's hand. He tried to keep his voice as calm as he could.

"Susan, honey, get down with your sister on the floorboard and stay there until I tell you to get up. OK?" Susan nodded and put her arm around Betsy. Just as the two girls squirmed off the seat, there was a loud explosion and the back side window shattered spraying small pieces of silver glass throughout the car. Steve pressed the brakes quickly down halfway, let off the pressure for a brief moment, then with more force pushed down all the way locking them up and at the same time fighting the wheel to keep the Jeep straight. As he had hoped, the other car, a white station wagon, had not anticipated the move and had overshot Steve's car and was now attempting to stop fifty yards ahead. Steve hoped the separation of the two vehicles was enough for his next maneuver. He flipped the four wheel drive lever on the left hand side of the steering column as he spun the wheel to the right and drove the Jeep straight down the ten foot embankment that ran along the highway all the way to Henderson. The nose of the Jeep hit a small berm at the bottom of the slope, the momentum porpoising the front of the car upward pushing the two front wheels clear and then nosing over onto the sand beyond, large rooster tails of dirt trailing out from the back of the vehicle. As soon as he leveled the car, he cut the headlights and began to make rapid turns through a thick area of large salt-bush each one only a few yards apart from its' neighbor. When he came to another smaller berm he turned sharply and pushed the nose of the car deep into a large saltbush growing from the edge of the sand wall. He quickly got out and climbed the soft sands of the wall and peered back at the highway now two hundred yards away. The white car was driving slowly along the shoulder of the highway. There were three men, one was driving, there was one in the back passenger seat and the third was following behind outside the car looking through a pair of binoculars.

Steve could see his own shadow sharply outlined in the moon-light and knew he had only a few more moments before he was spotted. He waited until it appeared the last man had the binocu-lars pointed in a direction away from the Jeep. He quickly stepped back down beside the car and opened the back door. The girls were huddled behind the passenger front seat. Betsy was sobbing softly. Steve reached in and stroked her hair and wiped several tears from her cheek. He put his finger to his lips and whispered. "You both have to be brave. There are some men after us. The ride might get rougher so hold on to each other and this." He pulled heavily on the long end of the seat belt and wrapped it around Susan's arm. "Hold on tight. I am taking you home." He closed the door and still in a crouch opened the driver door and slid into the front seat. If his sense of direction was working, he was only three miles from a desert track he and his brother had hiked many times when they were young. It had originally been a Mormon handcart trail and possibly an Indian trail before that. It was still used by those denizens of the desert that had four wheel transportation and though it was narrow and rocky, the Jeep would be able to negotiate it. He was hoping that it would prove too difficult for the low slung station wagon. As soon as he turned the jeep down the narrow wash, the windshield was lit up by the sweep of headlights coming down from the highway. In his side view mirror he could see the lights of the white car as it bounced up and down on the uneven terrain. The area where the Jeep was slowly maneuvering was more difficult and the pursuit car was shortening the distance between them. If they got much closer, they would be able to catch up on foot. A few yards later his fears were realized as he saw the silhouette of two figures pass in front of the headlights on the slow moving car. They were running in the light from the car and would arrive in five minutes at most. Steve gunned the engine and the Jeep fishtailed through the low shrubs wallowing almost to a stop until Steve spun the wheel and hit the gas again. Fifty yards later, the terrain in front of him dropped off sharply. He decided this was the best place he was going to find and his best chance to escape with the two children.

When he was sure he was out of the sight line of the pursuers he changed directions and swung in a wide arc away from the highway for about fifty yards. He eased the Jeep into a shallow arroyo that would make it hard to see unless someone were to come in the opposite direction of travel. He pulled a large battery operated lantern from beneath the seat and climbed across the seat and out the front passenger door. He again opened the back door and put his arms around both girls as they huddled on the floorboards.

He put his head between theirs and whispered in their ears. "No matter what you hear, do not come out until you hear my voice telling you to do so, OK?" They both nodded. Betsy looked about to cry again. Steve kissed her forehead. "It will be OK, I promise. Promise me you won't come out?" They both nodded as he quietly closed the door and begin to sprint in a low crouch down the shallow ditch using it for cover as long as he could. He could hear the station wagon laboring as it came upon the narrow rocky section. He could not see or hear the two men who were out in the darkness in front of the car. He dropped to the ground and crawled quickly for twenty yards until he was safely behind a large manzanita bush. He was about seventy-five yards away from the Jeep and as far as he could tell he was at least fifty yards off the line the searchers were taking. He turned on the lamp but kept it face down in the dirt until he was ready. He stood to a crouched position and holding the lantern at chest height and pointed towards the sound of the car, ran swiftly for twenty yards before ducking down behind another large bush. On the third dash, he heard a voice exclaim and shout something to someone else. The voice was much closer than Steve had guessed. He decided to change direction again and this time ran parallel to the highway quartering back toward the white car. Just as he ducked down into another shallow arroyo, there was a bright flash and explosion twenty yards to his right. Though he did not hear the bullet impact anywhere around him, the direction of the flash was only a few degrees off line. He switched off the lamp, crawled for another ten yards to where several low yucca plants were growing where the arroyo ended. When he was safely behind them he ran in a low crouch trying to make as little noise as possible. The ground leveled out into a wide swath of desert pavement, an area where the wind had scoured the soil away and the pebbles had settled over the years until they were almost as firm as a road. The station wagon could drive on this type of surface as if it were a hard packed dirt road. Steve decided to lead the chase away from this spot, but he made a mental note of the location.

After a long run, he stopped, turned on the lantern and placed it atop a large ant hill. He quickly moved twenty yards away and waited. Ten seconds later, he heard several shots accompanied by bright yellow orange flashes in the blackness as two bullets impacted the mound. When there were no more shots, Steve guessed that they were probably attempting to flank the light source and would not give away their location by firing again until they were right upon their target. Steve turned to look for better cover. On his second step he tripped over something and fell into a tangle of old wire and rusted tin cans. He lay still waiting to hear if the noise he had caused drew a response. When nothing stirred, he rolled over to see what he had tripped over. After some searching, his hand closed on a rusty bar of iron imbedded in the dirt with about six inches protruding above the ground. Steve tugged on the cold metal but it barely budged. He began to quickly dig the dirt out from around it with his hands. Four inches down he found a length of the rusty wire wound around the bar and as soon as he stripped the wire away the bar came loose. It was three feet long and was flattened at one end. Steve got to his knees, hefted it to test the weight and then crawled to a spot just in front and to the left of the ant hill. He figured at least one of the attackers would come that way. Steve crouched lower to blend his shadow in with the four foot bush he was hiding behind. He tried to memorize the shadows thrown off by the vegetation in front of him. The slight breeze he had noticed when he moved away from the Jeep had stilled and through his thin shirt he could feel the dew began to settle. From his hiding place he could turn his head to his right and see the mound that held the lantern. The battery was beginning to fail and the light was only as half as bright as before, the moon came out from behind a thin cloud and the shadows darkened. Before he could turn his gaze back to his front he heard the sound of a shoe scrape over coarse sand. He froze and shifted his eyes in the direction of the small sound. Nothing happened for several seconds, then a man of medium height dressed in a suit with a tie dangling from his open collar stepped in front of the bush ten yards in front of Steve. Steve recognized him as the driver of the blue Ford the day he encountered Angelo Sorelli at the gas station. The man was peering intently in the direction of the lamp and holding his gun with gloved hands at chest height, he was cautiously placing one foot in front of the other. Six more steps and he would be standing three feet in front of Steve.

Steve began to measure his breathing, forcing the calmness of the regular in and out down through all his major muscles. At the same time he focused his gaze intently on the eyes of the man before him. The man took two more steps then stopped. Though Steve could not see his eyes clearly, he saw the slight movement of the head in his direction.

"What the..? You son of a …" The man took a jerky involuntary step backward as he saw Steve's shadow for what it was. Before he could right himself and raise his gun, Steve took a step forward and swinging the bar once around his head, let it fly. The rusty bar helicoptered swiftly through the air and caught the man in the throat before he could take his next step. As Steve released the weapon and fell to the ground, he heard something land with a thud beside him. The man was lying on his back, gurgling sounds coming from his throat as his hands clawed the dirt beside him. Steve rolled to his right and his shoulder hit the smooth cold metal of the gun. He quickly snatched it up and crawled back behind the protection of the bush. In the moonlight he examined the weapon. It was a Browning Hi-Power nine millimeter. He slid the clip out and counted the rounds. Seven, and one in the chamber. He reinserted the clip and cocked the hammer. He rolled onto his elbows and peered around the side of the bush. The injured man was still groaning on his back unable to get up. Steve hopped to his feet and zig-zagged to the left of where the man lay and halting twenty yards beyond, stopped and listened. After hearing nothing for ten seconds he was about to make a dash for new cover ten yards away when he heard a hoarse whisper coming from his right.

"Jimmy is that you? Where are you?" As Steve straightened up he heard a twig break from the same location.

"Right here." Steve squeezed off two quick shots in the direction of the voice.

Steve turned and at a brisk trot retraced his steps back to where he had left the girls and the Jeep. As he crested the top of the sloping area he saw the car one hundred yards away high centered where the rocky path had narrowed. Even from that distance in the dark, Steve could tell it was Angelo Sorelli illuminated in the red taillights trying to lift the car off the rocky spine that trapped it. Steve smiled and picked up his pace until five minutes later he was back at the Jeep. He opened the back door and carefully lifted each girl onto the bench of the backseat. "Stay down and if I tell you to, roll back onto the floor. I am taking you to your dad." Steve backed the Jeep out of the arroyo and without turning on the headlights made his way the hundred yards to the desert pavement in the dark. The pavement ran for a half a mile and just when it began to peter out, the front wheels bumped onto the narrow two track trail. Steve turned left and two miles later stopped when the trail crested a small hill. He got out and looked at the huge sky overhead, the moonlight shading most of the stars. To the north the lights of Las Vegas sent an orange glow halfway up to the heavens. To the south he could see the bluish light of Henderson ten miles in the distance and from his vantage point he could just make out the dim gleam of headlights five miles behind. They were not moving. Steve pulled the girls one by one from the back seat, gave them each some water from a canteen he had under the front seat and made them walk a little bit around the Jeep. He put them back into the rear seat and strapped them in. He then continued to pick his way along the rough two track trail, pausing now and then to back up and change directions when he came upon sections that had been washed out.

An hour later he saw streetlights ahead as the trail stopped at a patch of flat desert that was bordered by a narrow paved road. Steve slowed down as he came to an area of cross streets and slowed even more to read each small street sign in the pale light the moon provided. When he thought he had found the one he was looking for, he turned onto it and then pulled over to check on the girls.

Horace Voorhees worked at EG&G in one of the smaller and more secret locations of the defense contractor. He had once taken Steve and the family on a drive that took them to a place where they could see the building from a distance, and Steve had remembered the name of the street that lead to the facility. As he drove down the deserted two lane road he wiped the sweat and dirt from his brow and tried to keep the girls talking and calm. He turned a corner and three blocks ahead saw several low buildings surrounded by a chain link fence topped with barbed wire. The small complex was lit brightly. Suddenly, a beam of light shone through the back of the Jeep and at almost the same time a large black van pulled directly in front of Steve, forcing him to brake hard. The driver of the vehicle that was shining two spotlights on Steve's car, spoke loudly through a megaphone mounted along with several lights on a bar on the front of the roof.

"Stay in your vehicle and turn off your engine." The voice commanded. Steve cut the engine and turned to look in the backseat. He smiled at the girls.

"This is where your dad works. Let's see if they let us talk to him." The girls nodded enthusiastically. Susan pointed towards the windshield, and when Steve turned around there was an armed security guard with a revolver aimed at him through the glass. Before Steve could react, another guard was tapping on his side window. A third was standing outside the back sweeping his flashlight through the broken out back window. Steve rolled down his window and made a great effort to keep his expression calm and casual.

"Good evening, officer."

"Do you know where you are?" The security guard demanded.

His tone was hard and irritated. "You drove past three signs saying this stretch of road is closed to traffic and is a prohibited area."

"I know where I am and no, I didn't see the signs." He said truthfully. "I have two young girls with me and I need to speak to their father who works in that building." Steve pointed casually to the middle and largest of the three buildings that could be seen from the street. The guard leaned partway into the jeep and shined his light on the two girls in the backseat as the other guard approached the window.

"How did that window get broken out?" He seemed calmer and the first guard deferred to him and moved out front and said something to the guard still holding a gun on the car.

"Someone heaved a rock at it out on the highway. The girls were scared and I thought it best to bring them to their father." He lied, but smiled at the guard. The guard studied Steve's face for a few seconds.

"Can I see your driver's license?" He did not return the smile. Steve reached in his pocket pulled out his wallet and extracted his license from behind the yellowed plastic window. He handed it to the guard without comment. The guard shined his light on it and then looked back at Steve.

"Who is the father, Mr. Cannon?" He didn't hand the license back. Steve decided not to push his luck. "Horace Voorhees." He continued the calm tone. The guard stepped across the front of the Jeep and summoned the other two officers over to the van that had cut Steve off. He reached through the driver's window and brought a small radio hand piece up to his mouth. He held up the license and spoke into the radio for several minutes. He let his hand drop down still holding the small black device and looked at the ground. After several more seconds he raised his hand, spoke again briefly and then replaced it back into the van. He said something to the other two guards and then came back to the front of the Jeep. He stood two feet away and shined the light directly in Steve's eyes.

"OK, Mister Cannon. Here is what we are going to do. You are going to follow this van through that gate and park it on the right hand side as soon as you get in. Leave the keys in the ignition and get out with the girls and wait by that sign over there. Someone is sending a vehicle out to pick you up. Do you understand?" Steve nodded and said "Yes." He noted that his license had now disappeared into the guard's pocket.

The van turned and Steve steered the Jeep slowly behind it and parked it where he was directed. He got the girls out of the back and holding both their hands, moved to the side near a sign proclaiming the area to be a prohibited one. The guard pulled his van up behind Steve's car and sat writing on a large clipboard. No one spoke further to either Steve or the girls. After a few minutes another van pulled up and a tall, bald, bespectacled man got out from the front passenger side and walked around the back of the vehicle.

"Daddy!" Betsy was the first to see him and he knelt as she ran ten feet to meet him. Susan let go of Steve's hand and held out her arms as her father put Betsy down and hugged her too. As he straightened up he looked at Steve.

"What's going on? Why aren't the girls at home? And why are you so filthy?" Steve looked down at his torn and dirt caked shirt and then back up at Horace. "Quite a bit of car trouble, actually, Horace. It was late and I figured if I came here we could call Val and she wouldn't have to worry so long." He glanced at his watch. It was 10:45. Horace looked away from Steve and addressed the guard who had Steve's license.

"Can I take my daughters over to the guard shack and call my wife?" The guard nodded and Horace turned the two girls away from Steve and started walking them to a small well lit building that Steve had not noticed until now. He was still watching their progress when the guard stepped in front of him.

"Would you mind coming with me, Mr. Cannon?" He pointed to the van that had brought Horace. Steve shrugged and climbed into the open door of the rear passenger compartment. The guard closed the door beside Steve and got into the front passenger seat.

The van made a U turn and they rode in silence for two blocks until they stopped in front of the only two story facility Steve had seen until now. The guard opened Steve's door and motioned him to step out. As soon as he placed his foot on the ground he was grabbed roughly by the driver who had come around the back and was now pinning Steve to the side of the van. Steve could hear the rattle of handcuffs as the first guard grabbed both wrists and twisted his hands behind his back. When he was secured to their satisfaction, they turned him around and pushed him up several concrete steps and into the building. They opened a side door just inside the main entrance and pushed him inside the darkened room. His knee hit a chair and he stumbled forward, the guard lifting him up by the cuffs to prevent him from falling. Someone switched on a light and a chair was shoved under his legs forcing him to lose his balance and to sit heavily down upon it. Both guards walked out the door locking it behind them, leaving Steve alone in the room.

Steve gazed slowly around the room. It looked more like a conference room than a detainment facility. There was a large blackboard with equations chalked on the dusty green surface and several paper coffee cups sat on the table just to Steve's right. The fact that they seemed ill-prepared for intruders made Steve relax a little. From their manner he guessed that the guards were ex-military police and would probably be fairly disciplined and would unlikely to be cowboys taking matters into their own hands. There was probably a protocol and Steve would just have to bear up under it until he could convince someone that he posed no threat.

By the large clock on the wall, Steve was alone in the room for twenty minutes until he heard voices in the hall and the guard with his license and another older man came into the room. They ignored Steve while they handed several papers back and forth between them. The guard pointing out several things to the new one who was dressed in civilian clothes. The civilian grunted a few times as he read the papers and then satisfied with his effort he picked up a chair and placed it in front of Steve. Steve shifted a little to relieve the pain in his right wrist and adopting an expectant look gazed at the man in front of him.

"So, how long do I have to stay here?" He figured he might as well get the ball rolling. The civilian looked at Steve impassively.

"I don't know, Mr, Cannon, that depends on your answers to several questions I have." He stared at Steve and didn't say anything more. Steve tried to keep his impatience from showing in his voice.

"Well let's get to asking them so I can get out of here." The man sighed and leaned back in the chair. The guard sat down at the table with the clipboard he had been writing on outside the gate and nodded to the man in front of Steve when he was ready.

"Well, Mr. Cannon, let's start with something concrete and work up from there. What are you doing approaching a restricted government controlled location with a semi-automatic pistol that has no serial number and has been recently fired?" The guard wrote something quickly and then looked up and waited with the civilian for Steve's reply.

"I was out target practicing earlier this afternoon. I found the gun out in the desert a year ago." Steve deciding brevity was probably the safest way to proceed.

"That sounds like fun, I like to target practice myself, Mr. Cannon, and maybe it's just me, but I always finish firing the whole clip and then I leave it empty or replace it with a full one. Yours had six rounds left in it." The man looked down and pulled the top paper off the short stack and glanced at the second page before replacing the top one. He looked up at Steve.

"Well?"

"I thought I did just that. I guess I didn't see that the new clip wasn't full." Steve was determined to keep his manner as casual as the civilian's.

The civilian looked at Steve for a few moments without comment. He got up from his chair and left the room. Steve looked at the guard, who ignored Steve and busied himself drinking coffee. Two minutes later, the man returned with an inch thick file in a blue folder. Steve could see the Atomic Energy Commission seal on the front. The file was put down on the table in front of Steve. The man leaned back in his chair and crossed his legs. He indicated the file with a small gesture.

"Your brother-in-law has a security clearance. And because of that, we have a file on his family, which is sitting in front of you now." He looked straight at Steve and continued. "Father killed building the Hoover Dam. Mother died of pleurisy. Brother killed in the Pacific. Wife filed for divorce while you were on Guadalcanal. Silver Star for bravery on Guadalcanal. Bronze star for action on Tarawa. Two purple hearts." He leaned forward and picked up the file and handed it to the guard.

"My job here is to assess threats to the facility. Now I have to decide if something you are working on or involved in as a result of your work as a private detective comes under that heading. Do we understand each other?" Steve shifted sidewise in his chair to relieve the pain in his wrists. "Because of you, a valuable member of the team has to leave mid-shift on personal business, bringing the whole process to a halt for the night." Steve smiled.

"Let me make your job easier and save us both some time. Call detective Polhaus with the Las Vegas Police. He will vouch for me." The men conferred for a few seconds, then rose from their chairs and left the room, leaving Steve alone. He stood up carefully, trying to unstiffen his bad knee and walked slowly around the room, shaking his leg every once in a while in an effort to get some circulation back.

After ten minutes he sat down and then repeated the process for the next forty minutes. He was sitting when the door swung slowly open and Tam walked three steps into the room and stopped. He looked down at Steve, his hands thrust into a long brown lightweight duster. He had the trace of a smile on his lips.

"Well the only good news here is that I got to leave that holy mess at the concert. The bad part is that it is 12:30 in the morning, and I gotta start again at six." He walked over to the blackboard and stared at the rows of equations. "What the hell are these? Is this what your brother-in-law does here?" When Steve didn't answer, Tam turned around and raised his eyebrows.

"No, he is more of a mechanical genius type. Keeps all the secret equipment working and modifies the parts that don't work." Steve replied wearily and leaned forward to take the pressure off his arms. Tam still stood by the board and shook his head slowly.

"A football star, huh? I learn more about you every day. Even I have heard of that team and the fact that they were a handful off the field and kept old man Donovan busy keeping them eligible..." Tam chuckled. "I should have guessed right there you would be involved."

"Yeah, well that was a long time ago. As I told you before, stuff happens in high school."

"Well, by all means let's keep up to date." Tam turned one of the chairs around and sat with his arms leaning on the back. "Heard a report on the radio from the Henderson police. Shots fired in the desert just off the highway. Wouldn't involve you though, right?" Tam grinned and pulled a pack of licorice gum from his coat pocket, unwrapped a piece, put it into his mouth and continued grinning at Steve as he chewed it enthusiastically. Steve glared at the detective.

"Sorelli and his little gang of two tried to ambush me on the way home from the concert with my nieces. I got one pretty good with a piece of rebar, may have shot the other one. Only saw Angelo from afar." He got up and began pacing around the room.

"I think they were gone by the time the police got there, so I wouldn't worry, there isn't much to connect you with the incident, but the sooner we get you out of here the better. Let me see if I can find the guy with the key to your bracelets." Tam stood and kicked the chair back underneath the table and walked out the door. Steve bent back and tried to stretch the muscles in his lower back. Tam returned five minutes later with the guard. Tam put a piece of paper down on the table and with a pen borrowed from the guard signed his name in two places. He handed the paper to the guard who handed it to the civilian who had just entered the room. He carried Steve's driver's license and a package wrapped in brown paper and tied with string, which he placed on the table. He picked up the paper and after glancing at the signatures, nodded at the guard. The guard stepped around behind Steve and quickly unlocked the handcuffs. Steve slowly pulled his arms in front of him and began to massage his wrists and forearms.

The guard left the room. The civilian picked up the package and the license and handed them to Tam. "I am releasing him into your custody. I expect you to note the incident in your log downtown and forward me a report." Tam nodded and indicated with a sideways movement of his head for Steve to follow him out the door. Steve fell in behind Tam and slowly walked out into the corridor without looking back at the civilian.

The Jeep was waiting at the curb with the keys hanging from the ignition. Tam indicated his car across the small street.

"There's an all-night diner four blocks in that direction." He indicated south with the hand that was in the coat of his pocket. "Let me buy you a cup of coffee." Steve nodded, the effects of the last three hour's events were starting to lessen, and when he followed Tam out the front gate, the cooler air blowing through the large hole in the back window did even more to make him feel better.

The diner was deserted when Steve and Tam sat down in front of coffees and a piece of berry pie that Tam ordered and ate in three bites. Steve drank his coffee and feeling the caffeine began to work through his system, ordered another one. Tam was silent until he had finished the pie and most of his cup of coffee.

"Well this has been a busy day for you boy-o. I got cornered by a captain at the concert who said you accosted someone in Herb Slater's office. Seems Herb is a little put out, and since I am known far and wide as your protector and general man Friday, naturally this lands in my lap." Tam put the coffee cup carefully down in the saucer, poured in a small amount of cream and slowly stirred it with his spoon. Steve shrugged and gazed around the diner as he took a sip from his own cup. He put the cup down and pulled out his cigarettes.

"So here is what we are going to do. Tomorrow, you are going to bring me this evidence you found and we are going to have a little closed door meeting with the assistant DA." Tam let the spoon clatter onto the saucer as he lifted his cup and peered at Steve over the rim. Steve sat back in his chair and watched as Tam worked a piece of berry seed out of his teeth with his tongue.

"If that is what you want, Tam, sure. But I don't see the point right now. Still pretty early in the going." Tam picked up a toothpick from a small glass holder on the table, unwrapped it, placed it into the right corner of his mouth and looked across at Steve.

"Not when you threaten the staff of the next mayor. Look, I'm just covering your heinie here. If the DA's office gives it no credence, then the worst that will happen is that Herb will bitch and moan, and if it eventually goes away, he will leave well enough alone. If you got something, then it will be tough sledding, but the Feds can do the heavy lifting, you will just have to keep your head down and I will get used to cleaning up after traffic accidents." Tam smiled. Steve shrugged and nodded.

"I'll be there by ten."

"Good."

"So I got the information you wanted. First, the prints on the case belong to Wallace Beech. No surprise there. Second, he has a wife, Miriam. Two arrests on fraud charges, but no convictions. Seems that the fraud squad in Tucson thinks she is in with Wallace on all his schemes, just too smart to get caught. He did three years in Arizona, been out six months. They are sending up a picture, should be here tomorrow or the next day." Tam began to work the toothpick vigorously against the offending berry seed.

"Pretty obvious that when it comes in, it will be Audrey." Steve stretched and yawned.

"So where do you think she's gotten to?"

"Nowhere we will we find her, I am pretty convinced of that."

"When it comes in, I will put a BOLO out on her. She has to be somewhere."

"Yeah, well Angelo has to be somewhere, but he seems to turn up at will, and my movements don't seem to be much of a mystery to him."

"That was a pretty close call with your nieces. Why weren't you packing? Has your permit been revoked or something?"

"No, but I think the time has come." Steve replied wearily.

"Past time if you ask me." Tan pulled the package from his coat pocket and pushed it across the table. "I pick you for more of a .45 man, Cannon, but at least it might get you home. The serial number is gone, and I am sure the only prints on there on yours. I'll leave any mention of it out of my report. Doubt the EG&G guy will pick up on it."

Steve casually slid the package off the table and into his lap. "Thanks, I will give it back if he raises a fuss."

"So, can you give me a description of the car?" Tam pulled out his crumpled notebook and a pencil stub from the inside pocket of his duster. Steve made a disgusted face as he watched Tam riffle through the creased and folded pages.

"'61,'62 Dodge station wagon. White, blue vinyl interior, Clark county plates starting with the numbers 2 and 3. Back bumper missing." Tam looked up at the private detective across the table.

"I guess you were too busy to see what color the fuzzy dice were." He shook his head and shoved the notebook and the pencil back into his pocket. "It's late. Again. I gotta go home, see if I still have a wife, and try to get some sleep." He reached into his front pocket and threw two crumpled dollar bills on the table. Steve watched as the detective began a search through all his pockets for his car keys.

"I am grateful that you came out and got me released, thank you." Steve put out his hand to shake. Tam snorted and as usual ignored the hand.

"Oh, no problem, consider it my honor. I'm just grateful it was Henderson this time, instead of Reno." Tam grimaced and walked the five steps out the door. Steve finished his cigarette and walked out into the clear night. It was still 85 degrees, but it felt cool after the scorching daytime temperatures. He started up the Jeep and three minutes later turned onto the highway towards Las Vegas.

It was 3:30 in the morning when Steve parked in front of his house. He sat for several minutes, turning the Browning over in his hand. In the moonlight the black metal gleamed blue. Steve got out of the Jeep, shoved the gun down into his pants and walked to the garage door. He looked quickly around him and then pushed the door open as far as it would go.

The Corvette slid slowly out of the garage as Steve lightly feathered the throttle. He turned carefully in the loose gravel and eased the car up the slight incline onto the paved road. He kept the speed under twenty miles an hour as he moved past the few darkened houses on his street. Two blocks later he turned onto Lake Mead Boulevard and gained a little more speed as he traveled towards the blackened mountains. After a mile, he crested a small rise and slowed to a stop when the lights of the city disappeared behind him. The car burbled beneath him as the big camshaft turned over.

Steve fastened the two clasps on the racing harness, settled deeper into the bucket seats and pressed hard down onto the gas pedal. The frame of the Corvette flexed under the heavy engine as the wide slick back tires gripped the pavement and the car shot forward, fishtailing side to side as blue smoke swirled from the road. Ten seconds later 120 mph flashed past on the speedometer, the beefed-up suspension bobbing up and down on the uneven surface. The wind slammed against Steve's ears mixing with the scream of the engine and the sound of the big blower sucking in the night air. A section of short S curves rose up quickly as Steve wrestled the car from side to side on the narrow road. When the car shot up an incline towards a blind hill top, Steve slid the right side tires off the road and into the dirt in case there was oncoming traffic on the other side. Twenty minutes later he slowed as he dropped into a shallow canyon beside a still cove on the western edge of Lake Mead. Steve shut off the car and walked over the sandy pebbled dirt to the water. He stared blankly at the silver black surface of the lake. Suddenly he drew the pistol from his waistband and sent six shots quickly into the blackness twenty yards from shore. The sharp reports of the 9mm echoed off the red rocks. Large ripples spread out slowly from the splash until they disappeared at water's edge just below Steve's feet.

August 21

THE SUN STREAMED through the open curtains as Steve struggled awake. His right side was so stiff he had to roll to the other side of the bed to get out. He sat on the edge of the bed and looked over his shoulder at the clock on the nightstand. 8:40. He looked down at the scratches covering his arms and chest. Some had bled in the night and were surrounded by purple bruises. He made his way to the kitchen, filled a teakettle with water, lit the stove and sat down on the chair to wait on the boiling water. When it was done he put a spoonful of instant coffee in a large cup and stirred the beverage slowly as he looked out the window. Several minutes later he turned on the shower and stood motionless beneath the cascade of hot water for twenty minutes.

The phone rang in the middle of dressing, he picked up the extension that sat on the edge of a bureau near the bedroom window. It was Tam.

"Get down here as soon as you can. The 10 o'clock meeting is off, a body was found early this morning in the desert. The description fits Beech. The coroner is bringing him in now and he should be able to pull the prints and make an ID by the time you get here."

"How was he killed?"

"Two shots. One to the face and one to the chest. Bring those papers you found in Beech's suitcase and I will keep them in my safe here."

"I'll see you in half an hour." Steve hung up the phone and continued dressing. When he was done he called Gaudin Ford and asked for Dwayne, a friend from high school and the only one of his circle of friends that did not volunteer for the Marines, but instead joined the Army Air Corp and spent three years fixing B-17s in England. Dwayne thought that it might take three days to repair the window on the Jeep as the nearest parts were in Salt Lake City. Steve looked at his watch and figured he could drop off the Jeep, pick something else up to drive and make it downtown in forty–five minutes. When the door to the safe swung open he pulled out the plastic sheets protecting the documents first. He reached back in and retrieved a 1911 .45 in a holster. He strapped the gun around his torso so that the pistol lay in the small of his back. He turned and looked at himself in the mirror from several angles to make sure the bulge was not obvious. Satisfied, he locked the front door and pulled the Jeep up onto the paved road and drove towards downtown.

He should have thought to ask Tam who had notified them of the body. He would bet $100 that it was Polaski, the retired cop. Steve smiled when he thought of tomorrow's headlines in the Las Vegas Sun and the Review-Journal. 'Body Found in Shallow Grave'. He laughed to himself as he eased into the traffic heading west towards the strip. If any of the readers would just look up from their morning papers and out their windows, they would see the impossibility of accidently stumbling upon anything out in that expanse, especially if it was even halfway concealed. There could be a thousand bodies buried out there and no one would be any the wiser, except for one thing. His father had called them the 'hidden village', the collection of desert rats that daily roamed over much of the southern Nevada and Mojave deserts. Gold prospectors, uranium seekers, anti-socialites, southern Paiute Indians, wanted and dispossessed men, many of them alcoholics or suffering from various mental diseases or both. Steve first became aware of this invisible population when he hiked as a small boy with his father and older brother. His father taught him how to observe his back trail and how to tell if there was someone following or lying in wait up ahead. Most of the face to face encounters usually involved begging for whiskey or money. In some rare cases even water was requested. Steve's father usually carried several half pint bottles of rot-gut whiskey that he would bestow on the more familiar faces he came across. Everyone that Steve knew who took frequent outings into the desert, considered it a matter of course that at least one pair of eyes was watching at all times, and few traveled unarmed. Which is where the retired cop Polaski came in. As far back as anyone could remember, he was the one that received the anonymous tips that led to the grisly discoveries. The whole community of desert rats knew he was good for fifty bucks and several bottles of booze if the tip proved genuine. It was an arrangement that everyone involved deemed satisfactory and the practice continued even after Polaski retired in 1960. The other angle that would also be hinted at in the daily papers was the possibility that the body was the result of mob activity. This was nearly as far-fetched as the possibility of a typical tourist stumbling across a body in the first place. By common agreement among all concerned, dumping bodies in the desert was forbidden. Partially because of the aforementioned activity and partially as a way to keep peace, any type of 'liquidation' would happen in some other part of the country. This had led to some rather tragi-comic scenes in where wise-guys being promoted to duties elsewhere would steadfastly refuse to leave town until they received personal guarantees. Presumably some who did receive such assurances met a fateful end anyway in spite of all their precautions. In this case, it was very likely that someone saw who had dumped Beech's body into the desert and Steve thought he knew the best way to find out that particular information.

Gaudin Ford was located on a busy corner and the usual Friday morning traffic was thick. Steve parked the Jeep in the back lot by the repair bays. He tossed Dwayne the keys and walked down the three rows of used cars that were lined up under multi-colored pennants facing the street. Seeing nothing that held his interest, he crossed the lot and pushing through a side door entered the showroom. He stopped short when he saw the car displayed in the middle of the showroom. The '64 Mustang was sleek, low, black and a convertible. The top was down and the door clicked open when Steve tried it. He was examining the dashboard instruments when a salesman leaned in from the passenger side.

"Now you've picked a very special car, there, my friend." The salesman grinned and looked admiringly around at the black leather interior. Steve glanced at him briefly and began to operate the air conditioning controls.

"How much does 'special' cost today?"

"Well you know, they haven't made too many of these for this year with the 289 and the four-speed."

"The price for the hardtop is $1995. How much more is this one?" Steve turned and looked directly into the salesman's eyes.

"This is $2350." The salesman's voice was not as enthusiastic as it had been seconds before.

"If I can drive it out of here in the next twenty minutes, I will write you a check right now." Steve pulled a thin packet of checks from his back pocket and slapped it down on the seat beside him. The salesman hesitated.

"Well I'm not sure. The owner's daughter is pretty taken with it... and I might have to check..." Steve interrupted.

"Get me the owner or the sales manager. I haven't got all day to huckle chuckle around with you." He pointed toward the office doors ten feet away. The salesman turned and was about to leave when Steve became aware of someone standing behind him. He turned as the man spoke.

"Give him the car, Max, my daughter can wait until her grades get better anyway." He extended his hand to Steve.

"Dwayne told me to find you in here and help you out." The man smiled as Steve reached up from inside the car and shook his hand.

"This is a great car. If you are in a hurry, and have proof of insurance, we can complete the rest of the transaction later." The man stepped back as Steve opened the door and climbed out.

"That would be great. Let me write you a check as a deposit." The owner motioned for Max to come around to their side of the car.

"Max, take his check and drive it out of the showroom." The man clasped Steve's hand again.

"Thank you for your business, Mr..?"

"Cannon, Steve Cannon." Steve released his grip as he saw the man's eyes light up.

"Say, are you related to Howard?" Steve waited for two beats before replying.

"No, no relation. But if I see him, I will definitely recommend he buy his next car here." Steve patted the man on the shoulder and after retrieving his checkbook from the front seat, followed Max through the office doors.

Ten minutes later he pulled onto Las Vegas Boulevard and headed downtown to the police station. The car drove smoothly and the powerful engine made Steve constantly glance at the speedometer to make sure he wasn't exceeding the speed limit by too much. It had been a long while since he had driven a convertible on a daily basis and he figured the wind buffeting would take some getting used to.

The station was busy as Steve walked through the corridor

towards Tam's office. He held on to a canvas satchel that contained the documents he had retrieved from Beech's suitcase. Tam's door was open and two other men were there talking with Tam and looking at something on the desk when he rapped lightly on the doorframe. All three looked up when Steve knocked. Tam pointed towards Steve.

"Detective Samuels, this is Steve Cannon. He has been investigating Beech since he first went missing. Detective Samuels is head of the homicide division." Steve nodded and stepped just inside the door. The one who was not Samuels nodded back. When both men turned their attention back to the desk, Steve held up the satchel and pointed to it. Tam nodded and indicated the file cabinet against the wall. Steve quietly stepped around the two men and placed it on top of a stack of papers perched precariously on the metal cabinet. After a few minutes, Samuels straightened up and turned to Steve.

"Well you can stop looking for him, Mr. Cannon, we have found him for you. The coroner thinks he has been dead for at least two weeks. Probably there all the time you were out looking." Samuels snorted and turned to Tam. Steve crossed his arms and leaned against the door frame.

"Well then, I suppose you must have a very good idea who would do such a thing." Steve looked away from Samuels and smiled at Tam. Tam raised his brows and shook his head as a warning to Steve. Steve smirked. Samuels returned to studying what Steve now saw was a map.

"We are in the early stages of gathering evidence at the crime scene, Mr. Cannon. Proper police procedure is a slow but sure process." Steve leaned forward from the doorframe and took two steps farther into the room. From his new position he could see a small red 'x' on the map. It was off a small road that was just south of the rural community of Pahrump. Steve knew exactly where that was. He smiled to himself, this is going to be easier than I thought, he mused. He looked at Tam.

"Well Tam, if you don't need me for anything else, perhaps I should get out of Mr. Samuels way and go find out who dumped that body on the other side of Pahrump." Samuels straightened slightly and looked over at Steve but said nothing. Behind Samuels, Tam held up a piece of paper and turned his body slightly so that only Steve could see what he was holding. It was a picture that had come over the teletype. It was a mug shot of Audrey Sizemore. Steve smiled at Tam, and walked out the door.

As Steve cleared the front door of the police station, he saw a man that worked for Tommy Carmino fold up a newspaper and detaching himself from the metal banister he had been leaning on began to amble towards Steve. He walked past Steve, pivoted and fell in two steps behind him.

"Keep walking straight, Mr. Cannon, and don't look back."

"Sure thing, pal, I'm just heading for my car."

"Tommy wants to see you today at the Plush Horse at 4:00 sharp. Got it?"

"Yep, got it. Tell Tommy I'll be there." The wise guy veered off and disappeared between two patrol cars parked at the curb. Steve continued on across the street and over to his car. He turned out of the parking lot and drove for two blocks until he saw a phone booth that was tucked away and not obvious from the street. As a further precaution he parked the Mustang at an angle to obscure it. Steve stepped inside, pivoted to face the street and dialed Val's number. When Val answered the phone she sounded out of breath as if she had been outside when she heard the ring. After Steve announced himself, there was a long silence.

"How could you, Steve?" Val said in a quiet voice. Steve had been hoping that she would be in more of a raging mood. This was going to be worse.

"I am sorry, Val." He couldn't think of any else to say.

"You are always sorry, Steve, but it never seems to make you treat people better does it?"

"Val,..I.." She cut him off.

"You know what, Steve? I lost the wrong brother in the war."

The phone clicked. Steve held on to the receiver for several seconds hoping it was just a momentary interruption in the transmission. When he was sure that she had hung up, he gently replaced the receiver back on the hook, waited until the extra coins he had put in came clanging down the chute, then left the booth and got into his car. He lit up a cigarette and watched the traffic move by on the way to the police station and city hall. After a few minutes he drove the three blocks to Skipper's motel and knocked on the door. After receiving no answer, he went to the office and spoke to a man who was filling in for the one that Steve normally dealt with. After a short fruitless conversation with the new clerk, Steve went back and knocked again. He waited outside the motel for ten minutes, then drove around the neighborhood for several blocks before turning onto Fremont street. He drove slowly west along the street, searching the thin crowds and peering into the open doors of the smaller casinos and bars. Seeing no Skipper or anyone that might know him, he turned left onto Las Vegas Boulevard and headed south.

*

BERNIE GOLD WAS in a good mood. Steve could see him laughing at the counter with a customer as Steve walked by the glass windows on his way to the front door. A few minutes later as he watched Steve tuck into a breakfast of bacon and eggs, he was not so cheery. The recounting of the previous night's events had dampened his demeanor considerably.

"Steve, this crap has got to stop." Bernie shook his head. "I don't have a good feeling at all about all this, somebody has got to find this maniac before more people get hurt." His eyes were wide and for the first time Steve realized that they held a bit of sadness all the time.

"I know, Bernie, but I think I am getting closer to figuring this out. Angelo is going to make a mistake and that will be that."

"I wish I shared your optimism, my friend, but I'm sorry, it's just my nature and the nature of my people." Bernie shook his head again and looked down at his cold coffee.

"You want another cup?" He asked hopefully. Steve nodded.

"And when you come back I need to ask you yet another favor." Bernie paused and grew serious again.

"When I come back, we need to talk about Remy." At the mention of Remy, Steve felt his stomach do a small flip. He nodded to Bernie and watched him as he made his way over to the counter.

Bernie returned with two fresh cups in saucers and placed them on the table before sitting down himself. He poured some cream into his and after stirring it for a few seconds, waited until Steve had taken a sip from his cup and replaced it in the saucer.

"I talked to Remy last night. I called her sister yesterday after you left. The sister was being cagey and rightfully so, so I just gave her my number and told her to tell Remy to give me a call." Bernie shrugged. "So she called me late last night, she is in Palm Springs. I remember Nash saying he had a place on one of the golf courses there, she didn't say where she was exactly, but I assume that is where she is staying." Bernie paused while Steve took another sip of his coffee and set it down.

"So how is she doing, Bern?" He voice was low and he had been frowning since Bernie returned with the coffee.

"From what she said she is ok, so I wouldn't worry on that score, Steve, but I think the main reason she called me was to tell me that she thinks Nash has gone missing."

"Missing? Why does she think that?"

"She has tried to call him several times, got the maid on the phone, who said she hadn't seen him since he left for LA five days ago. She called the Dunes, and they haven't seen him since then and he hasn't checked in with them either. She's pretty scared, Steve. That I do know." Bernie had leaned in for emphasis as he finished.

Steve looked thoughtfully down at his cup then back up at Bernie. He was still scowling.

"I don't like that she is staying in one of Nash's places. Did she say she was going to call me?" He watched as Bernie looked away.

"She asked how you were doing, but I didn't get that she was going to tell you any of this. But she didn't she didn't tell me not to tell you." Bernie looked up sheepishly.

"Thanks, Bern, Nash going missing is a new angle I didn't anticipate. But there isn't anything I can do about that right now, I have to keep on the trail I have been following and keep putting the pieces together as best I can. But there is something you can do for me in that regard. Do you think that you can locate Mike Hunter?"

"Yeah, I think so, Steve. You think he is mixed up in this because of the land deal?"

"Well, he was the first one that mentioned it to you and he was on Sorelli's hit list the last I heard, so yeah, I think I would like to hear what he has to say."

"He isn't in town anymore, I know that. He knows a lot of people in the South Lake Tahoe area, used to work in several of the casinos there. I'll poke around and see if anyone's seen him or knows where he is. I'll get back to you on that." Bernie smiled for the first time since Steve walked in.

"Better yet, Bernie, just give him my number and have him call me after ten at night. I don't want you to put a whole lot of effort into this."

"No effort? Look, Steve, people I care about are in danger. I will do what I can to keep them safe. If you found yourself without a family one day, you would know what I am talking about." Bernie's smile from earlier was gone, replaced by a hardness that Steve had rarely if ever seen in his friend.

"Don't worry, Bernie, everything is going to be alright. I just need a little more time and a little luck to corner Angelo." He slurped the last of his coffee, put two silver dollars on the table and got up to leave. Bernie picked up the coins and shook his head.

"No way, brother, everything you eat or drink here is on me." He held out his hand to Steve. Steve smiled, took the silver and called Walter over from where he had just taken the order of a couple nearby. Walter came over, acknowledged Bernie, and looked expectantly at Steve.

"Walter, I want you to know that you make it a pleasure to come into this dump every time I do. As a token of my gratitude, here is something to make up for all the times I have neglected to mention it." He took Walter's hand and dropped the two coins in and closed the surprised man's fingers over them. He smiled down at Bernie who was still shaking his head.

"Get outta here!" Bernie laughed, got up and walked Steve the few steps to the door.

"Keep safe Steve. I will get on the Mike Hunter thing right now." He waved as Steve backed out of the door and headed for the Mustang parked four spaces away.

*

THE TWO LANE highway that wound high above Las Vegas cut through the pinion forests that grew on the eastern flanks of the Spring Mountains. The air had become noticeably cooler and the hot wind that had swirled around Steve's head as he climbed from the valley floor was gone and had been replaced by pine scented fresh air. Just beyond the summit, he turned off the highway and cut down a short road and into the parking lot of the Summit Inn. He parked near a station wagon pulling a large silver Airstream and walked through the casino to the back where there was a bar and a package store. He waited as the bartender served a pair of tourists. He turned and surveyed the small gambling scene behind him and spied a familiar face. The man smiled at Steve and came up the two steps from the casino floor and held out his hand.

"How are you, haven't seen you in a while, maybe been a year right?" The man who was almost as tall as Steve widened his smile. "I'm usually better with names, but I think you are the guy that isn't related to any of the Cannons, right?" He released Steve's hand and reached inside his coat pocket for a card which he offered to Steve.

Steve took it, looked at it briefly before dropping it in the outside pocket of his windbreaker.

"Yeah, Mitch, I'm that guy." He turned back to the bartender who was free now and asked him if he had a couple of pints of Heaven Hill whiskey. Mitch stepped up beside him and they both watched as the bartender slid open a door in the cabinet behind him and began looking through his stock. Steve turned to the manager.

"Say, Mitch, have you seen Marcus Boomer in here lately?" The bartender put two small thin bottles on the bar and Steve pulled his wallet out to pay for them.

"Yeah, he was in here last week. Bought the usual, just what you are buying. We always make sure that we have that brand in stock." He pointed at the two bottles that were now wrapped tightly in two paper bags and nestled in the crook of Steve's arm.

"Thanks, I just wanted to make sure he was around before I made the trip. He sometimes goes to stay with his sister in Searchlight and doesn't show back up for weeks." Steve held out his free hand and grasped Mitch's hand firmly when it was offered in return.

"Thanks, Mr. Cannon, please come again and try to stay a little longer next time. Tell Marcus I said hi." Steve had already started moving towards the steps and waved in acknowledgement at the request.

Back at the car, Steve placed the bottles on the front seat and then erected the black cloth top. When he had fully fastened the latches and rolled up the windows, he pulled back up the short entrance road and turned right onto the highway which started a slow descent away from the summit.

Two miles later, Steve steered across the highway and pulled the car onto a large gravel turnout making a sweeping turn so that the car faced in the opposite direction from the one in which he had been traveling. The car was twenty yards from a large cattle guard that stretched all the way across a dirt road which continued for one hundred yards and disappeared as it crested a small hill. Steve shut off the engine and waited. The wind had picked up and several small little dust devils played around the car, spinning across the yellow dirt and swirling off through the yuccas.

Steve leaned forward on the steering wheel and squinted down the dirt road. After about ten minutes, he saw the head and torso of a man appear, walking slowly as he came to the top of the hill from the other side. His steps were short and measured and his small frame arched under the heavy blanket coat that came nearly to his knees. Steve got out of the car and waited as the elder of the Southern Paiute tribe took several minutes to walk the last section down the hill. The man stopped when he got to the cattle guard. He ignored Steve and peered at the car for several seconds before he looked up. Steve walked over and stood just on his side of the thick black pipes of the guard. He gazed steadily at the man who was looking at him as if he was looking at a sunset. The man's features were small but finely honed in the brown leathery skin. He had a small fringe of gray hair encircling his otherwise bald head. He stood with his hands hanging by his sides taking deep breaths through his nose. Steve waited until the man was ready to speak. He pointed with a small gesture behind Steve.

"I don't think that car is very good for you." His voice was barely audible above the wind.

"It's just a temporary one, Marcus, I won't keep it very long." Steve tried to raise his voice just loud enough to be heard. Marcus gazed at the car.

"Try not to have it very long, Steve Cannon." He shifted his gaze to Steve's hands which were in the front pockets of his thin nylon jacket. Steve returned to the passenger side of the car and retrieved the two brown bags. He walked back to the guard and without stepping on the pipes leaned over and carefully set the two bottles on Marcus's side of the guard. He straightened up and waited. Marcus walked the five steps to the bottles, bent over slowly and peeked carefully into one of the brown bags. He then picked both of them up and tucked each away in different sides of his multi-striped coat. Without a word he turned and began to trudge slowly back the way he had come. Steve waited until Marcus had traveled fifty yards and then stepping over the cattle guard began to follow, keeping a pace that preserved the separation between the two men.

After a walk of three hundred yards up and down several small hills, the dirt road ended in a small bowled out area that contained a dirty white trailer and the remains of a '46 Chevy truck. Marcus reached a small table that was placed ten yards from the trailer. Next to it were two metal folding chairs. He carefully placed the bottles of whiskey on the table and from a nearby bucket he selected two small tin cups, wiped them out with his hand and put them next to the bottles. He then disappeared into the trailer. When Steve arrived, he sat down in the chair facing out towards the mountains and waited. After five minutes, the door to the trailer opened and Marcus reappeared carrying a large square piece of plywood. From where he sat, Steve could see a small hole in the golden grain of the wood. Marcus trudged over in the general direction of the table and began walking around in a circle. As he passed by, Steve could see that on the other side of the plywood was a painting. After several circumlocutions of the table, Marcus selected a spot half-way between the trailer and the table, and propping the painting up with a rock, he rotated it slightly until it could be seen equally well from either seat. He then came over and sat down in the chair opposite Steve. He gazed at the painting and said nothing. Steve turned a little in his chair and studied the painting. It was done in oils, Steve guessed, and most of the board was dominated by a large raven, the feathers a blue sheen over the black. Where his eye should have been there was the oval shaped hole that Steve had seen from the back. The bird was in flight over a large plateau that was painted in tones of red, orange and brown. One edge of the rim of the plateau held several clumps of green vegetation. For several minutes they both gazed at the painting, the wind flattening the small wisps of grass around them that had once been a front lawn.

Presently, Marcus turned away from the painting and carefully opened the bottle of whiskey nearest him. He poured the cup in front of Steve half full and did the same for his cup. When he put the bottle back down and screwed the cap back on, it was half empty. They sipped their whiskey in silence, Steve looked out over the series of arroyos leading to the mountains, Marcus staring blankly into space, occasionally glancing at his painting. After ten minutes or so, Marcus grunted to get Steve's attention.

"Why did you buy that car?" He looked at Steve as impassively as he had been looking at the painting seconds before. Steve shrugged.

"I needed a car because the Jeep is being fixed."

"That is a bad choice." Steve looked back at Marcus with the same impassive thousand-yard stare and said nothing. Marcus took another drink of the whiskey and Steve did the same, the jagged, fiery liquid sliding slowly down his throat. Marcus looked at the painting and did not speak again for several minutes.

"That raven knows me." He was still looking at the painting.

"Does he know you as well as I know you?" Steve put the cup back to his lips and took a much smaller sip of the whiskey.

"No, you and I do not know each other."

"I met you when I was twelve. I have known you for many years, Marcus." Steve waited as Marcus turned and his eyes focused on Steve's face.

"Not in these forms. Perhaps in others we know each other well. It is not likely to happen in these we are in now." He returned his gaze to the painting. Steve took another tiny sip and looked back over the mountains. Nothing was said for several more minutes. Marcus filled his empty cup with the rest of the whiskey in the bottle and took a long drink.

"You have come because of the body." He paused for several seconds and then resumed.

"You are part of that body. You should go stay with my sister for a while. She will cleanse you." He returned to his cup and his painting.

"Who found the body, Marcus?" Marcus did not turn but continued staring outward.

"I saw the body. I saw the men when they left the man there." Steve looked down at his cup and swirled the brown liquid in circles.

"That is twenty miles from here. I would have thought that maybe Jizzy Ron or his brother would have been the ones." He raised the cup to drink, thought better of it and looked over at Marcus. Marcus shrugged.

"I was there, I saw when they did it."

"How many of them were there, and what did they look like, Marcus?" Steve waited another several minutes before he received a reply.

"Three. All white. Two and one big man in charge. Blue car, one shovel."

"What did the big one in charge look like?"

"I could not look at him directly. The other two were ordinary. One of them is hurt now."

"Was the man alive or dead when you saw him?"

"Dead."

"But you didn't call it in, did you, Marcus?" Steve tried to make his expression as neutral as he could. Marcus didn't look at him anyway as he spoke.

"Others want the money and the whiskey. If not, there is trouble." Steve stretched his legs out in front of him, the sun was warm on his skin, while the breeze was cool.

"You shouldn't go back to Las Vegas. I am going to Searchlight to see my sister soon. You should come with me."

"I have to go back, Marcus, I have to make sure that those men do not get away with this."

Marcus turned and looked at Steve closely.

"You are not evil. There is not much you can do. He can do plenty." When Steve did not reply, Marcus got up and walked to the trailer opened the door and reached for something just inside. He came back and sat down. He kept the object inside his coat. He reached across the table and took Steve's cup in his free hand and drained the whiskey it contained in one gulp. He wiped the gray stubble on his chin with the back of his coat sleeve. He brought out the object and laid it on the table between them. It was a small piece of wood about six inches square. On one side was a painting of a desert scene. On the other there was a rendering of a desert big-horn sheep done in part with natural ochre. The desert scene looked as if it had been painted many years ago, the colors of the sheep were sharp and vibrant. Marcus picked up the other bottle of whis-key and put it inside his coat.

"Put this in your house, if you stay in there the protection will be great." Marcus slid the piece of wood slowly over to Steve's side of the table. Steve picked it up and turned it over slowly in his hands. Marcus stood up and looked down at Steve.

"Your time here is gone." He turned and walked back to the trailer and opened the door. He came halfway back, picked up the painting of the raven and put it inside before again entering the small doorway and swinging the aluminum door closed behind him. Steve walked back to the car and put the small piece of wood in the glove box. He looked at his watch. He would arrive back in town just in time to meet with Tommy.

*

THE PLUSH HORSE was tucked in a small strip mall on East Sahara about two blocks east of the hotel. Next to it was a barber shop that catered to most of the power brokers in town. Steve had been in the bar on two previous occasions and was not fond of the service if one was not a regular. As he walked to the entrance, he passed by the red Cadillac. He opened one side of the big oak doors and stepped into the foyer. He was immediately spotted by the host who was bearing down on him from across the room when he heard his name being called.

"Cannon. Over here." Steve looked past a large fern plant and into the main room. Tommy Carmino was sitting in a curved black leather booth. Beside him sat a young woman with long black hair. The manager met Steve halfway into the room with a big smile and turned to lead him to Tommy's table. Steve ignored him. He stood in front of the table which had a slick black mirror finish. A small tumbler of scotch on a napkin sat in front of Tommy and he had his arms spread out along the back of the booth. He wore a beige, three piece linen suit with a pale lilac shirt and a cream colored tie. Steve guessed he had just come in from the barber shop as the smell of talc was strong. Tommy smiled up at Steve.

"Steve Cannon, meet Della." Tommy nodded in the woman's direction. "Della here is a helluva manicurist, you should have her work on you sometime." Steve nodded at Della who smiled as she slid out of the booth. She waved back at Tommy and disappeared through a pair of black swinging doors that led into the barbershop. Tommy dropped his arms down to the table and pointed to a deep upholstered chair across from him. Steve pulled the chair back slightly and sat down. A waiter appeared and Tommy ordered a scotch for Steve and another for himself. Tommy seemed in an expansive mood, not quite what Steve had expected, but it was still early.

"It must be 105 degrees out there, why are you wearing a jacket for chrissakes?" Steve looked down at the light blue windbreaker.

"I was up in the pinions. It was a little chilly." Tommy snorted.

"I just don't understand some people's fascination with that wasteland out there, but, hey." Tommy shrugged. The waiter returned with the drinks and Steve waited until he had put them down on the table and left.

"I presume there is an agenda to this meeting?" Steve asked. He picked up the glass and let a small sip of the smooth peaty liquid warm in his mouth. Tommy chuckled.

"Oh you bet there is." He straightened his tie and sat back in the booth.

"So let me lay it out for you, so we both know what we are talking about here." Tommy waited until Steve nodded that he was listening, then continued.

"Nash Brannock comes to me and requests that I comp a friend of his into the big suite. I don't think too much of it because the Dunes is hosting a big gathering of somethin' or other and they maybe have too many high rollers and too few rooms. Fine, no problem. Except the guy doesn't gamble. Not once. I don't hear about it until the guy is there almost two weeks. He gets the boot. I'm giving you the Readers Digest version here. I call Nash and ask him what the hell's going on, and I get a lot of hemming and hawing and a bunch of who shot John. I don't really care, cause I got plenty of problems bigger than that every day. Except two weeks later you show up asking about the guy and four days after that they find him whacked and buried out in the dirt. And yesterday morning the word is that Nash is missing and because he lives on our goddam golf course, we are supposed to know something about it." Tommy leaned forward for emphasis.

"You get the agenda now?" Tommy sneered and then with a mock look of surprise on his face, he threw up his hands.

"Oh, and I forgot the best part. You are playing patty cake with Nash's wife and Nash hires Sorelli to whack you except he can't find you because you are busy running around looking for the guy who stayed in my hotel just before he checks out forever!" Tommy's voice rose to a crescendo gathering several looks from the nearby tables. Tommy sat back in his seat, took a big swig of his scotch and after swallowing, took a deep breath and looked across the table. His face was expressionless, but his eyes were hard and focused on Steve. Steve laughed.

"Well Tommy, I gotta admit, you seem to be in possession of most of the facts." He leveled his gaze at the gangster. Tommy's voice was lower now but even more intense.

"Yeah, well, if you have any other facts to go with the ones I just enumerated, you better spill them now." Steve could see that Tommy was trying hard to remain calm.

"Your facts are good as far as they go, but there are several more that fit in between the ones in your version. So here is how I see it, and I'll try to lay it out so it makes sense from your point of view."

"From my point of view? What the hell does that mean?" Tommy's forehead began to redden.

"It just means that there are several ways to look at the recent events and several theories that fit the facts. It will be a while before we know which one or if any of them are correct. Or we may never know." Steve held out his hands and shrugged. Tommy sat back in his seat and shook his head.

"Why are you so hard to deal with? Just tell me what's going on, so I can solve my problem." Steve shrugged again.

"OK, here's what I know. The real name of the guy that stayed in your hotel was Walter Beech. He was a con man that had done several stints in the can and specialized in financial scams. This time he was pushing a fake land deal out in the Vegas Wash area. He comes to town and hooks up with Nash and and…you know Mike Hunter?" Tommy nodded and Steve continued.

"Now whether the two of them are in on the scam or are the first of Beech's victims, I don't know. But either way, Nash sees a way to make a lot of money, so he starts promoting the scheme to people here and to his Hollywood friends. He hires Angelo Sorelli and two other guys from out of town somewhere to act as his minions to look like he is this big connected guy. He also puts Angelo onto me with late night chats to scare me off. But Angelo, impressed with his new status decides to settle some old scores, namely, me, and Tam, the cop downtown. At some point, Nash decides the pie is only big enough for him, and he sets Sorelli on Beech and Hunter. I'm still trying to find Hunter, but we know what happened to Beech. Add into the mix, Beech's wife shows up in town looking for Beech, hires me to find him and then disappears when I tumble to who Beech really is. She was another guest in one of your suites, by the way. So now, by all accounts, Nash has gone missing. Two possibilities there as far as I can see. One, he scooped up all the money and ran, or two, he is no longer among the living and breathing." Steve sat back into his chair and took another sip of his Johnny Walker. Tommy screwed up his mouth and arched his eyebrows at Steve.

"So, you're telling me that all this is over some fake land deal?" He shook his head when Steve nodded.

"This isn't making much sense."

Steve leaned forward and tapped his index finger on the table in front of Tommy.

"Think about it Tommy. It is just like you were telling me several months ago. Most of the organizations in this town are horizontal. A little slice right in the middle of the food chain that siphons off what is needed. Not a vertically structured group like yours, where the controls are tight and everybody knows their job. Across the street, guys like Nash start thinking they are the reason the world goes round, forgetting they are the window dressing, and guys like that eventually get big ideas." Steve sat back and looked at Tommy with a slight air of satisfaction.

"Nice speech. Funny how that all that adds up conveniently in your favor. Nash was where he was precisely because he wasn't bright enough to get wise. So why does he go solo and risk the wrath of his bosses?" Tommy smirked. "Maybe losing the loving attention of his wife sent him around the bend, whatta you think?"

"Well as someone recently told me, Tommy, why does anybody do anything? I don't think Nash's motives matter as much as where he is and more importantly, where is Angelo Sorelli?"

"Well let me fill you in on that score. When I heard that Nash was missing, I committed substantial resources to find Sorelli. After twenty-four hours I can definitely say that he is not in this burg. Jack figures he is holed up somewhere in some little town around here and only shows up when he needs too. But his two running buddies are Jimmy Scatho and Junior Bellsley, both out of Kansas

City, and both recently kicked out of the Prothro organization there. So fill in some of the holes in your theories with those facts." Tommy signaled the waiter for two refills.

"How is Jack so sure that Angelo isn't in town?"

"Because, Slick, Jack's brother did time with Angelo up north when he went in for the showgirl deal."

"He was in the same prison with Angelo?"

"Same cell. Like in 'the old folks at home'." Tommy chuckled into the last of his drink. "Jack says the kid was always spooked after that and six months after he got out he disappeared. Jack was the one who first told me that Angelo was back in town and his connection to you and Nash." Steve looked down at his drink.

"There is another angle to this that you should know about, Tommy. Either Beech or Nash or both got Herb Slater to sign papers that make it look like the county commissioners have given the deal their blessing. I found those papers hidden in Beech's suitcase.

"So?"

"So this, Tommy. If the DA gets hold of it, the papers get hold of it as well, and this close to the election a lot of, shall we say, 'aligned interests' are in danger of going away."

"Oh, so this is what has got your panties in a wad. Your finely honed sense of morality is keeping you up at night because some politician is involved in a shady deal?" Tommy laughed and looked up at the waiter as he leaned over the table to serve the drinks.

"Do you believe this guy?" Tommy pointed at Steve. The waiter said nothing, but smiling, left the table.

"Well I hate to break it to you at this late date, Slick, but if these guys couldn't enrich themselves and throw their weight around there wouldn't be any takers for those crappy jobs. As far as I am concerned, I would have no use for a guy that wasn't smart enough to look out for his own self-interest."

"Well I hate to break it to you, Tommy, but that is where you go wrong. You have this big vision of going legit and building up this town so much that the skim looks like milk money, right? Well you need people that are trustworthy and able to work for the common good to accomplish that and some of those people need to be in government and all the people that make this system turn have to have confidence that things are being done for the good of all not just for somebody's greed."

"That's how much you know, Cannon. There is this guy named Sarno who just leased thirty-four acres down the street from the D.I. Know what he is going to do? He is building a massive casino hotel resort with six restaurants and a shopping arcade, all built around a Roman motif. Gonna call it Nero's Palace, or something, crappy name, he needs to change it, but anyway. And you know who will come? Everybody. Not just the addicted card players and nickel cuppers. Not just the high rollers that I spend most of my day cajoling to come to my hotel instead of going somewhere else. Families, Cannon. Families and working stiffs who will save all year if they have to, just to spend a week here." Tommy stabbed his finger on Steve's side of the table and sneered.

"And how is he going to get the financing for this big resort, Tommy? The banks going to rush to his side? The city going to issue bonds to help him out? And when he takes the only money out there, is he going to get to run his casino as he sees fit? See what I mean, Tommy? You can't get there from here. I believe your vision for this town will eventually happen, but I don't think you and your kind of organization is going to be around to make it happen." Steve watched as Tommy took a sip of his drink and looked around the room. He sighed and looked at Steve.

"This is a cash business, Cannon, always has been, always will be. To make that work, there has to be order and discipline and everyone involved has to know what the consequences are if those two things break down. Very few organizations are equipped for that. That's why I hope for his sake, Nash is either far enough away never to be found or already dead.

"Cash is king, Tommy? As in $750,000 in hundreds in the trunk of a black Chevy? That is your big dream for tomorrow land?"

"Well, you are smarter than I sometimes give you credit for, Cannon, I will admit that."

"Not so smart, Tommy, I just know a good mechanic that can get anything open in ten seconds flat, especially if I motivate him with a third of the money you gave me. I don't know how smart you think I am if you thought I was driving that car to LA without knowing what was in it. Hope they counted it." Steve smiled broadly.

"No need for that, Cannon. If I thought I had to do that I wouldn't have picked you for the job in the first place. But I think we are getting away from the subject. So your big idea is that Herb Slater figures prominently in this little mystery?" Tommy was smiling now.

"I do. I don't think a lot this would have happened if he hadn't given the deal his seal of approval."

"Well, why don't we just ask him, he's sitting right over there." Tommy raised his voice on the last word and pointed across the room to two men having a drink at a table against the wall. Everyone looked over at Tommy and when the two men looked at him, Tommy motioned one of the men to come over.

When Herb Slater arrived at the table, Steve stuck out his hand before Tommy could speak.

"Hi, I'm Steve Cannon. I don't think we have met formally, but I have been to your office and spoken to one of your aides." He smiled up at the perplexed man. The man was in the act of extending his hand when a look of comprehension came across his face and he withdrew his hand and straightened up and looked at Tommy who had put his arms back along the backs of the booth again and was smiling at both men and softly chuckling.

"I don't think you know who are drinking with, Mr. Carmino. This guy is accusing me all over town of corruption." He shook a finger in Steve's direction while still looking at Tommy.

"Don't look at me Herb, I got no dog in this fight. I just thought you should have a chance to explain yourself."

"Explain myself! What is this…?" Steve interjected before Herb could finish his thought.

"For the record, Commissioner Slater, I didn't accuse you of anything publicly. I merely asked why your signature is on a piece of paper I have in my possession that gives the Good Housekeeping Seal of Approval to building some kind of planned community in the flood plain known as Vegas Wash?" Steve looked across at Tommy and then up at Herb Slater.

"Seems like an easy question to answer."

Herb Slater muttered something under his breath and started to back away from the table when Tommy stopped him.

"Whoa, whoa, Herb, relax, here, have a seat. Let's all have a drink and see if we can sort this out like gentlemen." Herb stopped, looked at Tommy and moved back toward the table. As Herb reluctantly pulled out the other chair, Tommy winked at Steve. Herb turned his chair slightly so that Steve was out of his vision and he could look at Tommy directly. When Herb was seated, Tommy leaned forward and put his hands on the table.

"Look, Herb, some people mixed up in this Vegas Wash deal, have gone dead and missing. If Cannon here says he's got a piece of paper with your name on it that proves that you are involved or at least know something about it, I believe him. We all answer to somebody and I personally can attest to be getting quite a bit of pressure in this deal and I don't think I need to go into details here. So, let me order you a drink and while we wait for it to come, I want you to think about your answer to my simple question. What do you know about this land deal that Cannon is talking about?" Tommy sat back and signaled the waiter for another round of drinks. Steve looked down at the two unfinished drinks in front of him and smiled. Before the waiter could arrive, the other man who had been sitting with Herb came over to the table and stood between Herb and Tommy. When Tommy did not acknowledge him he leaned over the table and looked directly into Tommy's face.

"I think I need to be a part of this conversation, Mr. Carmino."

He spoke in a low calm voice. Tommy straightened up and looked back at the man.

"And who are you?" His tone was off hand but irritated. He looked at Herb and opened his palms. Herb looked at his newly arrived drink and said nothing.

"I am Mr. Gleason. I am Herb Slater's lawyer." He straightened up and looked at Steve.

"We are looking at our options concerning Mr. Cannon's allegations and as such, I am advising my client not to answer any questions. Am I making myself clear, Mr. Carmino?"

Tommy took a large sip from his glass, set it down and ignoring the lawyer leaned in and looked at Herb.

"Herb, are you expecting me to take back the word that you won't answer my questions?" The lawyer interjected.

"Don't say a word, Mr. Slater." Tommy shook his head.

"Well I have to say, I am very disappointed in you, Herb, and I know I will not be the only one. I tell you what, though, I will keep this between the two of us for a couple of days. You think it over, talk it over with your wife, you know, get a woman's perspective, and call me over the weekend. You know I am always willing to listen." Tommy stood up and tossed a hundred dollar bill on the table. He slid gracefully out from behind the table, straightened his tie and walked through the swinging doors into the barbershop. Steve picked up his first drink, took a sip and stared straight ahead. His thoughts were interrupted by the voice of the lawyer as he leaned across the table and addressed Steve.

"I advise you to get yourself a lawyer, Mr. Cannon. I also advise you to refrain from talking to anyone else about this matter until we have talked to said lawyer and he has informed you properly of the jeopardy in which you have placed yourself." He stood erect and placed a hand on Herb's shoulder.

"Come on, Mr. Slater, let's go." Herb got slowly up from the table and glancing quickly at Steve out of the corner of his eye, he followed Mr. Gleason from the bar.

Steve pulled out a pack of cigarettes, lit one up and finished his first drink. As he was preparing to go, the manager appeared at the table.

"Mr. Cannon, please make sure that you come back soon. I have personally opened an account for you and if there is anything you need, please don't hesitate to call on me." The man placed a business card on the table, bowed slightly and left. Steve put his cigarettes back into his pocket, and ignoring the card made his way back out through the oak doors and into the parking lot. Even though he had left the windows down in the Mustang, the interior was scorching. It wasn't until he was driving at 40 miles per hour down the road that the cabin began to cool down.

When he arrived home, he went into the office and jotted down a few notes in his notebook. He included some of the additional information he had learned from Tommy. He picked up the phone and dialed Tam's number. When Tam picked up he wasn't alone, so he told Steve to stay there and he would call back in ten minutes. Tam wasn't in a good mood when he returned the call.

"What's on your mind, Cannon? This has been a bear of a day, so try to make it short."

"I assume that Samuels was in your office when I called. Most of what I have can wait, are you coming in tomorrow?"

"Of course, Saturday is the only day I get any peace and quiet to wade through this mountain of paper work. If you drop by at ten, we can have a little catch-up in private. Homicide all enjoy their weekends."

"One thing now, though. If you could check on two hoods named Jimmy Scatho and Junior Bellsley, out of KC. Maybe there are mug shots out there somewhere."

"Are these your two playmates from the desert?"

"Yes."

"I'll give it a shot, see you tomorrow." Tam rang off and Steve sat back on the small couch and gazed out the window. After a few minutes, he got up and went back out to the car. He opened the glove box and stood in the gravel looking at the small piece of wood. He walked back inside and propped it up on the mantle above the fireplace. He went into the kitchen and opened the refrigerator. After a quick search of the cupboards, he grabbed his car keys, locked the door and headed to a little market four blocks away. He returned a half hour later and dumped three bags of groceries on the kitchen table. He walked out the backdoor that led from the kitchen to a brick patio and dusted off the grate on a fire pit that was built into the low adobe wall that bordered the patio on three sides. He poured half a bag of briquettes in the pit and after stuffing several wadded up newspapers in among the coals, lit a fire.

An hour later, Steve sat on the wooden picnic table and watched the glow on Sunrise mountain fade into twilight. The orange of the coals grew brighter as the desert grew dark. He picked up the plate with the half eaten steak and carried it and the rest of a bottle of wine into the kitchen. He washed up the plate and utensils and then carried the bottle and his glass into the office. He put a new record on the turntable and sat down on the couch, remaining still as the first sweet notes of Louis Armstrong's trumpet on 'Le Vie En Rose' hung in the air, joined a few bars later by the raspy counterpoint of his voice, soft and yearning. Before Louis was able to start the next song on the record, the phone rang. He reached for it without getting up and then settled back down on the couch.

"Steve?" Remy's voice had the normal soft tones, but there was a huskiness that was new.

"Hi, Gem, I have been worried about you. I have missed you very much."

"I have missed you too, Steve."

"Are you OK?"

"Yeah, I'm OK, just tired and scared for Nash. I haven't heard from him for six days and nobody else has either." Steve thought he heard a slight catch in her voice when she mentioned his name. He tried to keep his voice as normal as possible.

"There could be several good reasons for that, Gem, maybe he is just staying somewhere in LA." Before he could add another reason, she spoke again.

"No, Steve, I called everyone I could find in his address book here in Palm Springs, nobody has seen him and the people he was going to see in LA on his last trip say he never showed. Steve what can I do?" He could now hear some desperation starting to creep into her voice. He decided to change the subject slightly.

"Gem, where are you right now, where are you staying?"

"At our place in Rancho Mirage."

"That might not be such a good idea, maybe you better consider checking into a hotel for a while." There was a four beat silence.

"I'm flying to Las Vegas tomorrow. I need to be there in case he comes back." Her voice had lost some of the desperation and she sounded more resolved.

"That is a bad idea Gem. It won't do any good and it might put you in danger. Listen, there are a lot of Tommy Carmino's people out looking for him. If he is here, they will find him soon."

"Tommy's people?" There was alarm now in her voice. "What does Tommy Carmino have to do with Nash?" Now it was Steve's turn to wait for a few beats.

"Listen, Gem, I tried to tell you on the way to LA, there are a lot of people asking questions about the land deal Nash was involved in. The guy who was missing two days ago is now dead. Because he stayed at the D.I. on Nash's say so without the guys at the Dunes knowing it, it looks bad for Tommy and his boss. Questions are being asked that don't have answers and you know as well as I do that bad things will happen if this goes on much longer. You coming back here is not going to help anything." He was out of breath and stopped to take in some air. His palms were sweating and his throat was dry. He took a drink from the wine glass and let it drip slowly down his throat.

"I'm already booked. I will be there at two o'clock."

"I will come and pick you up. I will be waiting at the gate."

"Steve... I... hope you know that I need some time to figure things out. You do know that don't you?"

"Yeah, Gem, I know that." Their voices were quiet. There was a long pause.

"I'll see you tomorrow, then?"

"Yes, Steve, tomorrow. Goodnight." Steve heard the click and hum of the long distance line going dead. He stood up and placed the receiver back onto the cradle, crossed the room and turned the stereo up. He looked out the window of the darkened room at the road. The gravel of his driveway shone almost white against the earth in the last phase of the full moon. An hour later, he pulled the curtains closed and went to bed.

August 22

TAM WAS STANDING in front of a vending machine in the lobby drinking a cup of coffee and wearing a maroon golf shirt and khaki chinos when Steve swung open the large glass doors. Though it was early on a Saturday morning, there was still the usual bustle of activity down the hall where the booking rooms led to the holding cells. Tam watched impassively as Steve walked across the marble floor and stopped in front of the vending machine.

"Tam, are you sure you should be drinking this stuff?" Steve bent over and peered through the glass at the selections available from the large tan machine. Tam snorted and turned towards the hall that led to his office.

"You're welcome to run down to the Bob's Big Boy and get us real coffee and a couple of burgers if you want." He laughed over his shoulder as he slowed to let Steve catch up.

"Maybe later. I seem to eat most of my meals with either you or Bernie anyway." They came to Tam's office, the detective stepped aside and let Steve enter first. Tam closed the door behind them and shifted several large files from the chair to the desk so that Steve could sit down. When he had seated himself behind the desk and shifted more files so that he could see the private detective, he folded his hands and waited as Steve lit a cigarette.

"So, I assume you have been busy."

"I have, though I am not sure that we have too much new information. I got confirmation that Sorelli and his boys were the ones who dumped Beech's body in the desert." He exhaled smoke and waited for the inevitable next question.

"Confirmation from who?" Tam decided to smoke as well and opened the top drawer to retrieve a pack of cigarettes.

"From Marcus Boomer." Tam tossed the pack back in the drawer and looked up.

"That's your source? That alcoholic desert rat? That isn't even the guy who called it in to Polaski. And the guy who did, definitely said he didn't see who did it." Tam gestured towards Steve with the unlighted cigarette.

"Desert politics, Tam, they got their own rules and pecking order just like everyone else. I have known Marcus most of my life and he wouldn't say it if it wasn't true."

"He would say it for a drink, wake up for gods' sake. What are you? Some sort of frustrated anthropologist? Hallucinating all these relationships and secret code crap with everyone you see?" Tam turned his chair and looking at the wall shook his head. When Steve didn't reply he looked over at him and saw a very tense look he had never seen before. When Steve spoke, his voice was hard.

"My brother flew P-38 Lightnings in the Pacific. He died in that war. All my mother got was a telegram telling her he was missing and presumed dead, and then another one saying that they couldn't locate the body. It nearly killed her. Ten days after the second telegram, Marcus showed up at her door. He had walked all the way from the summit near Mule Springs to Boulder City. He had a page out of an atlas in his hand. He had circled a tiny island in the Marshalls. Through the man she worked for, my mom contacted

Senator McCarran. Two weeks later they found the wreckage of the plane and my brother's body on that island. That was the last happy day of my mother's life." Steve leaned forward, though Tam had averted his eyes back to the wall. "If Marcus says that Sorelli and his two thugs were in that desert that night, there were there."

The low hum of the air conditioner was the only sound for several minutes. Tam swiveled his chair around carefully and looked at Steve.

"Sorry, Steve, I got carried away. I guess I was imagining how I was going to frame that information for Samuels. I didn't mean to take it out on you." Steve sat back in his chair and looking up at the ceiling tiles, sighed and took another drag on his cigarette.

"It's OK, Tam. I know how Marcus appears to everyone. But he was very kind to me and Pete after my father was killed. I guess I will always see him that way." He straightened up in his chair and looked over at Tam.

"The other good news if you can call it that, is that Tommy Carmino has joined in the hunt for Angelo. Seems he knew about Sorelli being in town and his connection to Nash before anyone else. So there is that. Also, Nash Brannock is missing or at least has not been heard from for several days." Steve took a last quick puff from the Pall Mall and put it out. Tam sat with his hands folded in his lap and swiveled slightly from side to side in his chair.

"Steve, things have changed since this went from a missing person case to a homicide investigation. I can't afford loose ends, not with Samuels around. So I have to ask you why you were on Sorelli's hit list along with me and Mike Hunter?" The hum continued as the only sound for several seconds. Steve looked Tam in the eyes.

"Nash's wife, Remy and I have a relationship." Tam's demeanor remained impassive.

"How long?"

"Fifteen months, give or take."

"So you think this relationship you have or had was the reason for Sorelli coming to town?"

"The timeline's right. Based on what I know, the calls I got from Angelo started well in advance or just before the first known appearance of Beech." Tam stood up and walked to the large map of Las Vegas on the far wall. He didn't say anything for a few seconds.

"Well I don't know what bearing this will have on the investigation. I just wanted to hear it from you." Tam stared at the map for a while before he came back and sat down in his chair.

"So, Tommy have any ideas we can use on where Angelo is?" Steve shook his head.

"Jack Cathay is pretty convinced that he is holed up somewhere out of town but close by. Tommy says they have pretty much turned the town upside down and nothing."

"Why is Jack's opinion so highly valued?"

"Jack's convinced that Angelo killed his brother Sammy, because he knew a lot about Angelos' activities sharing a cell with him up north. Jack has made Angelo a hobby and is pretty familiar with his habits. My guess is that if Jack finds him first, our work will be pretty much done for us." Tam shook his head.

"Sammy was a drug smuggler who went down to Mexico and never came back. Most of these guys don't realize that time moves on when they are in prison, and when they get out they start throwing their weight around like they used to. Somebody down there didn't like it, as simple as that." Steve shrugged.

'Maybe. But we need all the help we can get finding this guy. Did you get a picture of the other two?" Tam opened the drawer in his desk again and tossed two small pictures on the desk in front of Steve. Steve picked them up and looked at them quickly.

"Yeah, that's them. Are you going to put out a BOLO on these guys?"

"Not my call, I will huddle with Samuels on Monday morning, give him the rundown and he can decide." Steve sneered.

"Two more days? Do you think we have that much time? Two days could mean everything in trying to find these guys. Can't you work around this guy somehow?" Steve threw the pictures back on the desk in frustration.

"Calm down, Steve, I don't think you quite get the picture, so let me fill you in. My main function here is to monitor criminal activity and assist any department that needs me in the investigation, whether it is Robbery, Fraud or Homicide, or whatever. Now, when something comes along like the Beech case, I have a free hand until it reaches the level it has. The second thing you need to know is that Samuels carries a lot of weight in this department. He was brought in six months ago after a spike in homicides last year. He is an ex-FBI agent who was attached to the LA homicide unit. Did some very high profile stuff before accepting this job. So things are touchy around here in that regard. Understand?"

"Sure, Tam whatever you say, but I don't see him in here racking his brain."

"I would watch it if I were you, Steve. I have had to justify your participation in cases many times, and many times I have had to hide that participation, for your sake as well as mine. Let me handle this my way and stay as far away as you can from Samuels. He will come down on you like a ton of bricks just for the fun of it. Enough said." Steve shrugged and nodded.

"By the way, here are your papers back. I waited until Samuels cleared out before I looked them over. I have a pretty good idea of what's what. How do you want to handle this?"

"I need to go over to county records and see if there is any mention of this project in the minutes of the meetings. Other than that, I have been told by Slater's lawyer to keep my mouth shut or else." Steve chuckled and took the papers from Tam.

"Well you seem to be getting it from all sides in this deal."

"Comes with the territory, my friend. How about I buy you lunch?" Steve smiled and stood up.

"Sure, that will work. My wife won't be expecting me until around three. Tomorrow is my daughter's tenth birthday and we have several things we need to get done." Steve opened the door and followed Tam out into the hallway.

The Bob's Big Boy restaurant was half full when Tam and Steve arrived. After having deposited themselves in one of the orange vinyl booths, they both ordered coffee and burgers. Steve felt relaxed and comfortable amid the clinking of plates and cutlery. He smiled across at Tam.

"So tell me, Tam, what was Angelo Sorelli like in high school?" Tam gave Steve a quick glance, pursed his lips, took a sip out of his water glass and shook his head.

"Nuts." He shook his head again.

"Always wanted to fight. I mean really fight. Hated anything or anybody Irish. Didn't bother me or anyone smaller than him. Always looking for the next big guy to beat up. There were several big tough Irish guys that loved to mix it up, but even they started avoiding him. Said he didn't know when to quit. The priests tried to get him into boxing, but he could never follow the rules. He avoided the draft somehow and drifted into the wrestling world after the war." Tam shook his head and looked out at the rest of the patrons in the restaurant. He turned back to Steve.

"You want to hear the kicker? He had a kid sister that had polio and could barely get around even on crutches. He would carry her everywhere. He would take her down to the wharf, to Mass on Sundays, everywhere. And when he was with her, that was one of the only times anyone could approach him or even have any kind of a civilized conversation. Now square that with what he did to that poor showgirl. I don't know sometimes." He looked out again at the room and became lost in thought.

When their food came they ate without saying much and then drove back to the station in the Mustang. Steve pulled into the space right beside Tam's car. A small white sign attached to a pole in the sidewalk said: 'Reserved for Detective Samuels'. Tam gave a sidelong look at Steve but didn't say anything.

They stood for a moment on the sidewalk. Steve still had an hour until Remy's plane arrived.

"So what else did you glean from Mr. Boomer?" Tam stood with one hand in his pocket, the other working a toothpick in the side of his mouth.

"Nothing much, except he hates my car." Steve gestured toward the Mustang. Tam laughed.

"Can't say as I blame him much. Kinda puny looking isn't it? Now take my Biscayne there. Always been a Chevy man, so maybe I am biased, but that is one solid dependable car."

Steve looked at the chunky off white sedan parked next to the sleek Mustang.

"I don't know, Tam, that looks like something my dad would be driving if he were still with us." He grinned at Tam. "That Mustang is the future. You watch, that will become a classic. Tam snorted.

"Classic? I heard that they had to slow production, can't give them away. And you with that beautiful specimen of American automotive genius at home in your garage? What is the world coming too?" Tam laughed and slapped Steve lightly on the shoulder.

"I need to go. I want to do one or two things before I head home." As he passed in front of his car, Tam leaned down and patted the hood and smiled back at Steve. Steve waved and watched him disappear through the big glass doors.

*

STEVE PARKED IN front of Skipper's motel. He lit a cigarette and smoked it while he watched both sides of the street in front of him. After his smoke, he walked into the office and encountered the man he had spoken with on his previous visit. The man had his feet up on the desk and was reading a newspaper. Steve pushed the paper down with his hand and peered over the top of it.

"You seen my friend lately?" The man put the paper down and looked back at Steve.

"Two days ago, may still be sleeping it off." He turned his

attention back to the paper. Steve kept his hand on the pages and stared at the man.

"You call this number the next time you see him and ask for Bernie. He will get in touch with me. You got that?" Steve picked up a pen from the desk and wrote Bernie's name beneath the number for the deli. He handed it to the clerk and waited until the man acknowledged with a nod. Steve straightened up, looked down at the man and snorted. He held out his hand. The clerk sighed and pulled a set of keys from his pants pocket. He selected a key and slipping it off the ring and handed it to Steve. Steve turned on his heels and left the office.

Skipper's room had not changed much since the last time Steve had been there except there was no Skipper. Steve could not find any indications that Skipper had been there that day or the day before. He took out his notebook and pencil and wrote a short note, instructing him to call or take a cab out to his house any evening after eight and to wait for him there if he was gone. He folded a twenty dollar bill into the note, and pulling up the covers up on the unmade bed, he placed the note and the money in the middle of the blanket where Skipper would be more likely to see it. He returned to the office and without a word, tossed the key onto the table and left. He stood by his car for several minutes smoking a cigarette before he circled the block several times and headed for the airport.

McCarran terminal was crowded as Steve made his way down the long concourse to the gates. Steve seemed to be the only one going in that direction as he weaved in and out of small knots of tourists streaming up the wide hallway to the baggage carousels. When he reached the gates in the main part of the terminal, he scanned one of the automatic flip boards that listed all the flights and saw that the 2:05 Bonanza flight from Palm Springs was on time and would arrive in five minutes. He found a seat behind a pillar where he could look out on the runways and watch the jets as they landed and departed. He could also see his reflection in the slanted window and anyone that might try to approach him from the rear. He sat back in his seat and watched as a white Bonanza jet with a bright orange stripe along the fuselage moved slowly into the gate just below his position. Soon after the metal stairs were rolled up and the cabin door opened, he saw Remy walking down the steps. Her head was covered in a light blue scarf and she wore white capris with a pink silk blouse. A large overnight bag was in her hand and she seemed thinner than the last time he had seen her. He moved up the concourse to the greeting area and stood at the back of the small crowd that had gathered to meet the plane.

When she came through the door she spotted Steve at once over the heads of the other people waiting for their loved ones. He smiled and waved to make sure that she saw him. Steve held out his hand and Remy passed the case to him. He kissed her lightly on both cheeks and stood back for a moment.

"It is good to see you, Gem."

"It is good to see you, Steve, I am glad you came."

He placed his free arm around her shoulders and as they turned to walk down the concourse, she leaned her head into his shoulder for just a moment. After a few steps, Remy disengaged and they continued on in silence until they reached the luggage carousel. Remy looked up at Steve. She was wearing her large sunglasses, the ones with the lenses so dark that Steve could never see her eyes.

"I have a lot of things I need to do, Steve. I know that Nash needs me and I have to do everything I can to find him."

"I understand, Gem. Let me help you." He wanted to reach out and take hold of her hand, but he stopped himself. Instead he shifted his weight and passed her case to his other hand. Remy shook her head and turned to watch the bags that were beginning to circle on the silver conveyor belt.

"But I appreciate the offer and I will let you know if there is anything you can do."

"Just let me know, Gem, whatever you need."

"Have you eaten? Perhaps we could grab some lunch." Remy shook her head again.

"No, thanks, Steve, I ate something before I got on the plane." She moved towards the carousel and a large gray leather suitcase that had just come out of the chute. Steve moved forward quickly and with his free hand hefted it smoothly off the belt. Remy murmured her thanks and reached to take the smaller case from his other hand. She turned and started for the exit and Steve followed her until they got to the curb. He led them across the two lane street and into the parking lot. He had left the windows down in the Mustang and now he placed both of her bags in the compact trunk. Remy opened the door and sat in the passenger seat without comment. As they drove through the exit of the lot, Steve looked over at Remy who was staring straight ahead.

"What is your plan for finding Nash?" Remy looked out the window and shook her head, but said nothing. Steve waited a few minutes more before he spoke again.

"I am going to tell you everything I know about this case and everything that has happened. I think it is only fair. Whatever you decide to do, there are things you need to know."

Several minutes later, Steve turned the car into the short circular driveway of Remy's house. He put the car in neutral and turned off the engine. Remy was crying softly. Steve reached over and hugged her shoulders and kissing the top of her head, he settled back into his seat.

"Please listen to me, Gem. I want you to go and stay at Bernie's place out in the valley. Rocco will be able to keep an eye on you and you will be safe there." Remy looked over at Steve and shook her head.

"I know you are trying to protect me, Steve, but I have to stay here. I know that Nash must have left me a clue in there that will lead me to him. I'm sorry, but I have to stay here." She put her hand on the door handle pushing it both ways in an attempt to open it.

Steve got out of the car and walked around to her side and opened the door for her. He then went to the trunk and retrieved both cases and walked up the cobbled sidewalk to the front door where Remy was fumbling with her keys. When she had found the right one, Steve put his hand on hers and looked down at her.

"Gem, let me go in first and take a quick look around. Just to be safe." Remy looked at him for a few seconds then nodded her head.

Steve opened the door carefully and slipped sideways through it without opening it fully. He was in an expansive foyer with a curving staircase at one end. He quickly worked his way through all the downstairs rooms, glancing out the sliding glass door at the pool. Finding nothing amiss, he bounded up the staircase two steps at a time and checked all three bedrooms and bathrooms on the second floor. The last room he checked was a library that had a big oak desk in the center of the room. Several drawers were open and there were papers strewn in a haphazard way on top. He quickly looked through them, and finding nothing that he could see was connected to the case, he left them as he found them.

He returned to the front door and brought Remy's cases into the foyer. Remy walked slowly into the foyer and looked around. She looked up at Steve.

"Thanks, Steve. I appreciate everything you are trying to do for me." Steve smiled in an attempt to lighten the mood.

"Here's how I think we should work things, Gem. If you need me for anything, call Bernie at the deli. I will check in with him several times a day to see if you have called. Every night at eight, I will call you, if you don't call me first, OK?" He placed his hands on her shoulders and waited until she looked up at him.

"OK?" She nodded her assent and hugged him briefly. He carried her cases up to the master bedroom, kissed her on the cheek and left.

Steve drove around several times past the house before he turned back up Paradise road and drove to the deli.

Bernie was not pleased when he found out that Remy had returned to Las Vegas.

"So no dice on convincing her to stay out at my place, huh?" Bernie shook his head.

"No, but I got her to agree to call you if anything went wrong and to call me every night at eight. Not much, but something. If you don't mind I would like to check in with you several times a day in case she needs something."

"Sure, Steve, of course. What does she think she can do here?"

"I don't know. I don't think she is looking at things that way. She seems convinced that he left some kind of trail or clue to his whereabouts that will only make sense to her. I don't know, Bernie, your guess is as good as mine." Steve quaffed the last of his beer and Bernie ordered another.

"I don't like the fact that Nash is missing and Sorelli is out there, and she is all alone in that house." Bernie shook his head again. Steve put the new beer down after one sip.

"I am going to swing by there as much as I can. It's no secret she lives there, so even if Sorelli is following me or is somehow able to keep tabs on me, at least I can check and see if she is all right. Though I get the feeling that she will not appreciate it much." Bernie nodded, then looked up and snapped his fingers.

"Let me change the subject for a minute, Steve. I got a line on Mike Hunter, I didn't talk to him myself but a guy answered the number I was given, I don't know maybe a roommate or something, anyway, I think I was able to convince him that it would definitely be in Mike's best interest to give you a call." Bernie's mood had brightened somewhat.

"That's great, thanks, Bernie. I owe you more than I think I can ever repay." Bernie waved him off derisively.

"What are your friends for? You've helped me plenty over the years and truth be told I think I am in your debt." Bernie smiled.

"But there is something you can do if you are so inclined." Bernie took a drink of soda water and looked at Steve.

"Name it, Bernie and consider it done."

"Well, once or twice a year, usually once, now that I come to think of it, and hell, it could be longer, I don't remember, I host the newspaper and TV boys to a little casino night or just poker, depending on how many can show. How about joining in and helping out?"

"Of course I will, Bern, what night? "

"This coming Tuesday night."

"Great. I can do that. Who'll be there?

Well, let's see who you might know." Bernie stroked his chin and looked into space.

"Gus Guiffre, sweetheart of a guy, does that afternoon show where all the lounge acts are the guests, know that one? Ralph Pearl, you've met him several times. Don Diglio from the paper might be coming, haven't heard. Jack Cortez, you know him pretty well, I don't think Hank Greenspun is coming, hasn't made the last two. For some reason I have always included Jack Dennison, you know him from the Jungle Club, so he will be there even though he owns restaurants. Wild Bill Elliott, you know the old western star, has that western movie thing on Saturdays, and the deal is, each guy is supposed to bring someone from where they work so that there is new blood and in most cases it is a business expense to those who are set up that way. So, I am sure I have forgotten some, but you get the idea. I may call on you to deal blackjack, but most likely I will sit you in with the poker guys who need a little encouragement, shall we say." Bernie smiled and winked. "Of course, I cover all your losses if any, and I don't remember having had to shell out too many of those." Bernie laughed and finished his soda.

"Might be a good distraction."

"I thought so. You haven't made one of these in a while, might do you some good."

"I think I will cruise by Remy's before I head home, Bernie. I'll drop by tomorrow and fill you in if I hear from Mike." Bernie got up and walked Steve to the door. As Steve reached to open the door, Bernie put his hand on Steve's back.

"Steve, you packing?" Bernie stepped back surprised. Steve turned and stood in the doorway.

"Yeah, Bernie, ever since that desert deal. My gut told me I should have been when the calls started, but I have always looked at it as a last resort. Sure wish I had one that night though." Bernie smiled and opened the door again.

"I agree with you, but for some reason, I feel better knowing that you got that kind of protection." Steve backed out of the door and waved to Bernie as the door swung shut. He walked several spaces beyond the Mustang before he retraced his steps and got into the car.

Steve parked across the street from Remy's house for fifteen minutes monitoring the traffic. He drove slowly past the house turned on the golf course road and made a U turn and drove past the other way. Seeing nothing noteworthy, he turned northwest and home.

*

WHEN THE PHONE rang at seven-thirty that night, Steve's first thought was Remy. The voice on the other end was foreign and it took a second for Steve to make the connection.

"Mike?"

"Yeah, this is Mike Hunter. My cousin says Bernie told him to have me call this number."

"Mike, this is Steve Cannon."

"Cannon? Yeah, I remember, you helped us out with those card counters at the Castaways, manned the catwalk, seems like a lifetime ago. How you been?"

"Better than you and some of the guys you have been hanging around with lately, from what I hear and from what I have seen." Steve heard a small intake of breath on the other end.

"Yeah, I guess, but is that what this is about?" Mike's voice was not so positive now.

"Mike, let me get something straight with you right from the start here. I don't know where you are and I don't want to know, and my advice to you is to make sure that it stays that way. You understand?" Steve waited as there was a moment of silence on the other line. When he didn't get a further reply, he took a deep breath and kept on going.

"Look, Mike, Beech is dead. They found him in the desert yesterday morning, shot twice. All I want to know is the story as you know it. As little or as much as you want to tell me." Steve held his breath.

"I figured that was gonna be the deal." Mike paused. "You know what? I think that Beech had some idea it would be too." Steve could hear Mike take a deep breath.

"Oh, God, I don't want to be a part of this anymore."

"I know, Mike, but there are still lives at stake here, and I am pretty sure that you are the only one that has the information that can make the difference between someone living and dying. Are you willing to help?" Steve waited and prayed.

"What do you want to know?" Mike's voice was small and quiet.

"Start from the beginning. How did you get mixed up in this scheme to begin with?" Mike cleared his throat with a little cough.

"Well, a year ago, after I got let go from the Castaways, I started freelancing junkets. You know, putting together groups of high stakes gamblers and promoting that to the various casinos and taking the highest bid, that sort of thing. Started working pretty well. Kinda by accident, I stumbled onto the Phoenix area, and with a few contacts ran into a lot of quality players and I was doing pretty well. Nash at the Dunes was a regular customer and I was running two or three groups a month through there. One of the guys I met was Beech, though he was going by the name of Sizemore. He signed up for two trips in a row, but didn't make either of them. I wrote him off and didn't call him anymore. Then one day he shows up at my house and starts proposing this deal to me. Seems he somehow got the grazing rights to some BLM parcels in the south Paradise Valley area. All he needed he said, was some connections in Las Vegas and the take could be five million for a couple months' work. He gave me $50,000 up front and my take was gonna be $750,000 if I helped him." Mike stopped and took a big gulp of something, Steve could hear ice cubes jingle in the glass.

"Things went pretty well right from the start. I introduced him to a couple of guys who invested some right off the bat. I told Nash Brannock about the deal and he got very interested. He flew both of us up to Las Vegas and comped us a whole weekend. I think it was that weekend that he and Beech made a deal. All of a sudden, Nash was fifty-fifty partners and my take was down to $250,000. I should have skipped out right there and then, but by that time I was in too far in and I realized I had started counting on that money. Nash got an architect to draw up some phony blueprints for a planned community, you know, golf courses, shopping centers, schools, all that stuff. He even had a mock-up made of how it would look that Beech had in his suite at the D.I. It was a work of art. Then Nash's big idea was to get the county commissioners to give it their approval. How he did that I don't know but once Beech started flashing around the contracts and the approvals, the money really started rolling in." Steve cut in when Mike stopped to take a breath.

"Mike. Can you give me any other details about how Nash got Herb Slater to go along with the scheme?"

"Not really. By that time my role was strictly to bring investors to the table, and once Nash started promoting the deal to all his friends from LA, and that money started rolling in, I was kinda the odd man out. The only thing that kept me in was Beech always telling me that he needed me and my help to keep the deal afloat. He also kept slipping me a few thousand now and then. I don't know why, since I wasn't doing much, and then Nash brought in Angelo, and for me the handwriting was on the wall. Beech tried to make the best of it, but I guess we know how that has turned out." Mike stopped and didn't say anything for a few seconds.

"That is when your name came up. I wasn't there for the original conversation and as far as I know, neither was Beech as I remember him asking me who you were and why was Sorelli always talking about messing with you. When Nash took over all the money, that is when I told Beech the gig was up and we should both get out of Dodge. But Beech wouldn't listen. His plan was to muscle Nash and keep him in line by threatening to go to Nash's bosses and the papers with the whole deal. Beech had kept copies of a lot of incriminating stuff and he was using it to keep himself in the deal. The last time I saw him, he gave me a package to mail if I thought something was going to happen to him. I mailed it that night. I went around to the Bali Hai two days later, but he wasn't there and a maid that he had gotten friendly with told me that there were two men there the night before looking for him too. That was Jimmy and Junior. I left town that night and I may never come back."

"Mike, who did you send the package to?"

"His wife Miriam, who he said had come up with the land idea in the first place, though I never met her. I got the feeling she was working on something else and when she was done with that she was supposed to join Beech on this deal. Before Nash became a partner, he was expecting her to show anytime with a big load of cash."

"When was the last time you saw Beech? Do you remember the date?" Mike thought for a few seconds.

"It was early in the month and it was a Sunday. Nash was in LA and Angelo wasn't around, so I took the opportunity for one last try at getting Beech to leave town." Steve flipped quickly through his calendar. August the 2nd. Two days before the last time the clerk at the Bali Hai saw him.

"You didn't hear from him after that?"

"No, I left and even moved two or three times in the space of two weeks to cover my trail. Angelo is crazy and I knew when he found out I was gone, I was going on his list too."

"Mike, you also need to know that Nash has gone missing. It is still early, but my gut tells me he isn't coming back." There was a lengthy silence on the other end of the line.

"That's a twist. What do you think has gone on?"

"I don't know, but it doesn't bode well in my opinion. Mike, listen to me. A lot of people have been looking for Angelo the last three days. Some people who are in a position to know are convinced he is not in town. I don't think staying with anyone that can be linked to you is safe. Do you understand what I am saying?"

"Yes, I understand."

"Mike, do you have any idea where Sorelli might be hiding out? He has the two other hoods with him, but nobody can seem to get a line on him."

"The last I know, he was living in a house off Maryland Parkway, but he was always trying to get Nash to put him up in one of the suites at the Dunes."

"Thanks, but I think he has gone to ground and is hidden pretty well. Make sure you take my advice, Mike, and cover your tracks."

"Yeah. I understand, I had that thought myself, especially since Bernie didn't seem to have much trouble finding me. I was thinking about taking a little trip to San Francisco. Maybe I should saddle up and do that."

"I would make it San Diego, Mike. Trust me on this."

"OK, whatever you say. Thanks for listening and thanks for the heads-up."

"I'm just glad we talked. Call me later this week if you want when you are somewhere else and I will give you any updates I have. Your information has been very helpful."

Steve rang off the phone and after recording notes of the conversation, he looked at the clock. It was 8:10. He picked the phone up and rang Remy's number. Remy picked up on the second ring, and Steve thought he heard a hint of disappointment in her voice.

"I'm just checking in, Gem, like we agreed."

"I'm sorry, Steve, I didn't know what time it was."

"How are you getting along? Is there anything you need?" Steve could hear a stiffness in his voice echo back at him through the receiver.

"No, I have everything I need, but thanks for asking." He sensed that she wanted to get off the phone.

"Gem, you've been in the house all afternoon. What have you come up with?" Steve figured he may as well lay it out and see what happened.

"All his clothes are still here and a lot of things that only I would know he would take with him if he was leaving are still here."

"What about the safe in the garage?"

'I don't know, I hadn't thought to check."

"If you want, I will come over and check for you."

"No, wait for a minute I will go check now." Steve waited for several minutes until he heard the receiver being picked up.

"Steve?"

"Yes, I'm still here."

"The door is open and the safe is empty. What do you think that means?" Steve rubbed his brow.

"I don't know what to think, Gem. What about the bank accounts? Did you and Nash have a joint account anywhere?"

"Yes, we had a joint and Nash had a separate one and the joint account is what I have been using since you and I left and went to LA. I found a bank statement that came in the mail yesterday and Nash's account still has money in it."

"Any bank statement on the Vegas Wash account?"

"No, I haven't seen one. What does all this mean, Steve?"

"I don't know, Gem, some things don't add up only because we don't have all the facts. Once some time goes by and we get more information, I'm sure we will find him." He hoped his bland statement sounded convincing. She didn't seem to notice that he had not added the word 'alive' to the sentence. He had meant to, but somehow it didn't come out that way.

"Gem?"

"Yes?"

"I was wondering if you were up for it if we couldn't take a drive up to Mt. Charleston tomorrow. Maybe go to Deer Creek, pack a picnic, might be fun. Get your mind off of things for a little while."

"I'm sorry, Steve, I don't think so. I have too many things to check over to see if I have missed anything. I need to go now, goodnight." Two abrupt clicks and she was gone. Steve pulled the receiver away from his ear and looked at it for a few seconds, then put it back on the cradle. He smoked a quick cigarette and then went to the small closet in the office and pulled out some fishing gear. After an hour of organizing, he stacked the equipment by the front door and went to bed.

August 23

SUNDAY MORNING BROKE with a cloud layer that sat on the mountains and obscured the rays of the sunrise. Steve was up at six and made himself a large breakfast of eggs, bacon and toast. After his second cup of coffee, he began to load the fishing gear in the back of the Mustang. When some of it had to be stowed in the back seat, he promised himself he would call Dwayne early on Monday to see how soon he could get the Jeep back. Just before 7:30 he locked the front door and was about to close the car door when he heard his phone ringing faintly from inside. He hesitated for a few seconds, before climbing out of the car, unlocking the front door and heading for the extension on the kitchen wall. The ringing stopped just as he entered the room. He was almost back to the front door when it began to ring again. He did not recognize the voice on the other end though it sounded familiar.

"Is this Steve Cannon?" By the tone, Steve guessed this was not a social call.

"Yes, who is this?"

"This is Detective Samuels. There has been an explosion at Tam's house. A car bomb. I need you to meet me at Sunrise Hospital now." Steve's throat closed and for a split second he returned to the putrid jungle, the heat and the screams reverberating off the kitchen walls.

"Tam. How is Tam?" He forced his voice out past the huge lump that had formed in his throat. He pressed his eyes as hard as he could to get rid of the green images.

"Tam is OK. His daughter is OK. His wife is in surgery. I am leaving, now. I expect to see you there." The line went dead. Steve stood in the kitchen holding the phone and staring at the patterns in the linoleum. The jungle images were gone, replaced by a sharp cold clarity. He hung up the phone, locked the front door and sat down in the car. He stopped. The new edge in his vision had just seen something that hadn't registered right away, but now was burned into his memory as if he had seen it every day of his life. He rose slowly out of the car and looked at the ground. Three feet away from the car was a tiny piece of electrician's tape barely peeking up through the gray gravel. He reached down and picked it up. It was still shiny and had not been there for long. Steve got down on his belly beside the car and carefully inched his way under the frame. He inspected the frame and the muffler, running his hands carefully along the drivetrain, feeling for anything unusual. It was several minutes before he noticed that there was a black bulge on the front of the far side of the frame that didn't correspond to the frame on his side. He extracted himself from the driver's side of the car and shimmied under the car just behind the passenger side front wheel.

He inspected the bulge, resisting the urge to touch it. By carefully and slowly maneuvering himself under the car he was able to see a wire connected to the bulge that ran forward toward the wheel. When he crawled under the car from the front, he saw a small metal disc taped to the inside of the wheel and the wire now visible for its' entire length connecting the disc to the mysterious bulge. It was when he looked at the bulge from his new angle that his throat constricted for the second time that morning. The bulge was four pieces of dynamite taped into a bundle. The wire was inserted deep within a blasting cap. Steve stopped for a second, crawled out from beneath the car and went over to the garage. Once inside he pulled out a small tool box and began rummaging through a larger box adding a few tools to the smaller one. Back by the car, he crawled underneath again and studied the set-up with a flashlight. He figured the small disc was some sort of solenoid that would rotate when the wheel turned, pulling the wire from the cap and completing the circuit. He and his brother had played with blasting caps when they were children and Steve knew how to handle them. He selected a pair of needle nose pliers from the tool box and several seconds later the long silver cap lay harmlessly in his hand. He returned to the garage and dug out a small carpenter's bag and a pair of gloves from under the workbench. He unwound several lengths of electricians' tape from the package that contained the dynamite and freed it from the frame. He retrieved the solenoid and the wire and placed all of them along with the gloves in the bag. With the bag safely on the seat beside him he drove down his street and fifteen minutes later turned from Sahara onto Maryland Parkway, eight blocks from Sunrise Hospital.

The emergency entrance was a beehive of activity as Steve pulled into the parking lot. Several police cars and two ambulances were stationed outside, their red overhead orbs rotating slowly in the gray light. Steve backed out and driving carefully down an access road parked near a small entrance that he had seen a doctor use once. As he opened the door, he could see a dark narrow hall

that ran for fifty feet or more and then widened out into a larger
space that was brightly lit. Tam sat on a bench along the wall, his
elbows on his knees, staring at the floor. He was fully dressed but
was wearing bedroom slippers instead of shoes. Just past the spot
where Tam was sitting, the hallway continued on until it terminated as a back entrance to the emergency room. At the far end,
he could see Samuels with his back turned talking with two uni-
formed policemen.

Tam looked up briefly when Steve entered the room and stood
in front of him. As if he hadn't seen him, Tam dropped his eyes to
the floor and continued to stare. Steve walked over and sat next
to Tam on the bench. The wall across from them held a door that
opened every few minutes as nurses and doctors came and went
back into the emergency area. Tam seemed oblivious to the presence of everyone. Steve had brought the bag in with him from the
car and now he set it down carefully under the bench beside his feet.

"Tam, I am sorry." Everything else he thought of to say sounded
trite and strange. Tam did not reply. After a few more minutes of
silence a nurse came through the door and approached Tam. She
carried a clipboard and when Tam didn't sit up or acknowledge
her, she squatted down in front of him. She spoke slowly in a gentle voice.

"Mr. Polhaus, the doctor is done treating your daughter. Other
than a few cuts and contusions, she will be fine. He would like us to
keep her overnight to make sure that there are no lingering effects
from the blast." She waited a few seconds and when Tam did not
respond, she stood up and patted him gently on the shoulder. She
looked over at Steve. Steve nodded. She continued down the hall
and moving around Samuels and his group, she disappeared into
the ER. Steve looked over at Tam.

"Tam, did you hear what the nurse just said?" When there was
no answer, Steve sat back on the bench and sighed.

"That should have been me." Tam's voice sounded queer, as if it was being forced through a narrow tube. Steve held himself back from responding.

"She said she just wanted to run down to the store to get one last thing. Julie didn't understand why she couldn't go. I stopped her on the front steps and just after I stepped back into the house, it happened." Tam shook his head slowly from side to side.

"That was for me and it should have been me." Steve put his hand on Tam's shoulder. The muscles were tense under the thin shirt. The door opened again and a second nurse stood holding it open.

"Mr. Polhaus, would you come with me, please. The doctor would like to speak with you." Tam looked up at the nurse but did not change his expression or make a move to stand up. Steve leaned over and half whispered into Tam's right ear.

"Tam. You need to go with the nurse, the doctor is waiting for you." Tam turned and looked at Steve.

"When did you get here?" He looked back at the nurse and made a pointing gesture at his chest.

"Me?" He said in a quiet voice. The nurse nodded and Tam stood up carefully and with small steps walked through the door.

"When did you get here?" Samuel's irritated voice echoed in the small space. Steve looked over at him and stared without response.

"You were supposed to check in with me when you got here. Did you forget that?" Samuels stood in the middle of the room with his hands on his hips. He was shorter than Steve by about eight inches and had a gray fedora cocked at an angle on his head. Steve guessed that he wore a raincoat mostly to cover his slight physique.

"I didn't forget. I think you are forgetting that I don't work for you, and unless you are going to arrest me for something, I can come and go as I please." He sat back on the bench, stretched out his legs and put his hands behind his head.

"That's how you're going to play this? I can arrest you as a material witness, right now and keep you for three days without anybody saying boo." He glared at Steve and moved into the middle of the room only three steps from Steve. Steve stared straight ahead as he spoke.

"I don't think this is the time or the place, Detective, for threats. I am here because a friend is in trouble. If you want to make some for me, I can't stop you, but while you are deciding, put on a pair of gloves and look at this." Steve crooked his right foot behind the bag and with one swift motion sent it scooting across the floor. Before he could move out of the way the bag banged to a stop against Samuel's foot. He picked up the bag and pulled the two flaps apart.

"Holy...Where did you get this?" Samuels quickly bent over and put the bag back on the floor as carefully as he could. Steve snorted.

"Don't worry, Detective, it can't hurt you. Someone attached it to my car. I took care of it." Samuels stood and looked up from the bag to Steve and then back to the bag. His face was several shades whiter than it had been a few seconds before. He turned and hurried back down the hall and returned with the two uniforms he had been talking with earlier. Samuels pointed to the bag and stepped back into the hall. The bigger cop of the two entered the room.

"Hey, Steve, I didn't see you there, how are you doing?" The cop smiled and bent down and looked at the bag.

"This yours?" Steve smiled and nodded. The cop looked inside and whistled. He put on the gloves that were inside the bag and carefully lifted out the package of dynamite and slowly rotated it around looking at it from all angles. He turned and looked back over his shoulder.

"It's ok, Sir. The blasting cap has been removed." He held it up towards Samuels as he moved back into the room. Samuels stopped abruptly and pointed at the bag.

"Put it back in the bag, patrolman and call the bomb disposal squad." The patrolman stood up and placed the dynamite back into the bag.

"Gee, Sir, would be just as fast if I ran it downtown in my squad car."

"No, Officer Gateson, do as I tell you. Call the squad and then take it outside and wait for them." The patrolman, turned and winking at Steve started back down the hall. Steve heard him laughing quietly with someone as he went out the door. Samuels turned and faced Steve.

"Where did you get that and why did you bring it here?" He still glared, but the voice was calmer.

"Like I said, it was attached to my car. After you called, I went to have a look and there it was. Now you don't have to spend three weeks putting Tam's car back together to find the few scraps that are left over." Steve yawned and looked up at the ceiling.

"I will talk to you later." Samuels spun on his heels and disappeared down the hallway.

Ten minutes went by before the door opened and Tam stepped into the room and let the door close behind him. He looked across the room at Steve.

"She's gone."

Tam stood without moving and stared straight ahead. He held a small paper bag in his right hand. Steve moved to his side and took his arm. He led him over to the bench and sat down beside him.

"They wouldn't let me see her." Tears began streaming down Tam's red cheeks. Steve held on tightly to his hand.

"I needed to see her and tell her it was my fault." Through his hand, Steve could feel the suppressed sobs come in waves.

"It wasn't your fault, Tam, there was nothing you could have done to stop any of this." Tam turned and looked at Steve. His eyes were bloodshot and barely focused.

"You're wrong. I should have quit two years ago when I had the chance. That is what she wanted, that is what we both wanted, except I couldn't do it. Just couldn't do it." Tam stopped as a new wave of sobs convulsed his body. He bent over and put his head in his hands and sobbed in great heaving spasms. Steve held on to the detective and waited for the sobs to subside. Just before they did, a middle aged woman came into the room and put her arms around

Tam's head and shoulders and kissed him on his cheek. Steve recognized her from one of the pictures in Tam's office. She was Tam's older sister, Georgiana. She lived in North Las Vegas with her husband and two sons, and by most accounts she had raised Tam after their mother had died. Just behind her, Samuels appeared at the end of the hall and motioned Steve to come with him back into the emergency room. Steve patted Tam on the back, gave a quick nod to Georgiana and then followed Samuels down the hall. Samuels stopped before two plainclothes policemen and pointed at Steve.

"Here's your boy. Let me know if he refuses to cooperate." He threw a disgusted glance at Steve, went out the entrance and climbed into the back seat of one of the waiting squad cars. Steve saw that the cop he knew from earlier was driving. He looked back at the two policemen, one of whom motioned to a side room. Steve walked into the room ahead of the two and selected one of the four chairs at the table and sat down. One of the men sat down and put a large notebook on the table, the other paced back and forth. After a minute, he spoke.

"Mr. Cannon, I am Agent Brady and this is Agent Molini. We have been assigned to investigate the bombing. We have examined the contents of the bag that you provided to Detective Samuels, and we have some questions for you."

Steve nodded and took out his pack of cigarettes from his front shirt pocket. He looked around for an ashtray and settled for a small paper cup from the water dispenser. The agent at the table looked bored.

"Are you about ready, Mr. Cannon?" He asked dryly. Steve returned the lighter to his pocket, took a drag and smiled broadly at the agent.

"Sure, shoot." The agent who was sitting down with the pencil and the notebook looked over at Brady as he paced towards the door. He turned and folding his arms leaned back on the frame.

"Just for starters, Mr. Cannon, if Agent Molini gives you a sheet of paper, will you be able to draw a schematic of the undercarriage of your car and the bomb exactly as you found it this morning?"

"Yeah, sure." Steve reached for the notebook as Molini turned the book around and handed Steve his pencil. Steve took several minutes sketching the frame of the car and the location of the bundle. He drew a small circle and inside drew a close up of the wire and the small solenoid. When he was finished, he pushed the notebook and pencil back across the table to Molini, who held it up as Brady came over to the table and squinted down at the page.

"Where is your car, now Mr. Cannon?" Steve pointed in the general direction.

"Outside by the curb, in some doctor's spot."

"We are going to have to tow it in and examine it, Mr. Cannon. With your permission, of course." The agent stared hard at Steve. Steve shrugged.

"Sure, no problem, as long as you give it back to me the way you found it." He stood to leave.

One more thing, Mr. Cannon. Detective Samuels is under the impression that you think it was one Angelo Sorelli who is responsible for the bombing of Detective Polhaus's car and the attempted bombing of yours."

"There is no doubt of that, Agent Brady. I am sure you have access to Tam's file. Read it and ask him. You don't have to take my word for it." Steve snuffed out his cigarette in the small cup.

"As of twenty minutes ago, Detective Polhaus is on bereavement leave. We are opening a new file on this case." He was back leaning on the doorframe and half blocking the way out of the room. Steve moved toward the door.

"The more, the merrier, Agent Brady." He pushed by the FBI agent and walked into the hall. Brady followed him. "Take this." Steve stopped and took a small card from the agent's hand. It had two telephone numbers printed on it. "Call me first if have any information I should know. Other than that, stay out of the way,

Mr. Cannon. We are in charge, now." Steve turned halfway around and continued walking back to the waiting room.

"Glad to hear it, Agent Brady, I feel safer all ready." He entered the room where he had first found Tam and waited until a nurse came through the door.

"Have you seen where Mr. Polhaus has gone?"

"He is in with his daughter. His sister is with him as well."

"May I go in and wait outside the room for him?" The nurse nodded and turning, held the door open as Steve walked into another brightly lit hall. The nurse stopped at the first door she came to and indicating to Steve that he should wait where he was, she opened the door and slipped into the room. Ten seconds, later she emerged.

"Mr. Polhaus knows you are out here." She smiled and continued out the door she had first appeared in. Steve paced up and down the short corridor. He had not noticed the usual hospital smell when he had first come in, but now it hung heavy in the small space.

When Tam came out of the room closing the door softly behind him, Steve sensed that he was more in control of himself.

"How is she doing, Tam?"

"She is going to be OK, she is a strong kid like her mother." He caught himself a little when he mentioned his wife, but took a deep breath and continued.

"She seemed to know already that her mother was gone. They have given her a sedative and she should sleep for a while. They want me to pick her up in the morning but Georgie and I will stay here tonight with her in case she wakes up." He slumped against the wall of the corridor and put his hands on his knees. Steve put his hand on the older man's shoulder.

"Tam, tell me what I can do to help you." He looked down at the top of Tam's head and his reddish brown hair. Tam looked up at him, his eyes were still bloodshot, but there was a cold look Steve had seen on only one or two other occasions.

"You gotta get that S.O.B., Steve, promise me."

"I will, Tam, or I will die trying." Tam straightened up, put his face closer to Steve's and whispered.

"Samuels put me on leave. I took the file home two nights ago. Stop by the house tomorrow and I will give it to you. Samuels will shilly shally around and blow this case for sure."

"They got two FBI guys on it already, Tam. I just got what I am sure is the first of many third degree sessions from those guys." Tam nodded, his face grave.

"Brady?" Steve nodded back.

"All he is interested in is pinning anything he can on the mob. The last guy they are going to like for this job is Sorelli. You're it as far I can see." The door opened and Tam's sister looked out into the hallway.

"Tam, she is awake and is asking for you." Tam nodded and looking directly at Steve started towards the door. Just before he entered the room, he turned back and pointed at Steve.

"Tomorrow." Steve nodded and pushed back through the door into the small waiting room.

The Mustang was just being winched onto the flat bed of the tow truck when Steve exited the side door he had entered an hour before. The sky was a little less gray and the temperature was starting to climb, the humidity rising with it. He watched the final preparations as the tow truck driver tightened the chains on the four corners of the car. On the back of the large truck, the car looked small. Steve approached the driver as he was stowing his gloves in a tool box that was built into the back of his cab.

"Hey, which way you going to get this thing downtown?" The man looked up at the car and then back at Steve.

"This your car?"

"Yeah the cops want to examine it. You know, make sure all the spark plugs are accounted for, that type of thing." The driver snorted and wiped his hands on an already greasy rag.

"Can go several ways, I suppose. I guess you want a lift."

"Yeah, if it's not too much trouble. Drop me off at Sahara and the Strip if you can." The man nodded and pointed to the cab.

"Sure, hop in, that was the way I was going anyway." Steve stepped up into the cab of the truck. Ten minutes later he waved to the driver and judging the early morning traffic, jogged across the four lanes and into the parking lot in front of Foxy's Deli. It was only 9:30 when he slid into a seat near the kitchen, but he felt like he had been up for two days. The coffee that Walter set before him tasted good and he stretched his legs out under the table and looked around the restaurant for Bernie. As he finished his coffee, he called Walter over to his table.

"Walter, is Bernie available?"

"He just got in ten minutes before you arrived. In the back there doing paperwork. Want me to tell him you are here?" Steve nodded. Walter returned and indicated with a quick toss of his head that he should follow him back to the counter. Walter knocked three times in quick succession and opened the door for Steve. Steve stepped through the door and closed it quietly behind him. Bernie was sitting at a desk across the room talking on the phone. He waved at Steve and continued the conversation. While he waited, Steve wandered around the perimeter of the large room, gazing at the pictures of celebrities that covered most of the available space on the walls. If there was an entertainer that had played the strip more than once since the war, it was likely that he or she had a picture on Bernie's red flocked wall paper. For the first time, Steve noticed something that had escaped him before, even though he had been in this room dozens of times. All the pictures were grouped by the hotel at which they performed. Those that had graced the stages of more than one hotel through the years appeared in all the appropriate places. There was also a loose chronology to each hotel's space with the time line moving from left to right. Most had dates along with the dedications to Bernie. The earliest that Steve could find was the Mills Brothers from 1946. He was looking at a series of Louie Prima and Keely Smith pictures from the mid-fifties. Louie and Keely were standing over a kneeling Sam Butera, pretending to whip him as he played his sax, when he heard Bernie calling his name. He quickly descended the three steps down to the main floor of the room and crossed over to the familiar round table where Bernie was waiting. Bernie's smile faded as Steve pulled out a chair and sat down across from him.

"What's wrong?" Bernie sat down and leaned across the table, a frown spreading across the round face. Steve sighed and sat back.

"There was a car bombing early this morning over in the Huntington district, Tam's wife is dead, his daughter is slightly hurt, but she will be OK." Steve waited as Bernie struggled to comprehend the words he had just heard. Bernie started shaking his head slowly from side to side, his eyes were fastened on a spot in the middle of the green felt.

"No, that can't be....that just can't be."

"I'm sorry, Bernie, I wish I could tell you it was a bad dream or some awful mistake, but I just came from Sunrise and Tam." Bernie refocused and looked up at Steve.

"How's he doing?"

"He comes in and out of it. Mostly he is angry, naturally. He is worried about his daughter, thank god his sister is there to help him. He's on leave for the next few weeks at least."

"How are you doing?"

"Holding up. Feel kinda helpless and responsible at the same time."

"Cut that crap." Bernie's expression was as fierce as Steve had ever seen it. "You better start taking more precautions, or you'll be next...." Steve interrupted.

"Oh, yeah, about that....He did try. Planted two bombs last night. Lucky I got the call about Tam's wife before I got in my car." He tried to make it sound routine. Bernie was now visibly agitated.

"You gotta come stay with me until they catch this guy, I mean it." He had stood up from the table and was now pacing back and forth behind his chair. Steve tried to make his voice as soothing as possible.

"It's OK, Bern, the FBI is involved now. That's more people with more resources looking for Sorelli. Besides, he is unlikely to try any direct action at my house. He knows I am too well armed and too alerted to do much but get his people as well as himself hurt or worse." Bernie kept pacing. Steve decided to change the topic.

"Bernie, have you heard anything from Remy? She doesn't know yet." Bernie stopped and leaning on the back of the chair slowly started focusing back on Steve and his voice.

"Remy? No, she hasn't called, but that's good, right? Means everything is OK on her end, right?" Steve nodded his head up and down vigorously.

"That's right Bernie. That was the deal we have, she is to call you if there is something she needs to tell me." Bernie slumped back down into his chair. He looked up at Steve.

"What do we do now?" His voice was quietly resigned.

"Well, like I said, the FBI are now on the case because of the bombing." Bernie interjected.

"And attempted bombing, don't forget that."

"And the attempted bombing." Steve continued. "I am going to turn up the heat on the land deal starting tomorrow, which should force Nash and Sorelli to make a move sooner than later, and if they have to move on someone else's timetable, they might make a mistake."

'Nash." Bernie shook his head. "I don't figure Nash involved with someone like Angelo Sorelli. It don't make sense. I mean, I have known that guy for fifteen years, back when he was a box man at the Old El Rancho." He continued to shake his head. "Has the world suddenly gone mad around here?" He stood up and went to the door, said something to someone behind the counter and returned.

"Coffee coming." He sat down and looked across at Steve. "So what am I supposed to think? How does a guy like that go off the rails so badly?" He looked around at all of his memorabilia. "Maybe I didn't really know the guy. Maybe I don't much about anything anymore." He sighed and got up to let Walter and the coffee tray into the room. For a few minutes they sipped their coffee quietly.

"Nash changed quite a bit, Bernie. Once he got those extra points in the Dunes, he forgot who he was and how he got there. He is not the same man that you and Remy used to know." Bernie nodded slightly.

'Yeah, you're right, I know that. Truth be known, I saw it happening and knew it all along. He got deeper into the Hollywood thing, used to tell him that was a sucker play but he liked all the attention. Whatta ya gonna do?" Bernie shrugged and refilled their cups.

"For what? How much was there in this deal anyway?" He looked up at Steve. Steve saw Bernie's expression and realized the question wasn't an idle one.

"Mike Hunter says that Beech was talking five million." Bernie thought for a minute.

"What are six points in the Dunes worth do you think?"

"I don't know, Bern, maybe half a mil, maybe a little less. Question is how do you sell and to whom? You don't just announce one day that it would nice if everybody just ponied up so you can go retire. I don't think it will ever work that way for guys like Nash. They are on that train until the end of the line."

"Yeah, I guess you are right. But this town is getting ready to change big, Steve. A lot of us old-timers see it coming. Nash is very keen on it. He sees and hears about the plans guys like Sarno and Kerkorian have and I think he figures if he could put together that kind of money, he could be a player in that league too. Are you going over to see Remy today?"

"Well that is my plan. The cops impounded my car, so until I scare up another one, I am stuck in low gear for a while." Bernie brightened.

"Hey you can use mine. I got three, you know, can't drive them all with one behind." Bernie laughed. "Take the one I got outside. The Thunderbird. Great car, you'll love it."

"Thanks, Bernie, that will work out great." Bernie's mood had lifted considerably since Steve had first walked in.

"All I need is a ride out to my place. Have you eaten?" Steve shook his head.

"Let's stop by the Showboat on the way and get the thirty-nine cent breakfast. I sometimes forget that other people cook food too." Bernie grinned. Steve stood up to join him and as he did he noticed a large reel-to-reel tape deck on a credenza behind Bernie's desk. He thought for a moment as Bernie was opening drawers and placing the papers that had been scattered across the desk top into them.

"Bernie. Let me ask you something. That tape deck you have there. Do you think that it could be rigged to record a phone call?" He walked over and bending down, peered closely at the silver machine. Bernie smiled and reached back into the drawer he had just closed. He held up a black wire that had a rubber disc connected to one end and a small silver plug on the other.

"Like this, maybe?" He tossed the wire to Steve. Steve turned them over in his hand. The disc was a microphone. Steve smiled up at Bernie.

"Actually, I got that idea from Nick Montero six months ago. Says it cuts arguments about who said what to whom and when to zero." Steve turned back to the deck.

"Where can I get one of these today, Bern?"

"Not likely anywhere. With all the musicians hanging off every showroom curtain in town, you would think you could, but no dice. Rocco picked this up for me when he was in LA. But you are welcome to borrow it. Here, let me fish out some boxes of blank tape."

"Are you sure, Bernie? Won't you be needing it?"

"Way ahead of you, Steve. With the FBI involved, they are going to try to nail everybody for everything. The more you can back up with tape the better for all of us, including Remy. Here, let me put it in the case for you. Know how to run it?"

"Yeah, sure, I have used one like it a time or two. Helped record a few of the late night sessions at the Jungle Club with one just like it. I'll be careful with it and get it back to you as soon as I can."

"Don't worry, it can be replaced." Bernie handed the deck over to Steve and then picked up a small box that held the extra tapes and the microphones. Bernie locked the door to the back room and after a few words with Walter, they went down a dark narrow hall and through a door that opened into a small alley. Right up against the building a baby blue '63 Thunderbird sat parked next to the garbage cans. Bernie pointed and laughed.

"My own valet parking spot." He opened the trunk and held it up while Steve loaded the tape deck and the box into it. Bernie pulled the keys from the trunk lock and tossed them to Steve and grinned.

"Going to be nice to have a chauffeur for the day." Steve slipped behind the wheel and pulled out into the alley so that Bernie could get into the passenger door. They negotiated a tight corner at the end of the alley and then turned into the parking lot in front of the deli. Steve looked over at Bernie when he heard a small laugh.

"We should do this more often. Get out and see what the great big ol' wide world is up to." They both laughed as Steve turned left to head up the strip to Fremont Street.

The Showboat was hosting one of their bigger pro bowling tournaments, Steve and Bernie crowded into a small booth in front of one of the keno boards. The room was packed with tourists, locals, and waitresses moving quickly through the tables with breakfast platters, swerving to avoid the keno runners taking tickets back to the booth in back of the bar. Bernie looked around and smiled.

"This is the real Las Vegas, kiddo, the real thing. And notice I didn't say 'Vegas' like some outta town dope or even some of our own newspaper guys that have been doing that lately. Remind me to read 'em the riot act on Tuesday night." Bernie laughed and pulling two keno tickets and two crayons out of a glass cup on the table, tossed one of each to Steve and began to mark his numbers. Steve looked skeptically at the piece of paper in his hand.

"Bernie. You ever win anything worth shouting about in this game?"

"Naw, five hundred dollars once. Got an old friend from Chicago that comes out here once a year and stays with me, bless him, and he is crazy about keno. Funny thing is, he will tell you ten times a day about how he hit for twelve thousand five hundred at the Mint eight years ago. But does he ever mention the three thousand he loses every year for the last twenty years? You gotta love this town." Bernie finished his slip, and seeing the blank one still in Steve's hand, he grabbed it, quickly filled it out and after catching the attention of one of the runners, handed over the papers and the money. They sat back and waited for their breakfasts to arrive.

Later, as they walked to the edge of the large parking lot to where they had to park the Thunderbird, Bernie put his hand on Steve's arm and stopped him.

"Do you think that I could tag along when you go see Remy? If it's a fifth wheel deal, let me know, I can go over and see her later."

"Of course you come, Bernie, Remy will be glad to see you. Probably much gladder than she will be to see me." Steve unlocked Bernie's door before circling the car to get to the driver's side. When he had settled in his seat he looked over at Bernie. Bernie had a worried look.

"I don't get it Steve. What is up with you and Remy? You know I thought about it last night and I think you two would be great together." Steve laughed as he pulled onto the Boulder Highway to get to Desert Inn Road. He shivered just a little as he remembered the last time he was on this highway with Betsy and Susan. Luckily, Bernie interrupted his recollection.

"You know what we should do? We should go out one of these nights and catch Charlie Teagarden at the Silver Slipper. Whatta say? Get some of the guys who dig that kind of music and make a night of it. We haven't done something like that in at least a year." Bernie shook his head and smiled.

"Yeah. That sounds great. Include me in that." Bernie nodded and laughed.

"I will, you can count on that, I will."

When they pulled into the driveway in front of Remy's house, the sky had darkened and a light mist was starting to fall. Steve rang the bell and waved when he saw Remy look out from behind a nearby curtained window. She opened the door and smiled wanly at both of them. Bernie stepped through the door and hugged her.

"Good to see ya, Remy. How have you been doing?" He stepped back with his arms still around her and looked her in the eyes.

"Good, Bernie, good. You look well yourself." She turned and reached out to Steve. He took her in his arms and squeezed her hard. He kissed the top of her head and held her for several seconds. She kissed him lightly on the lips when he let her go. She reached out for Bernie's hand and walked them both into the round spacious living room. Bernie sat next to her on the gold sofa and patted her knee.

"I don't like the idea of you being alone here, Remy. You gotta come out to my place where we can protect you and take care of you. Steve, here will stay there too, if it will make you feel better. At least stay at his place for chrissakes." Bernie looked at Steve for help.

"Remy, I'm not telling you what to do, but Bernie is right. It is too dangerous out there with Sorelli around, especially after what happened this morning."

"What happened this morning?" She looked back and forth at them her voice rising in alarm. Steve made his voice low and reassuring.

"It's just that a policemans's wife was killed by a car bomb, and they are pretty sure that Sorelli was behind it." Bernie began to tag on to Steve's statement.

"And there was…" He stopped cold when he saw Steve quickly look over at him. Remy looked back and forth at them again.

"Is there something that you're not telling me? Something about Nash?" She began to cry and Bernie quickly wrapped his arms around her and tried to get her to calm down. Steve tried again.

"No, Gem, nothing about Nash. Nobody has any more information on him then we did last night, but we are all still looking." Remy straightened up and when Bernie offered his kerchief, she dabbed her eyes and looked at Steve.

"I know you would rather not hear it, Steve, but I love my husband and I can't sleep or eat or even think straight until I know he is safe."

"I know that, Gem, but I have to put all that aside for your safety. I don't know what will happen to us, any more than you do, but I love you and I am going to protect you from whatever wants to do you harm." Remy began to cry softly again and Bernie shifted uncomfortably in his perch on the sofa. He looked at both of them in turn.

"Well, we all can agree on that, right, Remy? So let's figure out where you need to be and get you packed." Remy shook her head and stood up, looking down at Bernie.

"You don't understand, either of you." Her fist was clenched tightly around Bernie's kerchief.

"I'm not going anywhere until I find out where my husband is and when I do, I'm going to him. Is everyone here clear on that?" She looked sharply at Steve, who nodded and threw up his hands in slight frustration. She ignored the gesture and looked down at Bernie. Bernie was looking down at his hands.

"Look at me, Bernie, you wonderful man." He glanced up and Steve could see tears in his pale eyes.

"I love you dearly, you know that." She reached out and placed her hand under his chin and rubbed the top of his head.

"But this is how I must do what I have to do. You just have to understand that for me, OK?" Bernie nodded slightly and with a small sniffle looked over at Steve. Steve chuckled.

"Don't look at me with those big cow eyes, you wanted to come." Steve stood up and threw an arm around Bernie.

"Come on. Let's get out of this lady's hair." He leaned over and kissed Remy on the cheek at the same time pulling Bernie up from the sofa. Bernie hugged Remy and went to wait in the foyer. Steve took Remy's hands in his and looked at her reddened eyes.

"Make sure that you call me if you hear anything and I will do the same." She nodded her assent and followed him into the foyer. She kissed Bernie on both cheeks and waved to them from the front door as Steve opened the car door for Bernie. He blew Remy a kiss as he walked to the driver's side and got in.

Bernie was in a quiet mood as they drove out Maryland Parkway toward his place.

"You know, maybe I should have married at some point along the way." He sighed and looked out the window as they passed Nevada Southern University.

"Why didn't you?" Steve switched on the car's windshield wipers as the mist turned into heavier rain.

"Aw.. I don't know. I guess I was too busy and maybe figured there was plenty of time and then I guess you look around and that time has kinda passed you by."

"I don't think it ever too late for that, Bernie. There are plenty of great women out there, you just gotta make yourself available."

"Well, you found one and you don't seem to be setting the world on fire." It was Steve's turn to sigh.

"Yeah, I guess I am unlucky that way. Right woman, wrong time." He slowed as they came to a large puddle that had formed on the road.

"But hey, Bern, we gave it the old college try, right. The woman knows her mind and that is all there is to that." He slowed again to turn into the short driveway that led to the gates behind which the driveway continued into the complex where Bernie lived and owned several units. When they were in front of Bernie's door, he looked over at Steve,

"Been a while since you been out here. Come in for a drink?"

"Sure, Bern, that would be great. I can use one." He parked the car and followed Bernie through an arched gateway and into a small courtyard that led to the front door. Bernie removed his shoes on the tile just inside the door and Steve did likewise. He followed Bernie as he padded down a short hall to a landing that led three steps down to the sunken living room. The carpet was white and very soft under Steve's unshod feet. Bernie pointed to a large rosewood cabinet that was below a long line of windows that overlooked his private pool.

"Pick out something to listen to that fits the mood. Scotch, OK?"

"Fine." Steve frowned as he flipped through one of four large stacks of record albums that were neatly loaded into a sliding metal rack. He pulled out a Lester Young album and put it on the turntable. He noticed that the record player and speakers were different than the ones he had used the last time he had been there.

"New rig, Bern?" He said as Bernie returned from the other room with two large glasses in his hand. Steve looked skeptically at the large drinks. Bernie smiled and shrugged.

"Saves trips." He offered one to Steve and pointed at the stereo.

"Yeah. Read about these new speakers, supposed to be great. Wait until you hear them." He looked down at the record that Steve had placed on the felt of the turntable.

"Ah, Lester Young, good choice, that is a half-speed master. I haven't played it through these yet, should sound great." Bernie motioned to the large white leather couch that curved around the center of the room in the middle of the four speakers that had been positioned at each corner. They both sat down, Steve just around the curve from Bernie so he could see him as they talked. The smooth tenor sax of the Prez filled the room with the first few bars of 'All of Me' and they were both quiet for the length of the record. Steve had never heard such lushness as he heard from the sound that came from the four speakers. Bernie smiled as his head swayed almost imperceptively to the jazz. They looked at each other as the last notes of 'The Prez and Teddy' faded from the room. Steve sipped his drink and looked past Bernie out to the pool and the stucco wall that surrounded it.

"You got a nice place here Bernie, I have always liked it here."

"You should buy something out here. In fact, I will give you a great deal on one of the ones I own." Bernie gestured with his glass in the general direction of the front gate.

"Naw, I like being out and away from everything."

"You think that is going to last long? They are going to start developing like crazy out where you are. You watch, not too many years they will have houses all up the side of Sunrise."

"Maybe, but hopefully I will be six feet under by then." Bernie snorted.

"I remember when I first came out here in '46. Most of the strip was just dirt and desert iguanas. That was only eighteen years ago. A lot can happen in half that time. I think everybody here has had it easy. Like I said, change is gonna come quicker and harder than people can even imagine." Steve shrugged and took another sip of his scotch.

"Let me ask you something, Steve, and give me your opinion, right off the top of your head."

"Sure, Bernie, what?"

"I got a chance to buy a small sliver of land on the strip. Roughly triangle shaped across from the Sands. It is a little piece left over from the lease deal Jay Sarno made with Kerkorian. Not much, but it could hold a decent sized casino with a small hotel on top." Whatta you think?"

"I dunno know, Bernie, that is not my expertise. I just found out a few days ago that you owned the one connected to the deli. Would you move that one out there?"

"Naw, it would be a whole new deal. Those little strip mall

casinos make good money. Know what I heard? Vegas Village is going to put in several banks of slots right down the middle of the concourse, you know, that separates the groceries from the dry goods? What do you think of that?"

"Figures. The Mormons won't be caught dead doing that stuff, but they will sure jump at a chance to make money off of those who do." Steve laughed and shook his head.

"Are you sure that you want to get that involved, Bern, I mean, and don't get me wrong, here, but a high profile strip operation is going to attract the wrong element. How are you going to keep them out of your operation?" Bernie shrugged.

"They are on the run, Steve. Their time is almost over. I can clear the commission tomorrow, there won't be any trouble from that corner."

"I don't know, Bern, those organizations have always been very resourceful and tenacious, especially the ones like Tommy's." Bernie laughed.

"Did I ever tell you that I knew Tommy back in Chicago? Ask him sometime. Might be good for a laugh. No, they wouldn't mess with 'ol Bern." Bernie suddenly grew quiet and watched as a sudden squall of wind and rain hit the large windows that led out to his deck.

Steve stood up. "I should get going, Bernie, I will try to get your car back a soon as I can, I really appreciate the loan.' Bernie waved him off and snorted.

"Keep it as long as you want, don't hurry." He got up and walked Steve to the door.

"Let's both keep checking in with Remy, I don't have a good feeling about any of this and I would cut off my arm before I should see that kid get hurt." Bernie shook his head and looked at the floor.

'Don't worry, Bern, between the two of us, she will pull through no matter what's ahead. Thanks for the scotch, I will call you tomorrow." Steve patted Bernie's shoulder and ducked into the light rain and walked quickly to the car. He was a half hour from home with the rain and the Sunday traffic. He pulled back onto Maryland Parkway and headed north. It was two hours later when the phone rang.

*

THE GRUFF VOICE laughed when Steve said hello. Steve leaned over and switched on the reel-to-reel tape machine he had borrowed from Bernie. The small microphone was already attached to the receiver.

"What do you want Sorelli?"

"I just wanted to see how my favorite dead man was doing and if maybe you're thinking of getting out of town like you should."

"I'm not going anywhere at least not until you are dead or behind bars."

"Ha, ha." Sorelli laughed. "I think recent events suggest that ain't gonna happen. But I tell you what will. You're going to regret the day you decided to tangle with me."

"I already regret that you were born, so I guess that will fit right in there somewhere." Steve laughed back.

"Well, you keep cracking wise, dead man, soon you are going to feel a whole lot worse than Tam O'Shanter. Go figure on that one. Jimmy shadows him three weeks in a row and what does he do every Sunday morning? He gets in his car and drives to Friendly Fergies, gets a cup of coffee, buys a paper, reads the sport pages while he finishes his cup and then goes home. On the one Sunday, he doesn't, it's his wife gets blown up. But I cry outta one eye and I'll tell you why. Now he knows what it's like to lose somebody close. One of my uncles was like a father to me, so now we are almost even. And speaking of Jimmy, he would say hi, except he can't talk very well on account of that cheap stunt you pulled in the desert. But you can be sure we will make it up to you." Sorelli chuckled.

"Well if Sunday morning was any indication, you do pretty sloppy work. A blind man could have seen that set-up."

"Naw, don't think so, Cannon. You got lucky and someone

probably tipped you off. Otherwise, we wouldn't be having this nice little chat. But that was just for starters. In fact, I am glad you didn't get scattered all over Clark County in pieces. Now I get to do it on a far more personal basis."

"I should have killed you when I had the chance in the desert."

"Too busy trying to save your own candy ass, and I don't think you got it in you."

"You are bound to make a mistake sometime Sorelli, and there are now a whole lot of people that are waiting for that moment."

"Well, once again, I wouldn't hold my breath on that one either."

"In any event, Sorelli, Tommy Carmino told me to tell you hello." Steve waited as there was a slight pause.

"What the hell does Tommy Carmino have to do with this?" Sorelli's voice was barely above a guttural growl.

"Well you know how it is, Angelo, you start thinking you are a bona fide wise guy, the real wise guys are gonna make you put up or shut up. In this case, he doesn't seem too pleased that you are running around town playing with fireworks. Kinda bad for business, if you know what I mean." Steve stopped when he heard Sorelli laugh.

"Carmino is a spineless wanna be businessman. He thinks because he is smooth and friendly that he can schmooze his way into polite society. He's got another think coming on that score too."

"Oh, and I forgot the FBI, they are now involved and I don't think whatever hole you've crawled into is going to hide you forever."

"Well, Cannon, here is another news flash for you. The word around the campfires I visit is that they don't even like me for any of this crap, and they are just as likely to blame Tommy and all those other creeps you seem so happy to hang around with. And if I was you, I would make sure I was somewhere else when they really need a scapegoat. See, Cannon, this town keeps getting more and more unhealthy for you by the minute."

"You've always talked big, Sorelli, but all you ever seem to do is come down hard on people that can't defend themselves. Unless you called for some other reason than to spin fairy tales, I've got more important business."

"Thanks for reminding me, dead man, I guess there is one more thing I got for you. Know Sunset Park out in the valley? Well, where Eastern meets Warm Springs road, right at the end of the park, on that little dirt road, there is a package there for you. Don't say I don't try and help out." The phone line went dead and was replaced by a small buzz from the microphone.

Steve looked at his watch. He dialed Tam's office number and got no answer. He dialed the first number on the card that agent Brady had given him. Agent Molini answered.

"This is Steve Cannon, I need to speak with Agent Brady."

"Not here. Went to get dinner."

"Have him call me, when he gets back, it's important." Steve hung up and rewound the tape. He hit 'play' and listened to the short conversation with Sorelli. Though the volume was uneven in parts, the voice was unmistakable if one had ever heard Sorelli speak in person and on close listening, all the words could be made out. Forty minutes later, the phone rang.

"This is Brady, why'd you call?" Steve could hear the skepticism in the agent's voice even though he was trying to sound casual.

"I just got a call from Sorelli. Among other things, he thinks we should check out a place he describes in the valley. Says there is a package there we need to retrieve." Steve heard a yawn on the other end of the line.

"It's late, Cannon, maybe I will check on it tomorrow." Steve laughed.

"I taped the conversation if you think I'm not square on this."

"Not admissible, even you should know that."

"Didn't tape it for evidence in court. I taped it because I figured this would be your attitude just like I am taping this one now. Might not stand up, but it might be interesting for some parties to hear someday." Steve waited in silence for several seconds.

"Give me the location. I will send a black and white out to see what, if anything this clown, whoever he is, thinks we should see." Steve relayed the description of the spot and then without further comment, hung up the phone. When it rang again three minutes later, Steve answered it after he started the tape machine.

"Is this Steve Cannon?" The female voice was deep and confident.

"Yes, who is this?"

"Rita Malone, from the Las Vegas Sun." Steve could hear her rustling papers on the other end.

"Well I guess this is my night, what can I do for you?"

"What do you mean 'your night'? If you would rather I call tomorrow, just say so."

"No, no, just a private joke, I'm sorry. Go on, you were saying?"

"I just have one or two questions about the car bombing this morning."

"Why call me? The police gave a briefing downtown at 3 o'clock, that was probably all the information they have so far." Rita chuckled.

"Hank said you would play it close to the chest."

"Hank put you onto me? Why would he do that?" Steve automatically reached for a pen and paper, but realized that the tape was spinning and sat down on the couch instead.

"Hank hired me two months ago. I was doing investigative journalism in LA and he convinced me to come here and work for him. He seems to think that I need to see the 'unofficial' side of the town, and he has given me the names of several people, yours being one. He said not to ask you about your last name."

"OK,..., but you mentioned the bombing this morning, what connection are you presuming there?"

"I guess you have a right to know. A source we have in the department, said that your name appeared several times in the police report of the incident. He also hinted that the body they found in the desert on Friday is somehow connected to the bombing. Care to comment?"

"No not at this point. But I tell you what. If you want to meet me somewhere tomorrow, I might have something for you."

"Sure where and what time?"

"How about noon at the Alpine Village Inn on the strip across from the Hacienda, know it?"

"No, but I have a tourist map, Mr. Cannon, and I'm getting pretty good at getting around. I will see you there."

"Fine, goodnight." Steve hung up the phone and turned off the tape. He dialed Bernie's number and waited until he picked up.

"Bernie, this is Steve. Sorry to bother you so late, but I need you to check with Hank Greenspun about someone. Can you do that for me?"

"Sure, sure, who is it?"

"Woman named Rita Malone. Says she is working as an investigative reporter for him, and wants to know all about the bombing and Beech in the desert. I need to know if she is who she says she is and what Hank's angle is on this deal."

"I'll call him right now. You going to be there a while?"

"Yep, call me back if you hear anything." Steve hung up and waited. When Bernie didn't call back an hour later, he turned off the light and went to sleep.

August 24

STEVE'S MONDAY MORNING started with a cop pounding on his front door and peering in through his kitchen window as he slowly made his way to the living room. He could see it was a city cop, but one he didn't recognize. He looked through the curtains at the squad car to make sure it was legitimate. He recognized Samuels sitting in the front seat, wearing his usual gray fedora. When he opened the front door, the brightness of the sun made him squint, the rainy weather of the day before having cleared out overnight. He looked at the cop, who jerked a thumb back toward the squad car.

"What? Now? I'm not even dressed yet. Tell him to wait." Steve slammed the door and walked back through the kitchen removing his bathrobe as he went. Ten minutes later he stepped again into the brightness and approached the passenger side of the car. Samuels slowly rolled down the window and regarded Cannon with a sour look. From just behind Sunrise mountain, two F-105 jets from Nellis Air Force base banked in unison and made their wide sweep over the east end of the valley as they prepared to land. In a matter of seconds they were already over the base, but the loud engine noise still lingered and reverbrated over the desert. When it was quiet enough to talk again, Steve stepped closer to the car.

"What's so important that you have to come all the way out here on a bright Monday morning and disturb the peace?" He crossed his arms and glared at the detective. Samuels didn't say anything, but reached into the breast pocket of his raincoat and held out a Polaroid photo.

"Thought you might have some idea who this was, since you seem to think that you are an infallible source on all matters pertaining to any investigation I make. Found him wrapped in a rug just off Warm Springs Road." Steve continued to glare at him for a few seconds before he looked down at the picture. The face was partially destroyed by at least one gunshot wound, but there was enough left to recognize. Steve sighed and handed the photo back to Samuels.

"Nash Brannock." He looked out over the valley in the direction of the Desert Inn. He could hear a cluster of grasshoppers singing in the manzanita bushes next to his garage.

"I want the Browning 9mm you kept from the incident in the desert." Samuel's face was grim. Steve again focused on the man before him.

"Sorelli carries a .45." He said flatly and recrossed his arms.

"Beech was killed with a .45." He glared even harder at the detective. He saw the shadow of the other cop move away from the front door and closer to Steve. Samuels smiled slightly.

"Yeah, you are right again as usual. And you also own a .45 if I am not mistaken. Give both of them to Officer Michaels there." Samuels rolled the window up and put the photo back in his breast pocket and adjusted the brim of the fedora in the rear view mirror. Steve stepped away from the car and turned toward the officer who was standing near the front door with his hands folded in front of him.

"Come in out of the sun, officer, I have a couple of things you need to take with you." Five minutes later as he watched the dust from the squad car settle back down onto the gravel, the phone rang. Steve smiled when he heard Bernie chirping at him on the other end.

"I finally got hold of Hank this morning. He was out at some big gala at the Sands last night. Anyway, he says that this Rita dame is legit and he seems to know quite a bit about this deal including the Slater angle. How you going to play this one?" Steve grimaced and paced in the small room as he spoke.

"Well based on very recent events, I need all the help I can get. Just give her the facts, I guess and see where it takes her. If Hank is backing her, that might pull some weight with the DA, though I doubt that Samuels or the FBI are going to be too impressed. But Bernie, listen to me. Samuels was just here and I have some bad news for you." He paused as he heard Bernie sigh.

"He's dead, right?" The voice was low and quiet.

"Yeah, Bernie, Samuels just showed me a polaroid they took a half hour ago. They are taking him downtown to make a formal ID, but it was him alright."

"Steve, was it bad? You know what I mean." Steve could hear Bernie's voice crack slightly.

"Yeah, Bern, it was bad, but let's not concentrate on that right now. Can you meet me at Remy's in ten minutes? I don't want her to hear it from them over the phone with no one there."

"Yeah, sure thing I will leave right now, goodbye."

Steve went quickly to the safe in the bedroom closet. He opened it and after a few minutes deliberation he chose a Smith&Wesson snub-nose .38 revolver, the same model of gun that Jack Ruby had used to gun down Oswald nine months before. He locked the door and pulled the blue T-Bird off the gravel driveway and onto the asphalt.

Bernie's car was not in the driveway when Steve pulled off of Twain Avenue and parked his car in Remy's driveway. He had just lit up the first cigarette of the morning when a large black Pontiac pulled in behind him. He saw Bernie's face behind the wheel and relaxed. He put his arm around the shorter man as they walked together toward the house. Steve rang the bell several times and stepped back from the door. When there was no answer, he rang again and walked back into the driveway and looked up at the front upstairs windows. All the curtains were shut tight. He had just indicated to Bernie to ring again, when Remy's white Jaguar XK120 pulled past the two cars at the end of the driveway and stopped beside Steve. She had a white scarf wrapped around her neck and her sunglasses sat on top of her head. Steve noticed her red nail polish matched the red interior of the convertible almost exactly. She opened the low-slung door and looked at Steve from behind the car. She also looked over at Bernie who had moved to a position just behind Steve.

"Steve, Bernie, it's not even nine o'clock in the morning, what are you two up too?" She laughed softly and lifted a brown paper grocery bag from behind the front seat. Steve walked around the front of the car and took the bag from her hand and passed it to Bernie, as Remy stopped short.

"Steve...I...what are you?..." Steve put his hand around her back and pulled her towards him, wrapping his arms around her.

Bernie watched as he said something to her that he could not hear. Remy shrieked and tried to claw away from Steve, turning in his grasp and sobbing on his shoulder at the same time. Remy's legs quivered, and Steve let her down gently on the hood of the car. Bernie put down the bag of groceries and held onto her as she cried. After a few minutes, Remy was able to gain her feet again and held onto Steve as he and Bernie walked her slowly to her front door. She held out her purse weakly to Bernie. He held it open in front of him and sorted through it until his fingers touched the jumble of keys. He held them up and she pointed to one. He opened the door and then helped Steve get Remy over to the couch. She wasn't crying as hard as she had been a few minutes before. She looked up at Steve.

"How?" She put her hand to his face. Her eyes were wide and the tears made dark tracks of mascara down her cheeks. She sobbed involuntarily every three or four seconds.

"I don't know the circumstances, Gem. I just got the word this morning." Remy started crying harder now, her face buried in her hands on her lap. Steve and Bernie took turns holding and consoling her. Bernie went into the next room and called a doctor he knew. When he came back he whispered to Steve and Steve nodded. Twenty minutes later the doctor arrived. Steve recognized him as the house doctor at the Dunes. Bernie and Steve helped Remy upstairs and into bed, and then waited downstairs for the doctor. Bernie shook his head and looked over at Steve.

"Did Angelo Sorelli do this?" His voice broke with emotion. Steve nodded.

"Yeah, I am positive. His MO, and he had the motive. He probably knew where the money was, and once he got it." Steve shrugged. "And so it goes." He shook his head and stretched his arms over his head. He saw the doctor descend the stairs and come into the living room.

"How is she, Doc?" Bernie stood up. "Can I go up and see her?" The doctor shook his head as he was writing something on his pad.

"I have given her a sedative. She should sleep for a while. I am having the pharmacy down the street send over some other medication for when she wakes up. Can someone stay with her for at least a few hours?" Both Steve and Bernie nodded their heads. Bernie looked at Steve.

"I'll stay. You got things to do, I'll call Walter at the deli, they will probably declare it a holiday down there."

"Thanks, Bernie, I will call you in a couple of hours to see how she is doing." He followed the doctor to the door. "I will put her car in the garage before I go, Bern." Bernie waved as Steve let the doctor out the front door and followed him down the long driveway. He opened the garage door and swung the Jag into an empty space. He turned on the garage light and examined the wall safe. There were no signs it had been forced or tampered with. There were several smudgy fingerprints on the chrome face and the handle. Steve made a mental note to tell Brady.

*

THE ALPINE VILLAGE Inn was three-quarters deserted a few minutes before noon, when Steve walked in. He moved up the steps to his right when he didn't see anyone that looked like she might be a Rita Malone in the downstairs Rathskeller area. As he entered the room he was met by a waiter in lederhosen who bowed slightly and was about to speak, when Steve saw the only other person in the room sitting at a table in the back against the wall. He smiled at the waiter and waved his hand toward the back of the room. The waiter smiled and backed out of the way so that Steve could pass. As he reached the middle of the room, Rita Malone stood up to greet him. She was only an inch or two shorter than Steve and as she held out her hand, her white teeth flashed a smile behind the red lipstick. Steve reached for her hand and shaking it gently, smiled back and moved to pull the chair on her side back from the table. Her shoulder length black hair swept forward from her dark face as she stepped in front of the proffered chair and sat down. Steve moved to the other side of the table and holding in his sport coat in at the waist, sat down. When he looked up he met a strong gaze from the light brown eyes. She was not smiling but her expression was one of bemusement.

"Well, the private detective, Steve Cannon in the flesh." She smiled again.

"Well Miss Malone, you say that like it was some kind of big deal. If that is the case, I am afraid you are going to be sorely disappointed." She continued to smile.

"Well things look OK so far." She reached into her purse that lay on the chair beside her and pulled out a small notebook. Steve looked at the notebook and then back into her eyes.

"Can I buy you a drink and then some lunch?" He signaled the waiter to come over to the table.

"I am working, Mr. Cannon, but do help yourself. And Mr. Greenspun insists that the tab is on him." She picked up the menu and flipped slowly through the pages, glancing now and then at Steve as he gave the waiter the drink order. He ordered a scotch and soda for himself and a club soda for Rita. When the waiter had gone, she picked up her notebook and looked at Steve.

"I heard that they found a Mr. Nash Brannock somewhere in the south part of the city shot dead. Mr. Greenspun seems very upset. What do you know about it?" She laid the notebook open on the table but didn't pick up her pen.

"Word gets around quick. Hank and Nash were friends. Ran in the same circles. I guess you know by now and if you don't, you should, that your boss is not the usual type you run across in your business. He is as much a mover and shaker as anyone in this town and knows everybody and I dare say pretty much everything about them as well. The fact that you even called me last night, gives my theories some credence, if only in my own mind." He chuckled and offered his newly arrived glass as a toast. She picked up her soda and clinked their glasses together softly. Steve frowned slightly and took a small sip of the scotch.

"So why has Hank decided that this is worth his time and resources?" He waited while she took a small sip and set down her glass.

"He thinks you are on to something. Wants to know what you know." She stopped as Steve waved his hand in a small gesture.

"I have a relationship with him that goes back a long way. I don't remember him being shy about buttonholing me at parties and sporting events if he wanted to know something. Why you?" He watched as her eyes shifted to the white German china in front of her. Steve waited until she looked up and then leaned in a few inches toward her.

"Listen to me. You and I are going to have to trust each other on this deal or it isn't going to work and it might even make things worse. There are a lot of bad things happening to a lot of people in this town and everyone refuses to see the big picture. So I have no patience for anyone that is going to sit in front of me and not play it straight. So make a choice right here and now, or leave me alone." Steve sat back in his chair. Rita didn't say anything.

"That's Ok, Miss Malone, I get the picture. I have become so persona non grata that even Hank touches me with a ten foot pole, but at least in this case he uses a beautiful one." He laughed sardonically and stood up to leave. Rita reached forward and gently grasped his hand.

"No, don't. Please sit back down, Mr. Cannon." Steve detected a slight bit of panic in her voice. He stood for a few seconds looking down at her and then he pulled the chair back under himself and sat down. He looked at her directly. This time she didn't look at her plate.

"You can trust me, Mr. Cannon. I am good at what I do, and I know how sensitive things can get and how the wrong information in a story can have very bad consequences. I want you to know that all I want to do is find out the reasons why there are two men and a policeman's wife dead in the space of a week. And you are right, Mr. Greenspun has to be cautious, he feels this whole episode needs careful handling." She picked up her notebook and held it up between them. "I think we both want the same thing." Steve nodded and sat back in his seat.

"Are you sure you are up to this?" She looked up quickly from her notebook. Her face was hard.

"Why, Mr. Cannon, because I'm a woman, maybe, and the wrong race on top of that?" They looked each other straight in the eyes for a full five seconds. Steve blinked first.

"So, where do we start? How much do you know about who the main characters are, and how they fit together?" She held up the notebook and riffled the pages. They were all blank. Steve took a deep breath and began to tell the tale as he knew it, only leaving out the Slater connection. When he had finished, she had filled several pages. They ordered a light lunch and while they waited for it to arrive, Steve watched as she bent over her notes, underlining several sections. Presently, she looked up at him.

"Do you mind if I call you Steve and you call me Rita?" Steve nodded. "I have some questions, then, Steve. How does Beech's wife who pretended to be his sister fit into all of this?" Steve took a sip of his drink and watched as the waiter approached their table with two bowls of chicken soup and a plate with a small loaf of pumpernickel surrounded by a mound of seasoned cottage cheese.

"I'm not sure, but I have an idea that she is playing more of a role than is apparent."

"What makes you think that?"

"Because in my experience, guys like Sorelli want to belong, and are used to taking orders. In his case it is just a question of who he takes orders from. I don't think he is smart enough to think up an operation like this, let alone run it on his own. According to the Arizona authorities, Miriam Beech was the suspected brains behind all of the scams they ran down there. And the fact that her husband was the one that was caught and jailed is even more persuading." Rita nodded and wrote something in the margin of one of the notebook pages, and then looked up. Steve could see that she had something to say and was trying to find the right place to start.

"Mr. Greenspun wanted me to tell you something. He and the paper have endorsed Herb Slater for mayor. Part of the reason that Mr. Greenspun wants me on this story is to substantiate or disprove the rumors that have been swirling around City Hall. He wanted me to tell you specifically that whatever evidence you give to me of wrongdoing on anyone's part will be treated fairly. I have to tell you that some of the reports have made him began to rethink the paper's endorsement." She paused and looked at Steve. When he didn't say anything, she continued. "So, Steve, what are you prepared to tell me at this point about Herb Slater's involvement?" Steve took a bite of the pumpernickel and chewed it slowly. When he was done he dabbed his mouth with his napkin.

"Simply this, Rita. I have papers that have Herb Slater's signature on them and are on the County Commission's letterhead, that attest that the commission has deemed the Vegas Wash area fit to be developed residentially and commercially." He looked at her, shrugged and held his palms open. She wrote for a few minutes before she spoke.

"I guess the $64,000 question is what are you going to do with the papers?"

"I'm turning them over to the District Attorney today. Then it will be his decision, not mine. I'm only interested in finding and stopping Sorelli. And before you think that I am on some kind of noble quest, I will hasten to add that he has threatened my life numerous times and attempted to kill me twice and killed the wife of a good friend and the husband of a better one. So to me it is personal. Nothing more, nothing less. If Herb Slater is mixed up and did something wrong or his name was misappropriated, I don't know, somebody else can decide that. I just rang a few doorbells to see if anybody was home, if you know what I mean."

"How does Tommy Carmino feel about that?"

"I don't know, why don't you or Hank ask him?" Steve scoffed. "I thought you didn't know how this town works?"

"I don't, yet, but Mr. Greenspun does and he is a little concerned that this situation may get out of hand and lead to some other unpleasantness."

"Well you can tell Hank for me that I have had a conversation with Tommy about Herb's involvement and I didn't get the feeling that he was going to make a federal case out of it. But here is something you should know, Rita. Tommy Carmino doesn't really care who ends up sitting in the mayor's office because guys like Tommy are always sure that they can get ambitious guys like Herb Slater to bend to their will." Steve sat back in his chair. "First class in Mob 101 is over." Rita smiled slightly and went to put her notebook away. Steve reached across the table and stopped her.

"I have some questions for you if you have the time?" She nodded and put her notebook beside her plate.

"What are you going to do with all the information I have just given to you?" She shrugged.

"I will take this to the law enforcement people handling the case, get their comments, if any, write a story and submit it to Mr. Greenspun."

"Well I can give you a little help there. Detective Polhaus was the lead on the case until they found Beech's body in the desert, then Detective Samuels, head of Homicide took over. Once the bomb went off, the FBI in the persons of Agent Brady and his partner Agent Molini took over at least that part of the investigation. Another place where I am persona non grata so I don't know the division of labor, but I do know that the only cooperation I ever got was from Tam Polhaus and he is on bereavement leave for the duration. So good luck."

Rita Malone smiled and started collecting her belongings. She stood up and offered her hand across the table. Steve stood up and shook it as gently as before.

"Thank you, Steve, this has been very helpful." Steve smiled.

"Well, maybe something good will come of it. Let's make a deal. I will call you with any additional information or ideas I have and you do the same. I have another request. Call me and read me any articles over the phone before they go to print. I don't want to change anything, I just need to know if I need to keep my head down." He held out his hand again. They shook and Rita smiled, patted Steve on the forearm and walked to the head of the stairs. He watched her walk carefully down the narrow steps and turned back to the table, pulled out a cigarette and finished his drink.

After he was finished he went down the stairs to the lobby. He waited a few minutes for the phone booth to become free. He dialed Remy's number and waited. After several rings Bernie picked up the receiver.

"How is she Bern?"

"OK, I guess, Steve, still asleep. Must have been some heavy knockout drops he gave her."

"That's probably all for the good, Bernie. I have to go see Tam for a few minutes and then I need to go to county records downtown and then get back there to you. Ok?"

"Sure thing, no problem, Steve, take your time. I don't think she will even be awake by then."

"Thanks Bern." Bernie laughed.

"Don't thank me, she's my girl too." Steve laughed and rang off. He opened the booth and walked slowly out of the restaurant.

*

THE LARGE SCORCHED spot on Tam's driveway still smelled like cordite as Steve stared at it in the afternoon heat. The front of the garage and part of the house had large irregular gashes left by pieces of the Chevy when it exploded. Steve stepped up onto the porch and rang the bell. As he waited his eyes swept the neat upper middle class neighborhood, one of the older ones south of Charleston Boulevard, home to bankers, lawyers and upwardly mobile family men. Tam opened the door in t-shirt and shorts, his feet were bare. It looked to Steve that he had attempted to shave but with indifferent results. His bloodshot eyes bore into Steve's as he opened the door wider to admit his guest. Inside, Steve felt the chill of real air conditioning and stood by the door until his eyes became accustomed to the lack of light. He turned back towards the detective as Tam closed the door behind him.

"How you holding up, Tam? I know you are probably sick of people asking, but it's just because we have no idea what else to say." Tam snorted, shrugged and indicated that Steve should follow him through the living room to a hall and then into a back bedroom that had been converted to an office. When they walked through the double doors, Steve looked at the spacious room and thought of the office space back at his house.

"Here." Tam held out two fat manila folders that were held together by a thick red rubber band. Steve took them from his hands and sat down on a low bench along the wall nearest the door. He carefully removed the band and began to let the pages of each file turn over slowly in his hands. Tam leaned back against a large oak desk in the middle of the room with his arms crossed.

"That is everything I have collected myself, most of it carbon copies from Samuels file. The only stuff missing is the reports from yesterday." Steve looked up from his study.

"They found Nash shot in the face and rolled up in a rug just off of Warm Springs by Sunset Park. Tam stared straight ahead as if he was looking at something in the middle distance. After a few seconds he looked down at Steve.

"What are you going to do about it?" His voice was calm, but for Tam, Steve thought it was weirdly void of inflection. Steve slid off the subject slightly.

"There is a lot to go over here. Most of it is stuff we have hashed over before, but there may be some details in here that I may have missed. Take me awhile." Tam shook his head slowly. The middle distance stare was back.

"You don't have the luxury of time, it is probably too late for everybody. What was it that old Indian told you? 'Nothing you can do, but he can do plenty'? Well, I think he was right for once." Steve waited for a few seconds.

"I told you Tam, and I meant it. I will kill Angelo Sorelli if it is the last thing I do." He stood up and put his hand on Tam's shoulder.

"You need to call me or Bernie if there is anything you need. Where is your daughter?"

"Georgie's." Tam stepped away from the desk and walked into the living room. When Steve came out of the hallway, Tam was standing with the front door open. Steve walked slowly across to the detective and looked into his eyes for several seconds, then stepped out onto the narrow porch, descended the three steps and walked toward the blue T-Bird. Before he drove away he sat and watched Tam staring at him from the open doorway.

After two hours at the county office of records, Steve had examined everything that pertained to the public business of the county commission for the last year. There was no discussion or any mention at all of any project in the Wash area or even near it. There was plenty of discussion and meeting agenda items devoted to various projects one quarter the size of the one proposed by Beech for Vegas Wash. He had also read much about the hotel resort deal that Jay Sarno was trying to bring to life. He made a mental note to tell Tommy that the name was now to be 'Caesars Palace'. He asked to borrow the phone at the front desk and dialed the office of the District Attorney. He asked for the name that Tam had given him several days ago.

"This is Assistant District Attorney Jim Larsen, to whom am I speaking?"

"Mr. Larsen, my name is Steve Cannon, I work from time-to-time with Detective Tam Polhaus. He gave me your name in connection with a case we have been working on. I wonder if I might stop by and run something by you that pertains to that investigation." There was a pause on the other end.

"Yes. I heard about the explosion yesterday that killed Tam's wife. How is he holding up?"

"Not well, I'm afraid. The matter I wish to see you about is directly connected to the bombing. I am in your building right now if you have some time." Steve heard a whispered conference take place.

"Yes, Mr. Cannon, if you come over right away, I can give you a half an hour."

"Thanks. I will be there shortly."

Steve walked through the marble rotunda of City Hall and through an indoor garden space connecting the city building with the Federal one just next door. He ascended a short staircase and opened the door to the District Attorney's office. On a hat rack just outside one of the inner office doors, a familiar gray fedora was perched. Steve snorted and rapped on the glass. Without a reply he entered into a reception area where a man and a woman sat behind one long table. A door was open to Steve's left and he saw Samuels sitting in a chair in front of a desk. When he saw Steve, he stood up and disappeared from Steve's view. The man was reading a file. The woman looked up expectantly at Steve.

"Can I help you?" Before Steve could answer he was addressed from the open door.

"Come in, Mr. Cannon." The speaker was a tall, dark haired man in his late forties, in his shirt sleeves and wearing a blue suit vest and pants. His tie was slightly loosened at the collar. Steve followed the man into the large office and sat down in a chair the DA indicated across from the desk. Samuels did not look at Steve or greet him, but leaned on the window sill and gazed out over the garden. Steve pushed the files down out of sight beside him in the leather chair. Larsen sat down behind the desk and glancing up at Samuels, leaned toward Steve.

"Well Mr. Cannon, I think I know what you have come about,

and since time is at a premium, let's start right away. You have some evidence in your possession that may implicate a city official in a land fraud, is that right?" Steve looked over at Samuels who made an obvious effort to avoid eye contact. Steve looked Larsen in the eye.

"If I had such information, what would you be prepared to do about it?" Larsen sat back and put a hand to his chin, his forefinger resting on his cheekbone.

"That would depend, of course Mr. Cannon, on what type of evidence it was, how it was obtained and whether or not it could be verified. What do you have to tell me about the three conditions I have just mentioned?" Steve took a deep breath and smiled.

"I have papers on County Commissioner stationary that bear Herb Slater's signature, signing off on the efficacy of developing the Vegas Wash area." He looked over at Samuels who was nervously tapping his fist softly against his mouth. "I retrieved them from the belongings of a man found killed and buried in the desert. I have been over at county records this afternoon and I have seen Herb Slater's signature several hundred times and I am convinced it is genuine."

"Can I see the papers in question, Mr. Cannon?" Samuels had now turned from the window and was glaring down at Steve. Steve shrugged.

"I have some handwritten copies I have produced out in the car that I can give you today." Neither man's eyes went to the files that Steve was sitting on. Samuels erupted angrily.

"What kind of fools to you take us for, Cannon? A copy is worthless. Either give us the originals or face charges." His face had reddened quickly. Steve calmly turned his gaze to Larsen.

"Let's take this step by step, shall we. One of the originals with the signature should be fine to verify if Herb Slater signed it. If that passes muster, then we can talk." Samuels began to sputter a reply, but Larsen held up his hand.

"I think that is a reasonable way to proceed, Mr. Cannon. Can

you please retrieve a signature page and bring it back to this office?"
Steve nodded and stood and turned from his chair concealing the
two file folders from Samuels view but not from Larsen. He looked
Larsen square in the eyes for a split second. A hint of a smile played
in the corners of the attorney's mouth. Steve took only two strides
to leave the office and enter the reception area. He slowed, took a
deep breath and descended the wide marble stairs to the floor of the
marble rotunda. He walked across the open expanse and into a side
alcove by the front door. On the far wall there were three rows of
lockers built into the marble facing. They were placed there for the
purpose of holding items that someone might not want to carry any
farther into a county or federal building. Steve smiled as he twisted
his torso slightly and felt the .38 resting in the holster in the middle
of his back. He removed the three sheets of originals, keeping one
and placing the two folders in the locker. He pocketed the key as he
made his way back up the steps toward the DA's office.

DA Larsen looked over the document carefully. Without comment he looked up at Samuels who was peering over his shoulder,
and who at first did not see the attorney's gaze and then abruptly
straightened when he became aware of it.

"Detective Samuels, do you mind waiting outside for a few
minutes while I speak to Mr. Cannon in private?" Samuels stepped
toward the desk and started to sputter a reply. Larsen held up
his hand.

"Detective Samuels, if you please." He pointed toward the door.
Samuels glared at Steve and stormed out the door. Larsen pressed
the intercom on his desk.

"Miss Rhodes, would you make sure that Detective Samuels is
comfortable in the outer reception area?" He sat back in his chair
and looked appraisingly at Steve.

"Mr. Cannon, I think we should have a private chat here so
that we understand each other and there are no misapprehensions
on either side. Agreed?"

"Yes, of course."

"This office has been investigating Herb Slater and two other board members for several months. There is a noisy group of citizens who have lodged complaints. Mostly unexplained cash deposits and living beyond the means of a councilman's pay, that sort of thing. These are the first documents, assuming they are genuine, that may come up to the standard of proof that will stand up in a court of law. But you can understand being a long time resident of this fair city that there are pressures and crosscurrents that complicate even the simplest of procedures." Steve nodded.

"So, I will pursue the authentication of the signature and we can go from there. In the mean time I am going to have to ask you to refrain from giving anyone else this information." Steve sat back in the chair and crossed his legs.

"Too late for that Mr. Larsen, plenty of people know about the papers and the fake land deal. Too many to keep a lid on it now. If that is the criteria, I would have to say that is not much of a plan." Steve wished he could have a cigarette, but glancing around the office, he got the impression that not much smoking was done.

"Let me be honest, Mr. Cannon. Detective Samuels, as much of a pain as he can be is not my only problem. The FBI is involved not only because of the bombing, but also because of the corruption allegations that have been made over the course of two years. You have just hit a nerve because you have something tangible. There are powerful factions in this county who want to see Herb Slater and his cronies running City Hall and they have not been too happy even before this. But let me tell you something you may not know. I don't care. If there is something here that requires a remedy that I am charged with enforcing, that is how it will be. I give you my word on that." He smiled quickly. "I hope those files you came in with are more secure than just inside your car." Steve laughed.

"Yes, they are. Thanks for asking."

"Mr. Cannon, I have to work with many people through this office. Let's take just one example of someone we both know: Mr. Carmino. He, shall we say, appreciates my position, and I appreciate his, and we both take great pains to sharply define our boundaries. I have found that our common ground is keeping our respective bosses happy. That way, things get done and the large important matters aren't held hostage by turf wars. Do I make myself clear?" Steve nodded.

"By the same token, Attorney Larsen, I can assure you that when Tommy Carmino looks at the candidates running for mayor, he sees more of a distinction than a difference."

"You are probably correct on that, but in this case it is more a matter of perception and whose ox might get gored in the future." Larsen stood up and extended his hand to Steve.

"I appreciate your cooperation and I will be in touch."

"Thanks for your time, it has been very enlightening." Steve shook back and walked out through the small reception room into the bigger one. Samuels was nowhere to be seen. Steve sauntered out to his car and looked casually around. The driver side door was unlocked. Pretending to look for something in his pockets, he went back into the building and removed the folders from the lockers. He moved to a bank of pay phones and dialed the number of Gaudin Ford. When he got Dwayne on the line he was able to confirm that the Jeep was ready and that Dwayne would follow him back to Remy's in the car and that a third employee would tail them and take Dwayne back to the dealership. When he arrived, he didn't feel comfortable letting someone else drive the T-Bird so Dwayne followed in Steve's car.

He arrived to find that Remy was still sleeping and Bernie was on the phone. He spent the next ten minutes carefully searching the desk in the library. Finding nothing helpful he went back downstairs to Bernie. Bernie was exasperated.

"Samuels calls two hours ago. Wanted Remy to go downtown right then to identify Nash. I told him that wasn't going to happen, he got steamed, so I got the doc to call him and tell him she was in no shape, then I got on the phone to Sheriff Ralph and he convinced Samuels that I can make the ID, so that's where I gotta get to now." Bernie threw up his hands.

"I wish you didn't have to do this, Bernie, it isn't going to be pleasant. I would go in your stead, but I know that Samuels would never go for that." Bernie waved him off.

"Don't worry about it, I saw plenty of stiffs on the South side, believe me. I don't care as long as Remy doesn't have to do it." Steve nodded.

"I got my car back and yours is outside for you, I will stay here with Remy. Probably stay the night." Bernie nodded and stood to go. Steve walked him to the door.

"Hey Bernie, one more thing. I think you should buy that piece of land you were telling me about. Only take your time developing it, OK?" Bernie stopped with his hand on the door handle.

"Why? What's wrong with it?" He frowned.

"Nothing, Bern, nothing at all. It's just that I think it got left out of the deal by mistake and based upon the updated plans I saw, Sarno isn't going to have enough room for his parking lot and tennis pavilion without that piece. Buy it, maybe sink five grand into an architect that can draw up some plans or build a scale model to make it look like you are serious, then sit back and wait." Bernie smiled.

"Badda boom, badda bing? Is that what you got in mind?" Bernie laughed. "I will do it if you let me lend you fifty grand for a percentage. You can pay me back when we sell it back to them. Whatta ya say?"

"Naw, Bernie, that kinda stuff never works out for me. I don't want to jinx it for you. Besides, you might need someone to help set up security for your new casino, right?" Bernie smiled.

"You bet, but the offer is still open, think it over and thanks for the advice. Where do you come up with this stuff? I'm supposed to come up with this kind of stuff." Bernie shook his head as he walked out the door and down the walkway to his car.

Steve took the stairs two at a time and quietly opened the door to Remy's bedroom. She was still asleep, so he went back down to his car and retrieved the files. Back up in her room he pulled a chair over to the side of the bed, turned on a light and adjusted it so it would not shine on Remy's face. He then began to carefully sort the files into two stacks. In one stack were documents he had already examined. In the second stack he placed those that were new to him or that appeared to contain information he had not seen before. The second stack was much smaller than the first and much of it appeared to come out of the files that Tam was able to liberate from Samuels. Samuels had used his contacts to gather more background information on all the principals and it appeared that Tam had enough time to collect the documents but not enough to organize or analyze them. It was on a page that had come from the FBI office in Los Angeles that Steve found what he was looking for. The page contained former aliases and addresses for Miriam Beech. At the bottom of the page was an address for her sister, Helen. The address was in North Las Vegas and only two miles from Steve's house as the crow flies. He copied the address down and put the paper in his wallet. He carefully examined each of the remaining documents. Nowhere could he find any mention of law enforcement following up on the location. He was just going over the options he had with this new information, when he saw Remy open her eyes and look around the room. When she saw Steve, she smiled.

"How long have I been asleep?" Steve looked at his watch. "Most of the day, at least eight hours. How are you feeling?" She moistened her lips carefully with her tongue.

"A little groggy. A few minutes ago I thought it was a dream, but it isn't is it?"

"No. Gem, it's not a dream." She moved to get out of bed. Steve stood up quickly.

"Careful. Take it slowly, I think the sedative the doc gave you was pretty potent." Remy ignored the remark and walked around the corner and into the bathroom. She returned five minutes later and had put on a new bathrobe.

"I'm hungry. Can we go downstairs and can get something to eat?"

"Sure, Gem, I will make something for you." He went to her side and she slipped her arm under his as he lead her out the bedroom door and down the stairs. He made her comfortable on the couch while he went into the kitchen and pulled out the ingredients he would need for scrambled eggs and toast. When he was finished and went into the living room, he found her asleep. He woke her gently and followed her to the breakfast bar in the kitchen where he had set down a plate and a place setting for her. Her poured her a cup of coffee and sat next to her while she ate. She ate slowly and deliberately. Steve got up and poured himself a cup of the coffee and leaned on the bar across from her and waited until she finished.

"I think I should spend the night here if you will let me." She pushed the plate a few inches away and took a sip of the coffee.

"I don't think I want that, Steve." She shook her head. "No. definitely not. I know you are trying to be kind, but I need to be by myself." Steve had been looking at the floor while she spoke. Now he looked over at her and waited until she was looking at him.

"Gem, I love you and I want what is best for you. I know you need time to sort things out, I know that, but I also know there are things I can help you with, and I don't think you should be alone tonight. I will stay in another part of the house. Don't you think you will feel safer if you know I am here?" Remy stared at her plate.

"I don't know, Steve, I don't know what I think and you know what? I don't even care. All I feel is numb. I want to be alone." She picked up her coffee cup and walked back into the living room. Steve followed her and remained standing after she sat back down on the couch.

"I am going right home and I will be there all night. Call me if you need anything at all. Promise me?" She looked at him briefly and nodded. "I will call you tomorrow, around eight, Ok?" She nodded.

"Steve, I am sorry the way I have been behaving. I know that you are just trying to help me. Since LA, I have spent most of that time confused. I have been trying to work out where I could have done something different, both for Nash and for you. I think today I know the answer is that there is no answer. We all follow our hearts in some way and those are decisions that can't be taken back."

He went over to her, and kissed the top of her head. 'Gem, don't worry about it. It will all work out the way it is supposed to, you'll see." He kissed her lips gently and then walked out of the living room and closed the front door behind him.

*

A WHITE PICKET fence in need of paint encircled the corner lot of the house that matched the address on the police report. Steve sat across the street and several doors down. He had parked in back of a pick-up truck and the adjacent driveway held two project cars that provided cover for the faded red Jeep. The house was dark and there were no cars visible either in the driveway or parked on the street. After half an hour, Steve was about to leave when a green '56 Chevy station wagon came slowly around the corner and pulled partway into the driveway. A medium height woman with dark hair left the driver's door open and pulled up the garage door. The first third of the garage that Steve could see from his vantage point was starkly empty, as if no one lived there. After turning on the inside garage light, the woman returned to the car and pulled it slowly into the garage. Just as she pulled the door down behind her, Steve thought he saw some movement in the back seat of the Chevy. He waited for several minutes, but no lights visible from the street came on. Steve drove around the corner and took a right down the next street. He could see the top quarter of the house and there were no lights on in that portion as well. He drove for five minutes and arrived back at his house, entering the driveway from the opposite direction than the one he usually used.

After filling several pages in his notebook, he dialed the number he used the day before to contact Agent Brady. This time it was Brady who picked up the phone. Steve decided to get to the point.

"I need to know Agent Brady, how much you want to find Miriam Beech."

"Miriam Beech? The murder victim's wife? Don't need her, our office has already signed off on the official ID of the victim. Why do you ask?" Steve took a deep breath.

"Because Agent Brady, I believe she is behind the land deal and the deaths of Nash Brannock and Tam Polhaus's wife. Did you read the file that Tam put together?"

"Yeah, Mr. Cannon, I read it. A whole lot of conjecture if you ask me. I don't see how you are connecting her to either killing." Steve decided to try a new tact.

"Who do you think planted the bomb in Tam's car as well as my own?" There was a short silence.

"Dunno. But we are putting together the profiles of person or persons who might have done it and we are checking it against criminals who are known to have this type of thing as part of their MO, and who may have been in town and who may have had the opportunity."

"And what could have been their motivation, do you think?" Steve had been only partially successful in keeping the sarcasm out of his voice.

"I am only giving you my time, Mr. Cannon, in recognition of the fact that you are a victim of attempted murder. When I make an arrest, I will make sure my office informs you. By the way, you can pick up your car tomorrow." The line went dead. Steve looked at the receiver in his hand for several seconds before he put it down in disgust. He dialed Remy's number but after ten unanswered rings hung up. He was just walking out of the office to check on her, when the phone rang again. He picked it up on the second ring.

"Hey, Slick, you are a hard man to get on the phone. Why don't you get yourself an office for chrissakes. I got room here, or if that don't float your boat, how about somewhere downtown which seems to be more your speed anyway?" Steve turned on the reel to reel.

"No, thanks, Tommy, I don't like being available all the time. Because when I am, I have too many conversations like this one. What is it now? Three homey chats in a week? I think you should start wearing my letter sweater and I should buy you a locket or something."

"Enough of the crap, funny guy, how you have made this situation worse than it was last week, I'll never know, but you got a rare talent for mucking up the works, I know that for a fact."

"Well if all the king's horses and all the king's men can't come up with Sorelli, I don't see how that is my doing, Tommy, do you? And this guy and his sidekicks that aren't anywhere to be found in this burg, was the way I think you put it, are still able to plant bombs in the same night at two locations six miles apart. So either they are ghosts or supernaturally good, or maybe they are useful idiots to someone who is big enough to protect them and who might be protesting too much. Whatta think Tommy?" There was a loud silence on the other end of the line.

"OK, Slick. This isn't getting either of us anywhere. I now got FBI crawling over all our interests and they are using the bombings as an 'open sesame' to bring up old charges and inquiries that were shut off years ago. So I need to come up with something or preferably someone that has a stronger scent than we do in this deal. And now I turn to you, who if I am not mistaken is the mastermind who produced this little jigsaw puzzle. So let's hear a plan that I can use to solve my problem." The loud silence was now on Steve's side.

"OK. Here it is. I know where Miriam Beech is probably holed up." Tommy interrupted.

"Why do I care where some broad chooses to squat? You better come up with something better than that." Steve continued as if Tommy hadn't spoken.

"If she is there, Sorelli is either hiding there or at least makes regular visits. Give me two guys to even the numbers and I think we can get Sorelli and Miriam Beech and Herb Slater in the bargain."

"I have no idea what you are talking about, but I am out of strategic options. I can give you Jack Cathay and Little Moe. They aren't doing anything productive at the moment anyways. Meet them at that coffee shop by The Blue Angel Motel in an hour. This better work, Slick, or all our heinies are in a sling." Tommy cursed under his breath and hung up.

Steve sat back and thought for a few seconds. He then went into his bedroom and pulled out a leather bomber jacket with large front pockets out of his closet. Reaching into the back of the safe he lifted out a sawed-off twelve gauge shotgun. Back at the closet he emptied a box of Double 00 shotguns shells into the pockets of the jacket, twelve in one side, thirteen in the other. He thought better of the number thirteen and threw a shell back into the box.

August 25

THE COFFEE SHOP that shared a parking lot with the Blue Angel Motel was empty except for the two mobsters when Steve came through the door at one in the morning. Steve had met Jack twice before, a taciturn no nonsense personality with a deep voice almost as rough as Angelo Sorelli's. He was six feet tall and 240, but he seemed puny next to the guy sharing the table. Little Moe, whose real name was Maurice Gladman, was six foot seven and had wrestled professionally where he had been billed as 'Little Moe, the Jewish Giant'. Steve had never met him before but neither man responded when Steve held out his hand. Steve shrugged his shoulders and pulled over a chair from a nearby table so he could face both men who were overfilling the small booth. He looked quickly around the dimly lit diner and caught the eye of the waitress on duty. She held up a pot of coffee and Steve nodded. He turned back to the table and looked at Jack who was staring at his jacket.

"You cold?" His deep blue eyes were slightly watery and his face seemed much redder than the last time he had seen him.

"No. Why?" Jack reached over and felt the sleeve of the leather jacket. Steve laughed.

"Lucky jacket." He looked over at Little Moe who suddenly became more interested in his coffee cup. Steve waited until the waitress put the cup and a small metal pitcher of cream on the table and left.

"Look, Jack, I don't know how much Tommy has told you, but this might be one of those situations that could get out of hand very quickly. I need to know if you are going to back me or scamper off and tell some tale to daddy and leave me hanging. I have always known you as a straight shooter, so if that is what's cooking you can tell me now, I will go alone and Tommy will never be any the wiser." He stared straight at Jack who held his gaze.

"No problem here, Cannon. I just got one question. Is there a chance I get Sorelli in my sights tonight?" Steve nodded.

"Then I am in. What's the plan?" Steve turned to Little Moe.

"What about you, Moe? Same deal goes for you." Jack cleared his throat to get Steve's attention.

"He don't talk much unless you know him awhile. I'll vouch for him. He will do all right." Steve looked quickly at Little Moe, then back at Jack, then shrugged.

"I figure that stealthing these guys is a waste of time. I will go up and knock on the door, see who is there. If anyone is there, at the very least, that should stir up something. You guys back me up and we will see how it goes." Jack arched his brows.

'That's it? That's the plan?" He snorted and took a big gulp of coffee.

"Well what would you rather do Jack? All three of us bust in the door and shoot up the place, hoping one of the bullets hits Sorelli and not some innocent civilian housesitting or something?"

Steve arched his brows as well. Jack screwed up his face and mumbled something under his breath into his coffee cup. Steve leaned forward.

"What are you carrying?" Jack looked casually around the room and opened his light windbreaker jacket. He had two under arm rigs, one with a .357 magnum on one side and a 1911 .45 on the other. Jack jerked his head slightly towards little Moe.

"He's got a little 9mm popper, but he is pretty good with it for a big guy. I suppose you have a boy scout knife, right?" Steve shook his head.

".38 snub nose and a sawed off twelve gauge that stays with you." Jack snorted again.

"You gonna knock on the door with that? I might as well shoot you now and tell Tommy you couldn't stand the pressure and took the easy way out." He laughed and looked over at Little Moe who snickered and looked down at his cup. He looked back over at Steve and quit laughing when he saw the look in Steve's eyes.

"Listen, Jack. I'm not here to huckle chuckle with you or your mute friend. I'm here to kill Sorelli, not take him down and let him wriggle out of the justice system. If you're not up to it, don't come. You are Tommy's idea not mine. If you go, we do it my way. If this doesn't work, you know where to start looking for Sorelli again and you can run that operation all by yourself. We understand each other?" Steve waited until the mobster nodded. He then looked directly at Little Moe. Little Moe looked quickly over at Jack and then nodded slowly as well.

"Ok, let's go. Keep close to me, the house is way out in North Las Vegas."

A half hour later, Steve pulled slowly up to the curb and parked just short of the entrance to the driveway. The black Ford station wagon with Jack at the wheel parked across the street far enough back so that Jack and Little Moe could see the front door and not be blocked by Steve's Jeep. Steve walked casually over to the car and leaned against the driver side door.

"Who has the shotgun?" Little Moe raised it up to just below the window.

"Good. Alright, let's see if anyone is at home."

Steve walked back across the street and skirting the back of his car, opened the short white gate. There was a light in the upstairs window behind the closed curtains. Steve moved casually down the narrow sidewalk, took a single step up onto the darkened porch and put his ear carefully to the door. With his ear still to the door he felt behind him with his right hand until he found the button for the doorbell. He pushed twice, but there was no sound of a chime from inside the house. He waited a few seconds, then straightened up and looked back toward the street. From his angle, Steve could just make out Little Moe's white face peering at the house from the back seat of the station wagon. Steve cursed softly under his breath and knocked heavily on the door. He quickly stepped to one side and slipped both hands into the slit pockets on the front of the leather jacket. His right hand closed around the little revolver. For several seconds there was no sound. Steve was looking at the front door when he heard the sound of a door opening, but it took two or three seconds for him to realize it was not the door in front of him, but was coming from behind. Steve spun around and leapt off the porch onto the lawn trying to get a better angle on the driveway and the garage door. At the same moment, the green Chevy hurtled from the garage at high speed, someone in the back pushing open the lift gate window. Instantly, there was a loud roar and an orange flame reached half way across the street as a shotgun blast tore off a corner of the picket fence, the pellets rattling against the side of the house just above Steve's head forcing him to stop moving and dive into the grass. The big Chevy careened backwards down the driveway and tore through the fence crashing into the front of the Jeep. Bright gun flashes spit out the far side of the Chevy towards Jack and Little Moe. Steve came up to one knee and sent two quick rounds into the windshield on the driver's side. As he fired he could not see who the driver was, but the impact of his bullets forced the man to turn his attention away from the street. Another blast from the shotgun tore up part of the lawn ten feet in front of Steve. As he turned around, Steve locked eyes with Jimmy Scatho, a large white bandage covering most of his neck and lower jaw. Steve took aim again, just as Jimmy pressed on the gas and spun the car in a wide arc toward the street and with two wheels on the sidewalk, the car screeched around the corner and was gone. Steve had started running as soon as Jimmy had made his move, but he was only able to get one aimed shot off at the back of the disappearing car. He quickly ran over to the black Ford. The windshield was spider webbed from six or seven bullets and there were several more in both side doors. There was also one in Little Moe's arm and even though he was pressing it hard against the side of the door frame, Steve could see plenty of blood leaking onto the floorboard. He whipped around and stuck his head through the driver door window.

"Jack. You OK?" Jack sprung up from the front seat with his belt in his hand and reaching over the back of the seat began to strap it tightly around Little Moe's upper arm.

"Yeah. Let me get this on him and then I am getting us out of here. That bastard took two point blank shots at me. I don't know why I am still walking and talking." The belt secured, he slid back down into the driver's seat and looked up at Cannon.

"You better disappear fast. This place is going to be crawling with cops in about ten seconds." Jack reved the car's engine and lurched away from the curb. Two seconds later he had disappeared around the same curve as Sorelli had thirty seconds before. Steve walked back over to the Jeep, placed his gun on top of the hood and was surveying the front end damage when the first black and white came to a noisy halt beside him. Steve turned away from the officers and interlocked the fingers of his hands on top of his head. Several more squad cars arrived as the one of the first officers placed handcuffs on both of Steve's wrists, while his partner moved toward the garage, his pistol drawn and held with two hands pointed to the ground.

*

STEVE WAS SEATED in the back of the squad car when Detective Samuels separated himself from a small knot of officers he had been conferring with and leaned into the back window the farthest from Steve.

"Well, Mr. Cannon, seems like you had yourselves quite the little party here tonight. Wanna get a beer and talk about it?" Samuels laughed at his little joke as he walked back over to the officers and gave instructions to two of them. They both turned and looked at Steve briefly and then nodded their heads. Steve craned his neck and watched as the officers who had entered the house now returned to the front lawn. By their body language, Steve was able to ascertain that there was no one else inside. Steve sat back in the seat and grimaced. Where were Miriam and her sister? How had Sorelli reacted so quickly and why did Little Moe shoot before they had barely cleared the garage? Jack and Little Moe had been only ten feet away from the Chevy for at least five seconds, yet it did not appear that anyone in the other car had been hit. Steve was still going over the events of the night when the two officers got into the car. Steve did not recognize either of them as they both glanced back at him and then at each other. Steve leaned very carefully over to his right and pressed against the door handle hoping they had forgotten to drop the lock, but it was tight and did not budge. The squad car pulled away from the scene and left the neighborhood, but turned left toward Nellis Air Force base instead of right toward downtown and the police station. After two blocks the car slowed and bumped over the curb, moving slowly through a large vacant lot. In the headlights, Steve could see a long line of bushes a little higher than the patrol car and several mounds of old tires and garbage scattered around. The cop driving cut the lights as the other emerged from the passenger side and checked out the immediate area. He bent down at the open door and nodded to the driver. The driver turned and smiled at Steve.

"Time for a little exercise, boy-o." He got out and walked around to Steve's door, yanked it open and pulled Steve out by his neck and onto the ground. Steve tried to get to his knees, but the cop put a shoe on his ribs and pushed him back down. The other cop had opened the trunk and now came around to stand in front of Steve. Steve could see the end of the dense rubber club that he held in his hand. The first cop grabbed Steve by his hair and pulled him up until he was sitting on his knees. The second cop put the end of the billy club under Steve's chin and forced him to look up.

"Now, you're going to tell us who else was there with you." He jabbed the end of the club into Steve's throat. Steve gagged and then spit on the cop's shoe.

"I don't know what you are talking about. I just went up and knocked on the door, they came barreling out of the garage guns blazing. I dropped to my knees and got off three shots before they took off. That was it." The club was pulled back and was starting back down when the other cop put his hand out to stop it.

"Way too many of the witnesses heard multiple shots from both sides of the street, at least one of which was a shotgun. You're lying and you got one more chance to give up the real story." He let go of the arm that held the club and stepped back.

"There was a shotgun. You can check the side of the house behind where I was standing. There are pellet marks all over it."

"Then what sawed off the top of the fence in back of your car?" Steve shrugged. The cop with the club had just taken a step back and was winding up to swing, when bright headlights illuminated the scene. Another squad car slid to a halt behind the first one and for a few seconds a large cloud of dust enveloped everyone. Steve quickly rose to his feet and feeling the car behind him retreated to the far side of the cruiser. When the dust cleared, Steve saw the cop, Gateson, he knew from the hospital standing in front of the two cops with his gun drawn but pointed at the ground.

"OK officers, stand down." He looked from one to the other. The one with the club threw it on the ground. The other cop briefly held his hands in the air and walked over to his car and got back into the driver's seat without even glancing at Steve.

"I will take the suspect in. I think you better get back to Samuels and see if he's got any more dirty work for you." He made a show of slowly putting his semi-automatic back in the holster. The cop bent over to pick up the club.

"Leave it." The cop who was bent halfway over, straightened, then walked around the front of the car where Steve was standing. Steve and the cop glared at each other until the squad car pulled around the biggest mound of tires and disappeared into a new cloud of dust.

Steve stood and watched as the dust settled down around them. The cop snorted.

"So predictable. They have to do everything the shortcut way." He shook his head.

"Thanks for saving me from a beating." The cop nodded. Steve followed him back to the squad car and slid into the backseat after the cop had opened the door for him. They drove in silence for a few blocks after they pulled back onto the paved street.

"A few of us old hands checked up on Samuels after he had been here a couple of months. Asked ourselves why someone would leave the LA police department to come here. Turns out that they were glad to get rid of him, the citizen complaints dried up after he left. Now it is our turn. What did it for me was that he is ex-FBI and none of them will have anything to do with him. Speaks volumes, if you ask me. So now he has his little cadre of cops who think they are going to get ahead, but we will make sure they regret it when he moves on." He looked at Steve in the rearview mirror, Steve nodded.

"Anyone you want me to call for you when we get to the station? You know. Unofficially?" Steve smiled.

"Yeah, call Tam. It will give him something to do." The cop nodded.

"Yeah. Maybe it will get his mind on something else." They were quiet until they reached the station. Steve followed the cop in through the garage entrance to the booking bays. A half hour later Steve sat alone in one of the interrogation rooms. The clock on the wall said it was quarter to four. The door opened and Agent Brady stood in the doorway finishing a conversation with someone in the hall. Presently he turned toward Steve and entered the room. He was smiling.

"I told you that I would inform you when I made an arrest. I guess I saved myself a phone call." He laughed to himself as he pulled out the chair across from Steve and sat down.

"I want a cigarette."

"Later. Plenty of time for that back in your cell." Brady slapped a thick file folder on the table and looked across at Steve.

"I just have a few questions for you, Mr. Cannon, and then Samuels can have you all to himself." Steve looked past him at the wall.

"Can you identify any of the people at the scene beside yourself?" Steve looked at the agent.

"There were three of them. The only one I could identify was Jimmy Scatho, he was driving." Brady gazed at Steve for a few seconds, then opened the file and pushed two pictures toward Steve. Steve looked down at the mug shots of Jack Cathay and Little Moe.

"Nope. Who are they?" Brady picked them up and went to slide them back in the file. Steve saw Tommy Carmino's mug shot before Brady closed the flap of the file.

"They were there all right, Mr. Cannon. Are you sure that you don't want to reconsider your statement?" Steve sighed.

"I knocked on a door and got into a gunfight with three guys in a green Chevy station wagon, only one of which I can identify. It was all over in five seconds and I was lucky to get off the three shots I did." He shrugged. Brady looked at him for several seconds and then without comment, stood up and left the room. Samuels pushed past Brady as soon as the door opened. He did not sit down but paced back and forth in front of the table. He had his gray hat on and his rain coat which was held open by his hands on his hips.

"Well you went and did it now." He laughed. "That was quite a stunt you pulled. Who put you up to it? A couple of names and I think you walk by eight this morning. What do you say?" He stopped in front of the table and looked at Steve with his head held back. He was smiling.

"Don't know what you are talking about Samuels. I have told you and the other cops what happened at least six times already. I don't see what else you can expect me to do."

"Oh really? Let's start with the fact that I got witnesses all up and down the street that all say that at least twenty shots were fired including at least one from a shotgun and the gun flashes were coming from both sides of the street. So you expect me to believe that out of that many, only three were yours and you are still sitting here in the pink?" Samuels snorted. Steve shrugged.

"Just lucky, I guess. It happened pretty fast. They came out of that garage shooting, might have taken them a few seconds to figure out where I was." Samuels began to pace again.

"So let me see if I got your story right here. You knock on the door at one thirty in the morning. They look out and see you standing on the porch and this makes them quake in their boots so much that they grab every gun they can and make like Bonnie and Clyde out the garage door? Is that what you are serving up here?" Steve shrugged again.

"That's how it happened. I guess you will have to ask them what they were thinking." Samuels stopped pacing and leaned on one hand against the wall."

"Well, you are going to get a lot of time to think up a new theory because you aren't getting out of here for a long while. You know why? Because I can keep you on ice until I gather enough evidence to keep you inside forever. And just to help you along with a new theory, let me tell you what I got. A black Ford station wagon was seen speeding along Nellis Boulevard three minutes after the call came in. Now once I find that car and the low lifes inside it, maybe they will give us both the real lowdown. What do you think now, Mr. Cannon?" Steve laughed.

"I think the number of cars of any description speeding around that time of night will probably keep you and your sidekicks busy for a month. But suit yourself, detective, don't let me spoil your fun." Samuels started to speak again, but was interrupted by the door opening and one of the cops from the vacant lot leaning in and whispering in Samuel's ear. They both quickly disappeared into the hallway. Three minutes later, the door opened and Tam walked into the center of the room and stood looking at Steve. Tam was fully dressed and was wearing a brown suit that Steve had never seen before. He was clean shaven and except for some puffiness in his face, he looked normal. Steve smiled up at the detective. Tam did not smile back.

"What?" Steve held out his palms. Tam looked at him for quite a while before he spoke.

"Is this supposed to be some type of psychological therapy for me? Or is my phone number the only one you can ever remember off the top of your head?" Steve smiled and shrugged.

"You seem to be very good at what you do, Tam, I can hardly deny you the pleasure of pulling those strings like you do to get me out of here."

"Well so happens, I am just killing time. You are in too deep in this mess for me. If you see the light of day, you can thank Larsen on this one." Tam sat down wearily in the chair across from Steve.

"You called Larsen?" Tam waved him off. Steve scoffed.

"This isn't that big a deal, Tam. I knock on a door and Sorelli got steamed about it and took it out on the neighborhood." Tam nodded slowly.

"Except they think you went there with a small army intending to wipe them all out, though there are several ideas about who you were after and why. Brady thinks that you and some mobsters were after another gang of mobsters that planted the bombs. Samuels thinks that you were part of the shady land deal from the start and bumped off Beech and Nash and the bombs were just retribution."

"And who was in this army of mine? Bernie and Skipper?" Tam was not in the mood to smile.

"I know you have access to other resources, shall we say, but I don't care. All I want to know is if Sorelli stopped a bullet?" Tam's jaw was flexing as he spoke.

"To tell you the truth, Tam, it was too dark and it happened too fast. I only saw Jimmy Scatho and shot twice at him, but since he was driving at the time and the car went around the curve like Parnelli Jones himself was behind the wheel, I am pretty sure he was in one piece when he left." Tam looked in Steve's eyes and nodded slowly.

"That's what I figured. That's how these things usually go. If you don't have consistent training to fall back on, it goes by in a flash and you are left wondering what the hell happened." He smiled weakly at Steve and got up slowly.

"I've done my job. I hope Larsen springs you soon. Stop by and see me if you have an update." He shuffled a little as he walked toward the door.

"See ya, Tam. Thanks for the quick thinking with Larsen." Tam waved wearily. The door closed behind Tam and Steve was alone again. After another twenty minutes the door opened again and Assistant DA Larsen entered the room. He was wearing a beige car coat over a black shirt and gray slacks. He sat down and shook his head.

"I guess this falls under the heading of taking the law into your own hands, wouldn't you say, Mr. Cannon." He held his hands in front of him, palms spread on the table.

"I think it comes more under the heading of someone doing what the cops refuse to do. I have been laying out the evidence on this one for everyone from the start and the only one that gives me any credence is Tam, who is off the case. So, yeah, I do what I always do, follow whatever leads I have until I find out what I need to find out." Larsen sat back in his chair and smiled briefly before his brow furrowed.

"Well, Mr. Cannon, I take everything you say seriously and along those lines, let me tell you that a handwriting expert has agreed with you that the signature you gave me is indeed Herb Slaters'. It is still early on that and I will have to eventually get the FBI to verify the handwriting, but I think I have enough to proceed. If you can get me all the originals, then I can begin." Steve nodded.

"Sure, I'm a little busy right now, but as soon as I can, you will have those." Larsen smiled.

"They are processing you out as we speak. Shouldn't take more than an hour. I have filed you as a material witness in a case under my jurisdiction and that takes precedent over Samuels, at least. Brady thinks you being out will lead him where he wants to go, wherever that is, but either of them could discover more evidence and put you right back in here, so be careful. Here take this." He handed a small business card to Steve.

"It has my home number on it. For those three in the morning calls." Steve laughed.

"Well, I am sure that Tam will appreciate this." Steve put it away in his pocket. Larsen stood up to leave. He looked down at Steve.

"One more thing, Mr. Cannon. Angelo Sorelli is now a federal fugitive and wanted for the bomb plants. That means federal marshals under my direction are now available to help should you get a line on him again. I assume that is who you were hoping to surprise last night, right?" Steve looked up impassively.

"Yeah, it was Miriam's sister's house. I thought that there was a good chance he might show." Larsen nodded gravely.

"Personal revenge is not the hand maiden of justice, Mr. Cannon. Think about that for me. Will you?" Larsen threw a small salute at Steve and turned and walked through the door before Steve could reply. Steve smiled and chuckled to himself.

Twenty-five minutes later, the cop who had rescued him from the vacant lot, opened the door and indicated that Steve should follow him. As he was being processed out at the window, he asked about the Mustang. Gateson volunteered to bring it around for him. Steve opened the brown paper bag he was given and was not surprised to see the empty holster inside. He smiled to himself as he looked down the short hall and saw three pay phone cubicles just ten feet away. He had just put away his small address book and dropped his coins into the slot when Officer Gateson came into the hall and pressed the keys to the Mustang into his hand.

"Thanks. I owe you one." The cop just smiled and nodded as he continued through the door into the holding cell area.

There were nine rings before the slightly groggy voice came on the line.

"Who is this?" The voice was irritated. Steve smiled into the receiver.

"Hey Tommy, have you been getting a good night's sleep?" There was a short snort on the other end.

"Yeah, I am hoping this is just a continuation of a nightmare I was having, because with you on the other end, I know this is gonna be bad news."

"Well, good and bad, Tommy, but I guess it all depends how you look at it."

"Who's dead?"

"Nobody for sure, but Little Moe won't be lifting weights for a while."

"How bad?"

"Not too. But Jack blew out of there so fast I couldn't really evaluate it, so you will have to ask him." Tommy sighed.

"Jack knows the procedures, he'll take care of it. Did everyone get away clean?"

"Well that is the good news, Tommy. Not only did they get

away, but since nobody is really sure who was there, nobody will likely know how useless your organization is when it comes to lowering the boom. Tommy, you are going to have to get those guys out of the casinos and into the sunshine on the pistol ranges."

"What are you talking about?"

"Jack and Little Moe exchanged at least twenty-five shots with Sorelli and company across a street twelve foot wide. Jack had two guns as did Little Moe, one of which was my sawed –off shotgun, and the only casualty was Little Moe, as they were still blazing away as they left."

"And what were you doing all this time, Cinderella, hiding in the pumpkin?" Steve could hear the sneer in Tommy's voice.

"Well, no, actually, Tommy, I was trying to put as many rounds as I could from my puny .38 into the driver's window from forty yards away, when I wasn't ducking Little Moe's bad shooting. And I am glad you brought that subject up, because the cops just handed me back my belongings and they kept my pistol. I figure you owe me, and I'm not walking out of here without one."

"What? Where the hell are you?" Tommy was wide awake now and his voice was in full roar.

"I am down here in the cop station, Tommy, where I have been for the last two hours. It took an Assistant DA no less, to get me out. Otherwise we would be having a different conversation."

"Are you telling me that you are calling my house from the cops?"

"Relax, Tommy, you watch too many TV crime shows. They have to go through the warrant process to tap a phone in here and that would take them considerably longer than the four minutes we've been chatting, so let's get back to my problem for once, OK?"

"What is it you are going on about here?" The irritation was back.

"I am not going to repeat what I just said with cops six feet away. I am not leaving here without protection, so get someone over here with something in the nine range or bigger, pronto." He laughed to himself as he imagined Tommy sitting in his pajamas trying to comprehend the conversation.

"I don't believe you, Slick, I really don't." There was silence as Steve waited. When Tommy spoke again, the voice was quieter but still tight.

"OK, Slick, here it is. Wait for twenty minutes, get a cup of coffee or yuk it up with your cop friends for a while. When you come out, come out the west exit, the one that leads to Fremont. There will be a silver Mercury parked in the second space on the curb just where the meters began. Park behind him in the open space. Walk up to the car on the passenger side. The package will be delivered through that window. Got it?"

"Yeah, Tommy, I got it, and Tommy?"

"What now?"

"Make sure it goes bang when I pull the trigger, OK?"

"Yeah and after you hang up Slick, pretend you don't know me."

"Gee Tommy, after all the time we have spent together, that is rather harsh, don't you think?" Steve laughed. Tommy hung up.

It was already warm when Steve eased the black Mustang in behind the Mercury. The sky was pale and it was only a few minutes until sunrise. Steve walked to the passenger side of the silver car and waited while the window was rolled down. A hand came part way out holding a towel wrapped in gray duct tape. Steve shook his head and took the package from the disembodied hand. He returned to his car, waiting until the Mercury was several yards down the street. He tore off the tape and slid the Smith & Wesson 9 mm semi-automatic out of the towel. He pulled back the slide to make sure there was a round in the chamber. The weight told him that the magazine was full. He opened the front flap pocket of the leather jacket and positioned the pistol handle up and left the flap unbuttoned. The streets were nearly deserted as he made good time driving home. He locked the Mustang and took a quick around the house looking for anything that seemed amiss. Satisfied, he unlocked the back door and took the same precautions inside. After satisfying himself that everything was as he left it, he placed the gun under his pillow and collapsed onto the bed.

*

IT WAS TWELVE noon before Steve rolled over and stretched. His head ached and he had a metallic taste in his mouth, a taste that was still there after two cups of coffee. He stripped and cleaned the gun that Tommy Carmino had delivered to him, replacing the spring in the magazine and switching out the cartridges for ones he had loaded himself. He called Dwayne at Gaudin Ford and gave him the instructions he had been given by the cops as to the whereabouts of the Jeep. Dwayne promised that he would send someone over to pick up the car and call him back with a time estimate. He retrieved the original documents from his safe and placed them in the canvas briefcase. He dialed Remy's number but got no answer. He called Bernie and tried to keep his manner casual.

"Hey, Bern, I thought I would come over and have a late lunch with you if that is OK ?"

"Of course, why do you think you need to ask? Are you going to make it tonight?"

"Wouldn't miss it, Bernie, what time does your shebang kick off?"

"Dinner is at eight, festivities at nine."

"I will see you in a little while, I have to stop by Remy's before I get there, so no set time, OK?"

"Sure thing, I will see you when I see you."

Remy was fully dressed when she opened the door. Much like Tam, her face was a little puffy around the eyes, but they were clear and to Steve it seemed as if some of her old personality was back. He hugged her and they held each other for several minutes. When they had settled down together on the couch, he pulled out his notebook.

"Gem, give me a list of things you need, and I will get them for you." She smiled and put her hand on top of his.

"No need right now, Steve, I am pretty well stocked. Do you think that Bernie would be able to cater a small dinner tonight? I have several people from the Dunes coming over to talk about a few things. They asked me some questions this morning about arrangements for the funeral that I was unable to answer, so I thought with a few hours to think about it, I might be of more help to them."

"Of course, Gem, I am sure Bernie would be glad to able to do something for you. What else did they say?" She shrugged slightly.

"They said I could stay here as long as I need to, and that I should contact Nash's attorney and make sure they get a copy of his will. A few things like that." Steve nodded slowly.

"Take your time, Gem, there is plenty of time for all of this. Make sure that you take care of yourself. Bernie and I can take some of this burden off your shoulders, so please use us." Remy nodded. Steve looked at her.

"I love you, Remy and I want to take care of you." Remy looked into his eyes and held his gaze for several seconds.

"I love you too, Steve Cannon." She held up her arms and they embraced and kissed, their bodies pressed together. They released each other and Steve stood to go.

"I am at Bernie's tonight for one of his casino nights. I will call you before I go, OK?" Remy nodded and followed him to the front door. They kissed quickly before she closed the door behind him.

*

STEVE DROVE AROUND the edge of the Desert Inn golf course and parked in a patch of desert by the cart barn. He walked up the cart path past the first tee, and entered the pool area. There were a few children swimming in the light blue pool, while most of the patrons remained ensconced under umbrellas and out of the sun. Several pool boys hustled towels and drinks around to the guests. From the pool there were three entrances to the main hotel, Steve chose to walk through the golf pro shop area, which was connected directly to the main concourse and a large bank of elevators. Steve pressed '2' when the large steel doors slid shut in front him. He exited into the large carpeted foyer and turned right, then stopped and retraced his steps back toward the glassed in offices.

John Bonine blanched when he looked up in response to the knock on the side of his open door. Steve smiled widely.

"Hi there, remember me?" Bonine swallowed and nodded. Steve pointed back down the hall.

"Tommy Carmino's office down this way?" He smiled even more broadly. Before he could get an answer he turned and walked quickly past the elevators and down a broad hall that ended at two large dark wooden doors. 'Thomas Carmino, President of Resort Operations' spilled across the span in large bright brass letters. Steve smiled and opened the door.

The outer office was half the size of Steve's house and a dark haired secretary sat behind a large curving desk. She had a view of the pool, the tennis courts and the first hole of the golf course. She looked up from her typing and coolly surveyed the person in front of her.

"May I help you?" The look on her face suggested that Steve might need to be directed to some other part of the hotel.

"I'd just like to yak with Tommy for a few minutes." Steve smiled. The secretary didn't smile back as she shook her head.

"I'm afraid that isn't possible. Mr. Carmino has a very busy schedule today."

"Oh, I bet he does, and since I am the likely cause of some of his busyness, I think he might want to see me." He smiled down at her and leaned on the desk. When she looked blankly back at him, he reached down and picked up the phone next to her typewriter. He handed the receiver to her and arched his brows. She took it from his hand and without changing expression, put it back in the cradle. As he contemplated his next move, he heard a door open behind him, and when he turned he saw Tommy standing in his doorway, wearing a light gray suit, dark French blue shirt and a gray silk tie.

"I heard you were here, Cannon, just the guy I want to see." He motioned back into his office. Steve smiled at the secretary, who resumed typing as if she had never been interrupted. Steve shrugged and followed Tommy into the office. Tommy's office was three times as big as the reception space and the windows curved around two sides producing panoramic views of the property. Steve could see all the way to Remy's house and beyond. He nodded.

"Not bad, Tommy, not bad." He looked over at the large rosewood desk where Tommy was looking through a stack of papers. Tommy pointed toward the other side of the room where a tufted leather couch and two chairs were positioned two steps down into a sunken space. Behind the seating area there was a large pool table and a bar that ran along the entire wall. The upper half of the wall was covered with mirrors. Steve settled into one of the leather chairs as he watched Tommy cross to the bar behind him.

"Cannon, you want a drink?"

"No thanks, Tommy, I haven't eaten lunch yet. Going to stop by Bernie's after this." Tommy sat down on the couch in front of him and placed a glass of scotch on a cocktail napkin.

"Funny you said that just now, because Bernie is what I want to hear about." Steve's brow furrowed.

"Bernie? What about Sorellli, and how is Little Moe doing?" Tommy waved toward Steve.

"Moe is going to live. Jack took him to our doc and he is going to be out of commission for a few weeks, but no problem. Jack thinks he has a lead on the car that Sorelli used and he is out beating the bushes, which is where I thought you were going to be this morning." Steve chuckled.

"My main purpose after making Sorelli pay, was to put pressure on Sorelli, Miriam Beech and indirectly, Herb Slater. That Sorelli escaped with his life was just bad luck. I think he will now do something desperate and make a mistake. Someone will be there when he does." Tommy shrugged.

"Your funeral." Tommy chuckled. "Your little cap gun fight

and the fact that the Feds are all over this case has relieved some of the outside pressure on our organization, so let's hope Jack comes through." Tommy leaned back and took a sip of his drink.

"So, Slick, tell me what your friend Bernie is up to these days. I haven't seen him in a long while." Steve snorted a small laugh.

"Well, Tommy you don't sound like a man that was having nightmares six hours ago. Why the sudden interest in Bernie?" Steve shifted over slightly on the couch to get out from under the air conditioning vent which was blowing down on him. Tommy smiled.

"Well Slick, you've never been shy about spitting it out so here's the deal. I heard that Bernie is buying a piece of land across the strip from here. I need to know what he has in mind."

"You should ask him yourself."

"I'm asking you. One reason I'm asking is that it doesn't make any sense to me. And the other reason I am asking you is that I am no dummy and I know who is in like Flynn with who. That parcel has only 50 feet of frontage on the strip, the rest is on Flamingo Road and whatever he builds there is going to be overshadowed by Sarno's joint, so what gives?" Steve smiled.

"Oh by the way, Tommy, Sarno's 'joint' as you put it is going to be called 'Caesars Palace."

"That's hardly an improvement. What connection does that name have to anything else on the strip? Only two themes work in this town, desert locales and the old west." Tommy snorted and shook his head.

"I don't know, ask Sarno." Steve stared at Tommy. "But back to Bernie. Why do you care what Bernie does with a small piece of land anyway?"

"I care about everything that happens on the strip, and if Bernie is buying it, there must be a very good reason, and because I don't know what that is, I have to be concerned." Steve shrugged and was about to answer when Tommy cut him off.

"Sometimes I think that you don't know a whole lot about your friend." Tommy was sitting forward now. Steve shrugged again.

"Well let me tell you just one Bernie Gold story from the old days." Tommy finished his drink and set the glass back down.

"When I was first coming up in Chicago, I worked for a guy who was trying to consolidate all of the business into one organization. It was still fragmented from the end of prohibition and the war and making the transition from bootlegging to other lines of work was busting our chops. Anyway, this other organization from New York moves in and sets up shop on the Southside. They set up a numbers racket and start throwing their weight around. The outfit I worked for was still too weak to do much, so they picked up quite a bit of steam very quickly. Then they started abusing their customers; not paying off, giving winning numbers to their cronies and intimidating the real winners to keep quiet, crap like that. So Bernie, who owns two delis in the neighborhood at this point, decides enough is enough, and so what does he do? He starts running his own numbers games. So, long story short, everyone quits playing the other outfit's games and they play Bernie's. Two months later and the other outfit completely packs up and leaves town. But here is the beauty part. Bernie walks into our clubhouse and announces that we are going to buy the racket from him. You know how much he wanted? A buck. A solitary buck. The only stipulation was that we run it fair and employ all the people he had set up." Tommy smiled and sat back into the couch. "From that moment on, our organization never looked back. That man deserves all the respect he gets. True story." Steve shook his head slowly. Tommy continued.

"So when I say that I am curious about what Bernie Gold is up to, it is just old habit, something is definitely up."

"Well, I am afraid it is going to have to remain a mystery, Tommy, cause outside of what you already know, I can't add anything." Tommy smiled.

"That's Ok, Slick, because I know that when you do know, you will whisper it into my ear like a good little birdie." Tommy stood up.

"I don't think Sorelli is going to be much of a problem anymore.

Jack thinks you guys scared him pretty straight last night." Steve followed Tommy to the door.

"I think that Jack is just whistling past the graveyard on this one, Tommy, Sorelli is still out there and he won't quit just because we took a few shots at him, but time will tell, it always does." Steve walked through the door, turned and waved at Tommy and ignoring the secretary, opened the front door and made his way to the elevators.

Steve was just about to take a bite of one of Bernie's large pastrami sandwiches when Bernie himself sat down across from Steve. He had a cup of coffee in his hand and the daily tally sheets from the casino.

"How is Remy doing?"

"I think better, Bern. Starting to look a little toward the future, which is good I guess. She is going to call you about catering for a small get together she is having with the Dunes brass tonight." Bernie nodded.

"Yeah I got that call. Because I've hired a bunch of extra waiters for tonight, a lot of people have been standing around without much to do all day, so I will send some of them over there to help her and give it some class." Steve smiled.

"That would be great Bernie, I told her I would call her before I come over here, though she will still be pretty busy then."

'Don't worry, I will tell Mel or one of the boys to stay by the phone so at least she knows you did try and call. I heard about your brouhaha last night. You are going to make an old man of me yet, Stevie boy." Steve laughed and put down his sandwich.

"Well as I was telling Tommy Carmino just a few minutes ago, I think we impressed upon Mr. Sorelli the fact that he is not the only one who can play this game. Know what else we talked about?" Bernie shrugged.

"What?"

"Your little piece of heaven on the strip. Tommy is all warm under the collar, wanted to know everything about it." Bernie smiled.

"Yeah, amazing how word gets around. Anyway, about that. I called my real estate guy, Norman Kaye, right after I saw you last. You know Norman, performs with his sister in the Mary Kaye trio?" Steve nodded. "Well, he got on it quick, and I am signing the papers this afternoon." Bernie smiled.

"Good for you, Bernie, that was smart. By tonight, everyone will be wondering what is up."

"Well, let's keep them wondering for a while. Norman has already had several calls on it."

"The one you want is from Sarno. That will be the big payday." They smiled and Steve clinked his beer glass against Bernie's coffee cup.

"I forgot to tell you, Steve, tonight got expanded a little bit. Some of the regulars heard there was a poker night coming up and they all wanted in on it, and it just kind of snowballed from there. A lot of the strip guys are going to be there, most of the usual entertainers and some of the higher-ups. Just wanted to give you a head's up in case you wanted to give it a pass." Steve put on a mock offended look.

"Bernie, how can you even think such a thing? I told you I was coming and that is the end of it. Besides the way you got it set up, there will be plenty of people to play with."

"The other interesting part of that is that I did get a call from Sarno." Steve sat up a little straighter in his chair. "No, not about that. He heard about the poker game, he is obsessed with the game, a big player and by all accounts loses a ton. So maybe if you get the chance and you are in the game, go a little easy from time to time. Who knows, we may get some info we can use." Bernie smiled and chuckled.

A few minutes later they said their goodbyes, Steve promising to make it by eight for the kick-off dinner. The Sahara board said

111 degrees as he pulled out of Bernie's parking lot. He left the strip and drove downtown to the federal building. When he stepped out of the car, the pavement beneath his soles felt slightly spongy. Radiation waves rose like mirages from the street as he crossed over to the building. Despite the marble floors and walls and the air conditioning on the highest setting, the main rotunda was only slightly cooler than the shade outside as Steve walked across the expanse and up the two flights of stairs.

Jim Larsen's office had all the doors and interior windows open and ceiling fans were going in all three rooms. There was no one in either outer office, so Steve rapped on the door frame of Larsen's private room. The Assistant District Attorney looked up from a table he was sitting at by the window and put down the paper he was reading.

"Ah, Mr. Cannon, I was wondering when I was going to see you." He rose and turned one of the chairs that was facing the empty desk around and indicated that Steve should sit down. Steve slid into the comfortably padded chair, placing the canvas bag on the table in front of him. Larsen poured a glassful of water from a big pitcher and placed it in front of Steve. Steve nodded his thanks.

"I have just been going over some of the information we have on this case so far. Most of it has come out of the file that Tam Polhaus worked up, with a small contribution from Detective Samuels. I have yet to receive anything from Agent Brady or Agent Molino."

"Well you can add these to your pile." Steve pulled out the originals of the papers he had discovered in Beech's suitcase, as well as some of the information sheets he had gotten from Tam in case they had not been included in the files that Larsen now had. The attorney looked them over carefully one by one and placed them into three separate piles. When he was done he sat back in his chair and looked at Steve.

"I think that you have connected the dots very cogently in this case, Mr. Cannon. I am going to have my staff work up a time-line on this case and we can start getting the subpoenas we need to move this investigation along. But now, I need you to tell me from the beginning, everything you know and how you have proceeded through this case." The DA turned on a tape recorder behind him.

Steve took over twenty minutes detailing every wrinkle in the case. When he finished Larsen thought for a moment and read over the notes he had been taking in shorthand as Steve had relayed the tale.

"Let me ask you a few questions, Mr. Cannon. Forgive me if one or two might seem insensitive to you." Steve nodded.

"Do you know the disposition of the funds that were in the Vegas Wash account at Valley Bank?"

"No. sir, I do not."

"Do you have any reason to believe that Remy Brannock would have that knowledge?"

"No, I don't. But I have not asked her directly about that account since her husband's body was found." Larsen nodded.

"I think we can get that information. I will bet I already have the number of that account. There are several transfers of money from an account at Valley Bank into Herb Slater's personal account at Nevada Savings and Loan. If they are a match, that will go a long way toward vindication, Mr. Cannon, and a long way towards moving the corruption charges against Slater forward." Larsen paused and then continued.

"Let me ask you, Mr. Cannon, how much of her husband's activity do you think Mrs. Brannock was aware of?" Steve thought for a few seconds and when he saw the DA studying his face, he answered.

"She knows there was a land deal that her husband was promoting, but she didn't know it was fraudulent. She knows about the Vegas Wash account, but not the origins of the money. She knows what he did at the Dunes and some of the particulars, but not a lot of details. Typically, guys like Brannock are pretty closed mouth about the real reason they get up in the morning, at least the smart ones are." Larsen nodded thoughtfully.

"In your opinion, do you think she would cooperate in the investigation, even if details come out, and they will come out, that will cast her husband in a less than stellar light?"

"I believe she would, but I should tell you that I am going to advise her to retain a lawyer as soon as possible." Larsen nodded.

"I think that would be a prudent move on her part, and it might actually make the process smoother for everyone." Steve nodded and started to rise from the chair. Larsen held up his hand and stopped him.

"I have just a few more comments I wish to make Mr. Cannon, before you go, if that is all right with you?" Steve shrugged and sat down again.

"Shoot."

"I think you are right that Angelo Sorelli murdered both Beech and Brannock. I also believe that it is highly likely that he and his cohorts planted the bombs in your car and the car of Detective Polhaus resulting in the death of his wife. What I am not sure about is the role that Miriam Beech has played in all this. I know you think she is behind the last two killings but why would she team up with Sorelli if, as it appears likely, he murdered her husband?" Larsen paused and furrowed his brow.

"My opinion, Mr. Larsen? I think she saw a way to use Sorelli to cut her losses, at least get the money that Nash had collected so far plus the dough he stole from Beech. My guess is that when his usefulness comes to an end, she has some plan, that if successful, will prove unhealthy for our big ugly friend." Larsen sighed and nodded.

"Well then, Mr. Cannon, and take what I am about to say as just friendly advice, why not sit back and let the agencies have the lead while the rest of this drama plays out?" Steve sighed as well and looked out the large windows. In the distance he could see the neon visage of Vegas Vic swinging his arm in front of the Pioneer Club.

"Because I think I am the only one that truly knows what Sorelli is capable of, and I have very little confidence, no offense intended Mr. Larsen, that any agency is able to do even one thing to slow this guy down. He pretty much has had his way so far and somebody has to stop him, and since he has made it personal, it looks like that person is me."

"I see your point, Mr. Cannon, I truly do, but I am also charged with keeping public order and vigilante activity runs very contrary to that charge. I have to do everything I can to avoid incidents like the one that occurred last night. So let's just leave it here shall we, and as events unfold one way or another, we both know where the other stands, OK?"

"Fine by me, I didn't ask for any of this; my nieces terrorized, Tam's wife dead, Remy's husband dead, my phone ringing off the hook with death threats. So I am going to help you and Samuels and Agent Brady find him, and if he surrenders peacefully, that will be that. If not, then one of us will be dead. So if that is the understanding we have, I am all for it." Steve smiled and rose up from his chair. Larsen grimaced but held out his hand.

The air felt like the inside of a blast furnace as Steve exited the building into the concrete plaza that was surrounded by stone buildings on three sides. Most locals would laugh and tell visitors that complained about the weather that at least it was a 'dry' heat. But the truth was; that dry or humid, the hot air that one breathed into their lungs on afternoons such as this one would quickly sap the strength from even the fittest person.

The air inside the house was bearable only because Steve had left the swamp cooler running even when he was gone. He pulled out a light gray suit from his closet and laid it out on the bed. He spent the next ten minutes in the shower, letting the cool water run off his body. He padded around the house in gym shorts rather than get fully dressed. Anticipating a long night, he chose a glass of ice tea from a pitcher in the fridge instead of the usual beer. He was standing in the office in front of a fan when the phone rang.

"Hi, Steve this is Rita. Rita Malone. Do you have a few minutes?"

"Sure, of course, what can I do for you?"

"We are running quite a long piece on the Vegas Wash affair in tomorrow's edition. As promised, I would like to read it to you and get your comments if any and consider any corrections before I submit it."

"Sure, go ahead."

For the next ten minutes Steve listened as Rita spun out the tale of the last ten days in almost the same way Steve had done for the District Attorney two hours before. There was a good amount of background detail especially on Nash and Slater, and Rita had gotten hold of more arrest information on Miriam and Walter Beech than even Steve had seen. When she was done, there was a brief silence before Steve spoke.

"You have done a good job, Rita, I can't say that I have any problems with any of it. Tommy Carmino may have a problem with the phrase 'reputed mobster', but he will get over it."

"My first version included the incident last night in North Las Vegas, but Mr. Greenspun felt that since I did not have a primary source that could definitely tie that in with the rest of the story it would have to wait. That is, unless you care to be that source." Steve thought for a few seconds.

"No, I think that should be part of the story." Steve quickly filled her in, being careful to stick closely to the story that he relayed to the authorities.

"Thanks, Steve, I will run this by Mr. Greenspun, hopefully he will give the ok to include it." Steve chuckled.

"If I see him tonight I will give it a plug myself. Good luck."

'Thanks, again, Steve. Goodbye."

*

THE PARKING LOT outside Bernie's deli was crowded by the time Steve arrived. Several limos were lined up on the curb in the heat which had only gone down to 98 degrees, even though the sun was low on the horizon and would be gone completely by nine o'clock. Walter was manning the door and looked a little harried when Steve approached.

"Good evening, Mr. Cannon, good to see you tonight."

"Hi, Walter, what are you doing out here in the heat?" Walter indicated the crowd of people standing several yards away. There was a group of news reporters and guys with cameras being held back by a city cop and a security guard Bernie had hired.

"A lot of crashers trying to get in. Bernie gave me the list, but I have had to tell some big names no go, and there are plenty of unhappy people in the parking lot." Steve stopped and surveyed the scene.

"I tell you what, Walter. You give me the list, I'll stay here, you go find Bernie, and tell him I will spell you until everyone gets here. I am sure you have better things to do." Walter blanched.

"Nothing doing, Mr. Cannon, Bernie would have my head on a pike, for something like that. He told me to tell you to check in with him as soon as you get here. So please do that soon so I am off the hook." Steve put a hand on Walter's shoulder.

"Don't worry, I will go find him right now." Steve stepped into the deli. The tables had been rearranged into a huge horseshoe shape and there were name cards on the fresh linen in front of every seat. At the head of the table, Steve spied Bernie with three fourths of the Rat Pack. He had his arm around Sammy Davis Jr and was regaling him with some sort of funny story as they were all roaring. Steve smiled. One of the things he had always admired about his friend was that he didn't ever see race or what a man did to make a living, he just saw people. There were many places in town where the diminutive song and dance man was not welcome, but Bernie had always made sure that the deli was not one of them. Steve hung back and waited until Bernie disengaged himself and started working his way through the dinner guests toward the kitchen. Steve intercepted him just as he was about to push through the swinging doors. Bernie smiled and patted him on the shoulder.

"Man, I have created a monster. I had to tell Mel Torme there was no room. And I don't think Shecky Greene is ever going to talk to me again." Steve laughed.

"You just have to do these soirees more often and keep track of who came the last time."

"No chance I could do that. Hey, here is the key to the back-room. Joe is in there setting up. I told him to expect you, he will take care of you." Bernie waved and disappeared through the swinging doors. Steve opened the door and watched as several employees of the casino were busy stacking chips on the bank table and distributing ashtrays and drink coasters around the room. Steve spied Joe behind the bar and weaved through the tables and leaned on the polished mahogany.

"Hey, Steve how are you?" Joe put down a glass and reached under the bar to retrieve a small leather satchel.

"Here you go. Don't lose it all on the first hand." He winked as Steve took the black bag and opened the zipper. The bag was full of chips that Bernie had made up just for the game nights. There was a likeness of Bernie on one side and the deli logo on the other.

"Geez, Joe, how much is in here?"

"50 large, my friend." Joe chuckled. "Bernie told me to tell you that if you lose it all, that's fine. Whatever's left is yours to keep."

"I can't accept this, I brought five thousand of my own." Joe laughed.

"Then you go argue with him, if you want to waste your time. Those are the orders I got." Joe went back to arranging glasses on the bar. The bag was too big to put into his pocket and he felt silly walking around with it and keeping an eye on it all through dinner. He called down the bar to Joe.

"Hey, Joe, do you think that you could put this in the safe for me until after dinner?" Joe nodded.

"Sure, toss it here." Steve slid the satchel down the bar and made his way back out to the main dining room. The place was almost full. He walked behind several seated guests until he found his name card. He was between Hank Greenspun and Ralph Pearl.

Steve smiled to himself. This would be a hoot of a night. Greenspun was serious and quiet most of the time, Ralph was loud and bombastic. He sat down and surveyed the crowd. Most of the press people who were the original purpose of the night were giddy with excitement that they were in the company of so many luminaries. Just in Steve's immediate vicinity there was Billy Eckstine, Phil Harris, and Benny Binion. Where the tables turned the corner on the horseshoe, Louie Prima was yukking it up with Xavier Cugat. There was a constant toing and froing as a new celebrity came through the door every few minutes and everyone would get up to greet them and pay their respects. There was a notable absence of wise guys and movers and shakers from that quarter. That was another gathering all together, smaller, quieter and much less publicity. It was at one of those affairs that Steve had first met Tommy Carmino four years earlier. A few minutes after eight, Walter closed and locked the doors. He handed the list to Bernie, who nodded after he had read it over. Bernie made his way to the head of the table and with the handle of a soup spoon rapped loudly on a glass for several seconds until everyone stopped their conversations and turned toward the head of the table. Bernie smiled as he looked up and down at his assembled guests.

"Welcome everybody." He began. "Thank you very much for coming out in this heat to share a little food and fun with some of the people you don't get to see very often. Also I am glad to announce that the two charities that are benefitting from your generosity tonight are Danny Thomas's St. Jude's Children's Hospital and the Southern Nevada Chapter of the Fight Against Muscular Dystrophy. As you old hands know, the only rule of these gatherings is to leave all old slights and disagreements out in the parking lot. Everyone is the same in here and there are no celebrities and other people, there are just people having a good time. When I realized that I had not had one of these shebangs for a while, I decided the only thing to do was to combine the two regular ones into one. So, we have a lot of the newspaper and TV people with us along with some of the entertainers they cover as part of their job. Hopefully, a few of you will leave here tonight with some new thoughts about how you go about your work. If this is the first one of these get togethers you have been to, please ask others around you or me about the rules of the games in the other room. This is still casino gambling though the odds are reduced in your favor. That being said, you can still lose your money, so please play well within the limits you feel comfortable with. Any money made by the house when you buy chips from the bank and don't redeem them goes to the charities. Above everything else, have fun and enjoy the company and the food." Bernie left the head of the table to a loud enthusiastic round of applause, as the waiters began immediately to circle with cold salads and baskets of bread. Steve made room as Hank Greenspun came to his seat after waiting by the door for Bernie to conclude his welcome. Steve smiled at the shorter man, whose full face was framed by short thinning hair. Hank smiled and snorted.

"I hear your name all day, so of course you were destined to be my dinner companion. How have you been, Steve? You have too many adventures for a guy who is past forty." Steve laughed and shook the proffered hand.

"Yeah, I agree with you. But as you know in your business, every day brings a new surprise." Hank nodded and picked up the short food and drink menu that was beside his plate.

"What's good here, Cannon? You eat Bernie's food all the time." One of the waiters that Bernie had hired just for the night was standing between the two men waiting to take their orders. Steve quickly perused the special menu.

"Pot roast is usually good. I'm told the meatloaf is good, never had it. Bernie does cook a good steak." Hank grunted and ordered the steak and a scotch on the rocks. Steve ordered the same. Hank waited until a small lull in the conversations around them swelled back up to the normal high decibels. He inclined his head toward Steve.

"Already getting flak on the story Rita's running tomorrow. Had two conversations with Slater's lawyer this afternoon and one just before I got here, that being the reason I was held up." Steve nodded.

"You have my sympathy, I had a short encounter with Mr. Gleason and that was plenty." Hank paused while the waiter returned with the two scotches.

"The DA Larsen is very tight lipped. You are the only other person that has seen these incriminating papers. I hope this isn't going to splash egg all over our faces." He looked at Steve and then took a small sip of his scotch.

"Well for what it is worth, Hank, at the very least, Slater has some explaining to do. I have combed the public records and there is no indication that anyone but Slater signed off on that fake land deal. Larsen has intimated that there are several large cash deposits that Slater and his lawyer are having no luck explaining away. So I think you are on pretty solid ground here." Steve looked over at Hank who was staring across the room but seeing little. After a few seconds, he turned back toward Steve.

"You know, this is the part of my job I love the most and hate the most. I can't operate any other way but shine a light, however feeble sometimes, on the corruption that saps the energy of this place. But you know what? Most of the people in this room probably look at me and wonder if their turn isn't next."

Hank sighed and dug into his salad. Steve nursed his drink and after a few minutes, turned and asked Ralph Pearl what his impressions were of Louis Armstrong when he interviewed him for his TV show. Not long after that, the entrees arrived and the noise from the conversations around the table subsided. As usual, Bernie had gone all out. The food was highly rated by everyone at the tables and Bernie received another ovation when he reappeared to announce the opening of the game room. Steve hung back and waited for most of the rest of the attendees that were so inclined to make themselves comfortable at the tables inside. There were only two or three small groups still conversing over cigars and cigarettes at the dining tables when Steve made his way through the door into the casino.

Some of the game nights that Steve had attended included roulette and craps as well as the card games, but tonight, Bernie had opted for just poker and twenty-one and there were sixteen tables in the room, eight of each game. Steve went over to the bank table where Bernie and Joe were exchanging players' money for house chips. When Joe looked up and saw Steve he retrieved the black satchel from under the table and handed it to Steve. Steve shook the bag and the contents at Bernie.

"What am I supposed to do with all this?" Bernie laughed.

"Hopefully lose it all to some philanthropic soul who won't redeem them." Steve smiled and shook his head.

"Bernie, do you need me to deal?"

'No, thanks, Steve, I got that covered. Betty Graco who runs the dealer school sent some of her people that are close to graduating over for the experience. And since any money the house makes goes to charity, I got the gaming commission to sign off on it. Unofficially of course." Bernie winked and grinned at Steve. Steve made way for a group of gamblers eager to buy chips and wandered around watching several hands at each table. The Rat Pack and a few of the other entertainers took over one of the twenty-one tables and were keeping Bernie's waiters busy with drink orders. Steve was drawn to a poker table over in the relative quiet of the corner by the long bar. The serious poker players had convened. Benny Binion was there along with several others Steve recognized as players he had shared the poker tables with at Nick's place, the Golden Nugget. At the head of the table sat Jay Sarno, behind an impressive stack of house chips and three tall stacks of hundred dollar bills, a mildly irritated look on his face at the good natured back and forth that was occurring between the other players. As Steve watched, Sarno's impatience also showed up in his play. He played fast and stayed in lost pots way too long and bluffed when there were likely stronger hands against him that clearly were going to call his bluff. After a few minutes, Steve noticed Hank Greenspun leaning against the bar and not playing.

"Hank, don't tell me you are against gambling?" Hank, who seemed lost in his own thoughts looked up quickly and smiled.

"No, no problem with gambling at all. I am just a poverty stricken newspaperman, this is way too rich for my blood." Steve opened the satchel and counted out $10,000 in chips onto the bar.

"Here Hank, this is just funny money that Bernie gave me to lose, we might as well both have fun with it." Hank smiled.

"Sure, Steve, I will help you lose it. Thanks." Steve waved dismissively as Hank sat down at a twenty-one table next to Alan King.

Steve played several hands of twenty-one at one of the tables, chatting with the people he knew and winning a little more than he lost. After an hour, he walked back over to the corner poker table. There were a few empty seats and when Benny Binion saw him he pointed to the one right beside Sarno.

"Hey, Cannon, you going to nursemaid whatever you got in your purse all night or are you going to give some of us a chance at it? Sit down here and help us pluck this chicken." Benny nodded in the direction of Sarno, whose pile of chips was larger than an hour earlier. Steve laughed.

"I don't know, Benny, but whenever I see you at a poker table, somehow it is always my feathers that start feeling a little loose." Binion and several of the players laughed heartily as Steve sat down next to a scowling Sarno and started stacking his chips in front of him. He pulled out his own stack of hundred dollar bills and placed then neatly next to the chips.

"What we playing, fellas?" The player next to Benny laughed.

"Texas hold'em. What else?" Steve smiled and waited as the dealer shuffled the cards and began to expertly spin them off the top of the deck to each player in turn.

An hour later, Steve had several more stacks of chips than when he started. He counted the stacks of bills. He now had thirty-two thousand dollars just in hundreds. He had increased the chips that Bernie had given him by twenty five thousand even with the portion he had given to Hank. Steve and Sarno were now the only players left. Several had tapped out and Benny Binion had been dragged over to another table where Frank Sinatra and friends had been playing poker for the last hour. Steve glanced at his watch. It was 11:25. Bernie would make the last hand call in a few minutes. He looked back over at Sarno.

"Care to put it all in on one hand?" He knew Sarno's penchant for gambling even though this was the first time he had ever met him. He also knew that based on the last hour's play that the odds were roughly 3 to 1 that Steve would win the last hand. Sarno snarled.

"No thanks. I have had quite a bit to drink but I am not that stupid. As soon as you sat down things started running your way. No, I'm going to save my powder and go back downtown with Benny later. I think this might be the night I finally get the better of him." Steve shrugged.

"Suit yourself, Jay. I am always obliging when a man wants to push away from the table." Sarno scowled at Steve briefly, but then turned his attention to pocketing the not small amount of chips and cash in front of him. Steve watched the pudgy fingers nimbly load the stacks of chips into a zippered canvas bag.

"Let me ask you something, Jay. I was downtown doing some research the other day and I was reading the minutes of some of the recent commissioner meetings. When your project manager, Mr. Wald, made his presentation on July 27th, were those the final plans for the property?" Sarno stopped counting his chips and stared at Steve.

"What business is that of yours?" Steve looked at the developer blankly.

"Probably no business of mine, but I was just wondering why the Tennis Pavillion and the southwest parking lot were in the original plans, then got dropped along the way for some reason and then reappeared in the final draft?" Sarno eyed Steve suspiciously, but then shrugged.

"We just decided a month ago to do it all at once instead of two phases." Steve nodded.

"Makes sense, I guess. But are you sure that you got all the land you are going to need in your final lease deal with Kerkorian?" Sarno snorted.

"What are you talking about? How would you know the particulars of my deal with Kerkorian?" There was more than an edge of irritation in Sarno's voice.

"Well, Jay, it's there in the public record for anyone that cares to see. If I were you I would get together tomorrow morning with that project manager of yours and see if you may have overlooked something. You know a word to the wise." Steve winked and began to slide stacks of chips into the satchel. He pushed three one hundred dollar bills over to the dealer. Sarno finished counting his chips and stood up from the table. When he didn't move off right away, Steve looked up at him. Sarno's face had reddened considerably.

"I don't know what your purpose is in sticking your nose into things that you can't possibly understand. But I think it would be better for everyone if you stay out of this." Steve shrugged.

"Mr. Sarno, that was as perfect a description of my job as I have ever heard. But I think you got me all wrong. I hope Caesars Palace is a big success and I hope that other people follow your lead. I am just a 'cross all your t's and dot all your i's kind of guy, and in this particular deal, I think you may have fallen a little short in that department. But don't worry, I think a man of your talents can shear that Binion sheep over there and have plenty left over to correct his mistake." Steve smirked and got up from the table and walked over to the bar. Sarno stared after him and then walked over to the Sinatra table where everyone was preparing to leave. Steve waited while Bernie said his goodbyes and ushered some of his closer friends to the door. When the last guest had left, Steve sat with Joe and Bernie at the bank table while Joe tallied up the night's take. He plopped the bulging satchel down on the green felt. Both Joe and Bernie stopped what they were doing and stared at the bag.

"Geez, Steve, what did you do, hold up some of the tables?" Steve opened the bag and pushed it across to Joe.

"For once I was able to hold my own with Benny and some of the boys. The fact that Sarno plays like he is using monopoly money didn't hurt either." Bernie whistled as Joe kept pulling wads of hundred dollar bills from the bag. They waited while Joe toted it all up.

"One hundred ten thousand and change boss." Joe turned his notepad toward Bernie so he could check the arithmetic.

"Wow, Steve you really raked it in. I think we are going to be able to split over two hundred fifty thousand between the two charities." Bernie shook his head as Joe and another employee wheeled the cart full of chips and cash over to the safe.

"Here, you should keep at least part of the cash. If I know you, you showed up with at least several grand for the cause, you always do." Steve waved Bernie off.

"I won't hear of it, Bern, I am just glad that I could contribute and not lose all that dough to some of these guys who don't hesitate to cash in the chips."

"Well, I have noticed that we are getting less of that as these things roll on. At the end of the night most of the guys just leave the chips on the tables and call it macaroni." He smiled and pushed a new drink across the table toward Steve.

"I had an interesting conversation with Jay Sarno at the end of the evening, Bern. I put the bug in his ear that maybe he or someone in his camp miscalculated the amount of land they would need to build out the whole project at once. As you can imagine, he was not too happy about the news. I am not sure he believed me, but I will bet he will be mourning the bad news by lunchtime tomorrow." Bernie grinned.

"Leave it to you to speed things up. I put the money in the escrow account this morning and signed the papers this afternoon."

"Well, Bern, I hope you got a good lawyer because there is a lot of negotiating ahead." Bernie nodded.

"Norman is already on it. He figures that Jay will have to pay whatever price we set. But he also told me something interesting as well that I don't think too many people know. Sarno owns the option on twelve acres right across the street from the Dunes, where the old Three Coins Motel was, with three hundred feet of frontage on the strip. Wadda think?" Steve whistled softly.

"Are you thinking a swap?"

"Yep. Norman thinks he will have to go for it, and there are better tax issues involved in the swap for both parties, so it will be at least a slight win-win for him."

"Well if anyone can pull something like this off, my money is on you, my friend." Steve slapped Bernie lightly on the shoulder and followed him as they left the deli. Bernie gave some last minute instructions to Walter and Joe and then let both of them out the front door. Outside the 88 degree night air felt almost cool.

"Want to come out to my place for a late nightcap, listen to some jazz?"

"No, thanks, Bernie, I need to get home. I have to do some things tomorrow for Remy, so let me have a raincheck, OK?"

"Sure, no problem, Steve. When it comes to Remy, you have to do what you have to do. Let me know if there is something I can help you with there."

"I will, Bernie. You know I wouldn't hesitate to ask." Steve waved as Bernie walked around the building to his parking space in the alley. Steve walked the fifty yards to where the Mustang sat by itself in the deserted parking lot.

August 26

WHEN THE PHONE rang at eight the next morning, Steve had been up for an hour going over some neglected paperwork and paying a few bills.

"Time to wake up, dead man, ready for the last day of your miserable life?" Sorelli's voice held an edge of excitement. Steve shook his head and sighed.

"And just how are you going to accomplish that, Sorelli? I tell you what. Why don't we just stop jimmy jacking around here and get to the point. I am just sitting here all alone at home. Why don't you just come over here and we can settle this once and for all?"

"What, like a duel?" Sorelli laughed. "I don't think so dead man. I got a much better idea. Here, someone wants to say hello."

"Stevie?"

The sound of Skipper's voice hit Steve like a sledge hammer. He caught his breath and tried to speak but for a few seconds he lost that ability.

"Stevie..don't come here..don't come.." Steve could hear a short scuffle and then Sorelli was back on the line.

"So, if you want to see your rummy friend alive, you will do as I say, capice, dead man?" Steve took several deep breaths and let the exhalation pulse through his muscles.

"What do you want me to do?" His voice was flat and devoid of inflection.

"Drive out Tonopah highway and take the turn-off to Tule Springs. Drive ten miles past the ranch and you will see us waiting for you. If I see anyone with you, I kill him on the spot. You got one hour before I kill this pain-in-the ass drunk. You got that? One hour, dead man." The phone went dead.

It took almost all of Steve's strength to rise from his desk chair and walk into the next room. He quickly regained his equilibrium and fastened the holster around his waist. He placed the .38

revolver snug into the holster and stuck the 9mm that Tommy had provided in his belt. He changed into the boots he usually used to hike in the desert and grabbed a faded baseball cap and his back pack as he headed out the door. He paused with his hand on the door knob, then retraced his steps back into the office. On a clean sheet of paper he wrote 'Tule Springs' in large block letters and placed it squarely in the middle of the desk. Outside, the morning was already warmer than the day before. He drove two blocks then turned left onto Cheyenne and drove west four miles until the road intersected with the Tonopah highway, the main artery leading north out of town. He gunned the Mustang's engine and pushed the needle on the speedometer past 120. Twenty minutes later he slowed as he neared the turn-off to Tule Springs. The ranch was a rundown resort catering mostly to people needing somewhere out of the way to stay while the six month period for obtaining a divorce expired. Steve slowed as he came over a rise and the dusty buildings came into view. There were few signs of life as Steve slowly motored through and continued on up the dirt road that wound east toward the Sheep Range Mountains. After nine miles had gone by on the odometer since he had passed the ranch, he pulled off the road at the bottom of a long hill. He pulled a pair of binoculars out of the pack in the backseat and walked quickly over to a line of pinions that snaked up the hill by the side of the road, their dark branches getting taller the farther up the hill they grew. He slowed as he neared the top and crouched behind a shorter pinion tree to view the terrain beyond. From his vantage point, he could see that the road in front of him wound over a series of smaller hills and then eventually turned sharply towards the brick red and white striped backside of the Sheep Range. Just around the bend and shielded from view of the road by a small stand of pinion, Steve could just make out the front end of the green Chevy. If he had continued on in the car, he would have come upon it before he saw it from any distance. For the next several minutes he appraised all the possible approaches that could be taken from his current position to where the Chevy was parked with the least possibility of being seen. None of the routes were very good. The best one required a short traverse of open ground fifty yards shy of the car. From his angle on the hill, he could not be sure if that spot could be seen from the car. If one of the hoods was stationed between him and the car as a lookout, he would probably be seen long before that in any event. He weighed his options, turning over the different scenarios in his head. When he looked at his watch, he realized that no option remained but to get to the car in the next twenty minutes.

Ten minutes later, Steve had come within one hundred yards of the car. He had found a shallow arroyo that while taking him at a slight angle away from the station wagon had allowed him to arrive at his current position without any obvious signs he had been seen. There was enough cover in front of him to shield him for the next eighty yards if he crawled at least part of the way. When he was as close to the back of the car as he could get without exposing himself he cautiously peered over a tall creosote bush. The car was only occupied by one person who was sitting in the back seat on the passenger side. There were several bullet holes in the back just below the window that Steve had seen open as the Chevy had careened down the driveway two nights before. Steve crawled five yards to his right for a better angle. When he looked again he could clearly see Skipper, his mouth taped and from the angles of his arms and his posture it was obvious that his hands were bound behind him. Steve spent the next five minutes crawling carefully from one vantage point to another, stopping every thirty seconds to watch and listen. Hearing nothing, he quickly crawled over to the car and crouched just below Skipper's window. He slowly rose up and looked directly into Skipper's eyes. When Skipper saw him, he began to shake his head violently. Even through the closed windows, Steve could hear the loud stifled screaming sound coming from behind the silver tape on his friend's mouth. At the same moment he saw something move behind him, the reflection captured in the side window. Before he could turn, a second figure sprang up from the backseat floorboard and placed a pistol to Skipper's head. It was Jimmy Scatho. He still wore the bandage on his throat and his eyes became wild when he saw Cannon.

"Just in the nick of time, dead man." Steve stood up slowly facing the car. He slipped the Smith & Wesson from his belt and pulled back the hammer in one smooth motion as he turned around to face Angelo Sorelli. Steve held the sights squarely between the hood's eyes. Angelo held his pistol trained at Steve at almost the same angle. Beside him was Junior Belsley with a sawed-off double barreled shotgun braced against his stomach. They were standing in front of a shallow opening to an old gypsum mine shaft that was recessed into the side of the hill. Steve had come upon the car from an angle that had placed him right above the cave and he had been prevented from seeing the opening. Steve shifted his weight slightly and at the same time he moved his legs a little farther apart for better stability.

"So what now, Sorelli?" Junior moved the stock of the shotgun up against his cheek when Steve spoke.

"Well, dead man, I see two choices for you. You can pull that trigger and you will probably get me, and if you are fast and lucky, you might get Junior here just as he cuts you in two. But then your friend dies. Your second choice is to throw down all your weapons, and I know you have more than just the one you got pointed at me. You do that, the rummy goes free. Simple choice, Cannon, what's it going to be?"

Steve squinted as sweat beaded up under the brim of his cap and trickled into the corners of his eyes. He took several deep breaths and on the last exhalation he slowly lowered the barrel of the gun until it pointed at the ground. Sorelli laughed.

"I figured you for that kind of sappy sucker, Cannon. That pathetic drunk will probably be dead in six months, tops. But have it your way. This just makes it that much easier for me. Now ditch the little popper you scratched my windshield with the other night."

Steve reached behind him and slipped the .38 from the holster and threw it in the dirt along with the nine millimeter. Junior quickly scooted over and keeping the shotgun trained on Steve, scooped up both guns and returned to the spot where Sorelli was standing. Sorelli started walking slowly toward Steve, the gun still pointed at his forehead. At the same time, Jimmy Scatho pulled Skipper out of the opposite door of the car and pushed him around the back until he was standing beside Steve. Skipper was trying to speak. Steve turned and put his hand over the tape that was wrapped over his mouth and around Skipper's head.

"Shhhh, Skip, it is going to be all right. None of this was your fault ok?"

He looked into Skippers eyes and at the large tears that streamed down over the edges of the tape and fell on the ground. The next thing Steve saw was dirt and bloody drops making little puffs of dust from the gash on the side of his head. When he tried to move, the world swirled in front of his eyes. He closed them tight and pressed on them with his fingers to stop the motion. He fell back against the rear tire of the car and looked up at Sorelli who was standing over him. In his left hand he held the pistol, in his right was a short leather whip.

"Listen to me, Cannon, because very soon you aren't going to be hearing anything at all. We are going to leave your little buddy tied up here for a while. Later we are going to pour about a half a gallon of booze down his throat. When they find him, he won't remember a damn thing, and they will just think that you wandered off into the desert to look for him, and lost your way. Beautiful ain't it? Another one they can never pin on me. And here is something else you can think about with your last thoughts on this planet. After I take care of you, me and the boys are leaving this dust bowl with three million and change for all our troubles. I already took care of Beech's wife and now all that is left is you." Sorelli laughed and before Steve could reply, Angelo quickly raised his right hand and whipped the thin strips of leather three times across Steve's eyes.

Behind the red and black swirls, and the searing pain, Steve could hear Skipper and Jimmy grunting at each other as the two mutes scuffled right over the spot where Steve was writhing on the ground. Jimmy Scatho snapped Skipper's head back against the top of the car, knocking him out. Skipper slid to the ground, his body on top of Steve's legs. Sorelli began to yell at Jimmy and Junior.

"Get that rummy into the mineshaft. We only got a little over an hour before the planes come." Steve felt Skippers limp body being dragged off of his legs. He reached out and grabbed one of Skipper's arms and for a few feet the two hoods were dragging them both across the rocky soil. Sorelli kicked at Steve's arm and his hand lost its' grip on his friend. Sorelli kicked Steve twice more in the ribs before he went over to make sure that Skipper was secured in the mineshaft. Steve tried to crawl underneath the car, but blacked out briefly and came to as Junior and Jimmy were pulling him free by his legs. They pulled him to a standing position by his arms and held him up in front of Sorelli. Steve could not see out of either of his eyes and he felt the warm blood from them running down his cheeks. He passed out again.

When he came to for the second time, he was lying face down on the floorboard of the Chevy. Junior and Jimmy had both of their feet on top of him. Sorelli was driving and Steve could feel the car rocking back and forth around the curves and then going up at a steep angle. He tried to stay conscious and estimate the distance the car was traveling on the rough dirt road. After ten minutes, Steve felt the car nose over the summit and head down. That meant that they were now on the north facing slope of the Sheep range. Steve knew that not too far ahead, the road ended abruptly at the secured southern edge of the Nevada Test Site. At the bottom of the grade, Sorelli slowed the Chevy to five miles per hour, and Steve felt the bump along his body when the car left the road and continued at low speed through the desert.

When the car finally stopped, Steve estimated the distance they had traveled from the point where they left the road to be about three miles. All three of the hoods left the car and Steve could hear their faint voices in heated conversation a few yards away. Without warning the door swung open and his legs were pinned together and he was hauled out quickly, his chin bumping on the doorsill, before he was thrown onto the dirt. Steve tried in vain to open his eyes. He was finally able to get one of his eyelids open, but was still unable to see anything but shadows. Jimmy and Junior each grabbed an arm, hoisted him up and turned him with his back against the car. When the large shadow in front of him spoke, it was with Sorelli's voice.

"Not too much farther, now, dead man. We have a little hiking to do, so don't try and drag this thing out or I kill you right here." Jimmy and Junior pushed Steve forward and began to steer him through the large bunches of salt bush. The sand was deep and soft and Steve had a hard time pulling his boots out of it to take the next step. Several times, the two hoods deliberately let him walk straight into a clump of the vegetation. Steve's feet would immediately fall out from under him and the branches would scratch his face as he fell head first down into the prickly plant. When Sorelli called a halt after a half hour, Steve was not sure how far they had traveled. It was unlikely they had been walking in a straight line and the distance could easily have been a few hundred yards or a couple of miles. Jimmy kicked Steve's legs out from under him and he fell heavily into some vegetation. The acrid smell that filled Steve's nostrils told him that the vegetation had been recently burned. He also noted that he seemed to be on top of a small hillock as his feet were below the level of the rest of his body. He felt someone grab his collar and pull him to an upright position. His head was swimming, and the sun was painfully bright even through his damaged eyelids. The large shadow loomed in front of him again. He felt jagged pain shoot through his right leg as Sorelli swung the shotgun by the barrel and caught him just above the right knee. Steve tried to spin as he fell to protect the shattered leg, but was only able to twist it painfully underneath him. He collapsed onto the scorched branches of a manzanita bush. He tried to push himself up but found that his right arm had also received a heavy blow and was immobile. Sorelli pressed the barrels of the shotgun down on the side of Steve's head.

"If you had any idea where you are right now, dead man, you would be begging me to pull this trigger. But for all the grief you have caused me, you get to suffer instead." Somewhere behind him, he heard Jimmy make a half grunting, half imploring squealing sound. Steve felt the pressure of the shotgun pull away from his head.

"What? What is he trying to say?" Sorelli's voice was irritated. Junior pointed over to the edge of the valley.

"He just saw the planes, boss. They're coming." Almost before he had finished, the rolling low rumble of the jets reached all their ears. Sorelli snorted and yelled over the noise as it grew louder and echoed off the sides of the Sheep range.

"Shut up you two chicken-livers. That is just the recon run before they blow in here. We got at least thirty minutes to get back to the car." Jimmy broke into a loud whimper as the two jets swung over the southern tip of the Sheep range and turned the shiny points of their noses northward. They were a hundred yards off the surface of the desert and their hot exhaust, mixed with the radiation waves from the ground rose in a swirling mirage of wispy black smoke and shimmering chrome. Steve could feel the ground shake as the roar of the engines made everything vibrate in front of the plunging planes. Junior yelled above the tempest.

"Boss, let's get out of here, now!" Steve heard Sorelli swear something unintelligible and he could hear Jimmy kneeling in the dirt beside him wailing through his damaged vocal chords. The thick air vibrated violently against Steve's body as he used his left arm to push himself up off the burned manzanita branch that had kept his upper torso several inches off the ground.

The two F-105 Thunderchiefs released their shiny canisters earthward and pulled up into a sharp arc and were halfway out of the valley before the silver tubes split open and spread their loads of jellied death over the middle of the Area 51 bombing range.

Steve heard the impact of the napalm bombs just as he gave one last heave with his left arm, his body turning over and tumbling down the face of the small rise. He buried his face in his hands as his body flopped into a shallow arroyo at the bottom of the slope. Even with his damaged eyes shut tightly against the dirt of the small depression, he could see the bright orange flash that arrived at the same moment as the searing heat. It splashed over Steve's back and legs, forcing him to open his mouth and scream into the earth. The orange flash became swirling black and crimson clouds as Steve felt himself falling into a whirlpool of fire and smoke.

When Steve came again to consciousness, the first indication that he might still be alive was the smell of gasoline and the sound of vegetation burning nearby. Steve slowly pried his left hand away from his face. The air was hot and every breath seared his lungs. Steve wheezed through his mouth into the yellow earth. He carefully put two fingers to his upper face and tried to find his left eyelid. The skin was slippery with blood and even when he was successful in parting the two thin folds of torn flesh, he could not see any better. Just the shadow of his hand as he passed it in front of his face was all the vision he had. He decided to wait to test the other eye. After a few minutes a small breeze cooled the air enough so that Steve could lift up his head a few inches. He began to take inventory. He first tried to stretch out his good left leg. The pain of the burns on the back of the leg caused him to gag and catch his breath. After several attempts he was able to bend the left leg at the knee and dig his foot into the side of the arroyo. With the use of this new limited leverage he was able to elevate his upper body slightly with his left arm and drag his right arm out from underneath his chest. Though painful and swollen, Steve figured he had about fifty percent mobility on that side, the right leg was another matter. Steve could feel the jagged edges of bone grind against each other with even the slightest movement below his waist. He knew he would have to do something about that if he had any hope of getting out of here under his own power.

Five minutes later, Steve had finished cataloging the particulars of his physical state. One badly broken right leg, torn ligaments in the right arm, burns on the back of the left leg and lower back, a head gash that was still bleeding, lacerations on the cheekbones and eyelids, and no vision in either eye except for the occasional shadow. The small breeze the napalm had created had died down and the smoke had gotten heavier, forcing Steve to enlarge the small pit below his face and spend long minutes breathing through the upturned collar of his shirt. The only sound that Steve could hear was the crackling of a nearby manzanita bush as the liquids in the branches turned to steam and released with loud pops. The searing temperature of the explosion was now replaced by the steady heat of the sun. Steve knew he had better get moving quickly, if only to get into some sort of shelter from the sun and the midday heat.

After several painful attempts, Steve was able to attain a partial sitting up posture with the help of the slope of the arroyo. He tore the tail of his shirt and wrapped it tightly around the wound on his head. He was also able to move by lying on his left side and keeping his right leg as immobile as possible, push with his left leg and pull with his left hand. Moving in a rough circle around his original position, Steve was able to reconnoiter a ten square yard area. He had just completed his first circle and was contemplating which direction to move in next, when his hand brushed against a hard object. Though still warm to the touch, the manzanita branch was about one inch in diameter and three feet long. It was straight at both ends with a small kink about midway along the length. Steve rolled over painfully with the stick in his right hand. He fumbled with his belt buckle for several seconds before freeing it. With gritted teeth he slowly inserted the branch into his heavy canvas pants while trying to keep the bones of his shattered leg as straight as possible. When he had it positioned as well as he could, he laid the belt out on the ground and painfully scooted his body into position over it. The exertion of the last ten minutes forced Steve to lie back and breathe slowly through the sleeve of his shirt as the last of the smoke swirled above him. When he had recovered what little strength he had left, he snugged the belt up around his upper thigh as tight as he could with his left hand. After resting for a few minutes to let the pain subside, Steve began to test the new arrangement. The immobilized leg now allowed him to move more efficiently, if not a small bit faster. Unless the terrain changed underneath him abruptly, he was able to positon the leg as he moved for the least amount of the searing pain.

Steve crawled back to the slight shelter of the shallow arroyo and began to go over in his mind everything he knew about the area where he now found himself. Once, many years ago, with his father and brother, he had stood at the top of the highest peak of the Sheep Range and looked out over the small desert valley which would become the weapons training range for the Air Force at Nellis Air Force Base. He tried to keep the image in his mind as long as possible, focusing on any of the terrain features he might have seen that day. The valley was narrow at the northwestern end where two jagged lines of the range came together, and then broader and shallower in the southeast as the Sheep Range lowered itself slowly into the desert. He had also once seen an Air Force training film at a gathering in downtown Las Vegas whose purpose was to get the civilian population on board with a proposed expansion of Nellis. Though it was a small snippet, and the area was not identified, Steve knew then exactly where the jets were as they dropped their ordnance. If that was still the case, he was in the upper third of the valley as it narrowed, far from any road or patrol route. He knew that his foremost need was to get out of the line of fire. He had no idea how many times a day the range came under bombardment, but he knew that any pace he was able to maintain would still require many hours or even days to crawl to safety. The main question was: Which way to go? Being sightless for the last two hours had rendered his usual excellent sense of direction useless. He must get to higher ground on one of the slopes to escape instant death and also to have any chance of rescue. It was while his mind was struggling with this problem that he heard a small movement off to his right and whatever it was, it was moving towards him. He was still trying to decipher the origin of the sound when the small dust devil whirled over his legs and continued on up the slope. He remembered the little wind storms from that afternoon many years ago. In his mind's eye he saw them cutting across the valley south to north. If that was true, then his outstretched left arm was pointing to the closest slope. He hesitated. If he was wrong about the direction he could end up crawling straight down the middle of the valley and even if escaped the planes, he would die of thirst and exhaustion long before he came within miles of any sign of civilization.

Ten minutes later Steve lay on his back, his arms outstretched on an axis in the direction the dust devil had been taking when it crossed over his body. If the small dust storm was moving true to form, he should feel a breeze coming from the left side of his body over to his right, or roughly, south to north. For several minutes there was nothing, then almost imperceptively, Steve felt a small puff of breeze on his left fingertips. Several minutes later, the hair on that side of his head lifted as the air current became stronger. He had been right. The rising temperatures had created the usual early afternoon winds and though faint, they were blowing in the same direction that the dust devil had taken in its' journey across the valley. Steve felt around with his left hand for two medium sized stones. When he had found them, he carefully placed one at the end of the fingertips of his right hand and then repeated the same task with his left. He then slowly and painfully oriented his body on a straight axis beside the two rocks being careful not to disturb them as he did so.

Crawling in the direction he had selected, Steve began to experiment with several variations on the basic mode of locomotion he had been reduced to. After several adjustments, he settled on a method that caused the least amount of pain, while allowing him to best judge the direction he was traveling. He would lie on his left side, and pull his left leg carefully under his right one. Then getting as best a foothold in the sand as he could, he would reach forward with his left hand and if he was lucky, he would find a bush or rock to grab a hold of. If not, he would claw his hand as deep as he could into the sand and pull with his left arm while he pushed his body with his left leg. With much exertion he was able to do this ten times in a row, before the need to rest and let the pain subside overcame him. Every other rest period would find him on his back and he would not continue until he was satisfied, by using his two rock method, that he was traveling in the right direction. When he came to any of the larger groups of salt bush or manzanita that offered even a modest amount of shade, he chose those spots as his rest stations.

It was late afternoon, and in the long shadows, the rest intervals had become longer. The pain from his leg and the burns on his back, combined with the heat of the dirt surface caused him to black out for several minutes at a time. Even though he was still fairly sure he was traveling in the right direction he had little idea of how far he had managed to crawl. Though with the effort the task required, it seemed like miles, Steve knew he was lucky if he had crawled two hundred yards in the six hours since he had left the small arroyo. Steve was just beginning his crawling again when he felt the edge of a cool shadow strike the right side of his body as he lined himself up between the two stones. Several seconds later he was covered in shadow as the sun slipped over the rim of the Sheep Range. The sun sinking in the west confirmed that Steve was indeed crawling southward. But was that the direction that the slope of the Sheep Range lay in? Before he could contemplate the question any further, he fell into a deep sleep.

His shivering awoke him to total darkness. For several minutes he reoriented himself before moving off at a faster pace to warm up his body. Though his felt as strong as when he had started in the morning before, he knew that he now had a fever and that the toll on his endurance would be great. Hours later, he was still crawling very slowly, the black curtain in front of his eyes turning soft gray as morning approached. An hour later the edge of the sun's rays touched the left side of his body as he paused for a rest break. He was grateful for the warmth that spread over his body. He was in the same position two hours later when he awoke from a deep sleep.

August 27

THOUGH THE SLEEP had rested his sore muscles somewhat, the ordeal of the day before left Steve feeling spent. His tongue had begun to thicken in his mouth and he found it hard to swallow even the small amounts of saliva he was able to produce by rolling a small pebble under his tongue. Near the dawn, he had crawled into a rocky area that held small ledges that even though only four inches high required twice the effort to surmount. It was just as he had begun to crawl again and was crossing one of these small ledges that he heard a loud hiss three feet in front of his face. He froze where he was and holding his breath, waited. He knew that the origin of the sound was a snake, probably a Mojave rattlesnake. His fears were confirmed ten seconds later when he heard the sharp buzz of the tail rattles off to his left, and even closer than the hiss had been. Steve had encountered numerous Mojave rattlers in his travels and he was well aware of their unique habits. Rather than slither away quickly whenever danger approached in the form of a bigger animal like most other snakes, the Mojave stood his ground as if it were defending territory, and had even been known to pursue men for quite some distance as it could move quickly for short periods over level ground. The buzzing would slow if Steve did not move except for breathing, but the snake became agitated whenever Steve tried to back down the small ledge. Steve could not tell if he was within striking distance. Normally the Mojave could strike a distance one and a third times his length, but not being able to judge the size of the animal, Steve had no way to know if he was within reach of the sharp fangs. After several minutes of the standoff, Steve's strength was ebbing and with it, his ability to keep himself suspended on the ledge. Using slow movements every several seconds, Steve pulled his left foot up an inch at a time. When his foot was in position and the buzzing slowed again, Steve pushed with all his strength backwards, pulling his exposed arms in tight against his chest as he rolled backwards for several feet, landing on a second ledge he had crawled over fifteen minutes before. Waves of pain washed over his body. He held his breath and waited. After a few minutes, he heard the sound of the snake's scales sliding over the rocks heading in the opposite direction. It took him another thirty minutes to move sideways and traverse the twenty yards he felt was far enough to avoid encountering the reptile when he resumed his course. It took another twenty minutes for the breeze to rise up and enable Steve to plot his course. At noon, three hours later, he was only one hundred yards beyond the ledge where he had encountered the snake. He had just finished lining up two rocks and was sliding into position when the air crackled with the sound of jet planes echoing off the mountain sides. He waited as the sound faded for a few seconds then roared to life again as the jets bore down on the narrow range. This time there was no place to hide. Steve pulled his arms in around his head and waited for the worst. The air sounded as if it were being ripped in two by a giant unseen force, the narrow canyon rocking with echoes cascading upon each other. The rock ledge that Steve was laying on vibrated with the air waves that rolled across the desert. For a few seconds there was almost silence as the jets peeled off in formation and swept off over the Test site. Steve heard the crump of the canisters hit the surface somewhere behind him. He prayed that he had been able to crawl far enough to avoid the worst. The sickening smell of gasoline washed over the ledge he clung to and the hot breeze that followed prickled Steve's burned skin. Ten minutes later, the area right around Steve had returned to normal. Except for some light smoke and the petroleum smell, nothing remained of the onslaught. His breathing rapid and jagged, Steve pulled himself weakly over the rocky surface. Ten minutes later he had taken three breaks just since the planes had left. His progress was getting slower by the hour. If he didn't get to the slopes soon, where he might find some water, he did not know how much longer he would last. Darkness found him in nearly the same position he was when the planes swept through the valley. Soon after the encounter with the snake he had crawled into a deep sandy area with a perceptible downward slope. He began to doubt his choice of direction. By now the ground should have started to slope upwards if his bearings were correct. His fatigued body was refusing to go farther and the doubts that swirled through his mind made any more progress even harder. He lay on his good side and felt the warmth slowing leaving the sand underneath him.

The broken leg had swollen to nearly twice the normal size, and the abrasion of crawling over sand and rock had shredded the sleeves of his shirt, leaving the skin on his arms and hands raw and weeping. Worst of all was the lack of water. His tongue was so thick, he would be unable to speak or even shout if he were to hear anyone about. He had been forced into lying in whatever shade he could find for hours rather than exert himself under the hot sun and lose even more precious fluid. The pounding in his head was only relieved when he slipped into unconsciousness, and then only for a short while. As it grew darker, the shivering increased, as he was unable to even pull himself into a fetal position to conserve body heat. The night was illuminated by starlight, but to Steve, the curtain in front of his face was either black for nine hours or bright yellow when he turned in the direction of the sun. He fell into a delirious sleep.

August 28

SOMETIME AFTER MIDNIGHT, Japanese voices began screaming from the salt bushes around him. He awoke to find himself yell-
ing hoarsely at the men around him to get ready for the next charge.
When he realized where he was, he lay back in sweaty relief. He
lay on his back and tried to imagine how the starry night appeared
above him as he fought to control his breathing. He remembered
the cool nights in the desert he had spent with his father and his
brother. He would lay awake in his sleeping bag long after the others and gaze up at the Milky Way, the crystal specks in sharp relief
away from the city lights. It was as his breathing began to slowly
return to normal that he heard the sound. He thought it sounded
as if a small rock had fallen. A few seconds later the sound repeated,
but in a short little series that was definitely not random rocks.
Something was there and it was getting closer. Steve could hear
whatever it was slow down as it approached him from his right side.
It stopped only a few feet beyond him. For several seconds nothing
happened, then Steve heard two more footfalls. Whatever it was,
it was now standing right over him. Try as he might, Steve could
not get the crusted shut eyelids to open. He held his breath. A couple of minutes later, he heard deep relaxed breathing coming from
near his right ear. It might be a desert burro, he thought. Perhaps
one of the descendents from burros that were lost or released by
miners over the years. They banded together and roamed at will
over the desert. Many rough campers were visited by them in the
night as they were always very curious about anything new or out
of place in their surroundings. As he was mulling over this possibility in his mind, he felt a soft gentle push on his ear. Steve tried to
lay as still as possible, as the action was repeated several more times.
Carefully, Steve raised his right hand and touched the stiff under
hairs of a large snout. The animal did not back away or react at all.
Curious, Steve ran his hand along the soft hair covered jawline. His

out stretched fingers came up against the hardness of horn and he traced the enormous curl around as it pointed to the ground. A Desert Bighorn Sheep. Even with the hopeless state he was in, Steve found himself awed by the animal. Elusive in the extreme, Steve had only ever seen one once, and that was from a great distance. After several minutes, he heard the animal turn and walk slowly off to Steve's right for a few yards and then stop. Steve heard the footsteps coming back. They stopped next to him as before. The ear nuzzle was repeated, then the animal retraced his steps only to stop again and repeat the process twice more. The third time the animal walked away, Steve thought the sound of the sheep's footfalls came from above him. The fourth time the sheep left, he didn't return to Steve's side, but let out a long slow moan almost as a young child would make if it was hungry or cold. Almost involuntarily, Steve rolled painfully over and began to crawl toward the sound. The second time he extended his left hand searching for a handhold, his fingers curled around the slim trunk of an immature pinion tree that was two feet above him. As he grabbed it and pulled his body upward, his left foot struck another small tree. Not only was he going up in elevation, he was in the middle of a pinion forest full of young trees perfectly suited to his method of propulsion. In thirty minutes he covered more ground then he had all the previous afternoon, even though he figured he had gained thirty or forty feet in elevation. As he lay on his back for his second rest period, he realized that the Big Horn sheep was gone. He lay still and listened for fifteen minutes, but heard nothing more. A few hours later, he settled down to sleep in soft sand under a four foot pinion tree.

*

IT TOOK SEVERAL minutes for Steve to realize that some sound had awakened him from a deep sleep. He was carefully stretching the muscles of his leg when he heard it again and separated it out from the noise of the light breeze through the pinions. Birds. Small birds. Steve guessed they were desert finches, flitting through the branches of the pinions all around him. There seemed to be a large flock of them and as they sang and moved from tree to tree, Steve realized they were not just moving through, but that something was keeping them here. In his experience, that was either food or water or both. He must be near a seep, a small crevice behind which snow collected during the winter and being on a northward facing slope melted slowly, providing water for many months into the dry season. Steve's dad had shown him several seeps that held water every year, even in the driest ones. He began to crawl in ever widening circles pulling himself from one pinion tree to the next, always being careful to follow the sound of the birds. After a half an hour, Steve was just pushing off the trunk of a pinion with his left foot when his left hand sank deep into mud. At the same moment, a fetid humid smell entered his nostrils. He crawled forward carefully. Steve had seen many seeps over the years, most of them were hidden packs of snow that seeped out from under rock formations and aside from turning the ground around them muddy, offered no real water. He was beginning to think that was the case once again, when his left hand skimmed across a flat rock and sank into three inches of cool water. He quickly felt around and discovered that a small bowl had formed in a depression on the smooth limestone rock. He tasted the water that was dripping off his fingers, barely noticing the sharp alkalai taste and slightly fishy mud smell. He rubbed several small handfuls over his swollen lips and let a few drops run over the cuts on his eyelids. The small cistern held a little over half a quart of water, and after several good mouthfuls, it was gone. Steve figured it would take at least an hour for the seep to fill the bowl again. He passed the time resting and exploring the immediate vicinity. Though he didn't find another water source he ate several small hard purple berries that the birds were feasting on in a group of bushes just near the seep. They had a bitter, dried apricot taste, but they stayed down and soon he had several pocketfulls to take with him.

The seep filled two more times before it fell into deep shadows and the snow melt slowed the filling time to several hours. Steve decided it was time to move on. If the terrain ahead was too rugged, he could always turn back and revisit the seep. The area the sheep had led him to was a deep arroyo carved into the side of the mountain. The soil was loose and the pinion trees were all uniformly small and it was ideal for the way that Steve was forced to travel. The farther he climbed, the narrower it became, and at times, Steve's fingers were touching both sides as he lay on his back during the rest intervals. The breezes through the arroyo created a small venturi effect and were useless for judging direction, if Steve had had any choice in the direction of travel anyway. He knew at this point he was committed and the small crease in the vast mountain was to be his salvation or his final resting spot. It was several hours after dark when Steve reached up to grab a large rock that was two feet higher than his head and pushed forward with all the strength left in his good leg. The earth gave way under him and he plunged headfirst over a precipice striking his head on a large boulder as he crumpled in a heap at the bottom of a ten foot cliff. The manzanita branch had broken in two and the pain from the contorted leg made his head swirl. He did not know if he was on his back or lying on his stomach. He reached out and felt only large rocks pinning him against the ground. After several minutes of trying to budge the nearest ones, he passed out.

August 29

STEVE FELT HIMSELF moving again. He reached out to touch the rocks but he couldn't extend his arms or even open and close his hands. He tried to move his left leg but it seemed it was caught on something and wouldn't respond. The only thing that was the same was the pain and it washed over him again moving him deeper into the blackness.

August 30

THE SHADOWS SWIRLING in front of his unseeing eyes were made even darker by the bright light behind them. At times they made sounds and Steve responded by trying to move his left leg and left arm. When he did so the shadows came closer and made more sounds. Sensing he was on his back, Steve strained to feel any breezes that might give him the clue to what direction he should try to start pushing his body. He felt himself moving backwards and he began to move his good arm and leg as if he was doing the backstroke. With very little effort on his part he was moving backwards as if on a cloud. He was vaguely aware that this position also had reduced the pain in his leg. The exertion began to make his head swim and he gave in to the swirling black vortex once again.

August 31

STEVE CAME SLOWLY to consciousness. He remembered the rocks that had pinned him down and he reached for the closest one with his left hand. At first all he felt was air and then his wrist banged on something slick and cold. The background light was as bright as the normal sunlight but was softer and bluer than normal. He reached to touch his lacerated eyelids and was stopped by a heavy bandage. He stopped moving and tried to make sense of his surroundings. He touched the bandage again and pressed on it lightly. He reached down and ran his left hand along the slick metal bar. He then put both hands to his face and for the first time in five days his eyes released a torrent of tears. He felt them seeping under the bandages and running down across his swollen lips. He felt something gently grasp his left shoulder. The first sound he heard was Bernie's voice.

"Steve, Steve can you hear me?" With great effort, Steve reached slowly over his body with his right hand and grasped the strong hand holding his shoulder. His tongue moved in slow motion thickly in his mouth. He tried to clear his throat several times. He concentrated all his efforts on putting pressure on his vocal chords. The first two tries were small squeaky grunts. On the third try something in his throat seemed to move and he let out a deep breath to help the process.

"Sk...Skip...per." He squeezed the hand on his shoulder harder.

"Steve, Skipper is OK, they found him walking along the road by Tule Springs Ranch, he is OK. Don't worry. He's OK. You gotta rest and get well." Steve's hand released its' grip on Bernie's and fell down to his side. For a few seconds Steve was back in the desert. He could feel the small breeze on his forehead, but instead of continuing to crawl, he decided to take a rest.

"He's going to be alright Doc, right?" Bernie looked up through his own tears at the doctor who had just entered the room and was examining Steve.

"Yes, Mr. Gold, he will eventually be just fine. The medications are too much for his system right now, he will need more rest. I am going to have to ask you to wait outside."

September 1

STEVE AWOKE AGAIN to the blackness beyond his eyes and lay very still for several seconds as he brought his breathing under control. When he was able to take in deep breaths through his nose and then control the exhalation through his mouth, he began to take inventory. His right arm was lying at a strange angle and had an IV needle in it. His right leg had a heavy cast on it that came up past his hip and was suspended in the air a few inches off the bed. Both his arms and his left hand were wrapped in bandages as were his eyes and the top of his head. Because of the traction on his leg, he could not move laterally at all, and when he did, he felt the uncomfortable pull of a catheter. Unlike when he was in the desert, the pain was not localized but felt as if it were a malevolent aura around his torso and all of his limbs. He thought back over the last six days and tried to place everything he remembered in a chronology, beginning with the drive out to Tule Springs. As he did so, he practiced vocalizing, his tongue was not as thick as the day before and he was able to put together short sentences in a loud whisper. Twenty minutes later, he was still whispering to himself when he drifted back to sleep.

Voices came to him in a dream and slowly the voices pulled him from deep inside himself back into the room where they attached themselves to the different shadows that moved in front of the soft blue light.

"Doctor, I think he is awake." Two shadows leaned closer to him.

"Mr. Cannon, how are we today?" The male voice had gone up a few decibels. Steve wet his lips with his tongue.

"We are alive, today." He croaked in his stage whisper.

"Well, that is just fine, Mr. Cannon. Just fine. We are just going to move you to another room where you will be more comfortable." The shadows receded and several more shadows joined them as they moved around Steve talking among themselves. Steve spent his time trying to stay awake through the entire process. Eventually he felt himself being wheeled along in his gurney. The new room was if anything, brighter than the last. All the shadows left except one. The female voice was right next to his ear.

"I am going to adjust the bed, Mr. Cannon. Let me know when it becomes more comfortable for you." He heard the bed creak and a crank turning below his left side. When the bed was still at a shallow incline, he raised his left hand and the cranking stopped.

"There Mr. Cannon. I will be in to check on you in fifteen minutes. If you need anything before that please use this." She raised his right hand and placed a small piece of plastic that was connected to a cord in his palm. Steve tugged at her sleeve as she was adjusting his pillow.

"What, Mr. Cannon?" He gathered his strength.

"Tam…Tam Polhaus.." His throat was sore from his earlier exertions and his voice was becoming fainter. The shadow straightened.

"I don't know who that is, Mr. Cannon but I will tell the floor nurse and see if we can contact a Mr. Polhaus." She patted his upper arm.

"No need, nurse, I am already here." Steve heard Tam's voice before his shadow joined the nurse's at the side of Steve's bed. Steve raised his left hand and Tam grasped it in his. The nurse shadow spoke.

"Mr. Polhaus, I am afraid that you will have to wait outside with the others. Mr. Cannon is not allowed visitors until the doctor gives his OK." Tam turned to her but still held onto Steve's hand.

"Police business, Ma'am. I will only be here a few minutes." The nurse said something that Steve did not catch as her shadow left the bedside. Tam waited until she had left the room and then turned back to Steve. Steve croaked hoarsely.

"Sorelli." Tam squeezed a little harder. He spoke in low measured tones leaning next to Steve's ear.

"We found two bodies in the middle of the Nellis Range. Both burned to a crisp. The FBI is examining them now and will have a positive identification by tomorrow or the next day. But I can tell you as I stand here that neither of them is Sorelli. One is short and heavyset, and the other is too short and too skinny. He is still out there somewhere, Steve." Steve shook his head slowly and made a small unintelligible sound. Tam decided to change the subject.

"When I visited the site with Samuels and Brady, I saw the trail you left as you crawled away. I followed it all the way up the side of that mountain to where you were found by a group of archeology students lying under some rocks on a jeep trail. I figure it was at least two miles up that slope from where you started." When Steve didn't respond, Tam cleared his throat.

"Miriam Beech was found shot to death in a Mesquite motel room two days ago. No sign of the money." Steve shook his head.

"Figures." He coughed at the effort to talk. He waited until the spell passed and then tried to pull Tam closer. His voice was just a soft whisper now.

"Tell Jack Cathay to come see me." Tam nodded, then realizing his mistake leaned in closer.

"I will, Steve, I will. I am going to go now, I will come back soon and keep you posted." He squeezed Steve's hand. Steve nodded as he watched the shadow disappear into the bright blue light. Steve fell back against the pillows. He was still turning over his short conversation with Tam in his mind as he dropped off to sleep.

Steve was awakened two hours later by a doctor who was standing by his bedside with a clipboard in his hands. The doctor spoke with Steve for ten minutes detailing his injuries and prognosis. His leg would be in a hard cast for six weeks, a soft one for three weeks after that. His eyes were healing quickly and the bandages would come off in two days. His burns were being cleaned twice a day and would heal completely. The blows to his head had caused a concussion and the effects of that would linger for at least another week. The doctor left the handwritten notes on the bedside table for the nurses to read to him in case Steve had any questions, and left. Steve went back to sleep and awoke once in the night when he had a dream that a mountain lion was pursuing him up the little pinion canyon in the Sheep Range.

September 2

STEVE AWOKE EARLY when a nurse came in to adjust his IV. She was followed by the head nurse who gave Steve a choice. Began to try to eat solid food or have the feeding tube inserted. He chose solid food. His voice was much better and even though he had to conserve it, there was not as much pain nor did it take as much effort as before. The nurse who spoon fed him jello and mashed potatoes had just left when Steve heard the door open and felt the small breeze that always announced the event if he had missed the sound of the slight hinge creak. The shadow did not approach the bed but crossed the room and stood in front of the large window. Steve could see the shadow's outline in the bright light.

"How are you feeling, Mr. Cannon?" The voice was smooth and matter of fact.

"If I am disturbing you, you have my apologies and I will leave." Steve cleared his throat carefully.

"It's your hospital." He didn't know if his voice was loud enough to be heard across the room.

"Our hospital, Mr. Cannon, the community's hospital. I simply saw the need and helped it along." Steve tried to chuckle, but it came out more as a burp.

"The Central States Pension Fund money." He coughed as he ended the incomplete sentence.

"Well there is truth in what you say, Mr. Cannon, but I daresay that they have been rewarded handsomely for their investment. That success insures their continued participation in projects that will make this a better place to live. Don't you think that is a good thing, Mr. Cannon?" Steve did not answer.

"I know you have been through quite an ordeal, Mr. Cannon, and I don't want to tire you, but I wanted to have a small talk with you in person, just to answer some questions I have." Steve waved his left hand slightly.

"I know most of the particulars in this whole affair, Mr. Cannon, but I would like for you to tell me if any of the people that I am associated with were involved in any aspects of putting the fraudulent land deal together?" The shadow moved away from the window and stood halfway between the light and the bed. Steve shook his head as he spoke.

"No, none at all as far as I know." The shadow turned and walked back to the window.

"That is good to know, Mr. Cannon. I just wanted to hear it directly from you. It pays to check things yourself. Sometimes it is hard to divine the motives of someone like Nash Brannock, even harder sometimes for those who are closest to him." The shadow moved toward the door, then stopped halfway.

"I trust that you found our organization cooperative and supportive of your efforts?" Steve swallowed hard and took a deep breath.

"Yeah, Tommy comes across when he has to." The shadow nodded and started for the door once again.

"I hope you are feeling better soon, Mr. Cannon. Thank you for your time." Steve felt the slight breeze across his face again as the door closed. Steve lay back in the bed and tried to will the pain in his leg away. Several minutes later he fell asleep.

*

WHEN HE AWOKE three hours later, a doctor and nurse were standing over him. They had been discussing something as he came to. The doctor waited until the nurse was done taking Steve's temperature.

"Mr. Cannon, if you are agreeable, I would like to take off the eye bandages today." Steve nodded. The nurse cranked the bed up higher by a few inches and brought over a small pan. The doctor snipped off the surgical gauze that encircled Steve's head, and then carefully removed the two gauze discs that had covered his eyes for three days. Immediately, Steve felt the coolness of the air conditioning on his cheeks and forehead. His eyelids were still crusted shut. The doctor stepped aside as the nurse bathed both eyes and repeated the process with cotton swabs. When she was done, the doctor carefully retracted each eyelid in turn. He then busied himself placing surgical strips on several of the cuts, two of which had started to bleed slightly. The nurse finished by placing several drops of a solution into each eye. Steve blinked several times as the warm liquid swam in his eyes and the blue light grew brighter and the shadows turned into shapes with patches of color here and there.

Steve lay back in the bed and the nurse lowered it to the former position. The side of the room with the window was still painful for Steve to look at, so he stared up at the beige ceiling tiles. The more he blinked, the more clarity returned, first around the edges and then in the middle with several dull and out of focus areas still present in each eye. He was still waiting for the drops to clear completely when he felt the soft breeze on his forehead as the door opened and closed.

The doctor leaned over the bed and rested his hand gently on his shoulder. Steve could see the doctors brown eyes and the gray hair above the spectacles.

"We have cleared you for visitors, Mr. Cannon, and this young lady has been waiting a long time and is first in line." Steve looked over as the doctor backed away from the bed. Remy moved into the clearest edge of his vision and reached for Steve's hand. His vision swam again as tears washed out the last of the drops and fell onto the front of his gown.

"Gem." His voice had grown hoarse again. She leaned across the bed and kissed him on the lips. He hugged her to him gently with his right arm.

"Steve, I have been so worried, they wouldn't let any of us see you." She smoothed his hair where the eye bandage had been.

"I was so afraid that I would never be able to do this again, Gem," He leaned forward and kissed her, longer this time.

The doctor stepped forward. "I'm sorry, Mr. Cannon, but I must limit the visits to one every hour for five minutes. Your ordeal has weakened your body a great deal and we are still worried about the possibility of infection. The more rest you get the better."

Steve kissed Remy several times before she moved from his bedside. She blew him a kiss as she disappeared behind the door.

Steve had been asleep for two hours when he was awakened

by one of the nurses as she checked his vital signs and adjusted the catheter. As soon as she had gone, Bernie's round face appeared by his bedside.

"Man, it is good to see you up and looking around. You scared the bejeezus out of me when I first saw you right after they brought you out of surgery." Before Steve could speak, Bernie opened his jacket and pointed to the inside pocket. Steve could see the top half of a cold can of Schlitz still beaded with condensation. Steve chuckled painfully.

"Bernie, how am I going to drink that in here?" He watched as Bernie produced a small dixie cup and a short straw from his other pocket. Bernie pulled out an opener and quickly opened the beer, poured several ounces in the cup and held up the straw to Steve's mouth. Steve took a large drink through the straw and laid back.

"That tastes like heaven, Bern. Only you would think of that." He watched as Bernie produced a pack of Pall Malls and a box of matches from his pants pocket. Steve laughed again, being careful not to start a coughing jag.

"Damn, Bernie, they aren't going to let me smoke in here." Bernie smiled and put the cigarettes into a small leather pouch and put them in the bedside drawer.

"I heard them talking outside. Tomorrow, they are going to put you in a wheelchair and take you out onto the lanai. I figure I volunteer to push and when no one is looking, 'puff', puff'. Bernie made an exaggerated charade of smoking.

"Bernie, you can't even stand to be around smoking, what were you thinking. And besides, don't you have a business to run?" Bernie's face became serious.

"When Tam called me and told me they found Skipper, but that Sorelli had you, I couldn't sleep or eat for the life of me, I swear. So if I have to breathe a little smoke, so what, I will be thankful watching you take every puff." Steve smiled as Bernie bent down to pour more beer into the cup.

"Bernie, where is Skipper, now?" Bernie handed Steve the cup full of beer and carefully concealed the can back inside his jacket.

"Damnedest thing, Steve, I went down and picked him up at the cop station when Tam called me. They had him in the infirmary, but he was OK, just a few cuts and bruises. I took him back home to my place and we sat up all night, just talking. Talking about all kinds of stuff. And the strange thing is, he wasn't drinking. Not a drop and I was with him for fifteen hours. Anyway, he comes to me the next day and tells me he wants to get sober and can I help? So, I call this guy I know real well in Huntington Beach who runs a clinic. That night I put him on the plane for LA. If all goes well, he should be back in a couple of months. Whadda'ya think of that?" Steve put down the small cup and dabbed his eyes with the back of his still bandaged hand.

"Thanks, Bernie, you don't know how much that means to me." Bernie waved dismissively. "Don't thank me, thank Skipper, he is going to have to do the work." Just as he spoke the head nurse came back into the room. Bernie winked at Steve and smiled.

"Mr. Gold. When did you get in here? I told you no more visitors today." She put her hand on Bernie's back and started steering him out of the room. Bernie shrugged back at Steve and waved as she followed him out the door. "Mr. Gold, have you been drinking beer?" "Just a little ma'am." Steve did not hear the rest of the conversation as the door closed behind them. When the nurses came with his dinner two hours later, they found him sleeping soundly. They decided the food could wait until the next day.

September 3

STEVE HAD JUST finished breakfast and had gotten comfortable when the head nurse opened the door and came into the room. She read his chart and checked his vitals for herself.

"You are going to have to start eating more, Mr. Cannon. It will take a lot of strength to pull that cast around." Steve smiled and coughed before he spoke.

"I tell you what, Mrs. Hockett, you have Bernie bring me one of his pastrami sandwiches the next time he comes." Mrs. Hockett scoffed. "If you were to eat one of those, Mr. Cannon, it would add an extra week to your stay, and I know that you don't want that." They both laughed as she fluffed the pillows.

"And now, Mr. Cannon, if you are up to company, they are two special visitors that are first in line to see you this morning." She went over and opened the door and beckoned someone in.

"Uncle Steve, Uncle Steve!!" Betsy and Susan ran through the door their voices ringing in unison.

Steve smiled down at the two little faces as Betsy pulled a chair over to the bed, climbed up and stood on top of the bottom cushion. Her face was on the same level as her uncle's and she reached as far over as she could and hugged his neck. Susan patted his head and with one hand steadied her sister on her perch.

"Are you going to be OK, Uncle Steve?" The younger girl whispered into his ear.

"Yes, honey, I will be OK, I will be out of here soon."

"Mom says that you shouldn't walk around in the desert anymore because you always get into trouble." Steve took the small arms from around his neck and kissed the tiny fingers.

"Your mom is right. Is she here?"

"I am here Steve." He looked up and saw Val standing just inside the door. She was holding a large bouquet of pink carnations. She walked toward the window and for the first time Steve saw that there were almost a dozen other flower arrangements on a narrow table against the wall. One of the bouquets towered over the rest and was made of pink and white roses. She placed the vase on one of the few free spaces on the table and then came over to Steve's bedside. Steve looked into her eyes.

"I was hoping I would see you again, Val." His voice was hoarse.

"I was praying for it, Steve, you are the only brother I have."
She lifted Betsy off the chair, sat down and pulled the youngest
child back up onto her lap.

"Horace will come see you tomorrow if you are up to it."

"Yes, I would like to see him and apologize for the other night."

"No need for that, Steve, that is all behind us now." Val smiled
at Steve and he looked into her eyes as he used his left arm to play
patty-cake with Betsy.

Later after all his visitors had gone, Steve had the nurse collect the cards from the flower arrangements. Bernie had sent two
and the largest one was from the Desert Inn. As he was placing all
the cards in an envelope, the door opened and Assistant District
Attorney Larson walked into the room. Steve smiled.

"Careful, Mr. Larsen, if the head nurse sees you in here after
visiting hours you will wish you were in my place." The DA smiled
and pulled the chair that Betsy had used over next to the bed.

"I don't think so, Steve, I called ahead and got permission from
your doctor. But now that you mention it, she did not seem all that
pleased when I checked in at the desk just now."

Steve looked down at the small cup of ice chips in his hand. He
held it up a few inches so that Larsen could see.

"You know what I would have given for this little cup a few
days ago?" He shook his head and ran his tongue over the blisters
that still covered his lips.

"It is a remarkable tale, Steve, truly remarkable." He reached
out and patted Steve on the shoulder.

"Well, I thought I should wrap some things up with you." Steve
nodded gravely and shook a small bit of the ice into his mouth.
Larsen took a deep breath.

"I am sure that Tam told you about Miriam Beech. Time of
death suggests that she was killed the night before Sorelli lured you
to the desert. According to Skipper, they nabbed him the night
before that and he was probably tied up out in the car when they
killed Miriam. According to the manager at Valley Bank, Nash

came in with Sorelli and had the funds transferred to another account, one that had Miriam Beech as the sole name on it. That happened the day that Nash was probably killed, if we believe the coroner's report. That account is empty. Presumably, Sorelli was able to get his hands on it as well as the money in Nash's home safe. In addition, we found evidence that once Miriam joined with Nash and Sorelli, an additional 1.2 million was raised from other investors. That money is missing as well. Now on to the subject of Herb Slater. Herb has pleaded through his lawyer, guilty of aiding and abetting fraud and receiving bribes. He has withdrawn from the mayoral race and he and his attorney are trying to negotiate a plea deal with the State Attorney's General office in Carson City. We have a pretty complete list of the swindled investors and several of them have already filed lawsuits. And there you have it. Oh, and your car was found burned out where you left it at Tule Springs." He looked over at Steve who was staring at the ceiling. He rolled his head to the side and looked at the attorney.

"Do you have any additional information on Sorelli?" Larsen shook his head slowly.

"No. Samuels thinks he died in the desert and that eventually someone will stumble across his body. FBI Agent Brady has his doubts but I think he is willing to come down on the side of getting this case closed for good." Their eyes met as Larsen looked up from his notes.

"And you, Mr. Larsen. What is your opinion?"

"On the record I have no official opinion, I am not required to have one in this case. Off the record, I think you and Tam should conduct yourselves as if he were still out there." Steve held the DA's gaze for several seconds.

"I think you are right." He lay back and sighed. Larsen stood up.

"I think I am tiring you, Mr. Cannon. I will leave it as it is for now. If you think of any more questions, please call me and I will call you if there are any further developments to report." Steve nodded.

"And Steve?" Steve looked up at the tall figure.

"Once you are up and around, come see me. I have several cases I want you to look at with me. The taxpayers don't pay top wages for what you do, but I think it will be worth your while. Would you be agreeable to that?" Steve nodded.

"Sure, I would happy to work with you. Thanks for the information." Larsen turned and waved as he swung open the large door.

Steve closed his eyes and thought about the day he had come in out of the desert and Bernie had told him about the simple missing person case that Tam had. It seemed like a million years ago. He looked over at the table filled with blossoms. Five minutes later he was asleep.

September 14

BERNIE WAS BEAMING as he hustled around the front of the car to open the door for Steve. One of the orderlies had rolled Steve's wheelchair through the front doors several minutes before. Though it was only 85 degrees, the heat felt oppressive after two weeks of around the clock air conditioning. Steve had stood and taken the wooden crutches from the nurse that had accompanied him to the curb. While he waited for Bernie, he hopped back and forth on the supports, testing the best method and timing to move along with the most efficiency. When Bernie had the door open, Steve smoothly slipped into the front seat and placed the crutches at an angle between the two bucket seats.

"Damn, Steve, it looks like you are already an expert with those things." Steve turned and smiled.

"Well, they tell me that I am going to be hopping along with them for quite a while. I just need to figure out how to drive." Bernie laughed.

"No, you are going to have me as your personal driver, I insist." Steve shook his head.

"No Bernie, you all have your own lives to go back to. The quicker we all put this behind us, the better." Bernie shook his head and smiled.

"Suit yourself, you always have."

"As if you haven't, my friend." Bernie shrugged and laughed.

"Yeah, I guess you are right." They both laughed as Bernie turned onto Nellis Boulevard.

When they pulled off the road and onto Steve's gravel driveway, he saw his Jeep parked in the usual place in front of the door.

"That was pretty quick work." Steve remarked. Bernie laughed.

"It got wrecked three weeks ago." Steve thought for a second and then nodded.

Bernie helped him inside and turned on the swamp cooler and showed Steve the refrigerator that had been stocked with groceries and beer.

"Bernie, I can't tell you how overwhelmed I am." Steve felt the hot tears welling in his still swollen eyes.

"You would do the same for me and probably have." He headed toward the door.

"If you need anything, my friend, please call me. I will call you tomorrow to check on you. Get some rest, will ya?" Steve waved from the front door as he watched Bernie's car disappear over the small hill.

Steve did rest for much of the afternoon. After a light dinner, he hopped on one crutch into his office. He saw the piece of paper on his desk with the words: 'Tule Springs' written on it. He picked it up and was going to crumple it up and throw it into the wastebasket when he thought better of it and carefully placed it in one of the desk drawers. He hobbled over to the stereo and selected a record. He lay back on the small corduroy couch and listened as a Stan

Getz melody filled the room. A few minutes after the record ended and the arm of the turntable had returned itself to the cradle, the phone rang.

"Hi, Steve, are you back home?"

"Yeah, Gem, I am back home."

Epilogue

Marcus Boomer sat back in the metal folding chair. Placed in a semi-circle around the small table on the little patch of dried up grass in front of him were three of his paintings. He looked from one to the other and once in a while he gazed into the middle distance as the early October sun hung just above the Spring Mountains. From time to time he rose and with one of the brushes he carried in an old Ford hubcap, he would make a few brush strokes and then sit back down and contemplate them anew. It was while he was sitting and looking at a painting of a lone pinion tree that he saw the shadow glide across the ground in front of him and heard the two caws as the raven flew over the trailer. Marcus sat for a few more minutes. Then slowly, one by one, he placed the paintings inside the trailer and closed the door. He came back and retrieved the hubcap from the table and when he again emerged from the trailer he had on his long woolen coat. He glanced over his shoulder as the raven flew back the way he had come, and then began trudging up the dirt road. Ten minutes later he was nearing the top of the last hill before the highway. He stopped just short of the crest and rising up slightly on his toes, peered over. Below he saw the red Jeep and the man standing in front of it. He was leaning on a cane and wearing sunglasses. There were two small paper bags with their tops twisted shut just inside the cattle guard. The old man smiled and began again his halting gait down the long hill.